Sherlock Holmes

and

Doctor Watson:
The Early
Adventures

Volume I

Sherlock Holmes
and
Doctor Watson:
The Early
Adventures

Volume I

Edited by
David Marcum

Belanger Books
2019

CONTENTS

Foreword

Adventures

(Continued on the next page . . . .)

The following adventures appear in the companion volumes of

Sherlock Holmes and Doctor Watson: The Early Adventures

Volume II:

Volume III:

Editor's Foreword:
They Were Young Once Too . . . .
by David Marcum

When I was a kid, every one of my literary heroes was older than me. It wasn't something to ponder or resent – that's just the way it was. I started reading mysteries in 1973 at age eight with the exceptional adventures of *The Three Investigators*, and while their ages were never definitely stated – they didn't drive yet, for instance – it was clear that they were several years past me. Then, not long after that, I found *The Hardy Boys*. Frank and Joe were definitely eighteen and seventeen respectively, driving cars and planes and speedboats, and traveling all around Bayport and to New York, and anywhere else in the world that they wanted to go – Down South, Out West, Canada, England, Mexico, Iceland, Greece, Morocco, and everywhere else too. I don't think that I believed all of that adventure would suddenly come my way when I turned seventeen or eighteen – but I don't recall *not* believing it either.

Not long after finding The Hardy Boys, I realized that what I was reading were the *Revised Texts*, cleaned up and severely shortened from the stories that were originally published from the 1920's to the 1950's, before the revisions began. In those earlier books, Frank and Joe were sixteen and fifteen – but that really made no difference to me, as that was still older than I was, and all just some mysterious vague maturity that I hadn't yet reached.

The path where I found my other "book friends" (as my son would call them years later) led me to encounter other series characters like Sandy Steele and Brains Benton and Tod Moran, and adventure books by Troy Nesbit and Capwell

1

Wyckoff, to name just a faction. I collected and read about Tom Swift, Jr., but he never interested me as much as the pure mystery and adventure stories. I read some Doc Savage (although not enough), and became a friend-for-life of Tarzan, and also a Star Trek fanatic. One thing that they all had in common was that they were older than me.

In high school, I discovered some of the other Great Detectives – Nero Wolfe and Ellery Queen and Hercule Poirot. All older. In 1980, when I was fifteen, I happened upon Clive Cussler's Dirk Pitt, showing me that "grown-up" books could be incredibly fun after all, and not boring as I'd feared. At one point in *Iceberg* (1975 – the second Pitt book published, and the third chronologically), Pitt is described as being thirty-two years, four months, and twelve days old. At age fifteen, that was just a vague out-there age, lumped in with all of those other ages that were beyond my experience. Years later, after having re-read that book at least two-dozen times, I somehow still see Pitt as older than me, although now I'm more than twenty years older than he was in that story. That perspective is entrenched in my head.

When I was ten years old in 1975, I first encountered Mr. Sherlock Holmes and Doctor John Watson, who have been my greatest heroes ever since. They were older than I was, of course, as was every other figure in the books that I liked, so it was no big deal. But I didn't realize then what a stubborn issue the mistaken perception of Holmes and Watson's ages would turn out to be.

Holmes and Watson are recognized everywhere. Certain items related to Holmes – a deerstalker, or a pipe, or a magnifying glass – are identified all over the world with detectives in general and Holmes in particular. Many people have some idea of Holmes and Watson even if they've never read a Holmes story or seen a Holmes film or television episode. Others may have seen some of these films, and from them believe that they have a true idea of Our Heroes. But usually they don't.

There is a persistent and incorrect idea, reinforced by countless film misrepresentations, that Holmes and Watson were always staid and dull British chaps of middle years (or older), with Holmes a spry, cranky, and impatient eccentric (at best), and Watson a white-haired and portly *Boobus Brittanicus*, *a la* Nigel Bruce. Students of the true and Canonical Sherlock Holmes know this to be a falsehood.

When we first meet Holmes at the beginning of *A Study in Scarlet*, on January 1st, 1881, he is still twenty-six years old (although he'll turn twenty-seven in just a few days, on January 6th.) Watson, already a wounded war veteran, is only twenty-eight. Granted, Holmes is brilliant, and has already established a practice as a consulting detective, and Watson is a qualified doctor who has been to war and seen terrible things that most will never face, not even counting his injuries and subsequent disability. That is to say, they are exceptional men. But the thing that gets lost and forgotten is that *they were only in their twenties then*.

I'm a civil engineer, and there are several employees at our firm who are just about the same age now that Holmes and Watson were when they met on January 1st, 1881. Sometimes, knowing these coworkers pretty well, I try to imagine Holmes and Watson at that age, instead of as the middle-aged (or older) versions that so often want to spring to mind. I see how these coworkers behave in meetings, or carrying out responsibilities, or deal with those who are older and either know more, or who now know less as time and technology have moved on. It's a very instructive thing to observe, and they respond, as Mr. Spock says in *The Wrath of Khan*, "each according to his

3

gifts". I try to picture how Sherlock Holmes in his twenties would act, and also how he would be perceived, especially by those who are a little older.

Much is often made of how Scotland Yard and the other officials didn't want to take Holmes seriously, especially in those early days. There's a tendency to explain it away as if they thought that Holmes was too eccentric, or his methods too unusual. But consider that it might also have been a function of their age. Who among us has had a young doctor, fresh from school and in his or her twenties, and wondered if this person has enough knowledge and experience and seasoning to *really* know what's what. Then think about Holmes in that same light.

There has been a marked reluctance to portray Holmes and Watson anywhere near these younger and often appropriate ages in television and film. There is always a middle-agedness in media performances. When I was younger, and everyone was older than me, it just seemed natural. I was fortunate – or not fortunate, depending upon one's perspective – to see practically no screen versions of Holmes whatsoever while growing up, thus cementing in my head the Canonical version that I found in the original adventures. (This was before cable television and VCR's, and way before DVD's, so finding Holmes on screen occurred almost not at all.) I obtained my first Holmes book, an abridged copy of Whitman edition of *The Adventures*, in 1975, and then promptly shelved it, unwanted. It was only a few weeks later, when I saw part – but only a part – of *A Study in Terror* (1965) during a Saturday afternoon re-run, that I was tempted to explore The World of Holmes more deeply. The Holmes of the film seemed intriguing, and I was prompted to retrieve my sole Holmes book and start reading. Soon after I found more Canonical titles, and then pastiches like Nicholas Meyer's *The West End*

Horror and *Enter the Lion* by Sean Wright and Michael Hodel. I discovered that my local library had some old 1940's Basil Rathbone radio shows, so I was able to *hear* Holmes for the first time. (And even then, with intelligence beyond my years, I knew that Nigel Bruce was just plain wrong.)

But I didn't *see* Holmes on screen for a long time. In 1979, my dad took me to the local movie theater – and we were the only ones in attendance – to view *Murder by Decree* starring Christopher Plummer and James Mason. Both actors were excellent, and Plummer absolutely defined the heroic aspects of Holmes that I've always admired with his outrage at the government's conspiracy, taking his anger right to the face of the corrupt Prime Minister. James Mason was fine too – or so I thought at the time. But hindsight has educated me, for when the movie was filmed in 1978, James Mason was sixty-eight years old – playing a man who was actually thirty-six during the events during that Autumn of Terror, 1888.

I went for great stretches without any visual Holmes input. There was once a story on the CBS Evening News that happened to be on while I was in the room and talking with my parents. I glanced over to see that it contained a very short clip, to make some point within the story, from Rathbone's 1939 *The Hound of the Baskervilles*: "*Murder, my dear Watson,*" he said. "*Refined, cold-blooded murder.*" It was a five-second blink-and-you'll-miss-it scene, but it was my first time at *seeing* Rathbone as Holmes, after several years of hearing his radio performances. He was perfect. He was wearing the deerstalker, and he *looked like Holmes was supposed to look.*

Little did I realize that in *The Hound*, his first time out as Holmes, he was already too old for the part. He was in his late-forties then, while Holmes was only thirty-four when *The Hound* actually occurred. Rathbone and Bruce at least tried to do Holmes and Watson correctly in their first two films, *The*

Hound and *The Adventures of Sherlock Holmes* (also made in 1939), with Bruce darkening his hair and the stories set in the correct era, but a few years later, in the twelve films that they would make for Universal, they gave up all pretense of doing it right. Both acted like their own ages – in their fifties by that time, with Bruce possibly seeming even older with his white hair and bumbling muttering behavior.

Other Holmes films have also cast actors well-along in middle age, further solidifying the common belief that Holmes and Watson were always just somehow *older*. Arthur Wontner, who was a perfectly visualized Holmes, played him in five films when he was between fifty-seven and sixty two – and with a rather genial, soft-spoken, and sometimes bemused attitude. Peter Cushing took on the role of Holmes on multiple occasions: In the 1959 version of *The Hound* (when he was forty-six), in the 1968 BBC television show *Sherlock Holmes* (when he was fifty-five), and in 1984's *The Masks of Death* (when he was seventy-one). Granted, this final portrayal is supposed to show an elderly Holmes, but when *The Hound* occurred, as mentioned, Holmes was in his middle-thirties, and in Cushing's BBC version, he was a couple of *decades* too old. As part of his BBC series, Cushing also filmed *A Study in Scarlet*, one of only a handful of film versions of this Canonical tale. It ignored the meeting between Holmes and Watson, and instead jumped straight to The Lauriston Gardens Mystery. Perhaps that's just as well, since Cushing was fifty-five then, and would have needed to be a fine actor indeed, with some structures pulling his skin quite tight, to pull off a portrayal of a fellow in his twenties.

Another version of Holmes and Watson's first meeting occurred in the television episode "The Adventure of the Cunningham Heritage" (October 1954), which showed Watson being introduced to Holmes before veering off into another mystery entirely. This was from the thirty-nine episode series, *Sherlock Holmes*, (1954-1955) which has been hailed as being light-hearted (for the most part) and set in the early days of Holmes and Watson's friendship. But the stars, Ronald Howard and C. Marion Crawford, at thirty-six and forty respectively, were also too old if they wanted to seem like young men – and the older images of Holmes and Watson were again perpetuated.

The same is true for other actors. Douglas Wilmer was in his mid-forties when he starred in the excellent 1964-1965 BBC series. (I wish that more of these episodes had survived.) Ian Richardson was forty-nine when he played the mid-thirties Holmes in 1983's *The Hound of the Baskervilles* and *The Sign of Four*. Jeremy Brett was already fifty-one when his first performance as a mid-thirties Holmes in "A Scandal in Bohemia" aired in 1984. He would continue to appear as Holmes for the next ten years, as both his mental and physical abilities substantially declined. As he unfortunately (and irritatingly) foisted more and more of his own health issues onto his portrayal of Holmes, along with the insistent doctrine that he was portraying a very accurate Holmes, a great many people accepted that his version, with mental illness and older unhealthy features included, was the correct one, and it's been a difficult legacy to shake ever since.

Sadly, with its many flaws, Jeremy Brett's performance as Holmes has been the last time whatsoever that a television series about Sherlock Holmes has been aired in either Great Britain or America since 1994. There have been a few stand-alone films, such as a version of *The Hound* starring Richard Roxburgh (2002), and some other films with Matt Frewer, Jonathan Pryce, and Rupert Everett. In theatres, Sir Ian McKellan played an intentionally elderly Holmes, while Robert Downey, Jr. was forty-four and then forty-six when he played, in two back-to-back films, a middle-aged Holmes who was decidedly damaged goods. Screen representations of the younger Holmes just aren't to be found.

Noted Sherlockian Bert Coules has scripted a series of television programs featuring an age-appropriate Holmes and Watson in their twenties, solving cases early in their friendship. Hopefully, these will be produced, so that, for the first time since 1994 and the end of the Brett performances, a Sherlock Holmes television series will once again be on the air.

In the meantime, the public image of Our Heroes is often that of elderly fellows, rather than the way that they were presented in most of The Canon. We meet Holmes and Watson when they are twenty-six and twenty-eight, respectively. Five of the Canonical tales occur when Holmes is in his twenties – "The *Gloria Scott*", "The Musgrave Ritual", *A Study in Scarlet*, "The Resident Patient", and "The Speckled Band". (Take a moment to recall "The Speckled Band", set in 1883, one of the most famous Holmes tales. Can you see it? Do you remember the terror that is conveyed? Now imagine being Holmes and solving that case . . . and only being twenty-nine years old.)

There are twenty-five Canonical adventures wherein Holmes and Watson are in their thirties, and twenty-eight when they are in their forties. Only two, "The Lion's Mane" and "His Last Bow" occur later. In the first, Holmes is fifty-three, and in the second he is sixty. And yet, so many times he and Watson are shown as older men, sixty years or more if they are a day.

In some screen adaptations, this cannot be helped. Unlike the amazing BBC radio adaptations of The Canon starring Clive Merrison and Michael Williams, overseen by Bert

Coules, where the actors can play Holmes and Watson at any of the correct ages through the use of their voices, visual actors cannot jump so easily from their mid-forties in one episode to their twenties in the next. Allowances for this, such as in episodes of the Wilmer and Cushing and Brett series, must be made. But still, some occasional effort ought to present all those times that Holmes and Watson *weren't older.*

Luckily, even though visual mediums continue to reinforce that incorrect idea, the printed stories can present the younger versions of Holmes and Watson.

Since the mid-1990's, I've maintained an ever-growing chronology related to the complete lives of Holmes and Watson, containing both The Canon and thousands of traditional Canonical pastiches. It's currently over nine-hundred dense pages, and likely to cross a thousand soon, and the years before Holmes and Watson initially "officially" meet on January 1st, 1881, are extremely full of narratives about what else occurred. (One should not be surprised that their paths crossed a few times in a few extra-Canonical stories before being introduced that fateful day in the laboratory at Barts Hospital.)

The entries in my chronology for 1881, 1882, and 1883 – the years covered by this new collection – cover over sixty pages, spreading from the events of *A Study in Scarlet* that occur on the morning of January 1st, 1881 to the evening of December 31st, 1883, as related in the opening and closing frame-tale segments of "The Adventure of the Vintner's Codex" by Lyndsay Faye.

These are dense years, explored broadly and deeply (but not yet completely) by many pasticheurs. For instance, there are fifteen versions (so far) of the meeting in Barts Lab, all providing extra details and perspectives to this momentous

9

event, while not contradicting the "official" version in any way:

- *A Study In Scarlet* – Dr. John H. Watson
- *Sherlock Holmes of Baker Street* (Chapter 6, pp. 53-56) – William S. Baring-Gould
- "A Study in Scarlet" (BBC Radio Broadcast) – Bert Coules
- *The Private Life of Dr Watson* (Epilogue) – Michael Hardwick
- "The Adventure of the Cunningham Heritage" – Sheldon Reynolds *Sherlock Holmes* (Television Episode – *Opening Segment*)
- "I Meet Dr. John Watson" (Chapter 2, pp. 19-24) – Michael Harrison *I, Sherlock Holmes*
- "The Detective and His Boswell" (Chapter 1) – Runa93
- *Death on a Pale Horse: Sherlock Holmes on Her Majesty's Secret Service* (Part II Chapter 4, pp. 89-94) – Donald Thomas
- *At the Mercy of the Mind* Chapter 90 – Gwendolyn Frame
- *When the Song of the Angels is Stilled* (Chapter 51, pp. 363-367) – A.S. Croyle
- "Only A Mild Acquaintance" (Chapter 1) – music97
- "A Pocketbook of Insanity" (Chapter 1, Segment 3) – Wraithwitch
- "The Bishop and the Horns of Plenty" (p. 87) – Karl Showler *Sherlock Holmes and the Watson Pastiche*
- *The Secret Diary of Mycroft Holmes, Esq.* (Chapter 17) – Westron Wynde (S.F. Bennett)
- *Worth and Choice* (Chapter 6) – KCS

And that doesn't even count all the other stories that are set earlier in the day of January 1st, before this meeting, all relating what else was happening then in addition to the few short paragraphs that Watson provides in the Canonical account later published in the 1887 *Beeton's Christmas Annual.*

There is an amazing array of traditional, Canonical, and excellent Holmes adventures to found under the collective umbrella of "fan-fiction", with nearly all of them published under many curious and unique *nom-de-plumes*. With the

10

paradigm shift that allowed so many delvers into Watson's Tin Dispatch Box to find a way to publicly release stories without the restriction of going through the narrow and obstructive channel of traditional publishing, an explosion of narratives has been revealed over the last few decades. Too many of those who declare themselves to be arms-wide-open Sherlockians are cheating themselves to an incredible degree by ignoring some really excellent examples of Holmes's adventures – often as good or better than those from traditional publishers, and sometimes better than The Canon itself.

Below is a list of some – but definitely not all – of these traditional and Canonical "fan-fictions" (as well as the modern literary agents who revealed them), covering the years from 1881 to 1883:

- "Barman" – Sigerson
- "What Providence Brought Together" – KaizokuShoju
- "Only A Mild Acquaintance" – music97
- "The Violin" – Haley Moore
- "Vexing Visitors" MONKrules
- "No Dogs Allowed" – KCS
- "The Houseplant" – KaizokuShoju
- "A Man's Limits" – KCS
- "Brown" – Monty Twain
- "Beginnings" *London Crime: The Detective and The Doctor*
- "The Art of Boxing" – Protector of the Gray Fortress
- "Lunch Money" – Monty Twain
- "The Most Winning Woman" – TeriyakiKat
- "A Pocketbook of Insanity, or Watson's First Case" – Wraithwitch
- "Sherlock Holmes – My Limits" – Monty Twain
- "Another Curse of Our Indian Possessions" – medcat
- "The Pursuit of Justice" – Lands End
- "Photograph" – MONKrules
- "The Case of the Baker Street Flatmate" – Bemj11 *Tales of Scotland Yard*
- "The Dreaded Band" *London Crime: The Detective and The Doctor*
- "Irregular Protectors" – Ancalime8301
- "The Unelucidated Casebook of Sherlock Holmes: The

11

Framingham Forgery" – infiniteviking
- "The Second List" – Be3
- "Contradictions" – Pompey
- "A Pound of Flesh" – Alone Dreaming
- "The Other's Limits" – Anony9
- "A Study in Tea Leaves" – Chewing Gum
- "The Case of the Startled Bay" – Westron Wynde (S.F. Bennett)
- "Bedside Manner" – Capt-Facepalm
- "The Tenants of Baker Street" – Protector of the Gray Fortress
- "Perfectly Insufferable" – Jack of All Suits
- "Combat" – shedoc
- "The Worth of a Friend" – pebbles66
- "Pocket Watch" – Capt-Facepalm
- "Deadly Loose Ends" – Blues Scale
- "A Man About the House" – pebbles66
- "A Row" – Monty Twain
- "My Heart's In the Highlands" – Capt-Facepalm
- "The Adventure of the Barchester Clergyman" – callensensei
- "Lines On the Face" – lew daney
- "All Hours" – Nanatsusaya
- "Baker Street Lodgings" – Wraithwitch
- "To Be Valuable" – Bartimus Crotchety
- "Decidedly So" (Chapters 2-4) – rabidsamfan (C.H. Dye)
- "Mind Over Memory" – KCS
- "The Case of the Thursday Rendezvous" – Alone Dreaming
- "Reveries" – smallrose
- "Watson's Finances" – Miss Roylott
- "Lost" – Monty Twain"
- "Will You Be My Friend" – bluedragon1836
- "Experimentation" – Bartimus Crotchety
- "These Are Deep Waters" – Igiveup
- "The Case of the Mottled Eyes" – Louann Qualls
- "Burden of Proof" – Capt-Facepalm
- "Dark Clouds" – Natalya Ilyinishna
- "The Whistle in the Attic" – wordybirdy
- "Found Pages (4)" – Dan Antidormi
- "Pain and Music" – Alone Dreaming
- "The Pink Reticule" – Tristan-the-Dreamer
- "Cold" – Bartimus Crotchety
- "Unexpected Complications" – E Phoenix
- "It's Christmastime in the City" – KCS
- "A Christmas Stocking" – Daniel A. Antidormi
- "Irregular Christmas" – callietitan

- "Their First Christmas" – Aleine Skyfire (Gwendolyn Frame)
- "Simple Gifts" – KCS
- "Friend" – KaizokuShoju
- "One Year" – KaizokuShoju
- "A Winter's Tale" – charleygirl
- "Surprising The Master" – xXBleedingRosesXx
- "Things Are Not As They Should Be" – MJ Azilem
- "Juxtaposition" – Bartimus Crotchety
- "The Case of the Attempted Vendetta" – Vishakha Sharma
- "The Beast of Hampton Moors" – Mike "The Baron" McManus
- "Hazards" – Pepipanda
- "Recruiting an Irregular" – juniper
- "The Egg" – Jon'ic Recheio
- "First Blood" – charleygirl
- "The Winning Woman" – Maryann Boyle Murray
- "February, 1882" – Crystal Rose of Pollux
- "Matters of Humanity" – Chuxter
- "The Case of the Black Group" – C.H. Baker
- "The Rescuer" – IrregularHonor
- "Peaceful Mornings" – Protector of the Gray Fortress
- "Prize Fighter" – KaizokuShoju
- "Back to the Beginning" – Curreeus
- "The Adventure of the Woman With the Cane" – Nitzchild
- "A Row with Mrs Hudson" – EchoValley26809
- "The Call of the Chickadee" – You Float My Boat
- "Unbidden Ghosts" – ScarletteQuill
- "Trains" – Chuxter
- "The Adventure of the Dubious Fiancé" – Gaia1
- "The Breaking Strain" – Bartimus Crotchety
- "Untitled Halloween Story" – Law Abiding Citizen
- "Memories" – medcat
- "Yes, Guv'Nor" – Ivy U Rhizzpi
- "A Friend and Associate" – MemorieLane
- "Duet" – Ketari Fang (Addy-kin)
- "Seaside Poison" – xMORIARTYx
- "Mrs Hudson's Misadventure" – IrregularHonor
- "Are You Feeling Adventurous?" – MadameGiry25
- "Professional" – Arhie
- "Three Weeks" – sherlockiantreky
- "Rose" – Gyroscope
- "Enchantment" – IrregularHonor
- "Untitled Air on G" – prettybrokenthings
- "Reflective Thoughts" – Jfreak

- "The World Stares" – shell less snail
- "Chaotic" – Hades Lord of the Dead
- "In Writing Only" – Hades Lord of the Dead
- "Not A Sidekick" – Aisho9
- "The Soft Underbelly of Civil Conversation" – aragonite (Marcia Wilson)
- "Colourful Experiments" – Jfreak
- "Painkiller" – Lemon Zinger
- "Moment of Panic" – Taleya
- "A Stronger Fear" – KCS
- "Humming To Ourselves" – Monty Twain
- "Death Waits For Nothing" – Rose H. McKellen
- "The Case of the Missing Box" – InTheRealWorld
- "A Little Bit of Fun" – PoeticPerson
- "Honor the Light Brigade" – beargirl1393
- "Deprivation" – Lemon Zinger
- "The Crime that Never Happened" – Ronald Carpenter *Sherlock Holmes: The One True Detective*
- "Who Would Kill Marwood?" – aragonite (Marcia Wilson)
- "Observations of a Lodger" – shedoc
- "The Catalyst Client" – Loki's Campaign Manager
- "The Baker's Bread" – Alan Downing *Armchair Mysteries of Sherlock Holmes*
- "The London Littoral" – aragonite (Marcia Wilson)
- "Rest in Torquay" – jenny starseed
- "The Fascinating Case of the Circular Cord" – Dennis L McKiernan
- "Stealth Tactics" – KCS
- "Diagnosed" – Science of Deduction
- "The Olive Affair" – Boston Manor
- "Essential" – Protector of the Gray Fortress
- "Between Pride and Insult" – You Float My Boat
- "Scar" – Alaylith
- "Irrational" – MONKrules
- "Unfortunate Mannerisms" – Lennon Drop
- "Afoot!" – ihedge
- "A Moment of Being" – charleygirl
- "Why The Case of the Velvet Female Thief" – Velvet Green
- "Hope" – Bowen Cates
- *On Afghanistan's Plains* – Pompey
- *Agreement and Disputation* – KCS
- "Lost and Found" – Arwen Jade Kenobi
- "In Good Hands" – Nunewesen

- "A Calculated Risk" – Msynergy
- "No Secret So Close" – Addy-kun
- "Loyalty" – Monty Twain
- "221 Words and a 'B'" – MD Hammer
- "The Art of Deduction" – Deana
- "The Adventure of the Secret Threat" – Kaizoku Shoju
- "Extrasensory Perception" – Dean King
- "Boom" – Knife86
- "When Master Met His Match" – Werewolf Master
- "Rainy Days and Board Games" – wordybirdy
- "The Best of Sherlock Holmes" – vraindall
- "Reminiscences of Miss Helen Stoner" – Miss Roylott
- "Holmes's Speckled Band" – Tehstrangeness
- "Untitled" – tunclr4
- "The Case of the Irregular Irregular" – Eyebrows2
- "Sherlock Holmes and the Pocket Watch Murders" – Forgotten Phoenix
- "Heredity" – Ingrid Matthews
- "The Problem of the Biggin Hill Duel" – Adrian Luciens
- "Summertime Wonderland" – The Liberal Admitted
- "The Case of the Baker Street Irregular" – Arctic Squirrel
- "The Sport of Kings" – Kadal
- "A Case of Twelve" – wordybirdy
- "The Pugilist, the Doctor, and the Detective" – Eyebrows2
- "The Adventure of the Blind Prophet" – Phantom Cavity
- "Realization" – Tristan-the-Dreamer
- "Indoor Shooting Practice" – Monty Twain
- "The Adventure of the Haunted House" – AnnCarter
- "Sherlock Holmes and the Mad Fakir" – shedoc
- "A Nagging Question" – Protector of the Gray Fortress
- "Terror" – anony9

For those who have to have their stories somehow legitimized by appearing by way of "acceptable" mediums, here is another tremendously incomplete list of Holmes and Watson's adventures, also set between January 1st, 1881 and December 31st, 1883, that have appeared in novels, short story collections, and television and radio broadcasts:

- "The First Cases" – Anon. *My Name is Sherlock Holmes*

- "The April Fool's Day Adventure" – Denis Green and Anthony Boucher *The Lost Adventures of Sherlock Holmes* and *The New Adventures of Sherlock Holmes* (Radio Broadcast)
- "The Adventure of the Slipshod Charlady" – John Hall *The MX Book of New Sherlock Holmes Stories" – Part I: 1881-1889*
- "The Speaking Machine" – Jim French *The Further Adventures of Sherlock Holmes* (Radio Broadcast)
- "The Italian Gourmet" – Roger Ricard *A Sherlock Holmes Alphabet of Cases" – Vol. II (F to J)*
- "The Darlington Substitution Scandal" – Denis Green and Anthony Boucher *The Forgotten Adventures of Sherlock Holmes* and *The New Adventures of Sherlock Holmes* (Radio Broadcast)
- "The Wandering Corpse" – John Taylor *The Unopened Casebook of Sherlock Holmes*
- "School For Scoundrels" – Jim French *The Further Adventures of Sherlock Holmes* (Radio Broadcast)
- "The Adventure of the Willow Pool" – Denis O. Smith. *The Chronicles of Sherlock Holmes Vol. IV*
- "The Adventure of the Temperance Society" – Deanna Baran *The MX Book of New Sherlock Holmes Stories – Part IX: 2018 Annual (1879-1895)*
- "The Diary of Anthony Moltaire" – Jim French *The Further Adventures of Sherlock Holmes* (Radio Broadcast)
- "The Adventure of the Traveling Orchestra" – Amy Thomas *The MX Book of New Sherlock Holmes Stories – Part I: 1881-1889*
- "The Adventure of the Double-Edged Hoard" – Craig Janacek *The MX Book of New Sherlock Holmes Stories – Part IV: 2016 Annual*
- "A Scandal in Tite Street" – Mike Hogan *Sherlock Holmes: Murder at the Savoy & Other Stories*
- "The Kingdom of the Blind" – Adrian Middleton *The MX Book of New Sherlock Holmes Stories" – Part I: 1881-1889*
- "The Case of the Ruby Necklace" – Bob Byrne *The MX Book of New Sherlock Holmes Stories" – Part V: Christmas Adventures*
- "The Jet Brooch" – Denis O. Smith *The MX Book of New Sherlock Holmes Stories" – Part V: Christmas Adventures*
- "The Adventure of the Naturalist's Stock Pin" – Jon L. Breen *More Holmes for the Holidays*
- "The Adventure of the Knighted Watchmaker" – Derrick Belanger *The MX Book of New Sherlock Holmes Stories – Part V: Christmas Adventures*
- "Christmas Eve" – S.C. Roberts *The Misadventures of Sherlock Holmes*
- "The Haunting of Sherlock Holmes" – Kevin David Barratt *The MX Book of New Sherlock Holmes Stories – Part I: 1881-1889*

- *You Buy Bones* – Marcia Wilson
- "The Adventure of the Dover Maiden" – Jim French *The Further Adventures of Sherlock Holmes* (Radio Broadcast)
- "The Adventure of the Velvet Lampshade" – Peter K. Andersson *The Cotswolds Werewolf*
- "The Case of the Thistle Killer" – Charles Early *Sherlock Holmes* (Television Episode)
- "The Case of the Honest Wife" – Lyndsay Faye *The Strand Magazine* and *The Whole Art of Detection*
- "The Stolen Relic" – David Marcum *The MX Book of New Sherlock Holmes Stories – Part V: Christmas Adventures*
- "The Adventure of the Serpent's Tooth" – Jim French *The Further Adventures of Sherlock Holmes* (Radio Broadcast)
- "The Singular Adventure of the Abandoned Bicycle" – Alan Stockwell *The Singular Adventures of Mr Sherlock Holmes*
- "The Adventure of the Pawnbroker's Daughter" – David Marcum *The MX Book of New Sherlock Holmes Stories" –Part I: 1881-1889*
- "The Eye Witnesses" – Alan Downing *Armchair Mysteries of Sherlock Holmes*
- "The Adventure of the Surrey Giant" Paul W. Nash *The Remains of Sherlock Holmes*
- "A Christmas Goose" – C.H. Dye *The MX Book of New Sherlock Holmes Stories – Part V: Christmas Adventures*
- "The American Ambassador" – David Scott *Holmes Redux*
- "The Case of the Vintner's Codex" Lyndsay Faye *The Strand Magazine* and *The Whole Art of Detection*
- "*Matilda Briggs* and the Giant Rat of Sumatra" – Ian Charnock *The Elementary Cases of Sherlock Holmes*
- "The Pearl of Death" – GC Rosenquist *Sherlock Holmes – The Pearl of Death*
- "The Adventure of the Paradol Chamber" – Alvin F. Rymsha *Sherlock Holmes: The Lost Cases*
- "The Mysterious Disappearance of the Good Ship *Alicia*" – Gerald Kelly *The Outstanding Mysteries of Sherlock Holmes*
- "Sherlock Holmes and the Tick Tock Man" – Roy Templeman *Sherlock Holmes: The Chinese Junk Affair and Other Stories*
- "The Case of the Vanishing Blueprint" – Liz Hedgecock *The Secret Notebooks of Sherlock Holmes*
- "The Plain Gold Wedding Ring" – Nick Cardillo *The Feats of Sherlock Holmes*
- "The Helverton Inheritance" – David Marcum *The MX Book of New Sherlock Holmes Stories – Part IX: 2018 Annual (1879-1895)*

17

- "The Great Zeffarini" – Richard Stone *Mysteries Suspended*
- "The Problem of Woolthshrap Prison" – Thomas G. Waddell and Thomas R. Rybolt *The Chemical Adventures of Sherlock Holmes*
- "The Case of the Vain Vixen" – Gayle Lange Puhl *Sherlock Holmes and the Folk Tale Mysteries" – Vol. I*
- "The Two Footmen" – Michael Gilbert *The New Adventures of Sherlock Holmes*
- "A Simple Solution" – David Marcum *The Strand Magazine*
- "The Adventure of the Defenestrated Princess" – Jayantika Ganguly *The MX Book of New Sherlock Holmes Stories – Part I: 1881-1889*
- "The Paddington Witch" – John Taylor *The Unopened Casebook of Sherlock Holmes and* (BBC Radio Broadcast"
- "The Adventure of the Christmas Visitor" – Denis O. Smith *The Chronicles of Sherlock Holmes Vol II*
- "The Night in the Asylum at Torence" – Herman Anthony Litzinger *Traveling With Sherlock Holmes and Dr. Watson*
- "The Battersea Worm" – John Taylor *The Unopened Casebook of Sherlock Holmes and* (BBC Radio Broadcast"
- "The Adventure of the Monstrous Blood" – Craig Janacek *Light in the Darkness*
- "The Adventure of the Old Russian Woman" – H. Paul Jeffers *The Confidential Casebook of Sherlock Holmes*
- "The Coffee House Girl" – David Marcum *The MX Book of New Sherlock Holmes Stories – Part XIII: 2019 Annual (1881-1890)*
- "Sherlock Holmes and the Mummy's Curse" – H. Paul Jeffers *Ghosts in Baker Street*
- "The Moriarty Gambit" – Fritz Lieber *The Game Is Afoot*
- "The Gray Goose" [Author Unknown] *The Stories of Sherlock Holmes* (South African Radio Broadcast)
- "The Affair of the Friendly Tramp" – N.M. Scott *Sherlock Holmes – To A Country House Darkly*
- "On the Wall – Lenore Glen Offord *The Baker Street Journal*
- "The Seaside Horror" – Magda Josza *The Private Diaries of Dr Watson*
- "The Case of the Frightened Bookkeeper" – Howard Merrill *The Further Adventures of Sherlock Holmes* (Radio Broadcast)
- "The Adventure of the Inn on the Marsh" – Denis O. Smith *The MX Book of New Sherlock Holmes Stories – Part I: 1881-1889*
- "Sherlock Holmes and the Bradfield Push" – Hugh Ashton *Secrets From the Deed Box of John H. Watson MD*
- "The Endell Street Mystery" – Malcolm Knott *Sherlock Holmes: The Soldier's Daughter*
- "Watson's Christmas Trick" – Bob Byrne *Sherlock Magazine*

- "The Case of the Schweinitz Portrait" – Floyd R. Horowitz *The Baker Street Journal*
- "A Volume In Vermillion" – Kim Newman *Sherlock Holmes Mystery Magazine* and *Moriarty: The Hound of the D'Urbervilles*
- *The Surrogate Assassin* – Christopher Leppek
- *Murder at Sorrows Crown* – Steven Saville and Robert Greenberger
- *Sherlock Holmes and the Raleigh Legacy* – L.B. Greenwood
- *The Case of the Revolutionist's Daughter* – Lewis S. Feuer
- *Mrs. Hudson and the Spirit's Curse* – Martin Davies
- "Denoument" - Donald W. Jackson *The Baker Street Journal*
- *Mrs. Hudson and the Malabar Rose* – Martin Davies
- *Sherlock Holmes and the Case of the Edinburgh Haunting* – David Wilson
- *Sherlock Holmes and the London Zoo Mystery* – Willoughby Lane
- *Sherlock Holmes and the Portsmouth Plot* – Boston Manor
- *Sherlock Holmes Lost Adventure* – Laurel Steinhauer
- *Sherlock Holmes and the Somerset Hunt* – Rosemary Michaud
- *Sherlock Holmes Uncovered: The Eccentric Painter"* – Steven Ehrman
- *The Case of the Howling Dog* – Allen Sharp
- *The Adventure of the Bloody Tower* – Donald MacLachlan
- *Sherlock Holmes Uncovered: The Viking General* – Steven Ehrman
- *Holmes in the West Country – Patrick Campbell*
- *Test of the Professionals: Leap Year* – Marcia Wilson
- *Test of the Professionals I: The Adventure of the Flying Blue Pidgeon* – Marcia Wilson
- *Test of the Professionals II: The Peaceful Night Poisonings* – Marcia Wilson

This current collection of adventures – and there will never be enough of them to completely tell the whole story of Holmes and Watson – provides valuable additional information about those early years in Baker Street.

As usual, I've arranged the stories in this collection in chronological order. As a die-hard and passionate Sherlockian Chronologicist, I really believe that it adds to the enjoyment to progress through a volume of adventures while matching them with what was occurring at the same time in the lives of Holmes and Watson.

As with every project that I attempt, I want to thank my true love, soul mate, and wonderful wife (of over thirty years!) Rebecca, and our wonderful amazing son and my friend, Dan. I love you both, and you are everything to me!

Once again, I can't find words to express the gratitude I have to all of the contributors who have used their time to create this project. I'm so glad to have gotten to know all of you through this process. It's an undeniable fact that Sherlock Holmes authors are the *best* people!

Additionally, I'd also like to especially thank:

- Derrick Belanger – I'm very glad to have gotten to know Derrick, even though we've never actually met in person – yet. We've both been involved in many projects since we first started communicating back in the fall of 2014, initially discussing Sherlockian matters, and then progressing to writing stories and producing books, sometimes with Belanger Books, and others with different connections. As always, I'm having a wonderful time, and I can't wait to see what happens next. Thanks so very much!

- Brian Belanger – Brian is an incredibly talented and very busy graphic artist, and he's having fun on the same scale that I am by being able to play in the Sherlockian sandbox. He constantly amazes me with his gifts, and I can't wait to see what he'll come up with next. Many thanks!

Finally, last but certainly *not* least, **Sir Arthur Conan Doyle**: Author, doctor, adventurer, and the Founder of the Sherlockian Feast. Present in spirit, and honored by all of us here.

As always, this collection, like those before it, has been a labor of love by both the participants and myself. As I've explained before, once again everyone did their sincerest best to produce an anthology that truly represents why Holmes and Watson have been so popular for so long. These are just more tiny threads woven into the ongoing Great Holmes Tapestry, continuing to grow and grow, for there can *never* be enough stories about the man whom Watson described as "*the best and wisest . . . whom I have ever known.*"

David Marcum
August 7th, 2019
The 167th Birthday of Dr. John H. Watson

Questions, comments, and story submissions
may be addressed to David Marcum at
thepapersofsherlockholmes@gmail.com

21

Sherlock Holmes
and
Doctor Watson:
The Early
Adventures

Volume I

A Study in Scarlet
by Sir Arthur Conan Doyle

(An Excerpt)

*(Being a reprint from the
Reminiscences of John H. Watson, M.D.,
Late of the Army Medical Department)*

Chapter I – Mr. Sherlock Holmes

In the year 1878 I took my degree of Doctor of Medicine of
the University of London, and proceeded to Netley to go
through the course prescribed for surgeons in the army. Having
completed my studies there, I was duly attached to the Fifth
Northumberland Fusiliers as Assistant Surgeon. The regiment
was stationed in India at the time, and before I could join it, the
second Afghan war had broken out. On landing at Bombay, I
learned that my corps had advanced through the passes, and
was already deep in the enemy's country. I followed, however,
with many other officers who were in the same situation as
myself, and succeeded in reaching Candahar in safety, where I
found my regiment, and at once entered upon my new duties.
The campaign brought honours and promotion to many, but for
me it had nothing but misfortune and disaster. I was removed
from my brigade and attached to the Berkshires, with whom I
served at the fatal battle of Maiwand. There I was struck on the
shoulder by a Jezail bullet, which shattered the bone and
grazed the subclavian artery. I should have fallen into the
hands of the murderous Ghazis had it not been for the devotion
and courage shown by Murray, my orderly, who threw me
across a pack-horse, and succeeded in bringing me safely to
the British lines.

I should have fallen into the hands of the murderous Ghazis had it not been for the devotion and courage shown by Murray, my orderly.

Worn with pain, and weak from the prolonged hardships which I had undergone, I was removed, with a great train of wounded sufferers, to the base hospital at Peshawar. Here I rallied, and had already improved so far as to be able to walk about the wards, and even to bask a little upon the verandah, when I was struck down by enteric fever, that curse of our Indian possessions. For months my life was despaired of, and when at last I came to myself and became convalescent, I was

26

so weak and emaciated that a medical board determined that not a day should be lost in sending me back to England. I was despatched, accordingly, in the troopship *Orontes*, and landed a month later on Portsmouth jetty, with my health irretrievably ruined, but with permission from a paternal government to spend the next nine months in attempting to improve it.

I had neither kith nor kin in England, and was therefore as free as air – or as free as an income of eleven-shillings-and-six-pence a day will permit a man to be. Under such circumstances I naturally gravitated to London, that great cesspool into which all the loungers and idlers of the Empire are irresistibly drained. There I stayed for some time at a private hotel in the Strand, leading a comfortless, meaningless existence, and spending such money as I had, considerably more freely than I ought. So alarming did the state of my finances become that I soon realized that I must either leave the metropolis and rusticate somewhere in the country, or that I must make a complete alteration in my style of living. Choosing the latter alternative, I began by making up my mind to leave the hotel, and to take up my quarters in some less pretentious and less expensive domicile.

On the very day that I had come to this conclusion, I was standing at the Criterion Bar, when someone tapped me on the shoulder, and turning round I recognized young Stamford, who had been a dresser under me at Barts. The sight of a friendly face in the great wilderness of London is a pleasant thing indeed to a lonely man. In old days Stamford had never been a particular crony of mine, but now I hailed him with enthusiasm, and he, in his turn, appeared to be delighted to see me. In the exuberance of my joy, I asked him to lunch with me at the Holborn, and we started off together in a hansom.

"Whatever have you been doing with yourself, Watson?" he asked in undisguised wonder, as we rattled through the crowded London streets. "You are as thin as a lath and as brown as a nut."

I gave him a short sketch of my adventures, and had hardly concluded it by the time that we reached our destination.

"Poor devil!" he said, commiseratingly, after he had listened to my misfortunes. "What are you up to now?"

"Looking for lodgings," I answered. "Trying to solve the problem as to whether it is possible to get comfortable rooms at a reasonable price."

"That's a strange thing," remarked my companion, "you are the second man today that has used that expression to me."

"And who was the first?" I asked.

"A fellow who is working at the chemical laboratory up at the hospital. He was bemoaning himself this morning because he could not get someone to go halves with him in some nice rooms which he had found, and which were too much for his purse."

"By Jove!" I cried, "if he really wants someone to share the rooms and the expense, I am the very man for him. I should prefer having a partner to being alone."

Young Stamford looked rather strangely at me over his wine-glass. "You don't know Sherlock Holmes yet," he said, "perhaps you would not care for him as a constant companion."

"Why, what is there against him?"

"Oh, I didn't say there was anything against him. He is a little queer in his ideas – an enthusiast in some branches of science. As far as I know he is a decent fellow enough."

"A medical student, I suppose?" said I.

"No – I have no idea what he intends to go in for. I believe he is well up in anatomy, and he is a first-class chemist, but, as far as I know, he has never taken out any systematic medical classes. His studies are very desultory and eccentric, but he has amassed a lot of out-of-the-way knowledge which would astonish his professors."

"Did you never ask him what he was going in for?" I asked.

"No, he is not a man that it is easy to draw out, though he can be communicative enough when the fancy seizes him."

"I should like to meet him," I said. "If I am to lodge with anyone, I should prefer a man of studious and quiet habits. I am not strong enough yet to stand much noise or excitement: I had enough of both in Afghanistan to last me for the remainder or my natural existence. How could I meet this friend of yours?"

"He is sure to be at the laboratory," returned my companion. "He either avoids the place for weeks, or else he works there from morning till night. If you like we will drive round together after luncheon."

"Certainly," I answered, and the conversation drifted away into other channels.

As we made our way to the hospital after leaving the Holborn, Stamford gave me a few more particulars about the gentleman whom I proposed to take as a fellow-lodger.

"You mustn't blame me if you don't get on with him," he said, "I know nothing more of him than I have learned from meeting him occasionally in the laboratory. You proposed this arrangement so you must not hold me responsible."

"If we don't get on it will be easy to part company," I answered. "It seems to me, Stamford," I added, looking hard at my companion, "that you have some reason for washing your hands of the matter. Is this fellow's temper so formidable, or what is it? Don't be mealy-mouthed about it."

"It is not easy to express the inexpressible," he answered with a laugh. "Holmes is a little too scientific for my tastes – it approaches to cold-bloodedness. I could imagine his giving a friend a little pinch of the latest vegetable alkaloid, not out of malevolence, you understand, but simply out of a spirit of inquiry in order to have an accurate idea of the effects. To do him justice, I think that he would take it himself with the same readiness. He appears to have a passion for definite and exact knowledge."

"Very right too."

"Yes, but it may be pushed to excess. When it comes to beating the subjects in the dissecting-rooms with a stick, it is certainly taking rather a bizarre shape."

"Beating the subjects!"

"Yes, to verify how far bruises may be produced after death. I saw him at it with my own eyes."

"And yet you say he is not a medical student?"

"No. Heaven knows what the objects of his studies are. But here we are, and you must form your own impressions about him." As he spoke, we turned down a narrow lane and passed through a small side-door, which opened into a wing of the great hospital. It was familiar ground to me, and I needed no guiding as we ascended the bleak stone staircase and made our way down the long corridor with its vista of whitewashed wall and dun-coloured doors. Near the farther end a low arched passage branched away from it and led to the chemical laboratory.

This was a lofty chamber, lined and littered with countless bottles. Broad, low tables were scattered about, which bristled with retorts, test-tubes, and little Bunsen lamps, with their blue flickering flames. There was only one student in the room, who was bending over a distant table absorbed in his work. At the sound of our steps he glanced round and sprang to his feet with a cry of pleasure: "I've found it! I've found it!" he shouted to my companion, running towards us with a test-tube in his hand. "I have found a re-agent which is precipitated by hæmoglobin, and by nothing else." Had he discovered a gold mine, greater delight could not have shone upon his features.

"I've found it! I've found it!" he shouted to my companion.

"Dr. Watson, Mr. Sherlock Holmes," said Stamford, introducing us.

"How are you?" he said cordially, gripping my hand with a strength for which I should hardly have given him credit. "You have been in Afghanistan, I perceive."

"How on earth did you know that?" I asked in astonishment.

"Never mind," said he, chuckling to himself. "The question now is about hæmoglobin. No doubt you see the significance of this discovery of mine?"

"It is interesting, chemically, no doubt," I answered, "but practically – "

"Why, man, it is the most practical medico-legal discovery for years. Don't you see that it gives us an infallible test for bloodstains. Come over here now!" He seized me by the coat sleeve in his eagerness, and drew me over to the table at which he had been working. "Let us have some fresh blood," he said, digging a long bodkin into his finger, and drawing off the resulting drop of blood in a chemical pipette. "Now, I add this small quantity of blood to a litre of water. You perceive that the resulting mixture has the appearance of pure water. The proportion of blood cannot be more than one in a million. I have no doubt, however, that we shall be able to obtain the characteristic reaction." As he spoke, he threw into the vessel a few white crystals, and then added some drops of a transparent fluid. In an instant the contents assumed a dull mahogany colour, and a brownish dust was precipitated to the bottom of the glass jar.

"Ha! Ha!" he cried, clapping his hands, and looking as delighted as a child with a new toy. "What do you think of that?"

"It seems to be a very delicate test," I remarked.

"Beautiful! Beautiful! The old guaiacum test was very clumsy and uncertain. So is the microscopic examination for blood corpuscles. The latter is valueless if the stains are a few hours old. Now, this appears to act as well whether the blood is old or new. Had this test been invented, there are hundreds of men now walking the earth who would long ago have paid the penalty of their crimes."

"Indeed!" I murmured.

"Criminal cases are continually hinging upon that one point. A man is suspected of a crime months perhaps after it has been committed. His linen or clothes are examined and brownish stains discovered upon them. Are they blood stains, or mud stains, or rust stains, or fruit stains, or what are they? That is a question which has puzzled many an expert, and why? Because there was no reliable test. Now we have the Sherlock Holmes test, and there will no longer be any difficulty."

His eyes fairly glittered as he spoke, and he put his hand over his heart and bowed as if to some applauding crowd conjured up by his imagination.

"You are to be congratulated," I remarked, considerably surprised at his enthusiasm.

"There was the case of Von Bischoff at Frankfort last year. He would certainly have been hung had this test been in existence. Then there was Mason of Bradford, and the notorious Muller, and Lefevre of Montpellier, and Samson of New Orleans. I could name a score of cases in which it would have been decisive."

"You seem to be a walking calendar of crime," said Stamford with a laugh. "You might start a paper on those lines. Call it the *Police News of the Past*."

"Very interesting reading it might be made, too," remarked Sherlock Holmes, sticking a small piece of plaster over the prick on his finger. "I have to be careful," he continued, turning to me with a smile, "for I dabble with poisons a good deal." He held out his hand as he spoke, and I noticed that it was all mottled over with similar pieces of plaster, and discoloured with strong acids.

"We came here on business," said Stamford, sitting down on a high three-legged stool, and pushing another one in my direction with his foot. "My friend here wants to take diggings, and as you were complaining that you could get no one to go halves with you, I thought that I had better bring you together."

Sherlock Holmes seemed delighted at the idea of sharing his rooms with me. "I have my eye on a suite in Baker Street," he said, "which would suit us down to the ground. You don't mind the smell of strong tobacco, I hope?"

"I always smoke 'ship's' myself," I answered.

"That's good enough: I generally have chemicals about, and occasionally do experiments. Would that annoy you?"

"By no means."

"Let me see – what are my other shortcomings. I get in the dumps at times, and don't open my mouth for days on end. You must not think I am sulky when I do that. Just let me alone, and I'll soon be right. What have you to confess now? It's just as well for two fellows to know the worst of one another before they begin to live together."

I laughed at this cross-examination. "I keep a bull pup," I said, "and I object to rows because my nerves are shaken, and I get up at all sorts of ungodly hours, and I am extremely lazy. I have another set of vices when I'm well, but those are the principal ones at present."

"Do you include violin playing in your category of rows?" he asked, anxiously.

"It depends on the player," I answered. "A well-played violin is a treat for the gods – a badly-played one – "

"Oh, that's all right," he cried, with a merry laugh. "I think we may consider the thing as settled – that is, if the rooms are agreeable to you."

"When shall we see them?"

"Call for me here at noon tomorrow, and we'll go together and settle everything," he answered.

"All right – noon exactly," said I, shaking his hand.

We left him working among his chemicals, and we walked together towards my hotel.

"By the way," I asked suddenly, stopping and turning upon Stamford, "how the deuce did he know that I had come from Afghanistan?"

My companion smiled an enigmatical smile. "That's just his little peculiarity," he said. "A good many people have wanted to know how he finds things out."

"Oh! A mystery is it?" I cried, rubbing my hands. "This is very piquant. I am much obliged to you for bringing us together. '*The proper study of mankind is man*', you know."

"You must study him, then," Stamford said, as he bade me goodbye. "You'll find him a knotty problem, though. I'll wager he learns more about you than you about him. Goodbye."

"Goodbye," I answered, and strolled on to my hotel, considerably interested in my new acquaintance.

Chapter II – The Science of Deduction

We met the next day as he had arranged and inspected the rooms at No. 221b, Baker Street, of which he had spoken at our meeting. They consisted of a couple of comfortable bedrooms and a single large airy sitting room, cheerfully furnished, and illuminated by two broad windows. So desirable in every way were the apartments, and so moderate did the terms seem when divided between us, that the bargain was concluded upon the spot, and we at once entered into possession. That very evening I moved my things round from the hotel, and on the following morning Sherlock Holmes followed me with several boxes and portmanteaus. For a day or two we were busily employed in unpacking and laying out our property to the best advantage. That done, we gradually began to settle down and to accommodate ourselves to our new surroundings.

Holmes was certainly not a difficult man to live with. He was quiet in his ways, and his habits were regular. It was rare for him to be up after ten at night, and he had invariably breakfasted and gone out before I rose in the morning. Sometimes he spent his day at the chemical laboratory, sometimes in the dissecting rooms, and occasionally in long walks, which appeared to take him into the lowest portions of the city. Nothing could exceed his energy when the working fit was upon him, but now and again a reaction would seize him, and for days on end he would lie upon the sofa in the sitting room, hardly uttering a word or moving a muscle from morning to night. On these occasions I have noticed such a dreamy, vacant expression in his eyes, that I might have suspected him of being addicted to the use of some narcotic, had not the temperance and cleanliness of his whole life forbidden such a notion.

As the weeks went by, my interest in him and my curiosity as to his aims in life gradually deepened and increased. His very person and appearance were such as to strike the attention of the most casual observer. In height he was rather over six feet, and so excessively lean that he seemed to be considerably taller. His eyes were sharp and piercing, save during those intervals of torpor to which I have alluded, and his thin, hawk-like nose gave his whole expression an air of alertness and decision. His chin, too, had the prominence and squareness which mark the man of determination. His hands were invariably blotted with ink and stained with chemicals, yet he was possessed of extraordinary delicacy of touch, as I frequently had occasion to observe when I watched him manipulating his fragile philosophical instruments.

The reader may set me down as a hopeless busybody, when I confess how much this man stimulated my curiosity, and how often I endeavoured to break through the reticence which he showed on all that concerned himself. Before pronouncing judgment, however, be it remembered, how objectless was my life, and how little there was to engage my attention. My health forbade me from venturing out unless the weather was exceptionally genial, and I had no friends who would call upon me and break the monotony of my daily existence. Under these circumstances, I eagerly hailed the little mystery which hung around my companion, and spent much of my time in endeavouring to unravel it.

He was not studying medicine. He had himself, in reply to a question, confirmed Stamford's opinion upon that point. Neither did he appear to have pursued any course of reading which might fit him for a degree in science or any other recognized portal which would give him an entrance into the learned world. Yet his zeal for certain studies was remarkable, and within eccentric limits his knowledge was so extraordinarily ample and minute that his observations have fairly astounded me. Surely no man would work so hard or attain such precise information unless he had some definite end in view. Desultory readers arc seldom remarkable for the exactness of their learning. No man burdens his mind with small matters unless he has some very good reason for doing so.

His ignorance was as remarkable as his knowledge. Of contemporary literature, philosophy, and politics he appeared to know next to nothing. Upon my quoting Thomas Carlyle, he enquired in the naivest way who he might be and what he had done. My surprise reached a climax, however, when I found incidentally that he was ignorant of the Copernican Theory and of the composition of the Solar System. That any civilized human being in this nineteenth century should not be aware that the earth travelled round the sun appeared to be to me such an extraordinary fact that I could hardly realize it.

"You appear to be astonished," he said, smiling at my expression of surprise. "Now that I do know it I shall do my best to forget it."

"To forget it!"

"You see," he explained, "I consider that a man's brain originally is like a little empty attic, and you have to stock it with such furniture as you choose. A fool takes in all the lumber of every sort that he comes across, so that the knowledge which might be useful to him gets crowded out, or at best is jumbled up with a lot of other things, so that he has a difficulty in laying his hands upon it. Now the skilful workman is very careful indeed as to what he takes into his brain attic. He will have nothing but the tools which may help him in doing his work, but of these he has a large assortment, and all in the most perfect order. It is a mistake to think that that little room has elastic walls and can distend to any extent. Depend upon it – there comes a time when for every addition of knowledge you forget something that you knew before. It is of the highest importance, therefore, not to have useless facts elbowing out the useful ones."

"But the Solar System!" I protested.

"What the deuce is it to me?" he interrupted impatiently. "You say that we go round the sun. If we went round the moon it would not make a pennyworth of difference to me or to my work."

I was on the point of asking him what that work might be, but something in his manner showed me that the question would be an unwelcome one. I pondered over our short conversation, however, and endeavoured to draw my deductions from it. He said that he would acquire no knowledge which did not bear upon his object. Therefore all the knowledge which he possessed was such as would be useful to him. I enumerated in my own mind all the various points upon which he had shown me that he was exceptionally well-informed. I even took a pencil and jotted them down. I could not help smiling at the document when I had completed it. It ran in this way:

Sherlock Holmes – His Limits

1. *Knowledge of literature. – Nil.*
2. *Knowledge of Philosophy. – Nil.*
3. *Knowledge of Astronomy. – Nil.*
4. *Knowledge of Politics. – Feeble.*
5. *Knowledge of Botany. – Variable. Well up in belladonna, opium, and poisons generally. Knows nothing of practical gardening.*
6. *Knowledge of Geology. – Practical, but limited. Tells at a glance different soils from each other. After walks has shown me splashes upon his trousers, and told me by their colour and consistence in what part of London he had received them.*
7. *Knowledge of Chemistry. – Profound.*
8. *Knowledge of Anatomy. – Accurate, but unsystematic.*
9. *Knowledge of Sensational Literature. – Immense. He appears to know every detail of every horror perpetrated in the century.*
10. *Plays the violin well.*

*11. Is an expert singlestick player, boxer, and
    swordsman.*

12. Has a good practical knowledge of British law.

When I got so far in my list I threw it into the fire in despair. "If I could only find what the fellow is driving at by reconciling all these accomplishments, and discovering a calling which needs them all," I said to myself, "I may as well give up the attempt at once."

*Leaning back in his arm-chair of an evening, he would close his eyes and
scrape carelessly at the fiddle which was thrown across his knee*

I see that I have alluded above to his powers upon the violin. These were very remarkable, but as eccentric as all his other accomplishments. That he could play pieces, and difficult pieces, I knew well, because at my request he has played me some of Mendelssohn's Lieder, and other favourites. When left to himself, however, he would seldom produce any music or attempt any recognised air. Leaning back in his arm-chair of an evening, he would close his eyes and scrape carelessly at the fiddle which was thrown across his knee. Sometimes the chords were sonorous and melancholy. Occasionally they were fantastic and cheerful. Clearly they reflected the thoughts which possessed him, but whether the music aided those thoughts, or whether the playing was simply the result of a whim or fancy, was more than I could determine. I might have rebelled against these exasperating solos had it not been that he usually terminated them by playing in quick succession a whole series of my favourite airs as a slight compensation for the trial upon my patience.

During the first week or so we had no callers, and I had begun to think that my companion was as friendless a man as I was myself. Presently, however, I found that he had many acquaintances, and those in the most different classes of society. There was one little sallow, rat-faced, dark-eyed fellow, who was introduced to me as Mr. Lestrade, and who came three or four times in a single week. One morning a young girl called, fashionably dressed, and stayed for half-an-hour or more. The same afternoon brought a grey-headed, seedy visitor, looking like a Jew pedlar, who appeared to me to be much excited, and who was closely followed by a slip-shod elderly woman. On another occasion an old white-haired gentleman had an interview with my companion, and on another, a railway porter in his velveteen uniform. When any of these non-descript individuals put in an appearance, Sherlock Holmes used to beg for the use of the sitting room, and I would retire to my bedroom. He always apologized to me for putting me to this inconvenience. "I have to use this room as a place of business," he said, "and these people are my clients." Again I had an opportunity of asking him a point-blank question, and again my delicacy prevented me from forcing another man to confide in me. I imagined at the time that he had some strong reason for not alluding to it, but he soon dispelled the idea by coming round to the subject of his own accord.

It was upon the 4th of March, as I have good reason to remember, that I rose somewhat earlier than usual, and found that Sherlock Holmes had not yet finished his breakfast. The landlady had become so accustomed to my late habits that my place had not been laid nor my coffee prepared. With the unreasonable petulance of mankind I rang the bell and gave a curt intimation that I was ready. Then I picked up a magazine from the table and attempted to while away the time with it, while my companion munched silently at his toast. One of the articles had a pencil mark at the heading, and I naturally began to run my eye through it.

Its somewhat ambitious title was *"The Book of Life"*, and it attempted to show how much an observant man might learn by an accurate and systematic examination of all that came in his way. It struck me as being a remarkable mixture of shrewdness and of absurdity. The reasoning was close and intense, but the deductions appeared to me to be far-fetched and exaggerated. The writer claimed by a momentary expression, a twitch of a muscle or a glance of an eye, to fathom a man's inmost thoughts. Deceit, according to him, was an impossibility in the case of one trained to observation and analysis. His conclusions were as infallible as so many propositions of Euclid. So startling would his results appear to the uninitiated that until they learned the processes by which he had arrived at them they might well consider him as a necromancer.

From a drop of water, said the writer, "*a logician could infer the possibility of an Atlantic or a Niagara without having seen or heard of one of the other. So all life is a great chain, the nature of which is known whenever we are shown a single link of it. Like all other arts, the Science of Deduction and Analysis is one which can only be acquired by long and patient study, nor is life long enough to allow any mortal to attain the highest possible perfection in it. Before turning to those moral and mental aspects of the matter which present the greatest difficulties, let the inquirer begin by mastering more elementary problems. Let him on meeting a fellow-mortal, learn at a glance to distinguish the history of the man, and the trade or profession to which he belongs. Puerile as such an exercise may seem, it sharpens the faculties of observation, and teaches one where to look and what to look for. By a man's finger-nails, by his coat-sleeve, by his boot, by his trouser-knees, by the callosities of his forefinger and thumb, by his expression, by his shirt-cuffs – by each of these things a man's calling is plainly revealed. That all united should fail to enlighten the competent inquirer in any case is almost inconceivable.*

"What ineffable twaddle!" I cried, slapping the magazine down on the table. "I never read such rubbish in my life."

"What is it?" asked Sherlock Holmes.

"Why this article," I said, pointing at it with my egg-spoon as I sat down to my breakfast.

"I see that you have read it since you have marked it. I don't deny that it is smartly written. It irritates me though. It is evidently the theory of some arm-chair lounger who evolves all these neat little paradoxes in the seclusion of his own study. It is not practical. I should like to see him clapped down in a third-class carriage on the Underground, and asked to give the trades of all his fellow-travellers. I would lay a thousand-to-one against him."

"You would lose your money," Holmes remarked calmly. "As for the article, I wrote it myself."

"You!"

"Yes. I have a turn both for observation and for deduction. The theories which I have expressed there, and which appear to you to be so chimerical, are really extremely practical – so practical that I depend upon them for my bread and cheese."

"And how?" I asked involuntarily.

"Well, I have a trade of my own. I suppose I am the only one in the world. I'm a consulting detective, if you can understand what that is. Here in London we have lots of Government detectives and lots of private ones. When these fellows are at fault, they come to me, and I manage to put them on the right scent. They lay all the evidence before me, and I am generally able, by the hold of my knowledge of the history of crime, to set them straight. There is a strong family resemblance about misdeeds, and if you have all the details of a thousand at your finger ends, it is odd if you can't unravel the thousand-and-first. Lestrade is a well-known detective. He got himself into a fog recently over a forgery case, and that was what brought him here."

"And these other people?"

"They are mostly sent on by private inquiry agencies. They are all people who are in trouble about something, and want a little enlightening. I listen to their story, they listen to my comments, and then I pocket my fee."

"But do you mean to say," I said, "that without leaving your room you can unravel some knot which other men can make nothing of, although they have seen every detail for themselves?"

"Quite so. I have a kind of intuition that way. Now and again a case turns up which is a little more complex. Then I have to bustle about and see things with my own eyes. You see I have a lot of special knowledge which I apply to the problem, and which facilitates matters wonderfully. Those rules of deduction laid down in that article which aroused your scorn are invaluable to me in practical work. Observation with me is second nature. You appeared to be surprised when I told you, on our first meeting, that you had come from Afghanistan."

"You were told, no doubt."

"Nothing of the sort. I *knew* you came from Afghanistan. From long habit the train of thoughts ran so swiftly through my mind that I arrived at the conclusion without being conscious of intermediate steps. There were such steps, however. The train of reasoning ran, 'Here is a gentleman of the medical type, but with the air of a military man. Clearly an army doctor, then. He has just come from the tropics, for his face is dark, and that is not the natural tint of his skin, for his wrists are fair. He has undergone hardship and sickness, as his haggard face says clearly. His left arm has been injured: He holds it in a stiff and unnatural manner. Where in the tropics could an English army doctor have seen much hardship and got his arm wounded? Clearly in Afghanistan.' The whole train of thought did not occupy a second. I then remarked that you came from Afghanistan, and you were astonished."

"It is simple enough as you explain it," I said smiling. "You remind me of Edgar Allen Poe's Dupin. I had no idea that such individuals did exist outside of stories."

Sherlock Holmes rose and lit his pipe. "No doubt you think that you are complimenting me in comparing me to Dupin," he observed. "Now, in my opinion, Dupin was a very inferior fellow. That trick of his of breaking in on his friends' thoughts with an apropos remark after a quarter-of-an-hour's silence is really very showy and superficial. He had some analytical genius, no doubt, but he was by no means such a phenomenon as Poe appeared to imagine."

"Have you read Gaboriau's works?" I asked. "Does Lecoq come up to your idea of a detective?"

Sherlock Holmes sniffed sardonically. "Lecoq was a miserable bungler," he said, in an angry voice. "He had only one thing to recommend him, and that was his energy. That book made me positively ill. The question was how to identify an unknown prisoner. I could have done it in twenty-four hours. Lecoq took six months or so. It might be made a text-book for detectives to teach them what to avoid."

I felt rather indignant at having two characters whom I had admired treated in this cavalier style. I walked over to the window, and stood looking out into the busy street. "This fellow may be very clever," I said to myself, "but he is certainly very conceited."

"There are no crimes and no criminals in these days," he said, querulously. "What is the use of having brains in our profession. I know well that I have it in me to make my name famous. No man lives or has ever lived who has brought the same amount of study and of natural talent to the detection of crime which I have done. And what is the result? There is no crime to detect, or, at most, some bungling villainy with a motive so transparent that even a Scotland Yard official can see through it."

I was still annoyed at his bumptious style of conversation. I thought it best to change the topic.

"I wonder what that fellow is looking for?" I asked, pointing to a stalwart, plainly-dressed individual who was walking slowly down the other side of the street, looking anxiously at the numbers. He had a large blue envelope in his hand, and was evidently the bearer of a message.

"You mean the retired sergeant of Marines," said Sherlock Holmes.

"Brag and bounce!" thought I to myself. "He knows that I cannot verify his guess."

The thought had hardly passed through my mind when the man whom we were watching caught sight of the number on our door, and ran rapidly across the roadway. We heard a loud knock, a deep voice below, and heavy steps ascending the stairs.

"For Mr. Sherlock Holmes," he said, stepping into the room and handing my friend the letter.

Here was an opportunity of taking the conceit out of him. He little thought of this when he made that random shot. "May I ask, my lad," I said, in the blandest voice, "what your trade may be?"

"Commissionaire, sir," he said, gruffly. "Uniform away for repairs."

"And you were?" I asked, with a slightly malicious glance at my companion.

"A sergeant, sir, Royal Marine Light Infantry, sir. No answer? Right, sir."

He clicked his heels together, raised his hand in a salute, and was gone.

"For Mr. Sherlock Holmes," he said.

Chapter III – The Lauriston Gardens Mystery

I confess that I was considerably startled by this fresh proof of the practical nature of my companion's theories. My respect for his power of analysis increased wondrously. There still remained some lurking suspicion in my mind, however, that the whole thing was a prearranged episode, intended to dazzle me, though what earthly object he could have in taking me in was past my comprehension. When I looked at him, he had finished reading the note, and his eyes had assumed the vacant, lack-lustre expression which showed mental abstraction.

"How in the world did you deduce that?" I asked.

"Deduce what?" said he, petulantly.

"Why, that he was a retired sergeant of Marines."

"I have no time for trifles," he answered, brusquely. Then with a smile, "Excuse my rudeness. You broke the thread of my thoughts, but perhaps it is as well. So you actually were not able to see that that man was a sergeant of Marines?"

"No, indeed."

"It was easier to know it than to explain why I know it. If you were asked to prove that two and two made four, you might find some difficulty, and yet you are quite sure of the fact. Even across the street I could see a great blue anchor tattooed on the back of the fellow's hand. That smacked of the sea. He had a military carriage, however, and regulation side whiskers. There we have the marine. He was a man with some amount of self-importance and a certain air of command. You must have observed the way in which he held his head and swung his cane. A steady, respectable, middle-aged man, too, on the face of him – all facts which led me to believe that he had been a sergeant."

"Wonderful!" I ejaculated.

"Commonplace," said Holmes, though I thought from his expression that he was pleased at my evident surprise and admiration. "I said just now that there were no criminals. It appears that I am wrong – look at this!" He threw me over the note which the commissionaire had brought.

"Why," I cried, as I cast my eye over it, "this is terrible!"

"It does seem to be a little out of the common," he remarked, calmly. "Would you mind reading it to me aloud?"

And so it begins . . . .

49

The Adventure of the
Persistent Pugilist
by Thomas A. Burns, Jr.

After the singular and baffling affair at Lauriston Gardens, I had an occasion to reconsider my association with Sherlock Holmes, of whom I had learned was employed as a consulting detective, sometimes to Scotland Yard. Holmes was gracious enough to allow me to participate in the investigation and observe his methods, and he brought the perpetrator to heel in our very sitting room at 221b Baker Street. Whilst the investigation was in progress, I experienced a thrilling reintroduction to an active lifestyle, which I had eschewed since my return as a convalescent from Afghanistan, and I must say that I found it most invigorating. However, I had not reckoned with the subsequent *sequalae* that such exertions would bring.

Thus, it was on Monday, March 7th of 1881, I awoke in a bed of pain in the wee hours of the morning, my wounded shoulder throbbing as if the Jezail bullet that I received at Maiwand was still in place, with aches in every joint, and a debilitating headache as well. I tried to roll over and retreat once more to the blissful solace of sleep, but that simply was not to be. I dragged myself down to the sitting room. It was a mild night, so the windows overlooking Baker Street were thrown open wide. Of course, Holmes was not present – doubtless he was snug in his bed. I went to the sideboard and poured myself a stiff whisky, followed by a splash of soda from the gasogene. Then I sank into a comfortable chair to sip my drink and reflect on the probable reason for my sudden infirmity.

I have told elsewhere of my misadventures as an Army surgeon in Afghanistan and India. I had first-hand knowledge of the damage that enteric fever could do to a body, but during the thrills of last week's chase, I had forgotten that my Army doctors had informed me that my recovery was apt to be protracted, and that I should refrain from sustained physical activity and mental strain for many months. But I had been feeling so much better of late that I neglected the doctors' prescriptions. Now, I was likely paying for my recent lack of attention to my health.

The whisky worked its magic, however, and in a little while I was feeling nearly human again, when suddenly there arose a commotion at the downstairs door.

I struggled out of the soft chair and went to the window, where I beheld a street Arab, pounding on our door.

"I say!" I shouted from the window. "What is the meaning of this?"

"Doctor Watson?" the lad yelled. "Mr. 'Olmes wants youse to meet 'im at Davies Street and Brooks Mews!"

I was incredulous. "What? At this infernal hour?"

"E sez 'e needs youse, Doctor. He told me to say to youse, 'Come at once!'"

The unbridled cheek of the fellow! Come at once? Really? It was an open question whether I would even be able to dress myself, never mind hieing off all over London to satisfy Holmes's peremptory demand.

The boy was lingering at the door, so I tossed him a tanner for his trouble. My earlier pains had ameliorated somewhat, but I was still by no means in the pink. The thought of struggling into my clothes and venturing into the street to find a cab at this hour was disagreeable, to say the least. I flopped back into my chair.

51

Then the pangs of guilt began to assail me. Perhaps Holmes was in trouble, and had no one else to turn to for aid. One of the things that had attracted us as to share the same abode was that neither of us had family in the City. And Holmes had told me how much he appreciated my assistance with the murders of Drebber and Stangerson, even though I thought my contribution to the solution was minimal, if not non-existent.

The long and the short of it was that, fifteen minutes later, I found myself walking toward Marylebone Road, a major thoroughfare, where I would be much more likely to find a cab at this hour than in Baker Street. Brooks Mews off Davies Street was only about a mile away towards the centre city, but walking such a distance in my present condition was out of the question. I was in luck – I found a cabbie in Marylebone Road, either starving or an incontrovertible optimist, who agreed to take me to Holmes.

The ride was a rapid one, clattering through London's empty thoroughfares. Davies Street was just off Grosvenor Square, one of the toniest areas in all of London. As I exited the hansom in the yellow glow of the gas lamps, I noticed a group of men huddled just inside the mews, seemingly studying the pavement with rapt attention. Two of them were constables, recognisable by their tall helmets, and one was shining a bullseye lantern into the mews. I also thought I recognized that ferret-like fellow Inspector Lestrade, who had visited Holmes several times at 221b. I handed the cabbie one-and-six and approached the group. Then I saw that another man kneeling on the cobblestones a little way beyond them. It was Sherlock Holmes, intensively examining the prostrate form of a man.

"Here now!" exclaimed Lestrade as I neared, moving to block my access to the scene. Holmes turned his head and saw me.

"Watson!" he cried, springing to his feet, "How very good of you to come, old fellow!"

Lestrade moved aside to allow me to pass.

Holmes's obvious delectation at my presence went a long way towards expunging my earlier rancour about his peremptory summons. "What has happened here?" I inquired.

"That is what I trust you can help me to ascertain," said Holmes.

I looked down at the unfortunate chap splayed out on the pavement, obviously dead. He was a man in his prime, about Holmes's size, and his frock coat, waistcoat, and ascot identified him as a gentleman, as did the crumpled bowler hat lying just a few feet away from him. The dishevelled state of his clothing, coupled with the bruises and dried blood on his face, indicated that he had taken a terrific beating.

"What would you like me to do?" I asked Holmes.

"Please examine this gentleman, and tell me what you think was the cause of his demise."

I began to kneel, then asked, "I should have thought you had already done so."

"I have, but I am not a medical man. I want to see if your deductions agree with those of mine."

I sank to the pavement and began my examination with the chap's face. "He was battered while alive," I said, "as indicated by the extensive bruising." I tried to close his staring eyes with my thumb and met some resistance. "He seems to be in the early stages of *rigor mortis*, which would indicate that he died approximately two hours ago." I wiggled his jaw to be certain. Noticing the dried blood in his blond hair, I raised his head from the cobblestones and found a considerable depression in the back of his skull. "This head trauma likely killed him, but I don't understand how he could have suffered such a deeply depressed fracture like this by hitting his head on level pavement." I saw that Holmes was smiling at me now. "I really cannot tell you any more without a proper autopsy."

"That's very good, Watson, and it agrees with my observations and deductions perfectly. Constable, would you be so good as to hand me your lantern?" Holmes played the beam around in the mews, then out toward Davies Street. He continued, "In addition to the excellent reason that Watson stated, Lestrade, it is obvious that the fellow did not fall here, as indicated by the position of his hat off to one side. Also, the hat would not be in such a disreputable state if it had simply fallen from his head. Someone picked it up, crushed it, and threw it where it now lies. And consider his jacket, bunched up behind him, as it would be if he was dragged by his feet."

Looking directly at Lestrade, he accused, "Had you and your army not rushed into the mews before inspecting the pavement, we could doubtless follow the marks left when the victim was dragged to his present location, to ascertain the place at which the beating actually occurred. However, that should not prove to be an insurmountable difficulty." Holmes moved back towards Davies Street, the beam of the lantern dancing before him as a herald. He held out his arm when the rest of us attempted to follow. "Hold, gentlemen. Let us not make the same mistake twice." Holmes walked a little way toward Brook Street whilst scanning the ground. "Ha! Here is where our unfortunate pugilist met his doom! Watson, come forth!" He shined the lantern on a crimson splash on the kerbstone, then handed it to me. "Stand fast, all of you. The fight took place in the street. Watson, follow me with the light!"

Holmes whipped out a glass from his pocket and dropped to his knees, crawling about on the cobblestones like a child at play. I could see nothing special about the areas he scrutinized, but given the plethora of grunts, groans, and ejaculations he uttered, he must have been learning much.

Finally, he rose to his feet again. "All right, Lestrade. You and your men may approach." When the policemen arrived, Holmes clasped his hands behind his back and began lecturing them as if in a university hall.

"This was no common robbery, gentlemen, even though no valuables were found on the victim. My examination of the street revealed that two men engaged in fisticuffs there, and it is no difficult deduction that our man in the alley lost the match, likely when he was struck and fell to be mortally wounded by yon kerbstone."

"Then the assailant dragged His Lordship into the mews to get the body out of sight," offered Lestrade.

"His Lordship?" I asked. "Then you know who he is?"

"Yes," said Holmes. "The miscreants did an exceedingly poor job of searching the body. They left his calling cards in the inside pocket of his frock coat. He was Sir Aubrey Strongheart, Lord Redthorne, a sitting member of the House of Lords."

It suddenly became clear why Lestrade had summoned Holmes to assist in the investigation.

"What do you mean, the 'miscreants'?" asked Lestrade. "I thought you said there were only two men that were involved in the fight?"

"That is correct, Inspector. But as many as five men, one of whom was the assailant, participated in dragging the unfortunate peer into the mews."

"Then what were the other four doing while the fight was in progress," I asked.

"Due to the disturbance of the signs in the mews by the police, there is no clear indication," Holmes replied, "but it is probably a safe assumption that they were watching from just inside." Holmes paused, and then went on. "And there is one other confounding factor."

"Which is?" I asked.

"Lord Redthorne has all of the characteristics of an accomplished boxer." Holmes said. "His ears are thickened, his nose and hands show signs that they had been broken in the past, and he has more missing teeth than I would expect for a man of his age and status."

"Well, if he was a boxer," asked Lestrade. "then how in Hades did he get beaten so badly?"

"Elementary, Inspector," said Holmes. "The other fellow was the better fighter."

In Baker Street, the morning sun was peeping over the rooftops, but the cobblestones were still enveloped in a cool shadow when we finally returned. Lestrade had summoned a police wagon to convey the hapless Sir Aubrey to the morgue, then instructed Holmes and me to go home. But rest was not in the cards for us. Our landlady, Mrs. Hudson, apparently heard us arrive and delivered a fine, full English breakfast to our rooms before we scarcely had time to settle in. We were immersed in the midst of it when there came a rap upon the door, which quickly opened to admit Lestrade.

"I was just going by to see Lady Redthorne, and I wondered if you gents would care to come along," he asked.

"Have a spot of breakfast first, Inspector," said Holmes. "To paraphrase Balthasar, bringing bad news may be your job, but there's no need to be in a rush about it."

"It's the part of my job I care for the least, Mr. Holmes, and that's no lie," the inspector said.

So, it was about an hour later we found ourselves in Grosvenor Street, not far from Brooks Mews, seeking admittance to a venerable Georgian townhouse, Sir Aubrey's residence. A maidservant opened the door and conveyed Lestrade's card to the lady of the house. She returned with the message that Lady Redthorne would see us, and conducted us to a parlour with broad windows overlooking the street, now bustling with early matutinal traffic. Shortly thereafter, Lady Redthorne appeared, resplendent in a purple-and-white morning dress with a broad skirt. However, her hair was still down.

There is no need to recount in detail the delivery of our sad message to Her Ladyship. Lestrade prevailed upon me for the duty, because as a doctor, I've had to do this sort of thing much more often than I would have liked. First comes the disbelief. Then the grief emerges, and finally, the reluctant acceptance that a loved one will be seen no more. I must say that Lady Redthorne admirably controlled her emotions when she heard, although I was sure that would last only until our departure. She even had the equanimity to offer us coffee, which we politely declined.

Sherlock Holmes addressed her. "My Lady," he asked, "did His Lordship have any enemies?"

She looked at Inspector Lestrade before answering, as if to ascertain that this brash young fellow did indeed have the authority to question her. When Lestrade nodded, she replied, "Not really. Oh, there were a few in the Lords with whom he disagreed politically, but none of them would resort to physical violence against him."

"Do you know where he was last evening?"

"Not precisely, but I would guess either at a boxing match or at his club. I'm sure someone there would know."

"And his club was . . . ."

"Lockerman's, in St. James Street."

"He was fond of prize-fighting?"

"Oh heavens, yes!" she exclaimed. "You could almost say he was obsessed with it. He attended matches all over London, sometimes three or four a week."

"And he was a boxer himself?"

"He was. He trained at the West London Boxing Club in the Strand."

"Was he an accomplished pugilist?"

"He liked to think so. He won a few small purses at matches in the boxing clubs in the City, but the larger ones eluded him, likely because those matches drew the best fighters." She paused, shaking her head. "But I just cannot believe he would have fallen prey to a street tough, or even a gang of them. He was a better fighter than that."

"Did he wager on boxing matches?" I asked.

She gave me a peculiar look, but answered, "Of course he did, mostly at Lockerman's."

"Do you know if he habitually took the same route home from Lockerman's every night?" Holmes asked.

"I don't know, but it wouldn't surprise me. Aubrey liked his little routines." She suddenly stopped speaking, and her gaze rose to the ceiling.

"You've remembered something that might help us?" Holmes essayed.

"Possibly. I'm sorry to tell you that my husband had a most singular habit of challenging beggars and passers-by to fisticuffs."

"Really!" I exclaimed.

"He wouldn't give a penny to a mendicant unless the man would fight him for it. But if the fellow gave him a good show, he would reward him handsomely." She smiled. "A few months ago, Aubrey came home with a glorious black eye.

'Lucky shot from a fellow begging in the Haymarket! Gave him a guinea for his trouble,' he told me." She pulled a handkerchief from her bodice and dabbed at an errant tear running down her cheek. "Silly old fool!"

After Holmes confirmed with Lestrade that the inspector had no other questions for Lady Redthorne, we took our leave. On the street, Holmes said to me, "Watson, you're looking a bit peaked. Why don't you go back to Baker Street and get some rest?"

"I say, Holmes, I'm fine . . . ."

"I have a little investigating to do, best accomplished alone. If it would suit you, you can accompany me to Lockerman's this evening."

"Rather!" I replied. Truth be told, I was feeling a little under the weather, and didn't want to again find myself in a state where I was useless.

Upon returning to Baker Street for the second time that morning, I was surely beginning to feel the effects of my nocturnal excursion. I took to my bed and managed a few hours' slumber, arising in mid-afternoon. I rang Mrs. Hudson for tea, and the dear lady, probably taking note that I had gone without luncheon, included some biscuits and tea sandwiches on the tray. After such fortification, I picked up a new book by that excellent author Wilke Collins to while away the remainder of the afternoon.

Abruptly, I heard heavy footsteps on the stairs, not at all like Holmes's rapid tread, so I braced myself for a knock upon the door. However, it did not come. Instead, the door sprang open and a most singular, disreputable-looking chap invaded the flat.

He was tall, a tatterdemalion in mismatched garments – a filthy brown jacket over a bright blue waistcoat, a white cotton shirt, burgundy knickers, and hideous red-and-white striped knee socks, carrying a dirty tan cloth sack on his shoulder. And he affected the most curious headgear – a hat with a short, pointed brim in front that ballooned out in the rear like a cancerous growth, hanging halfway down his back. The blood came to my face as I sprang up in outrage against this untoward invasion of my home.

"See here, my good man, you cannot just waltz into a private residence – "

"Youse got any trash needs collectin', Guvnor?"

"I should say not! Take yourself back downstairs, go to the servant's entrance, and discuss it with the landlady!"

The fellow screwed up his disfigured face into a scowl, wheeled around and took two steps toward the door, then turned back to face me, removing his enormous hat.

"I must say that you are deucedly unkind to the tradespeople, Watson," said Sherlock Holmes.

My knees became weak, and I collapsed backwards, falling heavily into my chair.

"Watson!" exclaimed Holmes, rushing to take me by the hands. "I had no idea my little charade would affect you so! Please accept my humble apology."

I was chagrined as well, displaying such pathetic weakness to my friend. "I'm sorry too, Holmes. It's just that I'm not as strong as I would prefer to be, as yet."

"And I should have realised that." He stepped to the whisky cabinet to prepare a fortifying libation for me.

"Whatever are you doing in that outlandish attire?"

"Impersonating a venerable London dustman."

"But why?"

"Most of our class know the dustman as the chap who visits our homes to carry away our trash. But many do not realize that he is also a tradesman, engaging in buying and selling the second-hand merchandise that he collects in his travels. Given that Brooks Mews and Davies Street is a rather genteel neighbourhood, I suspected that Sir Aubrey's assailant was not native to the area, and may have left something of himself behind. Thus, I was happy when I was able to purchase these from a dustman who serves that area." He reached into his shoulder bag and withdrew another set of tattered clothing – trousers, shirt, and coat. "The dustman who had these said he collected them not far from Brooks Mews. While I cannot say for certain that our unknown aggressor wore them, I think it likely." He held up the shirt, indicating some brownish spots. "I am sure my reagent will show these to be bloodstains," he said. Throwing the shirt and coat on the sofa, he unrolled the trousers and held the waistband to his own waist. Several inches of cloth ran out over his shoes. "He was a large man, and as indicated by Sir Aubrey's condition, and a proficient boxer. In fact, I suspect he was a professional prize-fighter."

"What is your next step?" I asked him.

"As I alluded earlier, I think a visit to Lockerman's is in order. That is, if you feel up to it."

His remark stung, even though I knew he did not mean it in a deprecatory way. D--n my infirmities!

Lockerman's was a gentleman's club in St. James Street, situated in a grey stone building constructed early in this century. Unlike in many other such establishments, its members did not ascribe to a particular political stance, but rather were united by a love of gaming in all of its varied forms. Cards, backgammon, wagering on sporting contests, and races were all engaged in. As non-members were generally required to be accompanied by a member to be granted admittance, Holmes prevailed upon Lestrade to accompany us, so his police credentials could open the doors.

We were admitted by a liveried manservant who conducted us to the Club Secretary, Mr. Wystan York. A thickset man in his forties, he was attired in full evening dress and seemed to look down his nose at us, who were not. Holmes appeared not to notice.

After introductions were made, Holmes addressed him. "Please convey my condolences to the members concerning the death of Sir Aubrey Strongheart. We came here with the hope of meeting some of his friends, who might shed light on some of his predilections, thus providing insight into this sad affair."

"I really do not see how we can help you, Mr. Holmes," responded York, "even though it would be our fondest wish to do so," "It is my understanding that Sir Aubrey was waylaid by ruffians on his way home last night."

"It may have been meant to appear so, Mr. York, but there are unresolved issues that a discussion with some of His Lordship's acquaintances might elucidate."

At York's frown, Lestrade interjected, "Scotland Yard would be grateful for any assistance the members could give us, sir."

"Oh, very well," said York. Puckering his lips, he told us, "I suppose that Sir Aubrey's best mates were the Punters. I will ask them if they will meet with you in the Visitor's Lounge."

"The Punters?" I inquired. "What a curious sobriquet."

"Just a group of fellows linked by similar interests," said York dismissively. "Walters will conduct you to the lounge."

The Punters proved to be a motley band of gentlemen of similar age to Holmes and myself, causing me to wonder how Sir Aubrey, at least two decades older, came to be associated with them. The lot of them reeked with alcohol. Seeing them, I came to understand York's demeanour when discussing them.

"I was hoping that you could tell me of Sir Aubrey's personality and habits," said Holmes, "which might explain how he came to be targeted."

"Oh, Aubs was young at heart, y'know," said "Dinky" Peckham, a moustachioed, blond fellow attired in an outlandish grey-plaid suit and pink waistcoat. "He found many of the older members much, much too stodgy for his tastes."

"Rawther!" agreed "Fido" Drinkwater, who affected a brown long coat with broad, velvet lapels over a chequered vest and a polka-dotted ascot. "Said keeping our company made him feel like a child again, he did."

The other two Punters were Reggie Searles, a burly, morose man with a large, bulbous nose and a square jaw, who wore unorthodox garments similar to the other two, but a size too small for him, and Braddcy Bathgate, a short chap with a black moustache and a triangular beard, who eschewed jackets and waistcoats altogether. He was clad in black trousers, and a billowy black shirt with a high collar. He wore a remarkable gold medallion around his neck, comprising interlocking triangles with an Egyptian ankh in the centre.

"Did Sir Aubrey habitually follow the same route home from the club each evening?" Holmes asked.

"Yes," said Bathgate.

"No," said Peckham simultaneously.

Holmes raised an inquiring eyebrow. "Which is it, gentlemen?"

Tossing a bad eye at Bathgate, Peckham continued, "That is, I'm told he didn't."

Bathgate said, "Aubs had a lot of little 'abits. Way he fixed 'is pipe, that sort of thing. Said that a gentleman should have order in his life. Never cared much for it, myself."

I'll bet you didn't, I thought.

Looking at Searles, Holmes asked, "Did you ever box with him? How good of a fighter was he?"

"Yeah, I fought 'im," Searles replied. "Once."

"Beat you into the canvas too, didn't he?" Drinkwater chortled, earning a glare from Searles.

"I wouldn't say so," rejoined Searles. "He beat me all right, but I got my licks in too."

"Laid you right out like a piece of meat, he did," Drinkwater said.

"All in good fun, was it?" asked Holmes.

"Sure! Why wouldn't it be?" said Searles. "What are you inferrin'?

"I'm not implying anything, Mr. Searles." Holmes hesitated, then he asked, "How many opponents would you think would be necessary to take Sir Aubrey down?"

"Now that would depend on the opponents, wouldn't it," said Peckham.

"An astute observation, Mr. Peckham," said Holmes. "I was thinking along similar lines myself."

"What do you mean?" asked Peckham.

"Just that it's hard to believe Sir Aubrey would be beaten so badly by random street toughs."

Now the Punters were trading surreptitious glances. It was even obvious to me that something was being concealed here.

The room abruptly became quiet. It seemed that the Punters had mentally informed each other that silence was the order of the day.

"Very well," said Holmes, abruptly. "Lestrade, I think we've learned all that we're going to."

We parted from Lestrade in front of the club, engaging separate cabs to Scotland Yard and Baker Street. As we rode through the streets, I turned to Holmes and said, "It was them, wasn't it?

"Oh yes," said Holmes. "They didn't do it themselves, of course. They likely hired it out. But now, I must prove it."

"How will you do that?"

"By finding the man who pounded Sir Aubrey into the cobblestones," said Holmes.

Still feeling the effects of my exertions on this case, I slept late on Tuesday morning. Holmes had already eaten and was gone when I arose. I rang for breakfast and occupied myself with the papers for a while, and then turned back to Collins' excellent novel. Thus it was that I was feeling quite fit and relaxed when Holmes made his appearance close to suppertime. He was dressed in rough clothes, but unlike yesterday, his face was his own, and by the expression on it, I knew that he hadn't had any luck.

"I noticed in the paper this morning that the Belgian violinist Leopold Auer is playing at Willis's tonight," he said incongruously. "His playing is said to lack fire, but his technique is reportedly impeccable. Let us go and hear him for ourselves."

I am not nearly as fond of the violin as Holmes is, but it was obvious that he needed someone to commiserate with about his lack of success, so I agreed to accompany him. Since Mrs. Hudson already had supper on, we chose to dine at home, but we still had plenty of time to don our evening dress and make the eight p.m. performance in King Street.

All I can say about the performance is that I found that I preferred Holmes's playing to Auer's, which did indeed lack the emotion that my companion was able to evoke from the instrument. I told him so as we were exiting the venue, and he responded, "My blushes, Watson!" However, I could tell that he was pleased by my remark.

Once we were on the street, Holmes said, "It is still early, Watson, and it seems that we have much competition for cabs. Are you up for a walk across the square to the Red Lion for a pint?"

It was a mild evening, with a gentle breeze blowing from the east which carried much of the ever-present effluvial miasma away from the City. Just right for a brisk walk.

"That would suit me down to the ground," I told him.

So, we made our way into St. James's Square, intending to cut across the gardens to Duke of York Street. As we approached the statue of King Edward, a man stepped out of the bushes into the path, blocking our way. He was a very large fellow, and he stood balanced on the balls of his feet with his arms at his waist, his fists clenched.

"Yer Sherlock 'Olmes, ain't cha?" he grated.

"I am. And whom do I have the dubious honour of addressing?"

"Never you mind," the man said. "I'm 'ere t' tell ye t'quit meddlin' in things that don't concern ye."

"This is most gratifying," said Holmes. "I have spent the entire day searching in vain for you, and now, here you are."

"What do ye mean?"

"I mean that Inspector Lestrade of Scotland Yard would be delighted to have a conversation with you about the death of Sir Aubrey Strongheart."

"I guess that means I have t'teach ye t'mind yer business," the bruiser said, raising his fists in front of his face, and stalking towards us.

"Stay out of this, Watson," Holmes said, handing me his topper and his stick, and then taking a similar stance before advancing to meet the brute.

I wished mightily for my British Bull Dog, which was safely ensconced in my bureau at home, because it was totally inappropriate to carry it when in evening dress, and besides, I had no reason to think I would even need a revolver tonight. Holmes had told me previously that he had done considerable boxing while at university, but the ruffian advancing upon him must have weighed at least fifteen stone and was two heads taller, giving him a tremendous advantage in reach. I feared for the worst, and contemplated defying Holmes's injunction by making this fight two-on-one.

The big man stepped up and threw a jab that Holmes easily ducked, then a second and a third, which he similarly avoided. I could see that each fighter was taking the measure of the other. Suddenly, the giant uncorked a wicked roundhouse! Holmes let it whistle over his head, then dived inside, blocked a left uppercut, and landed several strong blows to the chest and the ribs. He worked his way to right, still punching, forcing his opponent to turn the same way to prevent Holmes from slipping behind him. His arms were so long that he couldn't effectively punch while Holmes was inside, but he could and did grab my friend by the shoulder and thrust him away, staggering him. Holmes just kept dancing backwards until he regained his footing.

"Is that all ye got?" the big man taunted, but I thought I detected a slight hitch in his step as he advanced.

Holmes did not reply. He went in again, ducking the jab and feinting, then inside once more, smashing a wicked right, followed by a crashing left to the ribs. Unfortunately, this time, the ensuing uppercut connected, knocking Holmes backward several feet and spilling him to the ground. I dropped Holmes's cane and hat and gripped my own stick tightly, ready to wade in and batter the colossus before he could reach the supine Holmes. But Holmes came up in a crouch like a Rugby player and rushed the giant, catching him just above the knees and taking him to the ground. Holmes then smashed a hard right into the brute's face before rolling away and regaining his feet.

"Oi, below the belt, that's not fair!" the big man growled as he rose, blood running freely from his nose. He took his boxing stance once more.

Now the two fighters circled warily, each imbued with a healthy respect for the prowess of the other, seeking an opening. Suddenly the big man rushed and Holmes went to meet him, but sidestepped at the last second, letting the behemoth run by. Holmes pivoted like a ballet dancer and drove two hard rights into the man's back just above the belt line. Kidney punches! The giant's mouth opened in agony and he went to one knee, his arms outstretched like a supplicant at an altar. Seeing my chance, I stepped in and with both arms, brought the knob of my stick crashing down on his head. I heard the stout wood crack, then the titan was splayed across the pavement.

Holmes glared at me with fury in his eyes. "I told you to stay out of this!" he snarled. "I would have bested him!"

"This was no contest with rules," I responded, panting. "This was a battle. In battle, you seize whatever opportunities you have."

My injured shoulder was burning like someone was thrusting a hot poker into the joint, and my breathing became ever more rapid, coming in fits and starts. I could feel the blood draining from my head as the air rippled grey in front of my eyes, then my knees abruptly buckled and everything went black.

When I regained consciousness, I found myself in my own bed in Baker Street. I tried to rise, but a cool hand pressed my forehead, pushing me back into bed. "Nae, Doctor," Mrs.

Hudson said. "Tak' some time to find yersel afore ye try t'rise. I'll bring Mister Holmes."

I did as she said, because my abortive attempt had left me as weak as a child. I lay there a few moments until the door opened, and Holmes entered the room.

"Watson! Thank God! How are you?"

"I've been better," I admitted. I struggled to sit up again, but failed. "Could you help me, please?"

Holmes came to my side and pushed me forward, placing a couple of pillows behind me as a prop. After ensuring that I was stable, he settled in the armchair next to my bed.

"Firstly," he said, "I must humbly apologise for snapping at you last evening. The only excuse I can offer is that my blood was up, and it is a poor one."

"Perfectly understandable. And I do believe that you would have beaten that ruffian, but you may have been severely injured in the process. I simply could not have that." I took a breath, then asked, "So you have Sir Aubrey's murderer?"

"I think so, but unfortunately, we do not know for sure. That was a mighty blow you struck with that fine ash stick of yours, and the recipient of it has not yet awakened." Holmes hesitated. Then, "Perhaps he will not ever awaken."

I was immediately saddened. Even a soldier despairs when he must take a life.

Holmes, noticing my dismay, continued, "You were right to do what you did. Even Lestrade said so, and he will speak with the Crown Prosecutors on your behalf. If the fellow regains consciousness, I have no proof it was he who beat Sir Aubrey unless he confesses. And even if he does, I am afraid that the actual instigators will go free."

"You mean the Punters." Holmes nodded.

69

"I feel sure it was they who engaged our boxer to fight Sir Aubrey. Remember, there was evidence that several men were in the mews that night, most probably at the time that the fight was going on, watching it."

"But what motive would they have to murder Sir Aubrey?"

"None, I think."

"What?"

"I suspect the entire incident was meant to be a joke," Holmes said. "The Punters obviously knew of Sir Aubrey's predilection for challenging street beggars, so they paid a professional prize fighter to dress as one and ask Sir Aubrey for alms as he returned home. What a surprise he'd have when he received the beating of his life! But no one imagined that he would be knocked down and crack his skull on a kerbstone. They were doubtless frantic when they realised what had happened, so they dragged his body into the mews, rifled his pockets to make it look like a robbery, and decamped."

"So, they're not actually guilty of murder?"

"They would certainly not be if they had summoned help. Sir Aubrey may have even lived for a time after the injury, and perhaps he could have been rescued if in hospital. But when they chose to conceal the incident, they moved into the realm of paying for a homicide. Unfortunately, without the testimony of the prize-fighter, I cannot put them in that alley. And even if he testifies, it is his word against theirs. I am certain that the Punters would alibi each other."

"So, what are you going to do?"

"I don't know. It is quite a three-pipe problem. Ask me in the morning."

Holmes left to summon Mrs. Hudson to bring me tea and a bowl of milk toast. When I protested the insipid fare, she promised me a proper breakfast tomorrow. "I have some lovely mutton kidneys on ice in the kitchen," she told me.

I woke with the sun on Wednesday. Most of my symptoms had abated, but that changed when I stepped from my bedroom into the sitting room, into a purple haze of tobacco smoke that burned my eyes and seared my lungs. I found Holmes in the centre of the room with the furniture pushed back, perched on a cushion like the caterpillar in *Alice in Wonderland* on his mushroom, eyes closed, with his pipe dangling from his lips. My head spinning, I fought my way through the misplaced furniture to the windows overlooking Baker Street and threw them open, allowing God's air to cleanse our dwelling of the noxious fumes.

"Great Scott, Holmes! Are you actually trying to suffocate yourself?"

He opened his eyes and assumed a dour expression. "I have found through experience that replacing the oxygen in my brain with nicotine stimulates creativity, allowing the solution of impenetrable conundrums."

"Have you solved this one?"

"I believe so."

"And what is your solution?"

"You are going to have one of the Punters confess to you," he said.

So, I found myself that evening in Sackville Street near Piccadilly, in front of a fine old townhouse, the residence of Mr. Braddey Bathgate. Holmes had sent a telegram at Lockerman's earlier in the day, which ran:

I know what you did to Sir Aubrey. If you will agree to meet with me alone at your residence at eight o'clock tonight, I will tell you how you can escape the consequences. If you chose to inform your associates of this message, I am afraid there is no hope for you.

John H. Watson

After I had read it, I asked Holmes what I should do when I met Bathgate.

"Just ask him to tell you what happened in Davies Street. I am sure he will cooperate."

I knocked on Bathgate's door, which swung open at the first impact of my fist. Strange. This was a genteel neighbourhood, but I still would not leave my door unlatched if I lived here. I stepped onto a black-and-white runner with an interlocking triangular pattern in a gaslit hallway, whose walls were sheathed with a greyish-black damask wall paper, all of which contributed to a dark, sombre atmosphere. As I advanced to a doorway on my right, my eyes were taken by a portrait adjacent to it. A round-faced woman with dark hair, wearing a shapeless black dress, stared out of it into my eyes, and I felt a shiver of dread run down my spine.

I rapped lightly on the door. "Bathgate!" I called. "Bathgate! It's Doctor Watson. Are you here?" Receiving no answer, I opened the door, and the smell of incense and old wood enveloped me. I entered the room.

It was a parlour overlooking the street, which was not visible because heavy maroon drapes masked the windows. The room was dark because the gas was low, but I could see that the decor was similar to that in the hallway. Floor-to-ceiling bookcases, interrupted by an open doorway, lined the wall to my left, and a large, carved desk lay at the far end of the room. Behind it, sprawled in a chair, was Bathgate. He wasn't moving!

As I hurried to him to check the pulse in his neck, I thought I heard a door slam in the rear of the house. I removed the medallion for easier access to the carotid artery, and confirmed that Bathgate was still in the realm of the living. I cast about until I spotted a decanter and glasses on a sideboard. The aroma that drifted up as I filled a glass told me it was brandy. I hurried to Bathgate and put the glass to his lips. His eyes soon opened and he sputtered, the spirits running down into his beard.

"Man, what has happened to you?"

He grabbed my wrists so strongly that I winced, looking into my eyes with terror in his.

"We did it," he said. "We killed him! We thought it would be a lark."

"What was it you did, Bathgate?"

"We hired Livermore to brace Aubs on his way home. Thought it would be fun to see him get his comcuppance. Never thought the brute was going to murder him!"

I did not have to work very hard to worm the story out of him. It was just as Holmes said. The Punters hadn't intended that Sir Aubrey be killed, but they committed a criminal act by trying to cover up what they'd done.

Finally, I asked him the question to which I was not sure I wanted an answer.

"Why are you telling me all of this now?"

He grasped my wrists again and said fervently, "Because I told him I would, Doctor! I told him I would, if he wouldn't haunt me no more!'"

A furious pounding on the door to the street arose. "This is Constable Warren! Open the door!"

I admitted the constable and prompted Bathgate to repeat his story, which he seemed most happy to do. The constable assured me that he would take the miscreant to Scotland Yard, where Lestrade would see to rounding up the rest of the Punters.

I returned to Baker Street to find our sitting room empty. Was Holmes out? I couldn't imagine he had gone to bed, knowing the errand on which he had dispatched me. I knocked on the door to his bedroom. It opened, and I found myself staring into the smiling face of Sir Aubrey Strongheart!

Sometime later, I was ensconced in my chair with a quilt over my legs, a fine Havana, and a glass of Holmes's best single malt. "It's the least I can offer after the shock I gave you, Watson."

"But it's marvellous, Holmes!" I said. "How could you so flawlessly assume the identity of Sir Aubrey?"

"I believe I have told you that I have had some little training as an actor. And my performance was hardly flawless. It helped that Sir Aubrey was a public figure, with many images of him available to me so I could get the make-up right. However, I having never met the man, I was unaware of any little mannerisms he might have had, as well as of the timbre of his voice. However, I did not think that my impersonation had to be perfect to fool Mr. Bathgate. That proved to be so."

"Whatever led you to choose him for this charade?"

"I noted his necklace when we met the Punter's at Lockerman's. It bore the symbol of Madam Blavatsky's Theosophical Society, which indicated that he might be vulnerable to spiritualism. I reasoned that if I could convince him that Sir Aubrey had come back from the other side to exact retribution, he might crack under the pressure. As you observed, I was correct.

"I arrived at Bathgate's townhouse shortly before you did," Holmes continued, "and let myself in through the front door. The wire I sent in your name ensured that Bathgate would be home, and given the air about him when we met at Lockerman's, probably inebriated. The look on his face when I found him in his parlour was priceless! I told him in a whispery voice that I would visit him nightly until he confessed to what he and the other Punters had done. He fainted into his chair, so I skedaddled before you arrived."

"I thought I heard you close the back door on your way out."

"Doubtless, you did. I met the good Constable Warren on my way home, so I directed him your way."

I took a long draw on my cigar, followed by a sip of the excellent Islay malt. "But you took a tremendous risk, Holmes. What if Bathgate had seen through your disguise – or worse still, produced a pistol and shot you as a burglar?"

"The risk was a calculated one. Bathgate and the other Punters are cowards, preferring to bedevil a man from the shadows instead of facing him directly, so I was not too worried about bullets. And even if he had seen though my disguise, then he would know indubitably that I was on to them, and they would likely make a mistake that would bring them down."

"Like they did when they set that unfortunate boxer on us in St. James Square," I observed. I was also glad to learn that our erstwhile assailant had regained consciousness, and that he corroborated Bathgate's confession in every respect. And I was very relieved that I had not killed the fellow after all. Lestrade assured me that no charges would be forthcoming, as

I was simply defending Holmes and myself from a scurrilous attack.

"Precisely. I knew they were shadowing us when we left Baker Street, but I chose to say nothing. They likely went to fetch the prize-fighter to threaten us while we were immersed in Auer's melodies at Willis's. Guilt is a powerful force, Watson," Holmes continued, "which has brought many a miscreant low. As the Bard said,

> *So full of artless jealousy is guilt,*
> *It spills itself in fearing to be spilt.*

The Two Bullets
by David Marcum

My friend, Mr. Sherlock Holmes, has never been particularly reticent about the nature of his gifts. He rightly feels that to hide one's light under a bushel is as disingenuous as falsifying data in a chemical experiment. "I have never," he has frequently told me, "felt modesty to be one of the virtues."

Therefore, it came as a surprise to me, one morning in mid-1881, when Holmes seemed reluctant to offer his assistance in what appeared to be a matter that would require little effort upon his part, while remunerating him handsomely – and this in the days when the rent money to Mrs. Hudson was dear and always of great concern to both of us.

I had returned late that morning from Barts, where I worked upon occasion when not filling in as a *locum*. Pausing at the bottom of the steps leading to our sitting room, I allowed a girl of about twenty to pass and depart. Upstairs, I found Holmes seated by the fire.

"A client?" I asked, dropping into my own chair.

He waved a hand. "The usual. Her mother has lost an article which was loaned to them. Fearing that it may have been stolen, she consulted me. I was able to offer a few words of advice."

That was the way in those early years, when Holmes would be visited by a number of different individuals – servants and nobility, policemen and criminals – on a daily basis. In most cases he never had to leave his armchair in order to arrive at a solution. A suggestion would be offered and he would pocket his fee. Only occasionally did he feel the need to arise and move about in order to determine the truth.

He reached to the side-table and lifted a small note. "Are you free this afternoon?"

I said yes, and he handed me the missive. It was a curt invitation from an Edgar Jessup, saying that he would send a carriage for Holmes, if that was acceptable. "Edgar Jessup?" I asked. "The textile king?"

"The same."

"I notice that I am not included in this invitation."

"Nevertheless, your assistance would be invaluable. Although," he added, "I am myself of two minds regarding this matter, and not at all sure that I wish to accept Mr. Jessup's summons."

I looked at the note. "Why ever not? There's money in this case, Holmes, if nothing else." I must confess that, in those days, fear of penury was always a motivation for the both of us. "He simply asks for your opinion on the measures he has undertaken to protect his art collection."

"True, Watson. But I recall too well another recent encounter between the two of us, although we never spoke a word."

This interested me greatly. Bear in mind that at that time in our friendship, Holmes had chosen to tell me almost nothing of his past. I had yet to learn where he attended University, or very much about his earlier days in Montague Street, or that he even had a brother, seven years his senior, who sometimes *is* the British Government.

"Just a few weeks after that Jefferson Hope business," Holmes began, "before you were quite so involved in my investigations, I was consulted by Inspector Plummer regarding a series of shop burglaries taking place in the area north of Bloomsbury. It was initially thought to be a routine affair, involving a local smash-and-grab gang that seemed to have formed spontaneously, as they do. You will know the place. The incidents were centered around shops near Woburn Place and Tavistock Square. The thieves always worked the same pattern, breaking a window and dashing in to steal the cashbox, and whatever else they could lay their hands upon. They were never in the shops for more than a moment, and gone before the inevitable alarm could be sounded."

"I remember reading something about it," I said, "although I had no idea that you were involved. It sounds as if they were rather foolhardy."

Holmes nodded. "Oh, they were. It was clearly the work of a group of ignorant thieves who were full of their own previous successes, and heading for a fall. In fact, they became more bold and careless as time went on. Eight shops had been hit over the course of a couple of months when the incidents finally caught the eye of the press. '*Crime Ring!*' proclaimed the headlines, as you may recall. A few of the shopkeepers were interviewed, and one, owner of a small bauble shop, foolishly proclaimed that the thieves had been so careless as to miss the cashbox in his store, along with a valuable sculpture that he kept on his front counter. As you might think, two days later, the man was robbed again, in the same manner, his newly repaired front door smashed, and the cashbox and statue taken this time before anyone could arrive on the scene."

"How could they do such a thing at the front door in a well-travelled street?"

"Not so well-travelled at three in the morning, my friend. Before I was ever involved, it was theorized – correctly as it turned out – that the gang consisted of only a few individuals – one or two to commit the robbery, and one or two others to serve as lookouts, keeping watch as to when the street was deserted."

"It appears to have been a routine police matter," I said, "in spite of how long it went on. Why did the inspector involve you?"

"It was by way of a referral. The last shopkeeper to be robbed, the same braggadocious fellow who had thoughtlessly informed the thieves what they had missed on the first visit to his establishment, had been a former client of mine, in a little matter regarding a cursed curio."

"Holmes," I interrupted while leaning forward. "Without derailing the current narrative, I would also love to hear an account of that one, to get a record of it for my notes."

He smiled tolerantly. "Perhaps another time." Then the smile faded. "Although considering the outcome of the case, one might almost believe there was a curse after all."

As I settled back in disappointment, realizing that he wasn't going to elaborate, he continued. "After he was immediately robbed a second time – as one might expect – this shopkeeper, an opinionated man named Mr. Silas, insisted to the police that I should be involved in the investigation. Knowing that he might have further dealings with the press, wherein Silas would shame the police if they didn't take his advice, Inspector Plummer was deputized to approach me. It didn't hurt at all that Plummer and I had worked successfully together on a few affairs in the past, when I lived in Montague Street.

"I examined the shop, and also several of the other more recent burglary sites, but could find nothing of any use. It seemed as if my contribution wasn't going to bring any credit to me at all. Mr. Silas, however, remained confident in my abilities, and the inspector was not unmindful of past instances when I had accomplished a thing or two.

"It was Mr. Silas who decided that if the thieves could be goaded once, it could be done again. I had my doubts about this, for who would be witless enough to return a third time, but I was to be proven wrong – unfortunately for Mr. Silas. He delayed an order that he had placed for new bars for his windows and door, and then reached out to the press once more, this time to suggest a story that once again the thieves had missed items of importance. As I said, I thought it unlikely that anyone would fall for it, undoubtedly sensing the trap, but I was mistaken.

"Working with Inspector Plummer, I helped to draw up a battle plan to keep the shop under observation during the nighttime. Some of his best officers, former military men, were selected from the Force to keep watch in the deepest hours of darkness. For the first two nights after Mr. Silas's latest pronouncement appeared in the newspapers, we arranged ourselves as planned, but nothing happened. Then, on the third night, tragedy struck.

"The fog was unfortunately quite thick that night. Plummer and I had planned for such an eventuality, but it still was not to our liking. The handpicked men drew in to closer positions, as they had been told to do, and we hoped that either the criminals wouldn't notice them, should they fall for the bait, or that they would postpone their efforts for another night. This, I may add, was also an unwelcome option, as the nights of lying in wait were becoming quite tedious.

"It was therefore with a mixture of surprise, relief, and anticipation when we heard the crash of breaking glass, indicating that the trap was being sprung. I had been hiding across the street in the Square with the inspector, and we both dashed toward Mr. Silas's shop. To my left and right, echoing in the fog, I could hear the heavy boot steps of constables running to join us.

"As we neared the shop, there was a combination of sounds that changed everything – two gunshots, one after the other, followed by an abbreviated scream that ominously stopped abruptly.

"We arrived in front of the shop just as two men stepped out of the doorway, straight into the arms of the policemen. Watson, if I am ever too critical of the official force, it is because they so often fail to show any imagination. On that night, however, it was this same 'failure' that let those brave men fearlessly disarm the two prisoners, without a thought to their own safety.

"Much as you would imagine, for a few moments there was a great deal of confusion, made up of the milling constables, the futile attempts by the prisoners to escape, and my effort, along with Inspector Plummer, to make our way past them all and into the shop in order to see who had screamed. I feared that I knew the answer, and I was correct.

"The plan had been for Mr. Silas, a widower who lived alone over his shop, to withdraw upstairs on each of the nights that we undertook his plan to capture the burglars. As we had known nothing about those responsible for the past violations, there was no way to ascertain just how dangerous the men might be. Mr. Silas had agreed willingly enough, but apparently it was only for show, as he was there in the shop when the two men broke open the door, and he had likely been hiding there on the previous nights as well.

"We found him on the floor, halfway behind the counter, and half into the main part of the shop, a shallow area stretching six or eight feet back from the front door. One of the constables lit the gas, and it was quickly determined that the man had died nearly instantly, the scream that we heard being his last sound on this earth.

"There did not seem to be any question as to what had happened. However, that was before we had a chance to interview the prisoners, whose stories muddled the issue. They were pulled into the shop, where the dead owner was quite visible to them, lying accusingly at their feet. Both men were in their mid-twenties, not much younger than we are, and upon seeing the body, one of them gave a great cry of grief and would have collapsed, had he not been securely in the constable's grip. The other prisoner looked at him in disgust.

"'Here now,' said Plummer to the distraught man, who now had tears running down his face. 'You're fair caught, and it's a hanging matter. What's your name?'

"The man swallowed and said, 'Edward. Edward Jessup.'

I must have shown some recognition, as Holmes nodded. "Exactly, Watson. The son of the same Edgar Jessup who has requested my presence today." He tapped the note from the man, lying on the table beside him. "The name meant nothing to us then, and the inspector continued his questioning. 'And you?' he asked the other man. 'Your name is – ?'

"'Abbott,' came the sneering reply. 'John Abbott.'

"'Well, you're both under arrest for the series of burglaries, along with murder.'

"At that instant, Jessup started. 'Oh, no!' he cried. 'I didn't murder him!' He looked with loathing at his companion. 'No! It was Abbott here. He's the one!'

"Abbott attempted to lunge at him, but the big officer holding him pulled him back and shook him like a terrier snapping a rat. 'Noon o' that,' he said in a broad Devonshire accent.

"Jessup raised his arms pleadingly. 'I admit to the burglaries. At first it seemed like a lark – something to do, a game almost. But as time went on, he became afraid.' Jessup pointed toward Abbott. 'The last couple of times, he insisted that we carry guns. I didn't want to, but somehow, I couldn't say no.'

"'Shut your mouth,' growled Abbott, trying again to step forward. 'I'm warning you – '

"'Go on,' said Plummer, sensing he could get the full story and a confession if he just let the man talk.

"'I didn't want to come back here, but John insisted. I thought it seemed like a trap, but he said that the old man couldn't help bragging. It would be just like before – that we'd be in and away before anyone knew a thing. But when the glass smashed and we stepped in, that man – ' and at this, he glanced toward Mr. Silas's body on the floor, ' – he rose up from behind the counter. John . . . John raised his gun then, and fired a shot.'

"Abbott growled and lunged ineffectively, whereupon Plummer said, 'We heard *two* shots. What of the other?'

"'That was my gun,' said Jessup. 'After John shot the poor man, he backed up into me, knocking my arm. I was so surprised, my own gun went off.'

"A sly expression crossed Abbott's face. 'You lie,' he said. '*You* were the one who shot him, and then backed into *me*, making *my* gun go off.'

"Jessup's face looked possibly more stricken than before. 'No!' he said. 'That isn't the way of it at all. You killed him! It was you!'

"A thought occurred to me then, although I supposed the question was moot in the end, as either way, one was a killer and the other an accomplice, and the law would treat them the same, no matter which name was associated with the actual death. 'The guns?' I asked. 'Where are they?'

"One constable answered, 'This one is on the ground, where I knocked it from that one's hand.' He nodded his head toward Abbott.

"'And I have the other,' said an officer beside me. 'In my pocket. I took it from him.' And he indicated Jessup.

"I nodded. 'Please keep them separate. It is important to keep track of who held which gun.' At that point, I asked everyone to remain still for a moment as I moved around and between them, observing what I could upon the floor. The prisoners' footprints were clearly identifiable, having tracked in the damp of the night fog, and each had a different pattern matching their shoes. It was evident that they had only proceeded a few feet into the shop, as there was no evidence that either had approached any closer to the counter. Of course, this did not contradict that part of their stories, or what we had heard at the time of the crime, when the breaking glass was followed so quickly by the two gunshots. The prints were too muddled to see who had advanced further into the shop.

"Additional examination quickly revealed one of the bullets lodged in the soft plaster, off to the right side of the counter. Clearly, this weapon had been aimed at a very different angle from that of the shot that killed the proprietor. Stepping behind the counter, I used my pocket knife to dig out the projectile, wrapping it carefully in my handkerchief.

"Plummer gestured toward me and, pulling me outside, asked what I was doing. 'It may or may not be important,' I answered, 'but I have been doing some research of late that may determine which of the two men fired the fatal shot.'

"He shook his head. 'It's obvious that it was Abbott. He is just claiming Jessup's version of events as his own in order to save himself, or to confuse things.'

"'I agree. However, if it is possible to settle the matter in a more exact manner, I expect that we should do so.'

"Plummer agreed and, after the two men were removed, he made sure that the two weapons were clearly identified and saved for my later examination.

"What," Holmes then asked unexpectedly, "is your knowledge of firearms, Watson?"

I pursed my lips. "As much as any common fellow's, I suppose."

"Are you familiar with rifling?"

I nodded. "I am. The placement of spiraling grooves within the barrel of a gun, running from back to front, so to speak, that put a spin on the bullet, thus allowing it to have a longer and straighter course."

"Exactly. Invented in the sixteenth century by the Germans, who have always had some skill with these matters, it vastly improved the performance of earlier weapons, such as the aptly named 'smooth-bores'."

"But what has such a thing to do with this investigation?"

"Well you might ask, as the inspector did at the time. I had been doing some experiments with firearms, having observed that this rifling action marks a bullet as it passes through the gun barrel.'

"What of it? I would be surprised if it did not."

"Ah, Watson, an idea should not remain thoroughly unexplored simply because something has occurred as one expected it to. Not long before the incident in Mr. Silas's shop, I had researched the nature of these marks upon bullets, and whether a projectile could be identified by the markings of a particular gun in a particular way, thus showing that it was fired from that same gun."

"But surely, Holmes, a bullet moving at such high speeds would be damaged in a different way from another bullet coming from the same gun, regardless of the permanent rifling marks. And what of the differences that already exist in the bullets themselves?"

"Those differences are there, to be sure. But a microscopic examination of the rifling marks on the soft lead of bullets are very sharply defined, I assure you, and in fact are reproducible time and again on different bullets fired from the same gun."

"I see where you are going with this. You hoped to establish conclusively through these rifling marks that it was Abbott who held the gun that matched the fatal bullet."

"Absolutely correct, my dear Watson. I set myself up in one of the labs at Barts, where I still have an arrangement, as you know. Following the autopsy, Plummer arranged for me to receive the bullet from Mr. Silas's body, and I set about examining it under a microscope, along with the other bullet removed from the wall. Luckily, both objects were in excellent shape, the one from the wall having simply imbedded itself into the soft plaster, while the one from the body hadn't been deflected or deformed by impact with a bone.

"First I examined the bullets fired on the night of the crime, and sketched the markings that I observed. The murder bullet, as I shall call it, had a full set of rifling marks, while the wall bullet had only 'false' rifling markings from what appeared to come from the tip of the muzzle. Then, I fired additional test bullets from each of the guns – both Webleys by the way, same caliber, different models – in order that I might see comparative examples of each. The bullets were fired into a great wad of bedding, to protect them from any deforming damage.

"When these were also examined and sketched, it was easy to see that the test bullets had markings matching the two bullets from the crime, and it was definitive which gun had shot which. I had conclusive evidence as to whose gun had fired the bullet into the shopkeeper, and whose had shot at the wall.

"Needless to say, the inspector was with me throughout the process, and saw what I saw in the microscope. He agreed with my sketches completely. 'One question, however,' he said when we had finished. 'We now know for sure which gun fired the bullet that killed Mr. Silas – it was Abbott's, as we suspected all along. But who's to say that Abbott won't claim that Jessup still fired first, intending to hit Silas but *missing*, and then, when backing up, he nudged Abbott, who then accidentally fired and hit Silas by mistake?'

"I saw his point. We were both certain that Abbott had undoubtedly been the first to fire, and intentionally at the dead man. However, how to prove the order of events? And after our efforts, what did it matter anyway? In any case, Plummer was loathe to bring this new and unproven ballistic science into court, especially as the defense would raise the very questions that he had just shared.

"In the end, the inspector sat down with Abbott, using my sketches, and was able to overwhelm the man's defenses so well that a confession was inevitable. He was subsequently convicted and hanged."

"And Jessup?" I asked. "He would have been considered an accomplice – also a capital crime."

Holmes nodded. "He was convicted, although the appeals process was much more extensive in his case, due to the influence and resources of his family. It was argued, bolstered by Abbott's confession, that he was not responsible for the murder, and that it was only due to his weak character that he had allowed himself to be coerced into participating in the earlier robberies – a poor defense at best. However, in the end, it was indisputable that he had been present at the crime, carrying a firearm, and he was convicted and sentenced to death."

"And was the sentence carried out?"

"It was. Last month. Inspector Plummer sent a note asking if I wished to attend. I did not."

We both fell silent for a moment, pondering the unexpected choices and twists and turns in a man's life that can lead to such a bad end. Knowing nothing of Abbott, I could imagine his past, perhaps a steady decline until the unsurprising conclusion, terminating upon the gallows. But the other, Edward Jessup – he had been of a good family, with every opportunity. What could have happened? What turn left when he should have gone right had taken him to the same tragic destiny?

"I understand your reluctance at meeting with the boy's father," I said. "But do you think that he even knows of your involvement in the matter?"

"Without doubt. As a witness, I was called to testify in court. As expected, the evidence of the ballistic rifling was not used, but my testimony as to the first statements of the accused when arrested was considered useful. I well recall the expressionless stare of the man in the courtroom as I was questioned. It hasn't been long enough for him to forget."

"Do you intend to see him, then?"

With a sigh, Holmes stood. "I suppose so. When I chose this profession, I never expected that every encounter would be dripping with bonhomie and good cheer. Will you join me?"

A part of me did not want to go, as the circumstances sounded rather grim indeed. But I could sense that Holmes wished for me to accompany him and, as his friend, I could do no less. "Yes, of course," I agreed.

So that afternoon, Holmes and I found ourselves in the textile king's well-tricked carriage, making our way toward the man's home near Berkeley Square. My companion was silent, pondering his own thoughts, while I inhaled deeply, not looking forward to the upcoming encounter.

At the Jessup home, we were shown in by a cadaverous-looking butler. I could sense that this was a house of sadness. We were taken through to a sitting room, and within moments Mr. Jessup entered.

Both of us had remained standing. When the man entered the room, I could tell that Holmes was exhibiting some reserve, although anyone that knew him less might not have noticed it. He was as surprised as I when Mr. Jessup reached out and clasped his hand warmly.

"Mr. Holmes, it has been far too long. I apologize."

I rarely see Holmes speechless, but that was one of those times. Finally, as the man continued to grasp his hand, he uttered, "I beg your pardon?"

"I apologize. For taking so long to thank you. It has been . . . difficult." Releasing Holmes's grip, he turned to me. "I am Edgar Jessup." To me he also offered a hand, which I accepted out of reflex. "I understand that you are the doctor that assists Mr. Holmes in his investigations."

I started to speak, but Mr. Jessup continued. "Please. Don't be surprised. I have done some checking into Mr. Holmes's career. Since . . . since the arrest and conviction of my son, Edward . . . ." He gestured toward a grouping of chairs. "Please, have a seat. Collins!"

He called the butler over to see if we would have something to drink, but we both declined. With the departure of Collins, Holmes began to speak.

"Mr. Jessup, I understand that you wish to consult me about your collection – "

"Yes, yes, we'll get to that in a moment. But first, my apology. And you must forgive me, you see. I've wanted to thank you for quite a while, but . . . ." His voice faded, and he swallowed. Then, more softly, he said, "Since Edward's . . . death. My wife is still not over it – she may never be, you understand. He was our only . . . our only . . . ." At that point, his emotions overcame him, and for a moment he could not speak. Then, composing himself, he continued.

"All this time, Mr. Holmes, I've wanted to thank you, but the wound was too fresh. I suppose it still is, but when I needed someone to advise me upon the security of my collection, and your name was suggested, I realized that I might never have a better opportunity."

"Thank me? For what, Mr. Jessup?"

"Why, for proving my son did not shoot the owner of that shop."

"How do you know of that, sir?"

"The police inspector informed me."

"But Mr. Jessup, I'm afraid that my efforts did nothing to help save the life of your son. He was convicted as an accomplice of the crime."

"True, Mr. Holmes, true. But the statements of that . . . Mr. Abbott, attempting to lay the blame upon my son, might have made things more ambiguous than they would have been otherwise. My son's reputation, there at the end, would have been further destroyed, much more so than it was. My wife and I . . . we would have known the truth, but to others, there would always have been some doubt.

"My son and I had been estranged for a time before his death. I blame myself now. It was this that let him fall under the evil influence of John Abbott. But after his arrest, and during the time of the trial and the appeals, he and I were able to become much closer. I like to think that it would have been the same regardless, Mr. Holmes, but truth be told, the fact that you were able to clear him of the murder helped my peace of mind as he and I faced those last terrible days together."

He swallowed again before gaining control of himself. "You didn't have to do that, Mr. Holmes. He was caught, and conviction was certain, whether or not he pulled the trigger of that fatal shot. But you went to the effort to discover the truth anyway, and for that, I shall be forever grateful."

"But Mr. Jessup – " said my friend.

"That is all that needs to be said!" interrupted the textile king, showing the force of will that had gotten him to that successful perch he occupied. "But know this, Mr. Holmes. You have a friend. Whatever I can do to help you in your career, you have but to ask."

I didn't know what to expect from Sherlock Holmes. Perhaps he would don that mask of cold aloofness he often wears. Possibly he would dodge the issue by explaining that he'd arrived at his solution more for the sake of science than to prove young Jessup's innocence. Instead, he responded with that grace and tact which have always been his hallmark, replying with a simple, "Thank you."

We proceeded then to discuss Mr. Jessup's art collection, with valuable advice provided by Holmes. On that day, the consulting detective acquired a patron of sorts, one of many that would line up on his side as the years went by. Very rarely would he draw upon this well of good will, but he always knew that it was there, should he need it. My friend has many gifts, and he has never felt the need to hide them under a bushel, but it is a testament to his integrity that he is uncharacteristically modest about this, that large and disparate group of people that owes him so much.

Brother's Keeper
by Robert Perret

To say I found my new friend's occupation to be a bit unusual would be an understatement. The business with Jefferson Hope has been no small bother. Indeed, it had proved to be a matter of life and death, and yet Holmes had received but a pittance of a fee from Scotland Yard, and the official detectives had taken all of the credit, so Holmes could not even turn the thing to his advantage as a testimonial to his prodigious talents, and thereby at least obtain further clients. It was unclear to me how Holmes managed his part of the rent and our other expenses. I wondered if perhaps our landlady was overly liberal in extending her mercurial boarder a line of credit. He yet catered to the dispossessed of London, but at a bob here and a shilling there it wasn't much of a living. I even began to suspect that perhaps he was drawing upon familial resources – some stern pater somewhere reluctantly posting a cheque to Mrs. Hudson each month. It was no concern of mine if Holmes were some kind of eccentric scion, yet I feared he might grow bored of his current jape and return home, leaving me unable to meet my obligations and thrust once again unto the paving stones of London. Such were my ruminations over a crust of bread and thin tea when there came a knocking at the door. As the lone occupant of Baker Street at the moment it fell to me to answer, and so I stiffly made my way down the stairs, my injury yet objecting to each step.

I threw the door open wide only to discover a much-beloved face awaited me.

"Murray!" I declared. "I had no idea you were in London! Come in!"

"Ta, Doctor," Murray said. "I've been on British soil the last few months, but only just arrived in London. I'd have written to you, but I didn't know where you went to until I happened to see your name in the paper."

"What paper is that?" I asked. "I'm not aware of any such mention."

"I've got it in my bag," Murray said. "Brought it to you as a kind of souvenir. I see you are still feeling the effect of those Jezail kisses."

I had hoped he had not noticed how heavily I leaned on the banister as we made our way to the sitting room. "I'd be buried under the Afghanistan desert if it weren't for you. This is but a small inconvenience. A drink for the weary traveler?" I made my way to the tantalus.

"Ta, I still have dust in my throat. Probably will until my last breath."

I let my hand drift past the decanter of cheap whisky I had supplied and instead plucked out an aged Scotch Holmes had accepted as payment from one of his hard-scrabble clients. I didn't know if he worked at the distillery or had simply pilfered the bottle, but it was a finer potable than I'd ever tasted. I owed Murray my life, and Holmes didn't seem to be much of a connoisseur of liquors. It was a dark honey amber in color, and it smelled of sweet mahogany. For a moment I considered pouring a tipple for myself but stoppered it instead. When I turned, Murray had reclined in Holmes's chair by the mantel and he had produced a small tabloid. He placed it in my hand as I gave him the drink.

"*True Law*," I read from the masthead. "Never heard of it."

"You know these sensation rags," Murray said. "A dozen on every street corner, a hundred at every terminal. Picked this one up at some little one-room station on the train down.

Something about a New World cult of religious fanatics murdering innocents under the guise of a London hack business."

A quick glance at the story in question showed that the newspaper had done a remarkable job of getting some of the particulars correct while getting the facts of the case all wrong. They did, however, credit Holmes and me rather than Scotland Yard. "Remarkable," I said. "Piffle, but remarkable piffle."

"It's true enough," Murray said, gesturing to the room. "I found you, didn't I?"

"Yes. Well, I'm not sure that is a good thing. Mr. Holmes seems to attract eccentric characters, and I don't fancy meeting half of them on my doorstep."

"Perhaps it is not a good idea to run your amateur detective business from your domicile."

"Quite right. I shall have to speak to Mr. Holmes and put a stop to it. I shouldn't want 221b Baker Street to become synonymous with crime, nor even its resolution. I'd never have any peace and quiet."

"This thing," Murray poked at the paper in my hands, "will all be fishwrap within the week, so no worries there."

"It seems you came out of the war alright," I observed.

"I've got all my limbs and no nasty diseases, so in that sense, I have sailed through the storm."

"How, then, may I be of service? I'm still scraping by on my stipend so I'm afraid I'm not much help there."

"Nothing like that, Doctor. It's just . . . ."

"Yes? Out with it, Murray. You can always be frank with me."

"Well, I suppose I want to hire you."

"Hire me?"

"You are a detective now, aren't you?"

"No, I – "

"Watson is the second greatest detective in London," Holmes interrupted from the doorway. "Though admittedly there is little competition."

"Goodness, man!" I said. "Have you been here the whole time? I thought myself alone."

"I've just returned from the Museum," Holmes said, brushing a thick coat of what seemed to be plaster dust from his vest. "I'm a bit of an autodidact."

"A what?" Murray asked.

"He's a self-educated man, in some areas at least." From what I'd seen, Holmes was deeply versed in the *minutiae* of varied specialized fields and yet woefully naive in areas I would deem to be common knowledge.

"Me as well, sir," Murray said. "I've learned as I go, sir, and made myself into a rather good orderly, I like to think."

"As far as I'm concerned," I said, "you've got the makings of a physician in you, and I'll happily write a recommendation any time."

"That's quite kind of you, Doctor," Murray said, but it seemed that his spirit had left him. He was slumped down in the chair now, his head hanging above his knees.

"Steady on, Murray," I said. "What do you need a detective for?"

"His brother is missing," Holmes said.

"That's right!" Murray gasped. "How did you know?"

"You are not a man of means, so it is unlikely to be a material loss."

"Holmes!" I chided.

"You don't evince the despair of a broken heart, so it is not a troubled romance. A family member, then. Your story of self-reliance, as well as your age, both suggest that your parents are no longer a concern. If you had lost a child you would be inconsolable. An endangered sister would have

96

pricked your bravado. No, this is the quiet exasperation of a man who must be his brother's keeper yet again. I can sympathize."

"I apologize for Mr. Holmes's lack of tact," I said.

"That's all right," Murray said. "It's what I need – what my brother needs – that *'piercing gaze of justice'*, just like the story said."

"Story?" Holmes asked.

I gave over the copy of *True Law* that Murray had gifted me. Holmes ran a critical eye over the piece and then barked with laughter.

"You find it amusing?" I asked.

"You do not?"

"The public is going to think that we said and did those things."

"The public isn't going to think of it at all. These lurid pamphlets are the very definition of ephemeral. Read on the train and forgotten before supper."

"It brought Murray to us."

"And a good thing, too. Now, let us hear of your brother."

"He did not have the honor of serving in Her Majesty's army on account of his legs, sir. Stunted, they were, from rickets."

"You yourself show no sign of the disorder," Holmes observed.

"I'm a bit older, you see, and after our mum had passed and father was unable to manage us anymore, we were sent to live with mother's maiden sisters. Suffice it to say, there was a good reason why they remained unwed. I soon came across the opportunity to apprentice with a cooper and seized it."

"I never knew any of this," I said.

"I'm not exactly proud of it," Murray said. "While it was not my intention, I had left poor Jacob the sole recipient of my aunts' tender mercies. I consoled myself by sharing what little dosh I could spare with my aunts to aid in his care. I had visited him weekly at first, but the household was seeped through with such a miserable atmosphere that I regret my visits began to lapse, and I sometimes found that months had passed since I last saw Jacob. During this ordeal, his disposition soured, but he was always freshly scrubbed and well shod when I saw him. Only later did I learn that my aunts gussied him up for my benefit and that he spent his formative years barefoot and in rags, waiting upon those horrible women hand and foot. I don't know why he took so long to tell me – he wasn't shy about much else."

"Perhaps he blamed himself for his predicament, and shame sealed his lips," I suggested.

"As his legs faltered, he became slow and clumsy. My aunts responded with beatings until they found him to be useless, and then they cast him out. I only discovered this weeks after the fact when I came to visit him and Aunt Dahlia tucked my coins into her skirt before informing me that she had not seen Jacob in many happy weeks and she hoped never to again. I ran frantically through the streets that day until I found him propped up against the alley wall of a restaurant, where he picked through their refuse tip for sustenance. I have never been more devastated in my life than when I saw the pitiful wretch that he had become. At once I gathered him into my arms and carried him back to the room I shared with three others who worked as I did. I laid him in my bed and ran to fetch bread and beer from the grocer on the corner. He ate ravenously and I regretted I could not afford more that day. I washed him and gave him my coat and the next day set about finding him a job, which is no small feat to accomplish on behalf of a man who can neither read nor labor."

"I am rather more interested in the events that more immediately anticipate your arrival here," Holmes said, putting a match to his clay pipe.

"Of course, Mr. Holmes, I apologize. Ultimately he would not settle on an honest living, and he made his way through the world by the roll of a die and the turn of a card."

"He turned to gambling," Holmes said.

"Indeed."

"Was he successful?"

"His luck runs hot and cold, like anyone. Although his body is ruined, his mind is intact, and he likes to overplay his feebleness to ensnare his prey."

"He made enemies, then?"

"I don't know if I would go so far as to say enemies, but the kind of men he gambled with were the kind to get sore when beaten by an invalid. Of course, it was worse if they discovered he was a cardsharp as well."

"I should think such a man would soon become infamous in his circles and have difficulty finding new opponents," Holmes said.

"And so he traveled like a vagabond, up and down the country, anywhere the rails would carry him."

"What, then, makes you believe that he is now missing rather than gallivanting?" Holmes asked.

"This," Murray said, producing a knotted tangle of fabric from his pocket.

"I'm afraid that even I will need a little more help," Holmes said.

"It's a doll," Murray said. "At least, it was once upon a time. My mother made it herself from an old flannel. As I say, Jacob was quite young when we lost her. He is not a sentimental man by anybody's reckoning, but what little feeling he does have is tied up in this. He would rather die than abandon it."

"Yet it was abandoned?" Holmes asked.

"I received a bill from the Hotel Galahad, in Avondale. It was little surprise, as I have often been obliged to make good my brother's debts before. They held his luggage as collateral, and the doll was tucked inside."

"Your brother has no permanent address, and you yourself had just returned from Afghanistan, correct?"

"A few weeks before."

"And you had no contact with your brother in that time?"

"No, sir. I had no idea where he was."

"So how did the hotel manage to send you a bill?"

"I received it general delivery, as it were."

"Even so, the hotel management had to know to look for you in Doncaster when no party in Avondale would have reason to believe you might be found there, save perhaps for your brother himself. To be quite honest, Mr. Murray, if it were not for your bond with the Good Doctor, I should be sending you on your way."

"But you won't, will you, Mr. Holmes? I'll pay you, of course. Here are three pounds now," he carefully peeled the notes from his purse. "I'll get you the rest. Dr. Watson will tell you I'm good for it."

"There's no need for all that, Murray," I said. "I owe you my life. Mr. Holmes and I will be very happy to look into the matter."

"I must emphasize, Mr. Murray," Holmes said, "there is very little to go upon here, and no real sign of an abduction. You must steel yourself for the very likely outcome that your brother has simply skipped out on his hotel bill and may not show his face again anytime soon."

"But we will do our very best to discover the truth, whatever it may be," I added to soften Holmes's declaration.

"Thank you, Doctor! Thank you, Mr. Holmes! It is such a relief to me already that you are looking after things."

"Very good, Mr. Murray," Holmes said, taking my old friend by the elbow and escorting him to the stairs. "A pleasant evening to you."

"Do you have a place to stay, Murray?" I asked as I caught him on the stairs.

"There's a boarding house called the Candlewick that caters to old campaigners like us."

"I know of the place," I said. "It's a bit rough."

"Maybe by London standards, but after my time in the desert, it is a veritable palace. Besides, no one is going to bother the likes of me."

"Come back here if it doesn't work out, and I'll put you up."

"Ta, Doctor. I don't think Mr. Holmes would like a houseguest, and I want him as happy as possible until Jacob is found."

When I returned to the sitting room, Holmes had reclaimed his chair and was sending purple plumes of tobacco up to the ceiling.

"Do you really think the case is hopeless?" I asked.

"I don't think there is a case at all, but you don't even open the Duke's scotch for me, so it is clearly a matter of importance to you. A debt of honor, I suppose?"

"How did you know about the scotch? The decanter looks perfectly full."

"To the contrary, it is a generous two inches short of where it had been earlier. Of course, the scent upon the glass is a dead giveaway – like anise and sorghum, isn't it?"

"I didn't realize you had such a refined palate for drink."

101

"Can't stand the stuff. A barbarous and inefficient method of intoxication, but there is no confusing the contents of that glass with the abrasive swill you imbibe. Does my sinuses in every time. I believe if we catch the 5:40 tomorrow morning, we should make Avondale in time for a midday repast. With any luck, we can be back to Baker Street tomorrow night."

"That's before the sun rises!" I objected.

"It will be good for your constitution to take to the countryside before the first fingers of dawn," Holmes chuckled.

So it was that I found myself nodding to the sway of the northbound express as a new day broke over the dewey hills of the Midlands. Holmes, of course, was keen with the scent of the hunt in his nostrils.

"I spent an instructive night asking around a bit about Jacob Murray," Holmes said. "While not exhaustive, my inquiries indicate that he indeed has a bit of a reputation about London, but as an easy mark rather than a sharp. It seems he is easily goaded into rash play and soon parted from his money. The only grievances I could uncover were those to whom he yet owed trivial sums of money."

"Are you a gambling man, Holmes?" I asked.

"Ha! There's no sport in cards when one had honed his observational skills as I have. Every tic, every tell, every quirk of the other players is plain as day to me, and I can't help keeping track of the cards. I'm surprised anyone has trouble with it."

"That's a bit much, surely."

"Let us play a friendly game or two when we find the time, and you can see for yourself."

"What of dice then?"

"I can throw a die to show any number I please, and as for betting on the roll of another hand, that is merest chance and hardly holds any interest."

"It seems to me you could dedicate the occasional evening to a gaming table and have no need to share a flat – nor even rent one."

"Ah, but the boredom would be excruciating. My mind craves novel problems, not the rote statistical columns of a professional gambler. It has all the risk and skill of accountancy when you come down to it."

"If I could make my fortune with a deck of cards, I'd not hesitate for a moment," I said.

Holmes simply smiled to himself.

At last, we arrived at Avondale, a picturesque enclave of grey stone buildings set among the hills.

"Almost has a Bavarian ambiance," I observed.

"Classical Saxon architecture," Holmes said. "Rebuilt many times over the centuries, of course."

"You're an expert at architecture as well?"

"Buildings bear scars, which can be quite instructive," Holmes said.

I asked after the Hotel Galahad of a passing porter. He offered to have our bags sent over for a modest consideration. Holmes briskly informed him that such a service was unnecessary, as we had none, but directions would be worth a tuppence.

"Out the doors and to your left, gentlemen," he said, rubbing the coin between his fingers. "The place is covered with red crosses. You can't miss it."

Indeed, when we stepped outside we found that the large banners that ran down the face of the hotel were visible from the station.

"Not much for subtlety, are they?" I said.

"Vanity is a useful tool," Holmes said.

It took us only moments to complete our journey, but when we approached the steps, a man in a gold-trimmed red-and-white coat and a garish peaked cap stepped forward to bar us.

I took him for a doorman. "Excuse me, sir. We would like to enter," I said.

"Do you have an invitation?" the man asked.

"An invitation to a hotel?" I stammered.

"Ah, I see," the man said. "Hotel is a bit of a misnomer, at least in the modern sense. This building belongs to a private organization."

"And yet a bill for boarding and hospitality was recently sent to a Mr. Jacob Murray," Holmes said.

"As I say, it is a private organization, sir."

"Which as good as confirms Mr. Murray was here," I said. "You'd have refuted it otherwise."

"I didn't say any such thing," the man said.

"The porter at the station didn't seem to think it would be any trouble to have our baggage sent here," Holmes said.

"I don't know anything about that, sir." The man's eyes had turned hard and his jaw was clenched tight.

Holmes produced a calling card. "Sorry to have bothered you. Would you pass my name along to the head of this organization?"

The man took the card but said nothing.

"Might you also recommend a restaurant? My companion here is famished."

"The Seabird is alright," he said hooking a thumb further down the road.

"Funny name for a pub this far inland," I said.

The man turned his hard gaze on me.

"We shall dine at The Seabird, then," Holmes said. "We can be found there for at least an hour, I should say. Good day."

With that, Holmes tapped the brim of his cloth hat and spun on his heel. So unexpected was the maneuver that I had to hurry to catch pace with him.

"Giving up just like that?" I asked.

"I have a certain experience with this kind of unsociable social club. The harder we try to wedge our foot in the door, the more they will puff up their chests and bloviate. The most we could have hoped for was to be shown the curb by the major-domo rather than the footman. My card will manage the infiltration much more smoothly than we ever would."

My mind was soon drawn to the dressed ham sandwich before me at The Seabird. Holmes had ordered the same but hadn't yet touched it as the last bite of my own disappeared. The barmaid had been swift and generous when keeping my glass topped off and I was soon overcome with a satiated languor. "Further than I might have chosen to go for a sandwich, but all is well in the end."

Just as I had settled back comfortably in my chair the door opened and the man from The Galahad entered. He had a quick word with the barmaid and then came to us.

"Mr. Holmes, you and your associate have been invited to call upon The Galahad."

"Is that so?" Holmes replied.

"If you would follow me," he said. "Your tab has been taken care of."

"Very good of you," Holmes said.

Nevertheless, I was sure to thank the woman personally as we left, briefly taking her hand as I gave a quick bow.

"She's my sister, you know," the man said outside.

"Oh?"

105

"Just don't be getting any ideas about what local amenities there might be," he said.

"By no means," I said, red under the collar.

"I assure you that Doctor Watson is a perfect gentleman," Holmes said.

Another man stood watch at the door when we arrived, wearing a coat similar in cut to the footman, but all in black save for the golden trim. The two nodded to each other and the door was thrown open. The man in black led us inside.

"I'm Mr. Carrington," the man said. "I manage the practical affairs around here. The Master is quite pleased with your visit. The Holmes name carries weight even here. Of course, we were rather expecting your – "

"I do apologize," Holmes said. "It was an oversight of mine not to send word ahead. Is the Master available now?"

"Of course. He awaits you, Mr. Holmes."

The floor was a black-and-white parquet, like so many of these gentleman's clubs. The hallway was lined with impressive paintings of their namesake, and while I am not expert, I suspect any museum in the kingdom would have been proud of such a collection. Heavy vermillion curtains hung closed at the end of the hall.

"Just to be clear, this is an informal visit," Holmes said. "There is no need for any formalities."

"No formalities, as you say, have been offered," Carrington said.

"Very good," Holmes said.

"What's all that about," I whispered to him.

"For a moment, I was worried we'd be flogging a goat in a gown or somesuch nonsense."

"An initiation?"

"I am a resolute member of no club," Holmes said before we stepped through the curtain that Carrington was holding aside.

We passed inside to find a rather conventional, if well-appointed, lounge.

"This way, gentlemen," Carrington said as he deftly stepped around us and led us to a table at the far end of the room. Three men were set there already. To the left was a man in a crisp blue suit who wore the broad, flat features of a lad well-familiar with a rugby pitch. To the right sat a gaunt figure in a drab fisherman's sweater, although he otherwise looked as if he were born behind a desk and would die there as well. In the center was the man I took to be the Master. He wore a garish white dining jacket and had twirled his beard and forelock into eccentric curls. He regarded us through red-tinted spectacles.

"Mr. Holmes," the Master began. "I'm afraid you have come all of this way for nothing. A telegram would have resolved this matter with much less inconvenience."

"It is no bother," Holmes replied. "A day out of the London atmosphere is its own reward."

"Yes, well, Jacob Murray stayed here only a few days, and the only remarkable thing about that time is that he left without settling his bill."

"And, indeed, without his personal belongings," Holmes said. "Do your guests often flee?"

"If you are familiar with Mr. Murray, then you can probably imagine that he spent his time here playing at cards, and it seems he was unable to make good on his obligations."

"So you assume," Holmes replied. "If he truly disappeared, then you don't know what his motive might have been."

The Master conceded the point with a dismissive wave.

107

"I'm at a bit of a loss as to why he was here in the first place."

The other men at the table chuckled until the Master silenced them with a hiss.

Holmes simply waited for an answer.

"Old Reggie . . . ." the rugby player began.

"One of our members invited Mr. Murray as a guest. We were given the impression that the two were genuine acquaintances, but it was later revealed that they had only recently met."

"When Murray cleaned Old Reggie out," the rugby player laughed.

"It seems Reginald was coaxed into a friendly game of hearts to pass the time on the train," said the third man, "and by the time they reached the station, he was well in debt to Murray."

"Reginald Parkes comes from old money," the Master said, "and has the assets of a peer but not two shillings to rub together."

"I quite understand his predicament," replied Holmes. "Murray used the debt to pry an invitation from Mr. Parke's hands?"

"And immediately began to ply his trade at our tables," the Master gestured at the room.

"Whereupon the barracuda found himself in a shark tank," said the third man. "He lost heavily that first night, but made good on his wagers, and so we put him up in a spare room. At that point, he seemed like he might even be a candidate for membership."

"But appearances are deceiving," the Master said. "It seems he used every cent he had in this world to maintain appearances on that first night. Indeed, all the money he had was what he had just won from Reginald on the train. He kept the charade up for a few more evenings, gambling on credit and assuring us he'd write a draught for any shortcomings before he left."

"Were his losses especially large on the day he disappeared?" Holmes asked.

"Not particularly," the third man said.

"Had he had a confrontation? Was there any reason he might have left the day he did, rather than a day earlier or a day later?"

The three men muttered in the negative.

"What about this Reginald Parkes? Were there any sore feelings there?"

"He was a bit embarrassed, I think," said the rugby player. "He's rather old and feeble. Hasn't been in since his folly was revealed."

"Even now that Murray has gone?" Holmes asked. "Has anyone spoken to him in that time?"

To that, the three just muttered non-committedly.

"Give me his address," Holmes said.

The Master nodded and the third man rose from the table and exited through a rear door.

"Why are you billing Mr. Murray if he was Reginald's guest?" I asked.

"I suppose it sounds petty when heard aloud," the Master said, "but he availed himself of our hospitality under false pretenses. He ate our food, drank our liquor, and slept under our roof, all while trying to pick our pockets."

"And yet, he absconds without his personal belongings when he is in no immediate danger," Holmes said. "Surely he could have simply provided a false draught and walked right out the door. By the time you discovered the writ was not negotiable, he would be long gone."

"Panic, I suppose," the rugby player said. "He meant to fleece us and found himself sheared instead."

Holmes had a skeptical tilt to his head. "May we see his room?"

"Why?" asked the Master. "We returned his belongings, such as they were."

"There may still be some subtle clue," Holmes said.

"Mr. Holmes, this interview was a courtesy, but our members value their privacy."

"I see," Holmes replied as the third man returned with Reginald's address. "Thank you for your time."

"Please send my regards to your – "

"Off we go, Watson," Holmes said, taking me by the elbow and quick stepping us out of the building.

"I don't mean to tell you how to go about your business, Holmes," I said, "but it seems to me you didn't press very hard."

"To the contrary, Watson. I pressed just hard enough to confirm that they are hiding something. Had we forced the issue, I find it highly unlikely that they would have revealed any damning evidence. To the contrary, we would have been led around on a merry stroll to see nothing of consequence. Once that proved to be the case, I didn't want to put the so-called Master too much on his guard."

"Do you think that Jacob might still be inside?"

"It seems unlikely. Unnecessary attention was drawn when they sent a bill to your Mr. Murray. Had they done nothing, no one would have ever connected Jacob with The Galahad."

"I'm afraid that I understand very little of this business," I said.

"Let us see if Mr. Reginald Parkes can shed any light upon the matter," Holmes said. With a decisive chop of his arm he hailed a carriage, and soon we stood in the ivy-spun garden of the disgraced club member. It was a picturesque cottage of grey stone, each of the cardinal directions sporting a trellis expertly decked in bluebonnets. Holmes knocked at the door but there was no answer.

"Perhaps he isn't at home," I said.

"I don't think anyone has been home for some time," Holmes replied. "Observe the ground."

"What of it?" I wondered.

"Do you see the imprints of these boot heels in the earth between the flagstones? Compare them to your own."

A previous visitor had left well define divots in the ground, while my own shoes left but a scant impression.

"And here," Holmes gestured, "note where the grass has been flattened. See the extra depression at each corner."

"Goodness! Do you think Mr. Parkes suffered a fall here, just outside his own door?"

"I don't think Mr. Parkes ever returned from his holiday and stopped at The Galahad. The bootmarks were made by a spry man carrying a heavy load. The disturbance of the grass just next to the door was likely created when Mr. Parke's luggage was set down as the porter knocked. Like us, he found no one at home, and was forced to retreat with the luggage in tow."

"Remarkable, Holmes!"

"We shall have to return to the train station to see if I am correct. Yet, while we are here, let us be certain that Mr. Parkes is not."

Holmes produced a small leather satchel from his coat. He turned away from me and seemed to be fiddling with the lock on the door. A few moments later it opened.

"Holmes, I am quite sure this is not legal."

"Doctor, we have an elderly man of a vulnerable disposition who has gone missing. What if he should be here gasping on the floor, straining to keep hold of that slender thread of life, and you could help him?"

"Do you think so?" I asked.

Holmes was already inside. I followed to find him closing the pantry door. "Nothing perishable." He ran his hand through the ashes in the fireplace. "Not a spark of warmth." Finally, he entered Parke's bed chamber and slapped at the pillows. "Dusty."

"No one to miss him, it seems," I said. The place was decidedly Spartan. It always struck me as melancholy when I encountered those who had lived their life and come to the end alone. I had seen many during my residency, and those lonely last vigils where a strange doctor is the only person to sit by the deathbed helped prompt me to seek a military career rather than general practice. A Jezail bullet had ended those ambitions, and here I found myself at loose ends, trailing after an eccentric idler on what was proving to be a wild goose chase.

Lost in this revelry, I did not observe when Holmes had left, but I suddenly realized that I myself was alone. I sprinted outside and hurriedly closed the door. In the distance, I saw Holmes perambulating with great haste. I cursed as I tried to close the distance but soon gave it up as Holmes disappeared from view. Was he intentionally giving me the slip, I wondered, or was he so focused on his investigation that all else had fallen away from his notice? Neither possibility seemed very complimentary. I continued to follow along, tacking towards the cluster of tall buildings at the center of Avondale. Cutting through an ancient alley, I came across a beggar, the first I'd seen since arriving. In London, the downtrodden are ever-present such that they become invisible, but here, this man very much stood out. He had a tangle of white beard that reached to his belt and his eyes were held shut, even as he seemed to survey the bricks around him. The clothes he wore were many sizes too large, and yet he seemed at home in them. I felt in my pocket for a few loose pence.

"Here you are, my fellow," I said, pressing the coins to his hand.

To my surprise, he returned the gesture by producing a pamphlet.

"No need," I said, having long since read my share of religious tracts and political screeds passed out by the fanatical and the disconsolate. "I'm happy to help where I can."

The man seized my arm with surprising strength. "Wait, please," he rasped. He pressed the pamphlet into my chest.

I sighed and took it. "*The Holy Grail Rests Under Avondale*," I read. It was much the same pap as I had seen across Europe anywhere holiday-goers congregate. A mishmash of Bible verses and outlandish claims about local history. The man likely had a treasure map he could sell me or a compass wrought with a nail from the crucifix, or some other mumbo jumbo meant to part fools from their money. "I'm expected on the next train," I said, only stretching the truth a bit. Holmes would notice if I were gone. Wouldn't he? "I'm afraid I don't have time for this sort of thing."

As I moved to break his grip on my arm I noticed that the jacket he wore beneath his coat had a label sewn on the inside. "This jacket belonged to Reginald Parkes?" I asked. "When did you get it? How did you get it?"

"Mr. Parkes," the man replied with a grin.

I briefly considered that this vagrant might have robbed the frail old man, but the jacket had a sheen of grime to it that suggested months, if not years, of rough wearing. "Do you know Mr. Parkes?"

"Mr. Parkes!" He tapped emphatically upon the pamphlet.

Upon a renewed inspection, I discovered that the pamphlet was published, such as it were, by a Mr. R. Parkes.

"Do you know where Mr. Parkes is now?" I asked. "Have you seen him today? Or yesterday?"

At this, the beggar's face fell. "Under," he said, making a gesture with his hands that suggested falling leaves to me.

"Under where?" I continued.

The man gestured up the alley and my gaze naturally followed. When I turned back he had disappeared. If I had not still held the pamphlet in my hand, I would have thought him a figment of my imagination.

I proceeded up the alley but saw no place where anyone could possibly have gone under anything. At the far end, I found myself standing across from the Hotel Galahad again.

"Where have you been?" demanded a voice to my right. I turned to see a man in the red-and-white uniform of an employee of the Galahad.

"Beg your pardon?" I asked.

"You must stay focused on the task at hand, Watson."

Only when I heard my name spoken did I recognize the man I was speaking to. Holmes had somehow grown a trim, pointed beard since I had seen him only minutes before. I could also swear that his hair was several shades lighter, bordering on blonde. Even the shape of his face seemed altered as if he had somehow gained at his jawline what he had lost in his cheeks.

"Put this on," he said, handing me a bloody butcher's smock.

"Why do I have to be the one to wear this?" I asked.

"If you can produce another passable disguise in the next few minutes, by all means, do so," Holmes replied. "I've yet to find a social club that will refuse delivery of meat, yet being

114

a member of the toiling castes will make you invisible to the men in there."

"From where are we supposed to get this delivery of meat?" I asked.

Holmes gestured behind himself and I peered over his shoulder to discover two crates of the butcher's art stacked on the curb.

"What would you have done had I not arrived in time?" I asked.

"I never had any doubt that you would. Now, quickly."

Holmes lifted the first of the crates and began pushing his way across the crowded afternoon street. I threw on the rank apron and followed suit. Holmes passed the entrance without so much as a glance and led me around the the building, kicking at a plain door set in the side.

"What's all this racket then?" came a gruff voice from inside.

"This box weighs as much as an ox, and it is leaking onto my uniform besides," Holmes said in an affected voice. "You going to let me in or do I let the cobblestones have all this fine meat? That would be a fine thing for us both."

"I've never seen you before."

"I'm usually stationed – well, you know," Holmes said. "It was my bad luck to be passing by when this lout arrived." Holmes nodded towards me. An angry bald head popped around the door to squint at me.

"All right," the man said. "Bring it in."

Feeling that the muscles of my injured shoulder were already at their limit, I lurched after Holmes and gratefully set the crate down on a large table in the kitchen.

"I wasn't expecting any deliveries today," the bald man said.

"I don't think he speaks the Queen's English," Holmes replied, shaking his head at me with disdain.

My look of genuine confusion seemed to play well, as the man simply grunted and turned to inventory the crates. "That will be all," he said without looking back.

As I stood flat-footed, Holmes gave me a shove and yelled overly loud, "That is all. You may leave."

Holmes herded me to the door, but at the last moment pushed me down behind the far side of the table so that I was hidden, before making a show of wrenching open and then slamming the outer door shut. I could then hear him making derisive clucking sounds.

"This isn't right at all," the chef said. "Look at this random hodgepodge of sausages and tripe. Actual tripe! I'll not be paying for it, and McGulkin will be getting an earful besides. Sending some ignorant clod here with scraps not fit for a dog."

"Best to be certain the Master didn't place the order before creating a stir."

"The Master never interferes with my kitchen."

"Still, best to be sure. McGulkin will suffer your wrath just as sorely tomorrow."

"You'd best get back before you are missed," the man said.

Holmes gave a curt nod before coming behind the table and yanking at my collar. I crawled along beside him as he ambled toward an inner passage. I had managed to stay behind cover but I would be exposed in the last few feet, just within eyeshot of the disgruntled chef.

Holmes pounced upon the sausages that had been laid out. "Any chance I could have a few of these? You weren't expecting them anyway."

The chef turned to slap Holmes's hands. "Keep your hands off. If I see you in my kitchen again I'll make you regret it."

"Just a thought," Holmes said, still eyeing the meat longingly.

As this transpired, I had effected my escape and waited for Holmes in the shadows of the unlit passage.

"What if he goes asking about the meat?" I asked.

"In a place like this, the servants are conditioned to mind their own affairs," Holmes said. "He'll bark down at us, but won't dare draw the attention of his betters. Now, do you suppose the Galahads are the sort to hide their secrets in the cellar or the attic?"

"Cellar," I said.

"You seem uncharacteristically sure of yourself, Watson."

I produced the pamphlet I had received from the itinerant man in the alley opposite. "Published by R. Parkes," I said.

"Where did you come across this novelty?"

"When we were separated, a man approached me and gave me this."

"Might it have been Mr. Parkes himself?"

"He did not appear to be a man of means, nor even a man with a roof to sleep under. He told me Parkes was 'under'."

"Under what?" Holmes asked.

"Here, I begin to expect. This building, I mean."

We felt our way along the darkened hall, pausing to poke our heads through what doors were presented to us. The better rooms were given to the storage of linens and dry goods, while the lesser rooms seemed to serve as dormitories for the staff. My billets in the deserts of Afghanistan had been more luxe. No stairs were to be found.

"It comes as little surprise," Holmes whispered. "The Galahads would be unlikely to keep their treasure within easy reach of their grasping inferiors."

"What are you looking for, then?" I asked.

"This," Holmes said, throwing open a door to reveal a sea of crimson robes.

"How did you know this was here?" I asked.

"If it wasn't robes it would be aprons, or masks, or absurd hats." Holmes seized two of the garments, and I gratefully shed my butcher's apron.

"Surely they must only wear these on special occasions," I said. "What if no one else is dressed like this?"

"We can bluff anyone save the Master – at least for a few minutes, which should be all we need."

We tugged the hoods as far over our faces as they would go and I followed Holmes with as much bravado as I could muster. We found ourselves passing through a small study and out into a larger reading room. As I feared, our outlandish dress was drawing attention from the handful of men perusing the papers and smoking. Worse, the manservant in attendance gave us a hard look before turning to open a paneled door. Surely he meant to raise an alarm.

"Where do you think you are going?" Holmes shouted. "Skittering away when duty calls. I see you haven't informed these gentlemen of the special assembly."

"I've heard nothing of a special assembly, sir," the servant said, now hesitating in the doorway.

"Perhaps if you were more diligent in your duties, these little lapses would not occur," Holmes said. "I hope your successor shall rise to the occasion."

"Successor, sir?"

118

"While these fine fellows sit here ill-prepared, there is very little to recommend your continued employment. I'll speak to the Master at the first opportunity."

"There's no need for that, sir." The servant bowed as he made his way back to the passage from whence we had just come. "Begging your pardons, sirs, I'll retrieve your vestments presently."

Holmes scoffed loudly and then exited through the passage opposite. I hurried to keep pace.

"That was a bit much, wasn't it?" I said. "The poor man is just after his wages."

Holmes swatted my concern away. We continued on and there was now a thick carpet under my feet, and the wood-paneled walls once again were adorned by fine paintings. To our right, the passage opened up to the foyer. Holmes continued on to a small dogleg on the far side. It was so short it was almost a nook. Holmes began to tap at the wall, prying at the wainscoting and tugging at the fixtures.

"You suspect a secret door?" I asked.

"This stump of a hallway makes little sense otherwise, and you can see the rug abruptly stops."

Indeed there was bare hardwood beneath us now. Suddenly the floor lurched and gave way beneath me.

"The whole thing is a lift," Holmes said. "Ingenious."

We were being lowered into an unlit pit, and I kept a hand on the lip of the shaft for as long as I could as we continued.

"Stop looking up at the light," Holmes advised. "The sooner your eyes adjust to the dark the better."

The lift soon shuddered to a stop and Holmes guided me off before pushing a lever to send it back up again.

"Are you mad? We'll be trapped down here!"

"Perhaps," Holmes replied. He knelt by the mechanism for the lift and stuck a penny in the gear works. "At least we will have the place to ourselves for awhile."

As my eyes adjusted, I found we were in a passage lined with rough-hewn stone bricks. As we cautiously made our way forward, we found depressions in the walls, and in those depressions human remains.

"Catacombs?" I asked.

"Valiant knights of yore," Holmes said. "Now set dressing for the local business-men's club."

The passage opened out into a chamber built around what appeared to be a rather dour fountain in the center. It was a monolith maybe waist-high, too squat to be a headstone, but too short to be a tomb. Letterforms unfamiliar to me were carved into each side, and they seemed to weep, creating a ring of water like a shallow moat.

"Do you smell that?" I asked. The unmistakable scent of human decay was in the air.

Holmes cocked his head and his left index finger drifted through the air. Then he sprinted forward suddenly. "A-ha! Mr. Reginald Parkes, I presume."

I joined Holmes to find the body of a frail old man tucked into one of the far alcoves. I struck a match and leaned in to examine him. His skin was contoured in red with burst capillaries. When I gently pried his eye open, it looked like an overripe cherry. I parted his lips just enough to see that the gums were a bloody pulp and the teeth sat loose in their sockets.

"Fascinating," Holmes said, peering over my shoulder.

"This man's death was horrible beyond imagining!" I chided.

"True, but there hasn't been a reported case of Hezekiah's Scourge for nearly seven-hundred years."

"You have a working knowledge of ancient maladies, do you?"

"I have an interest in the grotesque and bizarre," Holmes said. "It has long been conjectured that the affliction was the result of a toxic algae bloom. These crusaders must have brought it home with them."

"And it has thrived in a puddle beneath an English resort town?"

"You would be distraught to discover what is hidden beneath these bucolic hamlets."

In the dark, it was impossible to tell if Holmes was in jest.

"Yet surely, if this club holds meetings down here, Mr. Parkes is not the first person to come in contact with the water."

"We could conjecture that his age or infirmity left him especially susceptible, or that the algae are particularly active at the moment, or any other of a dozen possibilities. Yet I draw your attention to the altar. What is unusual about it?"

"There is nothing usual about it at all!"

"In particular, I note that there is nothing upon it. Surely this whole chamber is designed to venerate some object."

"Suggesting that someone took the treasure and left Parkes to die."

"Perhaps Mr. Parkes was already deceased and the choice was not so fraught."

"Jacob Murray?"

"It would be in error to speculate without more facts in hand, but the situation is suggestive."

There was a disconcerting groan from the lift motor as the gears tried to chew through the penny that Holmes had placed inside.

"It seems we are discovered."

121

"Discovered with a dead man," I said. "This will take some explaining."

"I propose that we first discover the answers," Holmes said, before crossing to the far side of the chamber. Right before my astonished eyes he simply vanished. I stumbled forward to the spot I had last seen him, only to discover that there was a discontinuity in the wall, more regular than a fissure but not quite a door. With no small effort, I pressed through and found myself in a tunnel, rough-hewn from the rock and small enough that I had to walk ahead bent at the waist. Soon I was in the blackest of voids, with only my hands running along the walls to guide me. I heard nothing but my own breathing and my own footfalls. After what seemed like an eternity, there was a pillar of light ahead, and in it I saw Holmes's silhouette. I could hear a whimpering now, a quiet pleading echoing all around me.

"Ah, Watson, at last," Holmes said, turning towards me. "Step lively. A doctor is sorely needed."

I hurried as much as I was able, though I was careful not to stumble before Holmes, who had moved so fleet of foot through the very same passage. I was shocked for a moment to see my friend Murray lying upon the ground next to a spring. Only when I got closer did I see the foreshortened legs, one resting painfully askew. Once in the light, I could see that, although there was more than a passing resemblance, this man's countenance was rougher than my friend's. Hardship had chiseled deeply into his cheeks and brow. "Mr. Murray? I am Doctor Watson, a friend of your brother."

"You're a doctor?" Jacob said. "Do you have any morphine?"

"Not with me, I'm afraid."

"Opium then?"

"Not as such."

122

"What kind of a doctor are you then?"

"The kind that is going to splint your leg so you can be rescued." There was little enough to work with, but I tore my robe to ribbons and bound the broken leg as well as I could. In light of his condition, I feared the man's only recourse would be an amputation, but that wasn't a determination I was willing to make down here. "That's a well, I take it?"

"Indeed," Holmes said. "I suspect this access tunnel was made in service of the unfortunates who burrowed these catacombs out of the rock. It seems to continue to the surface."

"I don't see a rope."

"I'll see what can be scrounged from above."

"You don't mean to scale the well unaided? That would be reckless in the extreme."

"As our friend here can testify," Holmes said, gesturing to the broken leg. "What choice have we?"

"Return the way we came? I'd rather leave in handcuffs than on angel's wings."

"A bit presumptuous, Watson. Nonetheless, I don't fancy facing a vengeful mob with ready access to that deadly water. Imagine the torments Parkes endured."

"I'd prefer not to, but I doubt the Galahads will be vengeful. They are pompous, not dastardly."

"I'm afraid they have succumbed to a certain kind of madness. Mr. Murray?"

"They believe it," Murray sputtered. "All of it."

"All of what?"

"How versed are you in the Arthurian legends?" he asked me.

"As much as any British boy, I imagine."

"And Sir Galahad?"

"The son of Lancelot. He completes the quest for the Holy Grail."

"Indeed, in the Arthurian legends he is the last man known to possess the Grail, and it is not seen again after he is taken into Heaven."

"These men believe they possess the Holy Grail?" I asked.

"Of course they are no more correct than the dozens of others around the world that believe the same."

"How can you be certain?" I asked.

Holmes simply arched a brow in response. "Those are the stakes for which the Master and his cronies believe they are playing."

"So give them the blasted thing back and let's take Mr. Murray to a hospital."

"If only," Holmes chuckled, and nodded to Jacob.

"I'd been down here for at least a day, alone in the dark with a dead man," Murray began.

"Quite a few dead men," Holmes corrected.

"Yes, well, I wasn't in my right mind by the time I discovered this shaft, and I did my damnedest to scramble my way up to freedom."

"When you fell you broke your leg," I said.

"I thought I was done for until Mr. Holmes stepped from the shadows."

"And the grail?" Holmes prompted.

"This was all a bit impromptu," Murray said. "I made my jacket into a sling and tied the sleeves around my shoulders. That worked well enough when I was climbing up, but when I fell, it seems the impact with the water knocked the bundle loose."

I made my way to the edge of the spring and peered down. The water was perfectly clear, but the bottom was beyond sight.

"How deep is it?" I asked.

"Deep enough," Holmes said. "I can hold my own as a diver, but we can't risk that there might be a cross current down there that would sweep me into an untenable position. Any bump on the head, any tangle of vegetation, any of a thousand trivial obstacles would be fatal. And it is not just my life I would be playing with, but yours as well."

"I still don't see the climb as much safer," I objected.

"For all my skill as a diver, I am a better mountaineer," Holmes said. With that, he kicked off his shoes and tugged his stockings free. With no more preamble, he then walked to the edge of the water and reached a ropey arm across the shaft of the well, wedging his fingers into some minor crack. Next, his foot followed, and then another. Even Jacob Murray seemed to have forgotten his agony for a moment as we craned our necks to watch Holmes make the ascent. The rock was clearly wet and slick with moss, yet Holmes never hesitated as he clambered up. After making it out at the top he shouted something back down, but the echoes made it unintelligible.

"How did you end up down here in the first place?" I asked.

"The dead man back there is named Reginald Parkes. I met him on a train and he was an easy mark. Too easy. He ended up wagering more than he could pay. I'm not one to hassle an old man, though. I see he is wearing this club regalia, so I offer to forgive the remainder of his debt if he made an introduction."

"Holmes had pieced that together already."

"Well, one night he comes into my room. I figured he's angry that he's been snookered and he was there to thrash me until his dignity has been restored. It has happened once or twice before."

"I'm sure."

"Instead, he tells me about a treasure in the cellar. How the Master is very controlling of it, and how unfair it is that he is kept away from it. He says he can't trust any of his brothers, but he is afraid to go down there alone. We come to an agreement and he shows me the lift."

"And once you were alone down here with the Grail, you killed him."

"I'm no saint, Doctor Watson, but I'm not a killer. Old Reggie just runs forward as soon as we see the cup. He doesn't even touch it, just kneels down and starts scooping water from the ground into his mouth. By the time I catch up to him he is lolling about on the rocks, his senses had left him already. I heard voices from the lift and it begins working its way up. I realize we are about to be caught, so I shove Old Reggie into one of these holes and then I squeeze myself into another. The Master and two of his entourage enter the chamber and go right for the Grail. They don't even look at anything else. They kneel down and pray and then leave. I spend who knows how long fumbling around in the dark and wishing I'd just let them catch me. At that juncture, I'm sure I'm going to die in here."

"But you steal the cup anyway."

"I defy you to remain rational under those circumstances."

"Did you drink the water?"

"After seeing what happened to Reggie? No. I think the thirst is what drove me to find this spring."

A rope came tumbling down from above, and shortly thereafter Holmes descended. With his help, we tied Jacob into a makeshift harness. Holmes shouted up and the rope began to rise.

"Who is up there?" I asked.

"The porter we met when we first arrived," Holmes said. "He seemed amenable to taking on odd jobs with no questions asked."

After Jacob was hauled up, Holmes followed. When the rope returned for me, I worried for a moment about whether I could scale the wall with my weakened shoulder, and yet the thought of asking to be hauled up as well mortified me.

"Step into the loops!" Holmes shouted from above. "We've managed a rather clever pulley system, and we might as well put it to use."

The porter gave us a handcart ride back to the Avondale station, where I sent a telegraph to the Candlewick and advised Murray to meet us at St. Barts.

"Won't these Galahad chaps be out to get my brother?" Murray asked, as we smoked and waited for Jacob to come out of surgery.

"As far as they know, your brother is simply a shiftless gambler," Holmes said. "From their perspective, their Grail disappeared only after Watson and I snuck into their *sanctum sanctorum*."

"I didn't mean to put anyone in danger," Murray said.

"Tut," Holmes said. "With our friends from the Yard looking over their shoulders, the constabulary of Avondale have been quite industrious in taking the Hotel Galahad apart. I expect that the catacombs will join the national registry. As for the rest, it seems the Master, a certain Nigel Bairnes, was not completely forthcoming in his bookkeeping. As the establishment was licensed as a public hotel, he will be facing quite a few charges of malfeasance before even considering the fact that Reginald Parkes was found rotting in the cellar. He'll be occupied for some time. As for the rest of the group, with the artifact gone they have little reason to continue propping up the organization."

"I'll be forever in your debt, Doctor Watson and Mr. Holmes," Murray said, shaking our hands.

"It was an honor to come to the aid of a brother-in-arms," I said.

Jacob was brought out of the operating theatre, and the surgeon, a gruff old man by the name of Mortimer, assured the brothers that Jacob would walk once again. However, a dubious glance washed across his face as he turned away. After another round of grateful platitudes, Murray set off for the train station, and Holmes and I turned our feet towards Baker Street.

"Do you think it might have been real?" I asked.

"The so-called Grail?" Holmes scoffed. "Mark my words, if the thing is ever recovered, it will be found to be made of copper, which has natural properties toxic to bacteria. Those that drank from the cup lived, those who drank directly from the font perished. Voila, magic cup."

"How can you be sure?"

"When you have eliminated the impossible, whatever remains, however improbable, must be the truth."

I have often wondered since then whether Holmes had truly considered all possibilities in this case. Of course, any certainty is lost in the water-logged crags beneath Avondale. That Grail, regardless of its authenticity, will not be seen by human eyes again. It is funny to think that Jacob Murray, of all people, holds the honor of seeing it last.

In the weeks that followed, I watched the papers with interest as Nigel Bairnes was tried and ultimately sent to prison. At the same time, it seems a philanthropic society purchased the hotel and returned it to its intended purpose, save for a small museum of local history which charged no admission. It turned out Reginald Parkes had made provisions for all of this in his will, naming his brother the executor.

There was some excitement in that his brother had long been known as a local eccentric whom many thought would be found legally incompetent to take possession of the Parkes estate in light of his Bohemian proclivities for wandering the streets and mooning after fairy tales, not to mention his blindness. Yet when he presented himself to the courts, he was by all accounts of sound mind, perhaps even charming. Freshly shaven, there was no doubt he was Reginald's sibling. I have often thought of taking a holiday in Avondale and getting the truth of the place from the younger Mr. Parkes, but since meeting Holmes, I find that I am constantly drawn along on his quixotic episodes. Soon enough things will settle, I tell myself. Surely Sherlock Holmes does not mean to keep up these manic endeavors for long.

Bad Blood at Barts
by Harry DeMaio

Chapter I - Stamford

The year was 1881. The location was London – more specifically, the Criterion Bar. I was just preparing to depart when a slim figure limped across my field of vision. I wasn't sure if I truly recognized him, although his military bearing, moustache, and carefully trimmed brown hair rang a familiar bell. He was dressed in non-too fashionable tweeds, holding a coffee cup in one hand and a bowler in the other. I doubt if he was making any connection with me. But he did stop, and we briefly stared at each other.

"I say, is that you, Watson?"

He scrunched up his eyes, paused and then let a smile work its way across his face. "Stamford, you old reprobate. It *is* you! How are you, old fellow? It's been years."

It *had* been years since we both took up the discipline of medicine. Then, off he went to serve as an assistant surgeon in Her Majesty's Army during the Second Anglo-Afghan War. I remained a civilian practicing at St. Bartholomew's Hospital (Barts). Now in London after being invalided out of the service, thanks to a Jezail bullet wound incurred at the Battle of Maiwand, he was back in London, but also living on his nine-month half-pay pension. Besides seeking new sources of income, he was searching for a place to live. I thought that I could help him. After we'd done some more catching up, I said that there was someone else that I wanted him to meet. And so I introduced him to Sherlock Holmes.

Several months later, I was also able to introduce him to the Surgery Superintendent at Barts. We were short-staffed, and I knew that it was possible that Watson could help take up some slack on a part-time basis. To say that Barts is an impressive pile is to vastly understate the case. Physically, professionally, and historically, the huge hospital is unique in England – and perhaps throughout the world – in terms of the number of patients served, the medical discoveries made, the publications issued, the famous practitioners on staff, the students, nurses, orderlies on duty, and the physical facilities. They speak to a massive and effective enterprise. I had been part of this universe for several years, and I felt quite comfortable approaching the Superintendent on my old friend's behalf.

When I presented Watson to the Superintendent's clerk, mentioning that he was a Barts alumnus, a skilled surgeon, and a war veteran, the office door opened rapidly, and we were welcomed graciously. Our session with him lasted only long enough to secure John's vital information and to set up an appointment next day to work out the specifics of his part-time employment.

That evening, to celebrate Watson's new source of income at Barts, we joined his flatmate, Sherlock Holmes, for dinner. We made short work of aperitifs, ordered wine, and selected our appetizers and entrees. Then I asked Holmes if he had carried out any further blood experiments, as he'd been doing when I introduced the two of them.

The detective smiled fleetingly. "I spent some time on that just today. I'm developing a system to assist in identifying both criminal victims and perpetrators through the analysis of bloodstains. It isn't definitive in the sense that I can put an individual's name to a particular sample, but I can establish characteristics that will separate and eliminate suspects or confirm likelihood. Are you anemic, Doctor Stamford?"

"Not that I know of."

"How about you, Watson?"

"Indeed not. I have other ailments but not that one."

"Good! I can thus positively state that neither of you is the source of the stain I've obtained from a Mayfair crime scene – a fatal assault. A well-dressed man was found in a park with his throat cut. This sample came from his clothing, but the blood is not from his body. He was hematologically healthy. It came from an anemic culprit or culprits, suggesting, along with other evidence, that our victim engaged in a deadly exchange during which he inflicted as well as suffered physical mutilation.

"The victim is, or was, a prestigious physician who lived in the area. Robbery doesn't seem to be the case here. His personal possessions were intact. Inspector Lestrade of Scotland Yard has the situation in hand. As a result of my efforts, he is searching for a recently wounded attacker. When he finds him or her, we will test for anemia. If the test is positive, Lestrade will further pursue that lead. If not, he'll have to look elsewhere. He's dubious about the test, but isn't above accepting supporting evidence if such exists, even if it's negative."

I admitted to being fascinated and said so. Little did any of us know how soon another example, closer to home, would arise.

When I arrived at the hospital next morning, I was greeted by a pair of constables checking as people entered and left. Puzzled, I identified myself and inquired why they were there.

"There's been a violent murder, Doctor Stamford. In the laboratory wing. One of the interns has had his throat slit. Inspector Lestrade is there."

"I've never met the inspector, although Sherlock Holmes has spoken of him."

"Oh, do you know Mr. Holmes? Fine gentleman. The inspector is waiting for him."

No sooner had he said that when two figures stepped out of a hansom cab and advanced toward the hospital entrance. One tall, with clean shaven, aquiline features. The other somewhat shorter but slim and sporting a modest moustache. Holmes and Watson. They both looked quizzically at the constable and then at me.

I looked back at them. "It seems you're the man of the hour, Holmes. A murder! Inspector Lestrade is waiting for you in the laboratory wing. It may even be the room where you've been conducting your experiments."

"Good morning, Stamford. Good morning, Constable. A murder? Who's the victim?"

"An intern, sir. I don't have a name. Had his throat cut. The inspector can fill you in."

Watson looked torn. On the one hand, he had his scheduled meeting with the Surgical Superintendent. On the other, his curiosity was clearly overwhelming him.

He looked at Holmes. "I'd better keep my appointment with the Superintendent. I don't want to spoil my first chance at meaningful employment, but I'll look you up in the lab as soon as we're finished."

Holmes nodded assent. "Do you want to come along, Stamford? You know this hospital far better than I do. You may be able to provide some useful insights. You may even know the victim."

It hadn't occurred to me that I might become involved in a murder, but I had no assignments for several hours, and my inquisitiveness was gnawing at me.

"I'd be delighted!" I immediately realized how callous that response sounded. Delight at a death. A human had passed on violently and I, a follower of Hippocrates, was letting this bizarre event overwhelm my sense and sensitivities. A little soul-searching seemed in order.

The laboratories were in an annex a good distance from the entrance hall and, during our walk to the site, both Holmes and I maintained a pensive near-silence – no doubt for different reasons. I was wondering how Watson's interview was progressing. I hoped I could console myself that I had helped my friend with his employment. We arrived at the lab where the inspector was waiting.

"Good morning, Lestrade. Allow me to introduce Doctor Stamford, a long-time associate of mine and a member of the surgical staff here at the hospital."

"Good morning, Doctor. Mr. Holmes. We have a bit of a poser here. I understand you've been conducting your blood experiments in this very room."

"That's correct. I have been working on your Mayfair knife episode. Incidentally, those bloodstains you passed on did not come from the victim. You must look for a tall, wounded, anemic individual with blond hair as your culprit."

"In other words, half of London. Well, let's look at *this* victim, shall we?"

The inspector was a ferret-faced, dark-haired individual of medium height, well-dressed and clean shaven. His black eyes were inexpressive. His voice was an interesting mix of several accents – London plus some rural overtones. All told, it was impossible at first meeting to determine his intelligence, although Holmes had mentioned on our walk through the buildings that he was regarded as a senior detective at the Yard. Whether this was a result of skill or simple longevity remained to be seen.

I recognized the dead intern. He was tall, quite slim with a narrow hawk-like face, and clean-shaven with black hair. He reminded me of someone. I had seen him several times while conducting surgical rounds. His name didn't come immediately to mind, but I recalled that he was an intelligent, inquisitive, outspoken individual whose responses to clinical quizzing were, more often than not, well thought-out and thorough. We had lost a good candidate. I said as much.

Lestrade responded. "His name is Joseph Wrigley. It seems unusual for him to be here in the laboratory. Was he involved in any of your experiments, Mr. Holmes?"

"Yes and no. He had no formal remit to do hematology work, but he had a strong interest in it. Once he had heard of my efforts, he kept popping in to question me and check on my progress. Frankly, he was a bit of a pest – an intelligent pest, but a pest nonetheless. For the record, Lestrade, I was not motivated to kill him to rid myself of his presence."

"The thought never occurred to me."

"By the way, why is the Yard engaged? Isn't this a task for the locals?"

"We can hardly handle this as routine. Wrigley's father is the chairman of a very large wool exporting enterprise and a major financial contributor."

"I'm impressed with your knowledge. I assume someone here on the medical staff has established time of death."

"A Doctor Reynolds, who also serves part-time in the coroner's office, made the call. Death occurred between eleven and one last night."

"At a time when Wrigley felt secure that I would not be here, and he could roam freely through the lab and my materials. Annoying! I must check to see if anything is missing or displaced. Have you found the weapon?"

"Not yet. Finding a sharp instrument in a surgical venue is like looking for a single bee in a hive."

"Do you know this Doctor Reynolds, Stamford?" asked Holmes.

"Oh yes. He is one of the Surgical Staff stalwarts. A very skilled and reliable professional."

"I wonder, Lestrade, if there is any connection between the Mayfair death and this killing."

"If there is, Mr. Holmes, you seem to be it."

"Before you have his body carted off to the mortuary, I'd like to examine it in some detail and take a sample of his blood. There seems to be an ample supply. I wonder if it is all his. There are stains and several finger-marks on some of my notes and books. I'll have to do an analysis."

At this point, Watson entered the room. Although he was an experienced surgeon and used to seeing death both in war and peace, he still blanched at the sight of the gore covering Wrigley's face and body. "This looks like a vicious attack."

"Right you are, Doctor," answered Lestrade. "It's a bit of a puzzle. No apparent motive as of yet, and not much to identify the assailant."

We were interrupted by the sound of voices in the hallway. Wrigley Senior had arrived. He was an older, somewhat stouter version of his son. He was accompanied by a constable and the Hospital Director. He ran into the room, swayed, and held his hands up to his face.

"Oh, my God! It *is* my son! Joe! Dead! He was such a brilliant young man with a wonderful future ahead of him. Struck down in his prime. What a horrible way to die! Who did this? Which one of you is the police? I insist on a thorough investigation that will not cease until this madman is brought to book and hanged."

Lestrade responded. "Our sincere condolences, Mr. Wrigley. I am Inspector Lestrade of Scotland Yard."

"Do you have any leads?"

"We have nothing substantial as yet, but the crime is only hours old. An extensive inquiry and search are being organized as we speak. Let me introduce you to Mr. Sherlock Holmes, the consulting detective."

There was more than a touch of irony in the policeman's voice when he said, "consulting detective".

Wrigley looked over at Holmes and paused. "Yes, I've heard of you. Are you involved with the police in this? If not, I would like to engage you to represent my interests."

"I haven't had the opportunity to discuss my role, if any, with Inspector Lestrade. This is, of course, a police matter. I've been conducting blood-related experiments in this laboratory on an unrelated investigation. Your son had a professional interest in my work and would drop by occasionally to inquire and confer. I was away last night, and I don't know why he was here during the time that the coroner believes that he was killed."

"Well, make your peace with the inspector here and let me know if I can become your client."

Lestrade looked none too happy. Then he remembered Watson and me standing there. "These two gentlemen are physicians and associates of Mr. Holmes. Let me introduce Doctors Stamford and Watson. I believe that Doctor Stamford knew your son."

"I met him several times when I was conducting rounds with the surgical interns. We had no personal relations to speak of."

Holmes inquired. "Beside yourself, Mr. Wrigley, what family does your son have?"

"Joe was a bachelor and, to my knowledge, he had no immediate marital prospects. His mother passed away several years ago. I have two other children. Edwin, Joe's younger brother, and Louella, his older sister. Louella is newly married and recently moved to Edinburgh with her new husband. She will be devastated at her brother's death. Edwin resides with me in Belsize Park. Joe had taken rooms near the hospital because of the long and irregular hours. As a result, I have only seen him infrequently of late. He came by on some Sundays for dinner, and we would spend most of our time discussing the world of medicine. Edwin would join us occasionally but not often. I'm not familiar with any of Joe's friends or associates.

"Now, if you'll forgive me, gentlemen, I must return home and break the news to my children and our staff. I assume that you have *post mortems* and examinations to conduct before turning Joe's body over to us for burial. We have arrangements that must be made."

At this he broke down and sobbed. The Hospital Director took his arm and led him out.

The Surgical Superintendent made an appearance, acknowledged the three of us, introduced himself to Inspector Lestrade, and made a vague offer of assistance. Clearly, a murder in the halls of Barts was quite unsettling, even for an institution inured to death.

He shook his head and said, "I will make arrangements to have the body transferred to the hospital mortuary for the time being, if that is satisfactory. I'm not sure what the appropriate Police procedures are in a case like this."

Holmes intervened, "Please have this room sealed and do not have it cleaned until we've had a chance to carefully examine it. The killer may have left us with information vital to solving this case."

Lestrade concurred.

Chapter II – Watson

During our meeting with Josiah Wrigley, I had stood dumbly by, unable to add anything of value other than my own condolences. Stamford seemed similarly at a loss. I wondered at the dynamic taking place between Holmes and Lestrade. Their relationship was obviously complex, combining grudging respect with sharp rivalry. Holmes saw the inspector as a determined plodder. He, in turn, thought Holmes showed an annoying and interfering unorthodoxy that set his law enforcement teeth on edge. I gathered that while their egos clashed, Holmes softened the impact by letting Lestrade take the credit in cases they shared for any solutions that were forthcoming. The inspector was more than willing to accept this arrangement since it enhanced his reputation among the public, the press, the ministries, and some members of the Yard. Not everyone was impressed, however – especially several of his CID colleagues.

"Well, Mr. Holmes, what's it to be? Will you work with us, or are you going to accept Mr. Wrigley as your client?"

"Those choices are not mutually exclusive, Lestrade, as you well know. While serving my private clientele, I have always cooperated with Scotland Yard to the greatest degree possible. This time will be no different. I am going to accept Wrigley's offer. Any discoveries I make will be passed on to you. That will also have no effect on the work I've been doing for you in analyzing the blood samples from the Mayfair murder. By the way, Stamford – who here in the hospital is aware of my work?"

Stamford paused a moment and then said, "I don't think there has been any secret made of it. Any number of staff members know what you are doing – including, of course, poor Joe Wrigley, while he lived."

Holmes turned to me. "I would like your assistance, Watson, in extracting some of Joe Wrigley's blood from his body – not at the point of the wound. They will no doubt come to transfer the body to the morgue in short order, so we'll have to be swift about it. I also have the stains and bloody finger-marks on my notes. Stamford, do you think you could purloin Wrigley's hospital jacket? There are blood stains on it as well. I sincerely doubt they all came from the same source. I assume you have no difficulty with what I am doing, Lestrade."

The inspector frowned. "You are tampering with evidence, you know. However, I'll consider it as an extension of your Mayfair work – provided that I receive the coat and the results of your stained notes for the record."

Holmes bundled his blood-soaked notes into a small bag. I used a sterile syringe to obtain a sample of Wrigley's blood for his analysis. Stamford had hidden the coat while Lestrade carefully looked the other way. Just as we were finishing, two orderlies arrived with a gurney and took the body to the hospital mortuary where the coroner was waiting. Lestrade took his leave, saying he expected to see us tomorrow.

I hadn't yet been given any staff assignments. Stamford on the other hand, had several surgical patients that he had to visit.

Holmes smiled. "What say you, Watson? Shall we pay a visit to Mr. Josiah Wrigley of Belsize Park? I will then return here and begin my research."

I asked, "Do you think we might have a little lunch on the way?"

He frowned. Months before, I had I discovered Sherlock Holmes's erratic eating habits, or I should say "non-eating" habits, when he is in pursuit of facts and solutions, or when "The game is afoot." – a phrase he borrowed from Shakespeare and uses frequently. Thank heaven for Mrs. Hudson, who has pledged to keep me adequately nourished in spite of my flatmate's dietetic idiosyncrasies.

I had previously discovered another of Holmes's peculiarities. Founded on suspicion of kidnapping or assault, he always takes the third vehicle in a cab rank. We climbed aboard a four-wheeler and Holmes gave the driver the address of the Wrigley establishment. I don't remember him having asked Mr. Wrigley for it, but he had obviously gotten it from some unidentified source. Curiouser and curiouser!

The hour-long ride through the brisk late morning to Hampstead Belsize Park gave me a chance to query Holmes about our prospective client. The mystery of the detective's source of information was solved. It seems Joseph Wrigley, in one of his evening sojourns in Holmes's laboratory, saw fit to recount his family's situation, history, and relationships. At the time, Holmes treated it as distracting noise, but nevertheless his sharp memory stored the facts away. Now they were emerging.

Josiah Wrigley, he told me, was the leader of a successful group of merchants who, over the past century, had built an extensive empire of import-export establishments. They came close several times to cornering the market for woolens. Of the current generation, Edwin had chosen to spend most of his time in the pursuit of clubs, wine, attractive young women, song, and gambling, much to his father's extremely conservative chagrin. Louella was comfortably married to a Scottish merchant who was affiliated with the Wrigley empire. They had no children. Josiah's conventional religious background and Louella's urging caused him, somewhat regretfully, to approve Joseph's venture into medicine. Joe seemed the obvious choice to benefit from his father's will. Now, that situation would have to be rethought. Clearly, Joseph had been Josiah's favorite.

According to Joe, Louella had adored him. Her feelings toward Edwin were unknown. The Belsize establishment, as we were about to discover, was a substantial property supported by a relatively modest household staff. Since the death of the lady of the house and the departure of Louella to Scotland, socializing had been a rare event. Edwin spent most of his time away from the house and as noted, Joe had taken rooms close to the hospital during his internship.

That was the totality of Holmes's recollection.

Wrigley House was a sedate, red-brick, multi-storey structure surrounded by well-tended gardens and a modest stable. We pulled up under a sizeable portico. The entrance was already adorned with mourning drapery. We asked the driver to wait, assuming our visit would be a short one. Holmes gave the ornate bell-pull a gentle tug. After a few moments, the door opened revealing a butler in black livery.

"Gentlemen, as you can see, this house is in bereavement and we are not receiving callers."

Holmes replied, handing the butler his card, "My name is Sherlock Holmes, and this is my colleague, Doctor John Watson. We met with Mr. Josiah Wrigley this morning about the untimely death of his son, and I believe he will wish to see us. Will you please make our presence known."

The butler, who we learned was named Stevens, hesitated, shrugged, turned on his heel, and went inside, leaving us standing at the entrance. After several minutes, a young man bearing a striking resemblance to both Josiah and Joseph Wrigley came to the door.

"Gentlemen, I am Mr. Wrigley's son, Edwin. I am quite reluctant to disturb my father in his grief. Can you tell me the subject of your call?"

"I am a consulting detective and I have been requested by Mr. Wrigley to take up an investigation into death of your brother, Joseph. I'm here to confirm that I will accept him as my client, and wish to speak briefly with him as to the particulars of the assignment."

Edwin's eyebrows rose. "I was under the impression that the matter was in the hands of the police."

"Scotland Yard is certainly involved, but your father also wished me to participate."

"Well, you are here now. Let me speak to Father and see if he wishes to see you. Come in, please. Will you wait here?"

He stepped aside and we entered a large receiving room, passing the obviously annoyed butler. Shortly, the sound of male voices could be heard coming from what seemed to be a library. The door opened and Wrigley Senior stepped out, followed by Edwin.

"So, Mister Holmes, have you decided to take me on as a client?"

"I have, Mr. Wrigley. I found your son to be a very interesting and empathetic young man, and I share your regret at his loss. This may not be the appropriate time, but I have some questions that I wish to ask you both about Joseph. I realize he was not living with you, so your knowledge of his habits, acquaintances, residence, and the like may be shadowy at best. Nevertheless, I have found that small details can often be of great import."

Edwin looked at Holmes with a half-sneer on his face. "I'm sorry, but I am definitely *not* my brother's keeper and have nothing I can tell you. I thought that was what you detectives are paid to find out. Father, I'm going to my club. Stevens knows how to find me, if necessary. I assume we don't know when Joe's body will be released to us."

He stepped from the room, took up his coat, hat, and stick and walked outside, turning toward the stables. Clearly, Edwin would not be providing much comfort for his grieving father. Holmes turned back to Josiah who stood silent, shaking his head.

"My daughter. Louella, is coming down from Edinburgh with her husband, Alexander Campbell. They should arrive early tomorrow morning. She will be a comfort. Campbell owns several large woolen manufactories and is associated with Wrigley Enterprises Limited. Louella is a very astute businesswoman. Actually, she is more skilled and talented than her husband – probably a result of my influences on her. Oddly, it was she who encouraged Joe to enter the medical profession. He never had much preference for business. Neither does Edwin. The male strain in our family seems to be adverse to commerce.

"Once she convinced Joe and me that he would be an ideal practitioner, I was prepared to provide him with the wherewithal to set up a Harley Street establishment after he completed his training. That plan must now be abandoned."

I asked, "Did Joseph have a regular schedule for coming here to Belsize?"

"You're a physician, Doctor Watson. You know how difficult it is to deal with professional demands. No, he popped in when the spirit and opportunity presented itself. I'm sorry that I've seen so little of him in the past several years."

Holmes dropped his gaze. "I regret having to ask this, but I must. To your knowledge, did your son have any enemies who would have reason to do him in?"

"I have been asking myself that question all day and I can think of no one. Perhaps professional jealousy on the part of a colleague. I doubt if he had any debts that he couldn't handle, and if there was a woman, I don't know about her. I queried Edwin about it. He was no help. I didn't expect him to be."

The detective sighed. "There was no sign of robbery. There was a struggle, but the violence was deliberately fatal. Whoever killed him intended to do so."

Wrigley looked as if he was about be overcome yet again. I volunteered my services and proffered a sedative. He shook off my offer with thanks. We took our leave as Stevens, the butler, came to his assistance. The cab was still waiting for us at the doorstep.

"I'm going back to Barts, Watson, to continue my research. You may wish to join me later at the laboratory. Perhaps Mrs. Hudson will see fit to feed you beforehand." Then he continued, "I have a very deep disrespect for coincidences. However, there is a peculiar similarity to these two cases. Both victims – Joseph Wrigley and the man who was murdered in Mayfair, Sir Reginald Jeffers – were physicians. Or, in Joseph's case, a soon-to-be physician. As far as I can tell, they did not know each other. The Mayfair victim has no current affiliation with Barts. The mode of the attacks is comparable. We do not have the weapons, but the cuts are much the same. I hope to prove that the attacker in both cases suffers from anemia, possibly hemophilia, or both. That too, may be coincidental, but I strongly doubt it."

"What did the Mayfair victim look like, Holmes?"

"Sir Reginald was an older man, blue-eyed, of medium height, portly, balding, and with a fringe of grey hair. He had a grey Van Dyke beard. He lived well. He was married with two adult children. His practice was in Harley Street, where he was a rather famous specialist in female ailments, and he was

145

knighted for his work on women's nerve-related issues. He was definitely *not* anemic."

"In short, there was no resemblance to Joseph Wrigley."

"None that we can use to establish a relationship."

"I've noticed one interesting anomaly, however. Joseph Wrigley looked rather like you."

"From which you conclude what, Watson?"

"Just an observation, nothing more. The similarity is striking, however."

"But probably quite irrelevant, my friend."

I looked at him. "Perhaps."

We had arrived at the hospital and Holmes climbed down from the cab. He gave the driver a substantial tip and directed him to take me to Baker Street. Short as I was of coin of the realm, I was grateful for his generosity. I agreed to meet Holmes later at the lab, for I knew that he would be absorbed well into the night in tracking down the genesis of the blood stains on his papers and Joseph Wrigley's clothing.

Chapter III – Lestrade

In spite of what certain consulting detectives may think, we here at Scotland Yard are not totally without intelligence or resources. A search of the Mayfair park where Sir Reginald Jeffers was found dead provided several physical clues and two witnesses that led us to a known "murder-for-hire" low-life that we believed had carried out the heinous crime. The questions were: Who paid him, and why?

"Slasher Thompson" had a history that would normally have left him wasting away in Newgate Prison, awaiting the hangman. No such luck. He had been twice arrested, most recently after the murder of Sir Reginald, and twice had managed to escape confinement. He was still at large after his last escape a day or so earlier, but our forces were closing in. We believed that he was still in the city. The jailer who allowed – or abetted – his last breakout was himself now in custody and had confessed to assisting our alleged killer.

When Slasher was last in confinement, we had extracted some blood from him to pass along to Sherlock Holmes, at his request, for hemoglobin testing. Needless to say, this did not sit very well with the felon. When he protested, the big-mouthed constable who took the blood spelled out what they were doing, mentioned the laboratory at Barts, and told him that Sherlock Holmes was going to put another nail in his coffin by proving that he was anemic.

While Slasher didn't understand all of that, he concluded that he must eliminate the detective if he was going to maintain his freedom. Either by bribery or threat, he got his jailer to let him escape.

It was my belief, based on these facts, that Slasher went to Barts, concocted a clever and plausible story to explain the gash that he'd sustained when he earlier did in Sir Reginald Jeffers, and asked the staff for treatment. One of the night nurses took him in care, cleaned his injury, and signed him out. Then off he went in search of the lab and Holmes. I thought that he had never seen Holmes and had only a vague image of what he looked like. Tall, slim, dark-haired, intense eyes, clean shaven, wearing a lab coat, and surrounded by experimental equipment and notes – in short, Joseph Wrigley, who was alone in Holmes's laboratory.

He attacked the intern who fought back, opening Slasher's recently treated wound, causing his anemic blood to spill. But Wrigley lost the battle and succumbed, a victim of mistaken identity.

I presented this scenario to Sherlock Holmes who grudgingly admitted its likelihood, especially when faced with the concurring opinions of Doctors Watson and Stamford.

There remained three outstanding issues. Who hired Slasher to kill Jeffers? Why? And where was the killer at this moment?

Chapter IV – Holmes

I hate to admit it, but Lestrade may indeed be correct in his assumptions. *(I detest assumptions!)* When I returned to the Barts laboratory, intent on another evening of research in bodily fluids, I found a poorly spelled note scribbled in pencil on hospital stationery stuck to the desk.

"Sherlok Homes. I'm coming fer ya. I won't make the same misteak again. Yer a dead man."

There was no signature. If Lestrade is to be believed, the murderer still thought I stood between him and his ongoing freedom.

Watson came into the room. "What progress, if any?"

I showed him the note. He grimaced "So do you now believe Lestrade's theory?"

"It is still only a theory, but it's gaining credibility with me. It makes some modicum of sense. If the killer *(I still refuse to use the word "Slasher")* is intent on doing me in, he obviously did not intend to slaughter Joseph Wrigley. A stupid waste of a life! I don't know how I will explain it to his father."

"More to the point, Holmes, how do we prevent him from carrying out his threat to *you*?"

"I have some thoughts on that subject. Do you have a weapon with you?"

Like most veterans, the Doctor kept possession of his Webley service revolver when he was "demobbed" from the

Army. He kept it with him more out of habit than expectation of use.

"Yes, and I have recently cleaned and oiled it, although it's hardly an appropriate instrument for a physician's kit."

"We may need it."

I turned and found myself staring into the faces of Stamford and Inspector Lestrade.

"Well, this is turning into a merry little band. Have you come to witness my departure from this life?" I extended the note for both of them to examine.

Stamford whistled and Lestrade shook his head. "Cheeky!"

"We need to lure him out if we're going to discover who paid him to slaughter Doctor Jeffers and why. To say nothing of putting his neck in a noose."

Watson retorted, "I don't like the idea of you being a sacrificial lamb."

"Fear not, Watson. Ferocity seems to be our friend's strong suit, not intelligence. I doubt he'll make an appearance until much later in the night, when the laboratory area is apparently empty."

"Except for you."

"Well, Inspector, I would greatly appreciate it if the three of you were also nearby. A set of handcuffs, a cosh or two, some rope, eight strong hands, and Watson's revolver at the ready should make a difference. I shall also wear a heavy jacket under my lab coat, and I have several knives to hand. May I advise you to cover your hands and heads to ward off any stray lunges."

They retreated to a small conference space nearby, leaving me to my work. I situated myself with a clear view of the entrance. I wanted the element of surprise to be entirely on our side.

Several hours passed. Was our killer coming? I wondered if my small ambush was still prepared. Suddenly, I heard running footsteps and my attacker burst into the room wielding a large and formidable butcher's knife.

"I've got the right man this time, you rotten snoop! No one's gonna send Slasher Thompson to the gallows – not now, not never!"

As he swung the knife at me, I smashed at his wrist with a heavy glass retort. The knife fell away from his hand and slid across the floor. I leaped and kicked him in the vitals. He doubled over and, on cue, my cavalry arrived and seized him. Watson waved his revolver in the killer's face and Lestrade clamped on the handcuffs. Stamford sat on his legs and tied them together with a length of sturdy rope.

The inspector snarled, "All right, my lad, that puts an end to it. This time you're going to a special lock-up and there will be no crooked jailer to help you. You're going to swing and very soon."

He blew his whistle and three large constables appeared to drag him away.

"Wait," I asked. "Who paid you to kill Doctor Jeffers?"

"Who knows? Who cares? He was some old toff with lots of the ready. That was good enough for me. I didn't ask for his pedigree. Paid in advance, he did. Described the fat old sawbones and told me where to find him. After that, it was Bob's-yer-uncle. Then I found out you were onto me and my blood problem. You had to go. How was I to know that the bloke I killed here in the lab wasn't you? Just bad luck."

Watson stared at him. "Your bad luck is just beginning."

"Don't count me out so fast, Smart Boots. Slasher Thompson's nobody's fool. I'll be back for ya, Homes! You and yer pals."

Lestrade and the constables pulled him out of the room past a couple of shocked orderlies who had heard the noise and rushed to see what was happening.

I looked at them and said. "I wonder if you gentlemen could help clean up this mess. Don't touch that knife. It's evidence."

The next morning, Watson and I were joined by Lestrade and we journeyed out to Belsize to pay our respects to the Wrigley family.

When we arrived, a small contingent of mourners was in attendance. Josiah Wrigley was sitting in a large chair staring blankly at the sealed coffin. The three of us went over to him and offered our condolences. Lestrade leaned over and whispered, "We've caught his murderer. He is in custody and will no doubt hang."

The old man sat up. "Who? Why?"

I replied. "A professional killer named Thompson. It was a case of erroneous identity. I was his real target. I was working on a blood analysis technique that would have helped identify him as the killer of another doctor, Sir Reginald Jeffers. I needed to be eliminated. He mistook Joseph for me. We looked alike, you see. Thompson was engaged to kill Sir Reginald by someone who paid him in cash. He claims not to know the man's name. His only description was that he was tall, old, and wealthy."

"Oh God," said Wrigley. "This is all so horrible. Nevertheless, I thank you for your efforts. Please inform me of your fee, Mr. Holmes."

"There will be no fee, Mr. Wrigley. After all, I was the intended victim. I share a feeling of guilt, myself."

"Thank you! Most generous! And now, I must greet several of my business associates. Excuse me." But instead, he left the room in tears.

Outside in the hallway, I spied a tall young woman standing alone, dressed entirely in black with a veil folded back from her face. Her features were very similar to those of Joseph and Edwin Wrigley. Edwin stood nearby, obviously overcome with boredom at the whole event. I walked over to the woman.

"Good morning. Am I correct in assuming that you are Mrs. Louella Campbell? I am Sherlock Holmes, and these are my associates, Doctor John Watson and Inspector Lestrade of Scotland Yard. We have been pursuing your brother's murderer."

"Good morning, gentlemen. Yes, I am Louella Campbell, sister of poor Joseph. His death is such a blow. I was so terribly fond of him. It was I who encouraged him to pursue medicine. Now, I regret that decision. He would still be alive if he hadn't been engaged at Barts. Have you had any success in finding his killer?"

Lestrade intervened. "Yes, we have, Mrs. Campbell. In fact, we have the man in custody at the moment. We are certain he also murdered another victim earlier. Unfortunately, your brother was killed as a result of a mistaken identity."

I explained the circumstances of the murderers' mistake to her. Her reaction was unusual.

"How awful for you, Mr. Holmes. I can only imagine how you are feeling."

"Your father is suffering badly, Mrs. Campbell. You all have our deepest sympathy."

"Father's aspirations for the future of the Wrigley family have been shattered. He had hopes of building a dynasty. Now that has been destroyed. Joseph was the center of his plans. Edwin, as you may know, has no interest in business, nor any desire to wed or raise a family. His interests lie elsewhere. And as for me, I am now incapable of childbearing, thanks to an egregious error on the part of a physician. We only recently made the discovery. I'm devastated. My husband, Alexander, is taking the news with typical Scots reserve. We are, however, planning a lawsuit. My father is absolutely enraged at the doctor. And now, this tragedy with Joseph. Father keeps saying, 'I killed my son, I killed my son.' Which of course is sheer nonsense. He is simply overwhelmed."

"Out of curiosity, Mrs. Campbell, what is the name of your error-prone physician?"

"Sir Reginald Jeffers. Do you know him?"

The Inside Men
by M.J.H. Simmonds

It was a bright morning and I was taking my usual morning walk in the Regent's Park. My wounds were troubling me less and less as the days grew longer and warmth finally returned to the air. The park looked particularly beautiful. Colourful blossoms covered the trees and the new growth of grass almost glowed, fresh and alive, in the bright sunlight. It was such a fine day that by the time I returned to our rooms above Baker Street, I had worked up quite a sweat.

I removed my hat and climbed the stairs, keen to remove my unnecessarily thick overcoat. I pushed open the door and casually tossed my hat onto the stand, swiftly followed by my coat. It was only after I had stridden half the length of the sitting room that I noticed a figure sitting upon the sofa.

Momentarily startled, I managed a cautious greeting, at which our unexpected guest rose and turned towards me. The broad grin, the blonde hair, and the keen blue eyes were instantly recognisable and most welcome.

"Inspector Gregson, what an unexpected delight!" I declared, accepting his warm handshake. I gestured that he should return to the couch and offered the good inspector a drink.

"No, thank you, Doctor. However, much as I may desire a measure of your fine brandy, it is a bit early in the day for me, and I am already vexed to the point where alcohol may well drive me over the edge."

Gregson accepted a tonic water but refused a cigar, so I settled down into an opposite armchair, curious to know the reason for his visit.

"I apologise for calling unannounced, but I desperately need your advice regarding an issue which is causing me considerable distress."

Gregson's smile had now vanished. The man's face appeared pale. New lines appeared to have formed upon his brow. Whatever the issue, it had clearly disturbed this fine detective.

"My dear sir, please tell me all that troubles you. Whatever the problem, I can assure you that you will always find allies here. Holmes is currently involved in another matter, but when he left this morning, he was confident that he was close to a conclusion and should be home long before nightfall."

"I feel embarrassed, to be quite honest, Doctor. I've attempted to raise this issue back at the Yard, but my concerns have been met with either mild derision or, otherwise, open contempt. If only Lestrade wasn't away on leave, I would have, at least, one pair of ears that would listen to my concerns," Gregson trailed off, the frustration and sadness clear in his voice.

"Inspector, remember that I am a doctor, late of Afghanistan. After serving with the best and worst of the military, I can assure you that there is nothing that you can say to me that would be any way shocking."

"Very well. I apologise, Doctor, I know full well that I can trust you implicitly. Where should I begin? I suppose it all started last month. It had been a quiet day, relatively – a few fights, a robbery or two, but nothing serious. I was in my office, working my way through the day's reports, when a sergeant knocked on my door.

"'It's the queerest thing, Inspector,' he reported. 'You know that we are actively searching for old Pete Moseley and Mark Trewavas? Well, they have just presented themselves to the front desk. They declared that they were both guilty, had seen the light, and must be locked up as soon as possible.'"

"How very odd," I encouraged. "Do continue."

"As you can imagine, this caused considerable mirth around the station. However, after a day or two, it was soon forgotten amongst the myriad cases with which we deal each day. The pair of them were sent before the magistrate the very next day following their surrender and were sent down for a few months each."

"I'll be damned, though," continued Gregson, "if the exact same thing didn't happen, just a week later. Stephen Kelly and Mark Hogarth, both well-known recidivists, knocked upon our door, asking to be locked up for their sins."

"That is quite remarkable," I replied. "Unique even. I do, however, have the distinct feeling that there is still more to come."

Gregson nodded. I now realised why he had so coveted my friend's brandy, however much it was forbidden to him while still on duty.

"Earlier this week, I discovered that two more villains, John Mitchell and Craig Blundell, had turned themselves in. What's more, just yesterday, I walked into the Yard to catch the Rankin brothers in the very act of surrendering. Whomever I spoke with, I received the same replies: Be grateful. The fear of God has changed them. That sort of nonsense. However, do you know what else I learned? I had only witnessed the tip of the iceberg. Over the past month, at least twenty criminals have surrendered to the law. This is not normal, Doctor Watson. You must help me to find the truth of it."

The truth was that I was stunned. I had absolutely no clue as to why these men who, hitherto, would have done almost anything to avoid incarceration, would suddenly demand to be

156

locked away. Gregson could sense that I was floundering, so I attempted to apply some of Holmes's deductive logic.

"Well, let me see," I hummed, playing for time, desperate for any theory or thought to present itself. "It appears to me that, at the most basic level, there are but two possibilities," I began, uncertainly. "Either these men really have had a Damascene revelation, or something else, something nefarious, is occurring here."

I watched Gregson attempt to suppress a deep sigh. Holmes would never have been so polite.

"I am sorry. I have neither the knowledge nor the mental capacity for reasoning enjoyed by my colleague. I can, however, offer you one grain of comfort. From what I've heard of your tale, I can guarantee that Holmes will both take your concerns with the greatest seriousness and, also, come to a similar conclusion as I. Something distinctly untoward is afoot."

Gregson immediately perked up, invigorated by my promise of Holmes's involvement. I assured him that I would send word to Scotland Yard the minute that Holmes returned and, with that, the policeman thanked me, bade farewell, and left to pursue his day's activities with a far lighter step than that with which he had likely entered our rooms.

As it happened, Holmes swept back into our Baker Street apartment barely an hour after Gregson had departed. He cast his hat onto a coat-hook and threw his overcoat roughly in the same direction. He stopped, aimed, and flung his cane into the stand. It bounced off both sides of the rim and rattled its way inside. Holmes clapped with obvious delight.

"Watson, my dear friend!" He grinned widely. Clearly, he had solved his existing case to his complete satisfaction. "A brandy? It may seem early, but I have been out since four and

I deserve a drink." Holmes poured two large glasses and slumped down onto the couch.

"Is sounds as if you have had a very successful morning," I commented, unable to conceal a smile as I enjoyed this rare side of Holmes.

"The sins of men, Watson – they have no limits. There are no lengths to which a man will not go in order to achieve his goals." Holmes took a long gulp of finest Armagnac.

"Do you intend to share any details of your latest surreptitious assignment, or am I ever to be kept in the dark?" I enquired, taking out my pipe.

Holmes seemed to remember something. He jumped to his feet, strode back to his coat and rummaged through the pockets. He pulled out something indistinct and, before I could see clearly, flung it towards me. The shining, spinning object flew with considerable force. Unperturbed, I rose swiftly and cupped my hands, much as a wicketkeeper before a fast bowler. I caught the mysterious projectile easily and held it before me. It was a tiara, diamond-encrusted, and shaped from cleverly woven platinum, or white gold.

"Very beautiful, in its own way, I suppose, but not really my preference," I joked.

I fully understood, of course, that the jewellery was payment in kind for a service provided by my colleague, one so sensitive that there could be no trace left for anyone to exploit, not even a traditional method of payment. I placed the ornate bauble onto the mantelpiece and returned to my chair.

"You do have another case," I announced, neatly drawing a discrete line under Holmes's recent activities.

I proceeded to recount my earlier meeting with Inspector Gregson. To my considerable surprise, Holmes remained silent and, even after I had finished, did not speak for several minutes.

"Watson, there is devilry at work here," Holmes stated, darkly, finally breaking his silence. "What would make serious criminals voluntarily give themselves up to the authorities?"

"Fear?" I speculated. "I am assuming that we have discounted any thoughts that they might be acting out of any sense of altruism."

"Carrot or stick, incentive or fear," Holmes explained. "It must surely be one or the other. We must speak to Gregson. Come, we shall take a cab to Scotland Yard."

Just over half of an hour later, we pulled up outside the sturdy edifice that housed the capital's finest detectives. We swept along the long, featureless corridors and were soon outside Gregson's unspectacular office. I reached forwards to knock, but Holmes pushed the door open and swept inside, unannounced.

Gregson looked momentarily perturbed, but soon broke into a smile as he recognised my impatient colleague. Greetings were swiftly dealt with and, at Holmes's request, Gregson was soon, once again, recalling his unusual tale.

"Exactly what crimes did each of these men admit to having committed?" asked Holmes after a few minutes' reflection. "I shall require a list of every man and the crimes with which they claimed involvement, a list of their previous convictions, and a summary of their backgrounds, affiliations, and details of any other crimes with which they are suspected to have been involved."

Gregson nodded and scribbled down Holmes's request. He took the note to a colleague in an adjoining room and re-joined us just as Holmes was preparing to leave.

"Send the information to Watson back at Baker Street. I must now depart to make enquiries, the nature of which may require certain changes of accent, appearance, and attire."

Without further explanation, Holmes rushed from the inspector's office and on to whatever den of iniquity housed his best-placed contacts and informants. I sat facing Gregson for a moment, unsure of what to say.

"Have you had lunch, Inspector?" I asked, as it was now well past midday and the morning's excitement had given me quite an appetite.

I spent a pleasant hour with Gregson, taking a light lunch and comparing our experiences on the rugby fields of our youths. It came as no surprise to me that Gregson had once been a more-than-useful prop forward, and he had only stopped playing at a serious level once he had decided upon a career in the Metropolitan Police force.

I arrived back at our rooms just after three in the afternoon and decided to forgo my afternoon stroll. I had a feeling that my energy might be needed elsewhere later that day, so I settled down before the fire and treated myself to a cigar from Holmes's inky black-macassar humidor.

"Watson! Rise from your post-meridian snooze and gather your senses."

I felt a sharp poke in my ribs and opened my eyes to see Holmes's thin face looming over me. In sharp contrast, his eyes shone like quicksilver and he wore a wide, open smile.

"Apologies, old man, I must have drifted off," I muttered, pulling myself upright in my armchair.

"Perhaps you over-indulged during your lunch with Gregson," Holmes suggested, much to my surprise, lowering his cane. He still wore his hat and overcoat, having clearly just returned to our rooms.

"How on earth did you know that we – ?" I began.

"Your tie, Watson. Those stains are no match for anything Mrs. Hudson could conjure up at such short notice. As you rarely dine out alone, the obvious inference is that you took your midday meal with the inspector."

"Of course, how simple." I sighed, rising to my feet and removing the offending neckwear. "By the way, did you discover anything of interest on your travels?" I enquired.

"Perhaps, perhaps not," Holmes mumbled, inconclusively.

When I returned sporting a fresh tie, Holmes had divested himself of hat, coat, and cane and was standing at the dining table, staring intently at several sheets of paper which he had laid out before him.

"I arrived just as a messenger from Scotland Yard was delivering the information that I had requested," Holmes explained.

"I see," I said, now fully awake and alert. "Does anything strike you as being of interest?"

"All is of the greatest interest, Doctor. However, I have yet to discover an anomaly or identify a clear pattern which might aid us in our investigation. Please, feel free to cast your eye over the data. As a physician, you are experienced in dealing with large amounts of information."

I took a quick look at the sheets that Holmes appeared to have already examined.

"Actually," I remarked, rather cautiously, "there is one thing that stands out."

Holmes's head snapped up, "Out with it," he encouraged. "Now is not the time for timidity."

"These are all career criminals. Their records certainly attest to the fact. Their crimes are varied — robbery, violence, burglary, illegal gaming, fraud, extortion. They appear to cover almost the entire criminal spectrum. However, they do seem to share one thing: They have each confessed to but a *single* crime, and looking through their records, the crime to which

161

they admit guilt is, in every case, by far the least of what they've been accused over the years."

Holmes leant forward, so low that his nose was almost touching the papers. He remained in thought for a while, before responding.

"My friend, you have, once again, performed a service of the most vital importance. We now have a beginning. The case is opening up, and I believe that if we continue to apply pressure in the right areas, it may split open before us. Our immediate course of action is clear," Holmes barked as he picked up his coat and retrieved his hat and cane. "We must interview these self-incarcerated felons, for I very much doubt that the police made much effort to question them – certainly not once they had made their confessions."

By the time I had caught up with Holmes, he was climbing into a hansom. "Where exactly are we going," I eagerly inquired.

"It did not escape my attention that of those who have presented themselves, nearly all have done so at police stations within the City of London. Therefore, we must go to where the majority of our mysterious penitents will have been incarcerated: Newgate."

The thirty-minute drive eastwards passed quickly, the pale late afternoon sun dipping and shadows lengthening as we trotted along Oxford Street. Holmes pulled out the pages of names and crimes and read each one aloud, hoping we might discern any further, hidden patterns.

We had made little further progress when we pulled up outside the grim austere frontage of Newgate Prison – "*Architecture terrible*" indeed. I shuddered, eyeing the long, windowless frontage of the austere penitentiary. After some negotiation, some of which may well have been financial, Holmes had arranged for us to interview a selection of the prisoners appearing on our lists. We were led along several dark, dank corridors and into a plain, whitewashed chamber, lit by a sole, barred window, high up on the opposite wall. In the centre of the room sat a table, perhaps six-feet-by-three. There were but two chairs in the room and both were placed on our side of the table. Towards the right of the rear wall, an ironclad door would provide ingress for our interviewees.

The guard who had accompanied us grunted and gestured towards the chairs. He was tall, broad, and had a face that resembled a roast ham. I wondered if he had been a boxer in a previous occupation, such was the battering he appeared to have taken over the years. We took our seats, slightly uncomfortably.

"How many of them did you manage to arrange for us to see?" I whispered, as a loud clanking, followed by the sound of metal sliding against metal, announced the arrival of the first prisoner.

"Although the warden promised a half-dozen, I would be surprised if we get to see more than half of that number," Holmes replied.

Despite his misgivings, Holmes did not appear to be overly concerned. The heavy door swung open and our first subject entered the room. He blinked, even in the poor light of the interview space – heaven knows in what conditions these men were being kept. He was short and wiry, and a wispy beard and moustache partly covered his pale skin. His face and clothes were so filthy that it was almost impossible to correctly determine his age. He could have seen anything from thirty to fifty years.

To my great surprise, it was the captive that first spoke.

"Well, look who it is," he smirked. "Mister 'Olmes 'imself. Whatever brings you all the way down 'ere? There's none but us rats in 'ere."

"I believe that you know exactly why I am here," replied Holmes, with considerable force. "Watson, may I present Mr. John Mitchell: Housebreaker, and a man not averse to using extreme violence to achieve his aims. The real question is," Holmes leaned forwards and stared deeply into Mitchell's eyes. "Why are *you* here?"

Mitchell shrugged, "Maybe I just wanted atone for my, ah, mercifully few misdeeds," he grinned. "Or maybe I just see the bigger picture. I'll serve a short stretch here and wipe my slate clean."

"What of the others?" I interrupted, impatiently, "Dozens just like you have turned themselves in."

"Dozens, eh?" Mitchell seemed momentarily taken aback, but he recovered quickly. "Well, I guess it must be catching, like the French Plague," he sneered.

"Take him away," Holmes announced loudly, waving towards the guard who lurked in the darkness behind Mitchell. "He will be of no further help." The large, grey-bearded guard took the prisoner by the shoulder and guided him back into the stygian darkness from whence he had come.

"Well, that wasn't much use," I sighed. "Let's hope that the next one is more forthcoming."

Holmes turned to me with a look of exaggerated surprise. I reddened, instantly, as I knew full well what was to follow.

"On the contrary. We have learned several vital pieces of information, which I had rather hoped would be the case. It was, of course, exactly why I chose him."

The arrival of the second prisoner put paid to my immediate questions. A hulking brute this time, long of arm and leg, but clearly short of intelligence. His lower jaw must have protruded a full inch beyond his upper front teeth. It seemed to take the thug a moment to recognise my companion, and when he did, his reaction was in stark contrast to that of his predecessor.

"Hello there, Horace," began Holmes, carefully. "Do not be afraid. You see, I needed to speak to you, away from your brother."

The man nodded his huge head, and for the first time I noticed his eyes, wide open – the eyes of a frightened child.

"I am very sorry, Mr. Sherlock, but my bro' would be very angry if told you anything," announced Horace in a slow, monotonous drone.

"Of course," Holmes replied, with exaggerated sincerity. "There is no chance that you would ever give away the big secret, is there?"

Horace shook his head and folded his arms, as best his shackles would allow.

"I suppose it matters not," Holmes added, casually, "for you will soon be released, your job done, your freedom earned."

"Back home to mum," smiled Horace, unable to suppress a giggle. "Just like the advertisement says, when we all make it back out."

Once more, Holmes's attitude changed abruptly. He dismissed poor Horace without further comment, and we waited for our next subject to appear. Several minutes passed, during which we heard raised voices from behind the iron-bound door, but no further prisoners were brought forward.

"It seems I was rather optimistic," sighed Holmes. "I fear that our remaining witnesses may have just become, unexpectedly, unavailable."

After a further minute or so, from out of the shadows before us, skulked the large, grey-bearded guard. In his huge hands he nervously wrung his cap.

165

"I must apologise, gentlemen," he stammered, carefully, as if he was recalling a statement quickly learned by rote. "The other men that you requested for interview are now otherwise engaged by the authorities."

Holmes appeared to take this setback with unexpected ease and, taking up his papers, rose to leave. Almost as an afterthought, he paused, momentarily, to examine the room's walls and doorway as he departed.

"Ha!" he cried, as we left the oppressive edifice and once again breathed the air of freedom. "It is exactly as I thought. I have learned far more here than during my earlier failed efforts. I need but a few more pieces of data and we shall have them all, Watson."

"Is there any point to me asking you exactly what you mean?" I asked, resignedly. "I see nothing but strange, aberrant behaviour."

I waved down a cab and we settled inside, grateful for the tartan blankets stored within, the air having turned decidedly chilly. We trotted west, and I leaned forward, eager to hear more.

"Come on, Holmes. Share with me what you have determined. At the very least, you must explain how you could have learned anything from those two unfortunate characters."

I was poised to continue. However, Holmes raised a finger and the words stalled in my mouth, unspoken.

"Three people, Watson," Holmes corrected. "Not two. The words of the guard also hold great meaning."

"The guard?" I protested. "He made but a single statement, one which someone of both higher position and intelligence had clearly instructed him to memorise and repeat as best he could."

"My dear friend, it is not always about what you know, or even that which you *think* you know," smiled Holmes. "You must cast aside your thoughts, beliefs, and suspicions, momentarily, and simply *listen*. All of which has provided us with a multitude of data."

"Well, that is all very modern and enigmatic, but how does it help us to solve this mystery? Gregson had already convinced me that something strange was afoot, but that little episode back there has made me wonder if we might be looking at a deeper and more widespread conspiracy. Our interviews were deliberately cut short: Why? If I happened to be a gambling man –" I ignored Holmes's raised eyebrows at this point. " – I would wager that it was the news of your involvement having quickly reached those embroiled at the highest level that caused the curtailment of our interviews."

"And your money would be safe, Doctor. I had hoped that we might speak to one or two more of the 'self-incarcerated' before our involvement became apparent. However, we have been fortunate, in that what little has been recounted to us by these characters has contained enough information to move us on to the next level of this investigation."

"Information," I hissed through gritted teeth, "that you will, no doubt, now share with me, your associate and confidant."

"Very well," Holmes acquiesced. "I chose a selection of miscreants that I knew well, for various reasons. I knew that Mitchell was a braggard and would not be able to help himself from sharing with us vital information. He confirmed that there was reason behind the surrenders, that the confessions were for only their most minor crimes to ensure minimal sentencing, and hinted that the incentive was financial. His reaction of disappointment to your revelation that many dozens had turned themselves in showed that, at the lowest levels, at least, there was significant competition to be involved in this scheme.

"Poor Horace Rankin is a sweet, simple soul, horribly abused by his elder brother. However, he gave away possibly the most important clue of all. He also genuinely expects to be back home, and very shortly. This can mean only one of two things: The prisoners expect to be released soon or . . . ."

Holmes paused, struck a match and lit a slim, Turkish-and-Virginia blended cigarette, before continuing.

"The behaviour of the guard, allied with our premature dismissal, is yet more confirmation that this affair runs deep. Indeed, it has infiltrated the very hierarchy of the prison service itself."

We shortly turned into Baker Street and were back in our rooms just as the sun was dipping below the horizon, staining the sky a rather ominous blood red. Mrs. Hudson swiftly produced tea and sandwiches, which we gratefully consumed, surrounded by the papers which still covered the dining table. I flicked idly through some of the sheets.

"It is such a sad state of affairs, isn't it," I commented, as I noticed a pattern amongst the myriad entries.

Holmes, who was also examining the papers while picking at his food, looked up. "What is? What have you seen? Any detail, however small, might be crucial."

"These records are surprisingly comprehensive. Gregson has done a sterling job here. It appears that many of those who have turned themselves in are related or connected in some way. Some share a surname, but many also appear, repeatedly, in this column here: The known associates of various others. All of these connections rather bring up the old question: Are criminals created by nature or nurture? Whatever the truth may turn out to be, this conspiracy is certainly premeditated and coordinated."

"Excellent. You have, once again lit a beacon," declared Holmes. "It is, as I believed, a call-to-arms. These criminals have been brought together for a purpose – a reason that lies, tantalising, just out of reach.

"And wait," he continued. "You may have uncovered more than you thought. We must connect as many of these names as we can, rank their power and influence in the criminal community, and build a pyramid upwards. This is not the work of a minor figure. Only a major criminal could convince others to take such actions, and only one with deep social and familial connections could command such loyalty. Whomever sits atop our chart might well be the key to this entire affair."

The next three hours were spent in an effort to create, from the pages of disparate information laid before us, a chart of all the surrendered criminals that were known to us, in ascending order of their position in the underworld. At the bottom were the common criminals – a selection of pickpockets, opportunists, common thieves, and suchlike. Above these was, by far, the longest list – the careerists, those who had made a living from crime. The burglars, fraudsters, and receivers of stolen goods, for example.

At the very top, Holmes placed just six names. However, they were not the names that I had been expecting. Rather than being major crime figures, bosses, or leaders of any sort, they were, instead, a group of extremely successful, but largely unknown, experts in the practical fields of professional, high-value robbery, safecracking, and high-end burglary. They may not have been well-known, yet they sat in the rarefied air at the very peak of London's criminal mountain. Despite the short experience that I'd already gained working alongside Holmes, I recognised none of the names written high on the final page.

"If I were planning a major robbery," I suggested, "these would certainly seem to be the men best qualified for the task. However, the fact that they are now all behind bars, and that by their own volition, makes such a theory appear rather redundant."

"Watson, I must now leave you," announced Holmes, abruptly.

"You know something. Have you cracked the case?" I asked, expectantly.

"I may return late. Best we speak in the morning." Holmes swept up his hat and coat and was out of the door and halfway down the staircase before I could even formulate a reply.

Resigned to spending the remainder of the evening alone, I poured a large brandy, filled my briar, and settled down before the fireplace. I lay the pages filled with our lists of criminals and their activities beside me upon the small occasional table and picked up the first sheet. After just ten minutes, I had to admit defeat. I could divine nothing more from this database of delinquents. Determined not to waste any more time on a subject about which I knew so little, I spent the next hour pouring over the latest medical journals before retiring to bed.

Despite my concerns regarding our current case, I managed a good night's sleep and was up and dressed well before seven o'clock the following morning. Seeing no sign of Holmes, I decided that I would take a stroll in the park before breakfast, pausing at the base of the stairs on my way out to relay my plans to Mrs. Hudson. Without needing to specifically ask, I knew that a fine meal would await me upon my return.

My walk was particularly pleasant that fine morning, the low, milky sun slowly burning off a light mist, the ethereal fading back into the mundane. After an hour, I headed back to Baker Street, invigorated and confident that my friend would soon solve this most unusual of cases.

I wasn't surprised to find Holmes sitting at the dining table when I returned, although his physical appearance was most unexpected. A long, dark wig sat around his shoulders, apparently fallen from a head still wearing a form of hair net that I recognised from Holmes's theatrical makeup supplies. His face was unusually ruddy, again a result of the application of a pigment from his dramatic box. The smile that played upon his lips as he poked at a poached egg, however, was most recognisable.

"My word," I declared. "Whatever it is that you've been up to, I can clearly see from your expression that you have made a significant breakthrough."

"I have only just rid myself of my own foolishness regarding this matter," Holmes replied, pushing away his plate and pulling off his hair net. Casually casting the limp web of cotton aside, he gestured to the fine spread that lay on the table before him.

"Sit and take your fill. I must withdraw temporarily to remove the remnants of my disguise before friend Gregson graces us with his presence." Holmes ran his fingers across his face, smearing his makeup in a most comical fashion.

I laughed. "I would never have guessed in a million years that you could make a perfect circus clown."

I could still hear Holmes chuckling as I set about my breakfast, another triumph provided at short notice by our irreplaceable landlady. As I was mopping up the last of my egg yolk with a crust of bread, Holmes reappeared, now wrapped in his old fawn dressing gown, his face restored to its usual hue.

Holmes perched himself onto his armchair, legs pulled up, and lit a cigarette. I rose to join him by the fire just as the front doorbell rang. Our guest had arrived. I went down and opened the door to reveal Gregson, his right hand raised, ready to knock. His face was pale and drawn. He had surely spent another night without sleep.

"Please come in, Inspector," I smiled. "We have been expecting you."

Despite the early hour, I poured three brandies and offered Gregson a Sumatran cigar, which he gladly accepted. Once I had lit it and a companion for myself, I waited for Holmes to begin.

"I owe you an apology," began Holmes, hands spread in conciliatory gesture. "It has taken me far too long to grasp the substance of this case. Perhaps the most important thing that I've gleaned from this affair is the fact that I am still learning. Once explained, even the most convoluted and labyrinthine problem can become childishly simple. This is very much the case in this instance.

"My initial strategy was to approach criminals, similar to the ones who have surrendered to the authorities, to ascertain whether they had any knowledge of the reasons behind this mass capitulation. This was a mistake, and a predictable one, as how could those not involved in the scheme have any knowledge of it? I returned empty-handed and a little chastened.

"It was only after the interviews at Newgate that I began to suspect the true reasons behind these unprecedented events. Do you remember what Horace said, Watson?"

"Umm," I stumbled, "not word for word, but something about going home to his mother, wasn't it?"

"'Back home to mum, just like the advertisement says, when we all make it back out'," Holmes quoted precisely from memory. "I almost missed it but there it is, clear as day."

"What 'advertisement' was this?" asked Gregson, instantly spotting something that had completely evaded me. "An advertisement for what?"

"The key to this whole disturbing affair," declared Holmes. "A few simple words spoken without thought. Poor Horace had no idea, but in less than a sentence, he had given away the whole sordid plot."

The inspector and I sat on the very edges of our chairs. Our cigars, long since forgotten, now each sported an ash of well over an inch in length.

Holmes stuck out his right hand and picked up a slip of paper that had lain quite ignored on the small table beside him. He held this before us. It was rather tatty, frayed at the edges, stained, and had been folded and opened so many times that the creases that crossed the paper were almost worn through. It had clearly passed through many hands. The writing was crude and faded, but still clear enough for us both to understand.

Gregson took it upon himself to read the missive aloud. "'*Due to unforeseen circumstances, I am now alone and will need assistance. I don't have not much to pay. Can you help an old fella out?*'"

"A simple enough call for help, hidden in plain sight among many, but once the identity of the author is known, it takes on a completely different meaning," explained Holmes. "That is the genius of it. Without this knowledge, it appears as just another innocent notice, one of thousands posted every day around the city."

"Where did you find this missive?" I asked, still blindly lost in the fog of ignorance. "How did you identify its author, and what on earth do you see in its contents?"

"A little basic logic and an awful lot of hard work and patience," he replied, stubbing out the short remains of his cigarette. "It occurred to me that the only way to discover the truth behind this mystery was to locate and interrogate members of the criminal underworld with some connection to those who had surrendered to the authorities. The first part was fairly simple – identifying the associates of these well-known criminals was no great task. Gaining this information without them becoming aware of my intentions proved rather more of a challenge,"

Holmes was now clearly enjoying himself. He plucked a churchwarden from the coal scuttle and filled it from his Persian slipper. I passed him a cedar cigar match and he was soon wreathed in surprising pleasant curls of smoke.

"I have, over the past few years, created and nurtured a selection of identities, which I employ when I have the need to mix with various groups and levels of society that I would otherwise be unable to infiltrate. Last night, I assumed the disguise of the lowliest of my army of imposters and set about locating as many of those connected to the incarcerated men as I could.

"I knew that I had to see this so-called 'advertisement' for myself, so I set out for taverns close to the locations most associated with the six criminals at the top of our list. At each hostelry, I insinuated that I had knowledge of a large, profitable scheme that was afoot and begged for a part in it, or any knowledge of the affair. I hoped that my pathetic aspect and sorry circumstances might gain me sympathy and lead one of my targets to reveal something, but time after time I was rebuffed or, as was more often the case, warned, most seriously, not to investigate any further.

"I had almost given up, the hour having long past from late to early when, without warning, in a most sorry establishment, this shoddy piece of paper was thrust into my hand. The provider had been an unimportant thug, currently laid low with a badly injured leg. He simply scowled. 'Well, at least you might be able to make something for yourself out of this.' He offered no further comment and returned to his ale, his back now firmly turned to me."

"Wait a moment, Mr. Holmes," Gregson interjected, glancing again at the grubby note. "There is no mention here of what you claim Horace to have imparted. Certainly nothing about his mother."

"Which confirmed to me what I already believed to be the case," Holmes replied without skipping a beat. "That Horace's brother had told him a pack of lies to ensure his servile cooperation. I now had the note, but without knowing the identity of the author, I couldn't determine its true meaning. I discovered the answer in the papers that still lie upon our dining table.

"Watson, you had the perspicacity to realise that the criminals' associates might be the key to unravelling this mystery. I examined all of those connected to these six men and determined that they had, recently at least, worked for only four known groups or associations. Three are well-known criminal gangs, while the other was a family business four generations of nefarious activities."

Gregson's face lit up. He had clearly seen more than had I.

"It was the family, Holmes!" he exclaimed. "The tone of the note makes that obvious."

"The note," Holmes continued, nodding in agreement and sucking deeply upon his pipe, "was penned by a well-known, successful, but widely believed to have retired, local criminal. His father, however, has very recently been handed a twenty-year prison sentence for a violent armed robbery. Now, read the note again."

Gregson again scanned the message, his brow furrowed in concentration. A few seconds passed when, suddenly, his expression changed. His eyes widened as his mouth fell open, a huge grin spread across his face.

"We have them!" he declared. "By Jove, Mr. Holmes! We have them!"

"Whom do we have?" I ventured, carefully, rather embarrassed to be the last to remain in the dark.

"Doctor Watson, my dear friend," Holmes explained, kindly. "The message is hidden in plain sight. Take the message literally, word for word."

"'*Due to unforeseen circumstances*,'" I read aloud, slowly and with great care. "'*I am now alone and will need assistance. I don't have not much to pay. Can you help an old fella out?*'"

Realisation hit me, a flash as bright as a burst of morning sun, suddenly rising above a mountainous horizon. I felt simultaneously elated but ashamed that I had not seen through such an obvious ruse.

"'*Due to unforeseen circumstances, I am now alone and will need assistance*,'" I repeated. "The unforeseen circumstance being his father's *incarceration*. '*I don't have not much to pay*' – a simple double negative, offering a good return for any willing to help him. '*Can you help an old fella out?*' They mean to break the father out of gaol, but from the *inside*. That is why they have attracted such a group of experts."

"A mass breakout," Gregson whispered, hoarsely, shaking his head in amazement. "All designed to ensure that one single man gains his freedom. However," The inspector quickly recovered his nerve, "we will have them all now."

Holmes handed our list of conspirators to Gregson who tucked it, most gratefully, into his jacket pocket.

"With this list of accomplices, you would have a pretty decent chance of breaking out of any gaol in the land. However, I don't think that they left anything to chance. From what you recounted of your prison visit, there has clearly been collusion from within the gaol itself. The only question is, how high does it go?"

Holmes nodded, silently. He held his hands together, joined at the fingertips. His long fingers formed a pointed arch – or, perhaps, more accurately, a bony ivory ribcage as of a long dead and emaciated carcass.

"I must now take my leave gentlemen," said Gregson, "for I have serious work to perform this day." He moved swiftly to depart. However, at the last moment, he stopped and turned back to us and smiled. "Thank you, Mr. Holmes. I know that mention of your name may still elicit a mixed response back at the Yard, but I will always be grateful for the help that you have accorded us."

Once Gregson had left, we returned to our chairs before the fire. I broke up some brown Virginia flake and filled my bowl. Holmes lit and puffed upon a Turkish cigarette.

"What a remarkable scheme," I commented. "To offer a huge reward to whomever could break the fellow's father out of prison. Why, if the original crime hadn't been so egregious, it would almost be worthy of respect."

"Remarkable, indeed," Holmes agreed. "Perhaps even unique, but also far too successful for its own good. The son went about his task with more enthusiasm than discretion. Far too many criminals learned of the scheme and turned themselves in," he explained. "Even though I have no doubt that the family in question could afford to pay off all of those who surrendered, their sheer number was enough to guarantee that the authorities would eventually be alerted, and thus it proved."

"So, what will happen to all of those involved?"

"Those who have surrendered will serve their sentences, short as they are. Gregson will put the fear of God into all involved, but he can do little more. I have little hope that the conspirators within the prison will be unmasked.

"And what of the son who orchestrated the entire scheme?" I asked. "I am struggling to accept that any form of justice will ever be served in this case."

"Nature versus nurture," Holmes replied, rather obliquely, I thought. "Prevention is better than the cure. These are the two philosophical questions at work here."

"Darwin and Erasmus," I stated redundantly. "I understand the former. However, in this context, I fail to see how we can come to any conclusions. These characters all knew of each other, many were close associates, and some were even related. The latter, I will need you to explain in far greater detail."

"Take the Brothers Rankin." Holmes waved his right hand, creating a pleasing spiral of smoke. "They could well be used to illustrate either theory. Poor Horace is certainly not a criminal by nature. It was only his brother's evil influence that lead him down the path of miscreance. Similarly, one might argue that neither brother would have turned to crime if they hadn't been abandoned at such a young age and had to fight on the streets for their very survival. It could even be argued that Rankin senior, despite his terrible history, has actually succeeded in life, given the circumstances in which he found himself."

"Perhaps, more pertinently," I added, now that I had finally understood the details and scope of the scheme, "it explains why the son was not directly involved. It sounds as if he was certainly qualified enough to have been one of those working from the inside. However, he seems to have made a new life for himself, away from the world of his father, one that he would not abandon at any cost – even the continued incarceration of his own father."

Holmes nodded. "He chose to limit his involvement to merely financing the scheme. His time away from the criminal world also explains his need to send out the poorly coded note. He had lost touch with many of his previous associates and had no wish to return to his previous haunts in order to reconnect."

Holmes's predictions were, once again, proven to be uncannily accurate. Those voluntarily incarcerated duly served their sentences, but no one else involved in this affair was ever held to account. Gregson could find no compelling evidence of conspiracy at Newgate, and the whole affair was quietly forgotten.

I have one footnote to add: Those of an observant bent might have noticed an unusual omission within this particular account. I have named neither the man whose escape was deemed so essential, nor his son, who went to such extraordinary lengths in almost achieving this aim. To do so would be a gross betrayal of trust, for the son had forever turned his back on the criminal world and indeed went on to perform several great heroic deeds for Queen and Country. One of these included a small supporting role for a certain Mr. Sherlock Holmes.

The Adventure of the
Villainous Victim
by Chris Chan

I have lost count of all of the occasions where my friend solved a baffling mystery where the official police failed, only to allow the legal authorities to accept all of the credit for the resolution of the case. In contrast, I believe that there is only one instance of a case where my friend desired public recognition for catching a killer, but he was denied it due to a fluke of chance.

In June of 1881, shortly after our initial meeting, Holmes and I took a day trip to Brighton to make some purchases at a new tobacconist's shop that had rapidly gained a reputation for having a special house blend of fire-cured pipe tobacco that had smokers all over London raving about its quality. After making some purchases that severely strained both of our monthly budgets, we walked back towards the Preston Park Station to take a late lunch at a nearby café before catching the three o'clock train back to London.

Our plans for lunch were interrupted when we heard a man's screams coming from the station. We sprinted in the direction of the shrieks, and soon discovered that they were coming from a ticket collector. I am the first to admit that I lack my friend's observational skills, but it did not take a pair of eagle eyes to determine what was causing the poor man's distress. Sitting on the ground five feet away from the ticket collector was another man, whose entire body was covered in blood.

While Holmes delivered a firm yet gentle slap across the hysterical ticket collector's face in order to silence his earpicrcing cries, I examined the blood-covered man. After a minute's study, it became apparent that the blood was not his own. It was a disturbing realization. I shook his shoulder until he finally turned his head and met my eyes. "Look here, my good fellow, do you know what's happened to you?"

He stared at me with glassy eyes until finally he responded to my question. "I . . . don't remember. Not everything, anyway. After they attacked me . . . ."

His voice trailed off and I snapped my fingers in front of his face to keep his attention. "Listen, sir, please try to stay with me. I'm a medical doctor and I need to find out what's happened to you. You say you were attacked. Who did this to you? What did they do?"

"I don't know. After they struck me, everything's a blank."

My friend's voice made me jump. I hadn't expected him to join in on the questioning. "Perhaps you can start by telling us your name. If, of course, you can recall it."

I couldn't be sure because of all the blood, but I thought I observed a small flash of indignation in the bloodstained man's face. "I most certainly do know my own name."

"And that name is?"

"My name is Percy Lefroy. Two men attacked me as the train started travelling through the Merstham tunnels."

I remained silent, knowing that Holmes was far more skilled in asking questions about crimes than I was.

"Very well, Mr. Lefroy. Did you know your assailants?"

"No, they were strangers to me."

"Can you describe them?"

"Well . . . no, not really. They moved so quickly, I couldn't get a proper look at them. I remember that they were unusually tall and strong, though."

"You have no recollection of their hair or eye color? Their clothing? Did they have facial hair?"

"I . . . couldn't tell you. I just can't remember. They just came up to me, beat me, robbed me . . . and the next thing I know I'm here, and I don't have a clue what's happened to me."

A constable's arrival interrupted the conversation, and the official representative of the law quickly took charge of the bloodstained man, hurrying him off to the police station to lodge a complaint before receiving a full medical examination.

I could tell from the glint in my friend's eye that he had no intention of taking the train back to London. He was far too intrigued by the grisly discovery and, once he was on the scent of a case, there was no stopping him.

"That poor fellow," I murmured.

"Poor? I wonder . . . ."

"Well, surely he's the victim of a terrible crime."

"Nonsense! There's no 'surely' about it, Watson. His story is deficient in so many ways, I'm surprised that he didn't blush with embarrassment at his own perfidy. Although, due to all of the blood covering him, it's quite possible that his face did turn crimson without our realizing it."

"Deficient? Whatever do you mean?"

"Surely, my dear fellow, you realized right away that the blood covering that man was not his own."

"Well, yes. That was clear after a brief examination."

"And I realized that after only a second's glance. After all, a man who had lost that much blood would be at death's door and would probably be unable to move. No, that wasn't his own blood. Now it's possible that he had somehow wandered into an abattoir, but I am never one to embrace a comparatively innocent option when a far more sinister one will suffice. Judging by the spatter on the man we just met, it's entirely probable that the blood came from a particularly violent fight with another human being, and as noted earlier, the loss of that much blood means that the other party involved in the fight is more likely to be dead than alive. Now, you noticed no serious wounds on that blood-covered man. I submit that when a man is attacked by another man with a weapon that can draw a large amount of blood, the innocent victim is highly likely to be seriously injured, even if that person does manage to turn the tables in the end. But this man sustained no injury, a condition more probable in an assailant than a victim."

"I agree with you that it's more probable, but not necessarily. Suppose he was attacked by a drunkard or a madman. The assailant could have swung a knife or some other weapon about wildly, but his impaired condition could have made it fairly easy for his would-be victim to have turned the tables."

"Possibly, possibly. But did you observe the watch-chain on the bloodstained man?"

I allowed myself to smile a bit. My observational skills had improved quite a bit over the last few months, and I'd noticed that there was no watch or chain in the bloodstained man's jacket or vest pockets when I examined him. I said as much, and my fleeting sense of triumph was crushed by my friend's superior grin.

"The bloodstained man's watch-chain wasn't in his jacket or vest, Watson. It was sticking out of his boot."

"Was it?"

"Yes, a little under an inch of it was visible coming out of the top of his right boot. Now, that is suggestive, is it not?"

"Well, I suppose it's odd, but I don't see how it could be considered suggestive."

"My dear fellow, why would a man shove his watch-chain into his boot? If he wished to consult his pocket watch, he would leave it in his jacket or vest. If it were damaged or if he'd lost his watch, he might conceivably keep the chain it in his overcoat pocket. Under what circumstances might he have placed his watch-chain in his boots?"

"Perhaps if he were trying to protect it from being stolen? If he feared a pickpocket or an armed robber, he might have hidden the watch-chain there in the hopes that no one would look there."

"That is certainly within the realm of possibility, I agree with you. But you're missing a critical point. If an innocent man were taking care to protect his watch-chain, he would make quite certain it was completely hidden inside his boot. And if a man was attacked by a drunken madman, like you suggested, then he would have no time to secrete his watch-chain into a hiding place. A sudden attack would provide him with no opportunity to do so, and as we just discussed a few moments ago, an unexpected attack is by far the most likely way an innocent man might have escaped an assault unscathed. Therefore, the postulation that the watch-chain was hidden in the boot as a precaution will simply not hold water."

"Then why would the watch-chain be in his boot? Are you saying that he tucked away his own watch-chain to bolster his claim that he'd been robbed?"

"I very much suspect that the watch-chain in question doesn't actually belong to him, but to his victim. An intelligent criminal would have accepted the loss and disposed of the watch-chain, and if the chain truly belonged to him, he would have sold or pawned it if he were in dire need of money. It's more likely that he stole the watch-chain, and then hid it in his boot so that he would not have committed his crime for nothing. Being in a hurry to hide his ill-gotten gains, he neglected to conceal the chain completely."

"Then this man isn't an innocent victim of a crime, but a perpetrator."

"That is a reasonable idea at present. I shall need to investigate further in order to verify my theories."

"Will you tell the police to arrest him?"

"No point in that, I regret to say. We have no solid evidence that will justify an arrest. I need to collect some more clues before I can make a proper charge. If I were to go about accusing men of committing murders with no corpses, even if I were entirely correct, it's likely that I would wind up in court facing a lawsuit for slander – not my preferred use of time and funds, I can assure you. No, our investigation must commence, and quickly, before our gory friend vanishes. After he makes his statement to the police and cleans himself up, there's nothing to keep him here."

"Then what is our next step?"

"If you'll follow me, Watson, I want to take a look at the train currently waiting at the station. I daresay we shall find some useful information there."

And with that, Holmes led the way to the train and climbed aboard. He worked his way down the train car, glancing into each compartment of the carriage, until he finally scrutinized one door handle more closely.

"A-ha! Here we are, Watson! This is the one we want."

"How can you tell?"

"The smears of blood on the handle, of course. The dark color of the door handle makes them difficult for the untrained eye to see – the casual observer may mistake them for rust. I, however, have made a special study of how blood responds to various surfaces. I've started a very promising monograph that I really must finish some day on how bloodstains appear on various kinds of wood and metals. These little marks that could easily pass for rust? They have a far more sinister meaning, I assure you."

With that, Holmes withdrew a handkerchief from his pocket and gingerly opened the door. He took a very swift look around, and turned back to me.

"This is the scene of the crime, no doubt about that."

"Are you sure?"

"My dear Watson, the copious amounts of blood on most of the surfaces, the damage to the room indicating a struggle, the abandoned, bloodstained personal items, and the three bullet holes in the wall all lead to the unescapable conclusion that a violent crime has been committed here. It is beyond the bounds of probability to suppose that two particularly sanguineous attacks have taken place in the same train car within the past hour. The dampness of the larger patches of blood and the lingering scent of gunpowder prove the recentness of the violence that occurred here."

"Shall we speak to the police and have the man arrested now?"

"Of course not. We need to find the real victim of this case. But we will go straight to the authorities and tell them of our discovery."

We could have made it to the police station in less than five minutes, but we had the unfortunate poor luck to be confronted by a pair of train conductors who had wandered into the carriage, spotted the two of us amongst all of the carnage, and drew the erroneous conclusion that we were responsible for the mess. We tried to explain the situation to them, but the dim-witted pair were holding fast to their first impression, and they blew their whistles and summoned the police. Seeing as how they were disposed to make trouble if we attempted to flee, Holmes explained to me that we might as well stand and wait, and we ought to be able to explain away the situation in a matter of minutes.

Holmes's prediction proved overly optimistic, and it took nearly an hour to convince the local constabulary that we had only been investigating a crime. It was only Holmes's repeated pointing out of the facts that neither of us had any wounds upon us that could have caused the bloodshed, that neither of us were carrying a firearm, and that the state of the blood's coagulation indicated that whatever had happened there had taken place some time earlier, that the police reluctantly but wholeheartedly conceded that we had nothing to do with the carnage. Furthermore, the realization that this was the scene of the crime that had led to that mysterious man getting covered in blood had a galvanizing effect on the Chief Constable in charge of the case.

"Well, I thank you for bringing the possible murder scene to our attention, Mr. Holmes," the Chief Constable told us with a moderate amount of grace. "But we would've found it fairly quickly on our own. I'm sure you know that. And thank you for those very insightful theories about the case as well."

"Will you be holding that man?" I asked.

"I don't think that we can, sir. We've interviewed him, and I must say I've had my suspicions of him from the start. We policemen aren't fools, you know. You weren't here when Mr. Lefroy made his statement, but I noticed a fair number of holes in his story, though I did suppose that we might be able to chalk them up to mental distress over the incident. It could affect anybody's memory, don't you know."

"Where is Mr. Lefroy now?" Holmes inquired.

"I suppose he's at the hospital. They're giving him a full examination, and we'll see what he has to say for himself after a bit of rest and time to collect his thoughts."

"May we speak to him?"

187

"You'd have to check with his doctors. If the man's in a state of shock like one of the doctors suspected, they might not allow anybody to question him."

Holmes craned his neck and examined a small cardboard box on the Chief Constable's desk. "Are these Mr. Lefroy's possessions?" he asked, pointing at the label.

"They are. Care to examine them?"

"I would." Holmes picked up a pair of golden coins and held them up, one in each hand.

"Now, why would a man be desperate enough to rob someone else when he had a couple of sovereigns in his pocket?" the Chief Constable mused.

"Oh, these aren't sovereigns," Holmes replied, tossing them on the desk, where they made a dull clunking noise. He withdrew a pocket knife from his coat and scratched the face of both coins, leaving a dark scrape on them. "Gilded lead. These sovereigns are counterfeit."

There was silence for several moments, and I broke it. "At the very least, are you going to arrest him for possessing counterfeit coins?"

The Chief Constable did not respond, and eventually Holmes responded, "It would be very difficult to make a passable case out of that, Watson. After all, we have no proof that Mr. Lefroy actually knew that these sovereigns were not genuine coin of the realm. All he has to do is claim that he was unknowingly given these coins by a bank or business and that is enough to shed a reasonable doubt upon his guilt. In any case, why arrest him for a trifling crime when a much greater crime, possibly mere assault but more likely murder, has been committed?"

"Are you proposing a course of action, Mr. Holmes?" The Chief Constable seemed oddly willing to listen to a non-policeman's ideas for continuing the investigation. "I just got a message from one of my men telling me that the hospital's given him a clean bill of health and that he's on his way to board the next train to London."

"Surely that shows a guilty conscience," Holmes mused. "The man wants to flee as soon as possible. He's not bothering to pick up the so-called sovereigns. That's highly indicative that he knows they're counterfeit, and doesn't want to return to the police station to retrieve them. When does that train leave?"

"In just under nine minutes. Perhaps a bit less – my watch runs slow."

Holmes turned to me. "Watson! Hurry to the train station. Purchase a ticket to London, find Lefroy, and ride back with him. Don't let him out of your sight. And be on your guard. I believe that he's already seriously harmed one man today, I certainly do not want you to be the second. Meanwhile, Chief Constable, will you kindly allow me to assist your men with a search of the line?"

I followed my orders to the letter and I managed to board the train moments before it pulled away from the station. The train wasn't particularly crowded, so it was an easy matter to come across Lefroy. He was wearing a clean suit, but it was one of the old, worn, third-hand pieces that hospitals often keep on hand for the indigent. It didn't fit him well, and the legs of his trousers were considerably longer than necessary, so that the tops of his boots were completely covered and it was impossible for me to tell if he still had the watch-chain hidden inside one.

I maneuvered myself into a seat one row behind and across the aisle from Lefroy, who was slouched down and staring at his feet. My mind raced as I attempted to figure out what the best course of action would be. Did I introduce myself to him? Should I try to strike up a conversation? Twice, my mouth opened in order to speak to him, but a moment's thought led me to clamp my lips closed again, figuring that perhaps it was best to keep my presence a secret. After all, what if he remembered me from the train station? No, it was surely a more prudent course of action to try to follow him unobserved.

The train ride was uneventful, and one station before we reached London, a grubby-faced young boy poked me in the elbow. "This is for you, Doctor." He pushed a telegram into my hand. "Mr. Holmes said you'd have half-a-crown for me."

I thought it presumptuous of Holmes to dole out my half-crowns without my permission, but I figured that he and I could settle accounts when we met again. As I dropped the coin into the boy's hand, I wondered how he'd gotten aboard the train, but he turned around and vanished before I could ask him the question.

Opening the telegram, I read the message:

Watson –

Body found. Don't let Lefroy out of your sight. When you do lose track of him, wire me immediately.

– Holmes

My first reaction upon reading this telegram was indignation. Holmes had developed a frustrating habit of assuming the worst about my abilities, and the fact that he was often more correct than I'd like him to be was a continual source of irritation on my part. Still, though I had no real experience shadowing other people in the street without being detected, I noted that the sun had recently set, and a light London fog was drifting into the area. I reasoned that these new developments would help keep me hidden from my quarry, though I immediately realized that a tandem consequence of the darkness and fog was the fact that I would have increased difficulty keeping Lefroy in my sights.

I managed to maintain an average of ten paces behind Lefroy over the next three blocks, but a throng of churchgoers exiting a small chapel blocked my line of sight, and by the time I made my way through the group of worshippers, I found that Lefroy was nowhere to be found. I hurried ahead in the hopes of catching up with him, but I felt my heart leap up so high it nearly hit my chin when a hand reached out of the alley and gripped my shoulder firmly.

"Who the hell are you and why are you following me?"

I found myself quite unable to speak, and as I turned around, I realized that the man holding on to my shoulder was Lefroy himself. My muteness proved no serious problem, as he recognized me immediately.

"Here now — didn't I see you at the station in Brighton?"

Mercifully, I regained control of my vocal chords. "Yes. I'm a doctor, you see. My name is Watson. The hospital was very concerned about you and wanted someone to keep an eye on you. Since I was on my way back home to London, anyway, I volunteered to follow you and make sure that you got home safely. I didn't introduce myself because I didn't want to disturb your quiet time to yourself, you see. After a terrible shock like the one that you endured this afternoon, it seems only right that you should be given as much space as possible in order to comprehend everything."

I felt the overpowering desire to keep talking, but I realized that babbling would only serve to raise Lefroy's suspicions, and I forced myself to be silent.

Would he believe what I said? If he was the violent fiend that Holmes suspected him of being, might he attack me? I met

Lefroy's gaze directly and tried to make my eyes unsuspicious and unthreatening, hoping that he would view me as a well-meaning friend.

Lefroy's eyes remained focused on mine for what seemed like hours. His expression was hard and accusatory, but unexpectedly and instantaneously, it transformed, becoming relieved and amiable.

"Oh, I say. How very decent of you."

"Not at all, my dear fellow."

"I do appreciate your going to such lengths to look out for my well-being. But I don't want you to go to any trouble. I was just on my way to my relative's boarding-house where I've been staying." He fingered the shabby, ill-fitting suit he was wearing. "I need to change my clothes."

"I don't mind joining you if you don't mind my presence," I replied, trying to sound nonchalant. "It'd give me a clear conscience to make sure that you got home safely."

"All right, then, thank you! But you're in for a bit of a walk, I'm afraid. The boarding house is in the Wallington district."

That was indeed a bit of a trek for me, but I decided that despite my many purchases earlier that day, I could afford a small luxury. "I must insist that you let me pay for a cab."

He demurred, then agreed with minimal coaxing on my part. Soon afterwards, we arrived at the boarding house. He wished me good night and made his way into the building.

I abruptly realized that I was in a tricky situation. I didn't know if the boarding house had a back exit, and there was no convenient place for me to hide and observe unseen. There was no way that I could make sure that Lefroy was resting in his room. I was fretting over the best course of action when another young street urchin jumped into the carriage with me.

"Who are you, young fellow?"

"My name's Cookney, Doctor. I just heard from Mr. Holmes, and I'm to give you this telegram."

I opened it, and read:

Watson —

Victim identified. Isaac Gold, former corn merchant. Both gunshot and knife wounds. Have you lost Lefroy yet? If so, return to 221b and wait for me.

— Holmes

Once again, my initial response was indignation, but the abrupt realization that I did not, in fact, know for certain that Lefroy was securely in his room tempered my umbrage. After I hastily tossed the carriage driver his fee, I hurried into the boarding house, planning on making up some story about wishing to rent a room there, thereby giving me access to the building.

Before I could reach the door, I felt a faint tug at the back of my coat. Turning around, I saw Cookney.

"It's too late, Doctor. Didn't you hear the whistle?"

"What whistle?" I had been so lost in my thoughts, a cannon could've gone off without my noticing.

"A couple of my pals gave the signal. Mr. Holmes gave us all some special whistles a while back. If you're young – around our age – or if you have unusually sensitive ears like Mr. Holmes, you can hear them. Most adults can't. The whistles are very high-pitched. Anyway, Lefroy went out the window about two minutes after he entered the boarding house."

"We need to catch him!"

"Don't you worry, Doctor. My pals are right on his heels. About an hour ago, I got a message from Mr. Holmes to pick up this special preparation of his from his home."

"What special preparation?"

"Couldn't tell you for sure what was in it, but it smells like a mixture of anise and vanilla extract. Rather nice, really. Anyway, Mr. Holmes told us the address, and I hurried here, snuck in through the coal chute, found Lefroy's room, and sprayed all the clothes and boots in his closet with the preparation. Mr. Holmes figured Lefroy would change his clothes and make his escape. But my pals are tracking him. Bobby'll catch him."

"You seem to have a lot of faith in that boy Bobby."

"Bobby's not a boy, he's a spaniel. Best nose in London. Wherever Lefroy goes, Bobby will follow the scent."

I stood silently for a moment, reflecting on both Holmes's ingenuity and his absolute confidence in a dog and a bunch of street urchins. "So what am I to do?"

"Just what the telegram said. Go back to 221b and wait. One of my pals is wiring Mr. Holmes."

"My carriage is probably long gone by now."

"No, I told the driver to wait. May I ride back with you?"

And so, a little over an hour later, I found myself back at 221b, eating one of Mrs. Hudson's hot dinners and wondering just where Lefroy was at that moment.

I was two bites away from finishing my meal when Holmes walked in the door.

"Ah, Watson! Enjoying your meal, I hope? I've asked Mrs. Hudson to send up mine as well. You won't mind if I eat while I tell you the results of the last few hours, do you?"

"Not at all."

Mrs. Hudson entered and set down a large plate of stew with rolls in front of Holmes, who smiled and began enjoying it immediately.

I allowed Holmes some time to nourish himself, but after a few minutes my curiosity got the better of me and I practically begged him to provide me with some news on the case.

"Ah, yes. I must say, Watson, this case was a great disappointment to me. There was no artistry, no cleverness, no imagination. None of the hallmarks of the great criminal, or even an inspired miscreant. Simply a bare, bland case of brutality and greed, resulting in a wasted life. I tell you, this Lefroy, if that is his true name, which I very much doubt, has done nothing to distinguish himself as a criminal. Nothing more than a modern highwayman who sacrificed another human being with every right to live for a pittance."

"There was a murder, then?"

"Yes, and it required no real effort of my intellectual powers to resolve the case. It was obvious from the very beginning that a violent crime occurred in that train compartment, and that no man could survive such a substantial loss of blood. That left the question of what happened to the body, and I suspected that the killer had simply pushed it out the window, possibly in a place where it might not be spotted for quite some time. A tunnel might be a logical place for disposing of the body, where it could be jettisoned from the train in darkness and lie undiscovered for hours, even days.

"After analyzing the state of the coagulation of the blood in the carriage, I had a fair idea of how much earlier the crime had occurred. I therefore subtracted the amount of time since the train arrived in the station, and after calculating the average speed of the train, determined that there was only one tunnel in the estimated range, and asked the police to check it.

"There, they found a body that was quickly identified as one Isaac Gold, a gentleman of mature years who was now enjoying a comfortable retirement. He was an aged, rather frail man whose clothing illustrated his prosperous condition was a natural target for a marauder. The body suffered numerous bullet and knife wounds. His watch and chain had been ripped from his waistcoat, and all of his money was removed from his wallet and pockets. Poor fellow."

"And you think that Lefroy is the killer?"

"I'm quite sure of it, Watson. The motive was robbery, a crime of opportunity. It was just the late Mr. Gold's bad luck to have been the selected victim. It might have been any one of a hundred other people. Lefroy – or whatever his real name is – will not escape the grasp of justice for long. He was foolish enough to provide his card to the police, giving them – and me – his address, thus allowing the boys to get there first. I have utter confidence that between my ragtag collection of street urchins, the keen nose of Bobby, and the efforts of the police, Lefroy will be caught within a very short time, and will doubtless pay the ultimate price for his crimes."

Holmes's predictions proved completely accurate. Lefroy was swiftly arrested and charged with the crime. Holmes and I were among the prosecution witnesses at the trial, where it was revealed that Lefroy's true name was Mapleton, and that he'd attempted to rob the unfortunate Mr. Gold, but Gold's refusal to be cowed into compliance led to Lefroy – or rather Mapleton – to turn to lethal violence.

After the announcement of the guilty verdict, Holmes and I discussed the case back at our lodgings.

"A sad crime, but not without its points of interest," Holmes remarked.

"One point still bothers me, Holmes. Why was Lefroy – or rather, Mapleton – sitting down at the station when the ticket collector found him?"

"Most likely, he realized that he was covered in blood and knew that he couldn't get away without attracting attention, so he decided to collapse and act as if he'd been injured in order to deflect suspicion."

"That makes sense," I replied. "You know, I can't say that I came across very well in this case. I let him escape out from under my nose."

"You're new to the field of catching criminals, my dear fellow. Give yourself a bit more time and experience. And indeed, if you wish to write up this case, you can always utilize a touch of artistic license to make your role a bit more heroic."

"Thank you for your generosity of spirit, Holmes, but I think that if I do choose to record this case for posterity, I shall adhere strictly to the truth. Accuracy is very important to me."

Holmes laughed. "If only the newspapers were as scrupulous as you, Watson."

"What do you mean?"

Holmes withdrew the evening edition of a newspaper from his pocket and dropped it on the table. "Read the coverage of our case, Watson."

I did so. When I reached the last paragraph, I read aloud, "*'The police are particularly indebted to the assistance of an independent detective, Mr. George Holmes'* . . . George Holmes! Wherever did they come up with that name? Who in their right minds could ever mistake the name '*George*' for '*Sherlock*'?"

My friend smiled. "I have no idea, but I shall take this as a lesson. Never seek out fame in the popular press. Any attempt to catch the public eye is bound to have unintended consequences, especially when reporters have such difficulty keeping stories straight. No, I think that in the future, wherever possible, I shall refrain from accepting any public acknowledgement of my role in solving crimes. Unless, of course, you decide to record my exploits, Watson. You are the one person who I trust to get all of the details correct . . . ."

NOTE

The murder of Isaac Gold was a true case from 1881, and the basic narrative and most of the characters, including the mention of "*George Holmes*", are taken from history. The idea that the papers got Holmes's name wrong is of course, purely my own invention.

The Cable Street Mummy
by Paula Hammond

I had not long been a resident in Baker Street and was still learning to accommodate myself to the peculiar customs of a fellow lodger who imagined that a jack-knife plunged into the heart of an elegant, Georgian fireplace was a fine place to keep his correspondence.

I nevertheless considered myself fortunate to have landed so firmly on my feet in this great wilderness of a city, for I doubt that I will ever again find such well-appointed rooms or such a fascinating and agreeable companion as Sherlock Holmes.

While his moods could be extreme, and his habits trying, it was the very contradictions in his nature that I found so compelling. He could be thoughtless, but was never mean-spirited. His studies were well-ordered and methodical, but he was a bohemian at heart. He affected a detached coolness towards the world, but exalted in music and good food. And, while he professed to care neither for society nor company, I had quickly come to regard him as a loyal and true friend.

I had risen early – a practice formed in the long days of student study and forged into habit chasing Ghazi coattails through Afghanistan. Holmes had hurried off the previous evening on some mysterious mission and not yet returned. So it was that I found myself a watcher at the window, and quickly fell into a brown study, musing on the press and swell of London life – still so new to me.

Our diggings lie but three minutes from the Baker Street underground station, with Regent's Park to the north and Mayfair to the south. It's a handsome house, brick-built with – or so our redoubtable landlady, Mrs. Hudson, tells me – six bedchambers, three sitting rooms, and, in the basement, a kitchen, scullery, housekeeper's room, butler's pantry, China closet, and larder. Upon inheriting the freehold from her deceased husband, Mrs. Hudson had divided up the property and I found myself in the agreeable position of going halves on rooms that I would never have been able to afford with my own depleted finances.

Mrs. Hudson had once commented that "a property is a nice thing to have but an expensive thing to maintain", yet it appeared to me she cared less for financial gain than the pleasure of being a landlady. There was an element of proprietorial pride in that slow, dignified tread of hers – like a head of state inspecting her troops.

She had just laid the breakfast table and was turning to leave with the same unhurried air. I nodded my thanks and made a beeline for the coffee pot.

A pall of early morning chimney smoke filled the sky, and the day appeared to have settled into a resigned, uniform grayness. "My, but it's a gloomy day," she sighed.

"It is, indeed, Mrs. Hudson," I replied. "Does it never make you long for home? The open skies of the Highlands?"

"Oh, rarely" she said. "As I grow older, I find I've an independent streak that does not sit well with my Presbyterian kin. No, London suits me very well and lets me suit myself. Besides," she added, waving a hand at the unruly piles of books, clippings, file-boxes, retorts, test-tubes, and little Bunsen lamps scattered around the sitting room, "who else would put up with their home being so cruelly abused?"

"Ah, well, you should perhaps retire before I empty the contents of this bag onto that very welcome breakfast table," Holmes announced from the doorway, with a gleeful laugh.

The landlady turned, tutted, and, eyeing Holmes with the look of a woman indulging a recalcitrant child, quickly retreated.

"Give me a hand Watson, I don't think Mrs. Hudson would thank me if I ruined her best table cloth."

I moved the breakfast things over to the side table and watched Holmes pull a piece of oilcloth from the voluminous pockets of his overcoat. He rolled out the cloth and placed – rather gingerly, it seemed to me – a doctors' bag on top. It was of the common design but I noted, enviously, that while mine still had the scent and sheen of new leather, his was a venerable thing, covered in all manner of chemical burns and greasy stains.

He opened the brass clasp with a snap and, with the attitude of a magician pulling a rabbit out of a hat, produced an object roughly the size of an human head wrapped in a sack, tied with string. With a flourish, he pulled the cord that kept the cloth fastened and the sack's contents tumbled onto the oil cloth.

Dear Lord! It *was* a head! And what a thing! Blackened skin and clumps of matted hair still clung to the skull. Its eyes, surrounded by sunken hollows, were open, so that it seemed to regard one with a steady yet horribly vacant gaze. Its mouth was agog, its tongue emerging from an avenue of splintered teeth like a bloated slug. "Good grief!" I gagged. "Where on Earth did you get such a thing?"

"At the crossroads of Cable Street and Cannon Street where, in keeping with tradition, its owner had been buried, head first, with a stake through his heart.

"You can't be serious?" I spluttered. "But who is it?"

"Watson," Holmes replied with an amused smile, "meet Able Abless."

I blinked stupidly and Holmes returned my blank stare, looking rather deflated.

"The name means nothing to you, then?

"Should it?"

"Ah, Watson, you're no student of crime. Forty years ago, Able here," he said patting the thing affectionately, "was probably one of the most famous men in the empire."

Now, I'm a medical man, and have seen things that would make the strongest stomach protest, but for some reason this curious mummy and Holmes's evident glee at its acquisition quite turned my veins to ice. "For heavens sake, put the poor fellow back in the bag and tell me what this is all about!"

"Oh, my dear Doctor, forgive me!" Holmes said, sounding quite chastised. "I sometimes forget myself. You're right, of course. The breakfast table is no place for the head of one of London's most notorious murderers. Now, draw up a chair and, while I'm no storyteller, I guarantee that what I'm about to relate will make this grizzly interlude well worth your while."

I claimed myself a cup of thick, black coffee and settled myself in the basket chair. Holmes took his easy chair and assumed his usual position, his long, thin legs stretched out towards the fire. Eyes closed, fingers steepled, he began.

"On Saturday, 5th November, 1842, at around eleven p.m., Bartholomew Jameson, the owner of a tailor's shop at Number 25 Pennington Street, was preparing to close his business for the night. Saturday was then the usual day for workers to be paid, and being so near Christmas, businesses opened early and closed late. His wife was nursing their newborn son, so he sent out their serving girl, Maggie, for oysters as a treat, while he and his assistant closed up shop. This was to be the last time Maggie would see any of them alive again.

"Even in the gloom, winding her way through the close-pressed streets, the errand should have taken no more than twenty minutes. But that night, she was out of luck. Or maybe in luck, considering what was about to happen.

"It was a chill evening. A river mist was beginning to creep up the lanes, blanketing the houses, so that she had to stop several times to ensure she hadn't missed her turning. To make matters worse, every shop she tried was shuttered. Determined to find some oysters for her young mistress, she pressed on towards the High Street – a leery place at that time of night, with the Thames-side inns still doing lively business. It had gone midnight and she was beginning to despair of ever completing her errand when she literally stumbled into a street seller, weaving home with his barrow, who was happy to let the last of his oysters go for a penny.

"Rushing back, Maggie clearly heard the bells of St. George's ringing the quarter-hour. Increasingly anxious, worried she'd be in trouble for taking so long, she picked up the pace. Trotting the rest of the way – heeled boots on cobbles telegraphing her progress – she arrived at Pennington Street, red-faced and breathing hard.

"The shop was in darkness. She pulled the bell, but got no reply. She rang over and over. Still nothing. After almost ten minutes, feeling so sorely used, she began to kick the door, believing that the family had forgotten about her and left her out in the cold.

"It was a single sound that changed her growing frustration to fear. A scream, high and piercing, cut off by what she later described as a 'terrible gurgle, like someone drowning'.

"Once again the girl hoisted up her skirts and ran pell-mell towards the river, where she managed to persuade a young officer of the River Police to return with her to the house. They arrived to discover the neighbor, who owned the pawnbroker's next door, hammering on the door. He claimed to have been awakened by a loud thump 'as though something wet was being thrown against the adjoining wall', followed by an anguished cry.

"The officer, Peter Hore, made for the rear of the block of terraces and, finding the gate locked, scaled the high wall that enclosed the family's small back yard. Nothing, I think, could have prepared him for the scene that he found there. The smell reached him first – a tang of copper and human excrement: The scent of death.

"The back door was open, and in the feeble light of his lantern, he saw what he at first took to be a bag of coal. It was only as he moved closer that the flickering torch revealed the gory truth. The body of Bartholomew Jameson, lying in a corridor, painted red with his own blood. His head, or what remained of it, had been reduced to little more than a sack of pulp and bone shards. The young assistant lay beside his master, the lower half of his face missing. His neck was broken with such force that the coroner would note that several of the cervical vertebrae had been reduced to dust. A shipwright's maul, which seemed to have inflicted such terrible violence, was found at the foot of the stairs.

"Officer Hore later speculated that the master and his assistant had died first, and the assailant had dropped the maul as he was making for first floor bedroom. Not an unreasonable assumption and, as it turns out, entirely correct.

"It was in those upper chambers that perhaps the most pitiful scene was to be found. The young mother lay by the crib, a carpenter's chisel forced with such violence into her neck that it had pinned her to the floor boards. The body of the young boy, still wrapped in his swaddling clothes, was found close by. On the wall was a scarlet smear where the child had been hurled against the brick – accounting for the strange damp thud heard by the neighbor.

"As shocking as these events were, however, this was just the beginning of the evening's horrors. While Officer Hore was busy searching the scene, a few streets away, a second, equally monstrous, and equally senseless attack was taking place. This time, there was a witness.

"Ichabod Monmouth had lived at Number 17 Waterman Way for two years. He rented a modest room from his employer, Samuel Black, for whom he worked as an arkwright, making sea chests for the sailors in nearby Tobacco Dock. At 10:30 p.m., Saturday, being his half-day, he returned from a convivial night in The Painted Stag, made small talk with his employer, and retired to bed. He was awakened two hours later by the sounds of, as he put it, 'bloody murder being done'. Opening his bedroom door, he was confronted by the shadowy outline of two figures. The intruders were evidently too intent on their work to notice they were being observed. One was slight of frame with a perceptible limp The other he described as 'a square, mountainous brute'.

"Although he'd later be branded a coward, it's clear from his account that Monmouth exhibited remarkable presence of mind. Knowing he couldn't tackle the intruders alone, he quietly closed his bedroom door and, using his sheets as a rope, clambered from his window and – barefoot, in his nightshirt – ran for help.

"By the time the police arrived, the murderers had bolted, leaving behind a trail of gory bootprints and three mangled bodies. There was also one tangible clue that was filed away as evidence and never referred to again – a handprint left on the apprentice's nightshirt by the cut and still-bleeding hand of his murderer."

For a while Holmes sat in silence. I knew from his drawn brows and keen face that his mind was busy, as was mine, in picturing those tragic events. Finally, it was I who broke the silence.

"And this is the man who committed these atrocities?" I asked, looking across at the doctor's bag with a renewed and, admittedly, somewhat morbid interest.

"He was certainly arrested for the deeds but no one – not even, I fear, the authorities – truly believed that he was guilty. The evidence was flimsy to say the least. Our only witness, Monmouth, described two assailants, and Abless fitted neither description. And, while he was known to the first victim, he had no connection to the second. A shipwright's maul, which was supposed to have the initials *A.A.* carved into its handle, miraculously materialized some time after his arrest. The original case notes make no mention of any such detail, nor do contemporary illustrations show any inscriptions on the murder weapon."

"But, then why – ?

"Conjure, if you will, the scene. Seven brutal deaths. Two women. One child. Innocents. A close-knit community. Emotions running hot. So hot, that the police feared a riot. The Magistrate at the time wrote '*I am vexed with myself . . . my desire for discovering the atrocious murderers may have run me into error . . . . I fear my zeal has not been within proper bounds.*' Note he said '*murderers*'.

"So you think it was what our American friends would call a 'frame-up'?"

"I have long suspected so but, as of some weeks ago, I can confidently say that I now know Able Abless was completely innocent."

"Yet he was still hanged?"

"Not at all. I believe he was murdered before his name could be cleared. The authorities claimed that he had taken his own life, which explains why he was buried in such a bizarre manner. Suicides are prone to spectral wanderings – or so I hear," Holmes added with a ghoulish grin

I was lost and admitted as much. "Now, look Holmes, I agree that all this makes for a spectacularly grotesque breakfast. But you say you can now *prove* that he was innocent. How? And how the deuce do you come to have his head?"

"I said that I knew that he was innocent. Proof is something else entirely. But courtesy of the gentlemen who unearthed Mr. Abless for me yesterday evening, that's exactly what I hope to be able to do. Now," Holmes sprang up with one of his characteristic bursts of energy, "if you're free, I would be very pleased if you could accompany me to Wapping. I'd like to introduce you to the rest of poor Able." And that was all he could be compelled to say until we alighted at the Church St. George in the East, where the little mortuary stood, looking sadly forlorn in the shadow of Hawksmoor's grand Baroque church.

Able Abless was dead and buried ten years before I was born. He had been interred without coffin or shroud and his corpse seeded with quicklime. After forty years lying in thick mud, there should have been very little left of him beyond softened bones. The fact that he was in such a remarkable state of preservation was, according to Holmes, due to a combination of waterlogged London clay, a succession of cold winters, and the quicklime itself, which destroyed the very bacteria that, ordinarily, would have made a feast of Abless' sorry remains.

I have noted previously the eccentric nature of Holmes's knowledge and it now appeared that I was to add "a disturbing understanding of the decomposition process" to the plus side of his tally. "I've been testing pig corpses under a variety of conditions," was his alarming admission. "Rather than aid decomposition, quicklime appears to act as a preservative," he noted, his dark eyes sparking. I made a mental note not to follow up on that particular conversation.

I was already acquainted with his uncannily preserved head, but Abless' body was even more of a surprise. His skin, though as tanned as leather and lying on his bones like a deflated hydrogen balloon, was soft and moist. His muscles still allowed for the arms and legs to flex at the joints. I could see that an autopsy had been recently completed, and Holmes confirmed that the organs and blood vessels were also intact. More amazing was that there was still liquid blood in his veins. It was all so uncanny that I found myself imagining that the cloying London clay in which Abless had been lying had seeped into his body, replacing flesh and bone with some Golem-esque simulacrum – and I shuddered at the thought of it

"I have long held that science lies at the heart of detection," Holmes commented, in a tone of barely suppressed excitement. "It may, one day, be possible to look at a body such as this and know the entirety of its history with absolute certainty . . . ." He paused a moment, looking wistful for, as I imagined it, some far-future discoveries, and then he continued. "No matter. Mr. Abless may keep his secrets for now, but he can still be of assistance. In this instance, I believe comparative *dactylography* may offer some intriguing possibilities."

"Finger . . . *graph*?" I hazarded, my Greek not being what it should be

"Exactly so. As you are no doubt aware, the front or palmar surface of the hands are marked with *rugae* – folds and ridges. Dr. Faulds' article in *Nature*, 'On the Skin Furrows of the Hand', contended that the scroll-like patterns found on the fingertips display infinite variety, and he even outlined a technique for their capture. As a matter of interest, he postulated that this technique could be used both on mummies and bloody finger-marks left on objects where crimes have occurred," Holmes added with an amused bark.

"Well, we certainly have a mummy. But do we have any bloody finger-marks?" I asked, fairly certain what Holmes's response would be.

For a reply, he hauled a large basket from beneath the work bench which contained, amongst other curious items, what was quickly identified as a soiled nightshirt. "We do, thanks to the foresight of Officer Hore and the archives of Thames River Police. We're lucky this was such a notable case. But to whom do they belong, hmm? That's the question."

Holmes plundered the basket once more and pulled out a piece of slate, a bottle of black, lithographic ink, a small printer's roller, a sea sponge, some sheets of paper, and – most curious of all – a magic lantern and a collection of glass slides to use within.

"Now, Watson, if you could moisten this sponge, and use it to dampen one of these sheets of paper, I'd very obliged. Damp, mind, not wet."

I did as requested while Holmes splashed some of the pungent, viscous ink onto the slate, using the roller to spread it evenly over the surface. "Now, we shall see!" he exclaimed.

I watched, spellbound for a moment, as Holmes manipulated Abless' corpse – all the more terrible for its unnatural suppleness. He rolled the right thumb onto the inked slate, and then, motioning me to hand him the paper, transferred the sticky print to sheet. He strode over to the bench once more and pressed the paper onto one of the glass slides.

He then took out his watch and, as he counted off the seconds, I saw his apprehension grow. My friend Stamford had once called Holmes "cold-blooded", but I had come to recognize a thousand tiny signs which reflected the great emotions that assaulted him in moments such as this: When he pitted his titanic intellect against the world.

As the minute-hand completed its sweep, Holmes, with a remarkable delicateness of touch, peeled the paper from the glass. Success!

"Ha! Ha!" he cried, clapping his hands in a paroxysm of excitement. "Magnificent! Just magnificent! A little faint, but it will do, Watson! It will do! Now come here, and we'll see what we shall see."

I edged around the autopsy table, crammed as it was into the woefully small work space, to stand beside him. He lit a candle and closed the mortuary's heavy shutters. Then, popping the candle into the space behind the projector, he angled the magic lantern towards the blank wall. "Look, now. Here is a slide I prepared from a photograph of the blooded thumb left on the poor victim's nightshirt. And here – " He placed the slide he had just prepared in the slot behind, so that the two images were superimposed one upon the other. " – is the imprint of Abless' thumb. You'll agree that, even with the difficulties involved in getting a clear image from the cloth, there's no possibility of these belonging to the same man?"

I admitted as much.

"And now?" He removed the new slide and replaced it with another from the pile. Heavens! It was a match! "But where did you get this imprint?" I asked – not for the first time in my dealings with Holmes feeling a little lost.

Holmes raised his hand. "I promise you, Watson, that within the hour you'll know everything that I do, but for now, allow me to indulge my sense of dramatic by admitting that I have an unfair advantage. I know something that only one other living person knows."

Back at Baker Street, we were informed by Mrs. Hudson that there was a caller awaiting our return.

I recognized the white-haired gentleman from several previous visits over the last few weeks, and had already extended my hand in welcome as Holmes began to make the formal introductions. So it was that I found myself in the uncomfortable position of shaking the hand of a man I'd much rather have knocked to the ground.

"Watson," Holmes said, "I'd like you to meet David Mathers, whom the press so luridly dubbed at the time as 'The Shadwell Slaughterer'."

I recoiled, as though bitten by a cobra, and shot Holmes a look of protest.

"Please, Watson, do sit down and allow Mr. Mathers the courtesy of telling you his story in his own words."

I confess I didn't like the way that everything, from the morning's exposition over the breakfast table to Mathers' appearance in our rooms, seemed to have been orchestrated. Nor did I care to be told to extend the social niceties to a murderer. But I did as Holmes requested, while our guest paced the floor and related one of the most ghastly tales it's been my misfortune to hear.

Despite his white hair, Mathers was still a vigorous-looking man – large, square of shoulders, with the sort of ruddy complexion that comes from years of drink and manual labour. "I didn't come 'ere to ask for forgiveness for what I done," he began, casting me a look that seemed to suggest otherwise. "I've been to the police and got nowhere. Not that I blame them. I ain't got no proof of what I say. That's why I came to

Mr. Holmes. A fine turnabout when a criminal needs a private copper to help prove his guilt – and no mistake.

"Well," he coughed, settling into his tale, in a curious sing-song accent I recognized as hailing from the Antipodes, "life's been good to me of late, but it weren't always that way. I've a knack of finding trouble, and I reckon I found the worst of it when I met Charlie Higgins. Him and me were inmates on the *Dromedary* – a prison hulk moored off Woolwich. An old fifty-gun two-decker, made after the Rum Rebellion. Stripped of its masts, rigging, and sails, it was a sorry old beast.

"Now, I ain't a good bloke. I'm a brawler and thief, but I believe in paying my dues. That's as much honesty as my old man beat into me. But this place was a floating hell that no human being deserved – and that's the truth of it. Home to six-hundred souls, each with a sleeping space of five-feet eleven-inches long and eighteen-inches wide – and me six-foot tall and a couple more across. In the winter, our blankets froze solid and there were many a mate who ended up just as cold and stiff in the morning. In the summer, we spent our nights choking in the dust and heat below decks, while vermin and disease ate us up. Our days we spent unloading ballast, hefting cables, dredging channels – all the dirty, dangerous work they usually pay the Paddies to do. But we were free labour for the docks. Making rich men richer. And we did it with both ankles chained. Misbehave, and the weight of the leg irons would be increased. It was that what left my mate, Charlie, lame.

"We was in for a year, Charlie and me. Damn near broke us. To this day I have nightmares where I'm wrapped in cold iron, rats eating my face." As he spoke, I saw that big man grow pale, his hands clenching convulsively. He paused, gave a visible judder, and pressed on with his tale.

"At the end of it, no one would look at us or give us honest work. We were sleeping rough, stealing food. Then we fell

212

lucky. I'd been trained as a carpenter and heard Samuel Black was looking for help. So I went along and he agreed to take me on at half-pay to see how things'd work out. Charlie got some odd jobs for a shop down on Cable Street, and it felt like life was on the up.

'Well, Charlie could never keep his eyes off a pretty woman, and he gets it into his head that the lady of the house is keen on him. She's laid up in bed awaiting a new baby and, naturally, calling on him to do little errands while her husband's busy. But he sees more to it than that and, once he'd got an idea fixed in his mind, no amount of talking would shake it. Eventually the lady complains to her husband and he's out on his ear. Round the same time, my gaffer found out I'd been in the hulks and that was the end of that.

"Later, I learnt that the sneaky beggar had gone and got himself an apprentice. So he didn't even have to pay half-wages. That got my blood boiling and no mistake. Then Charlie tells me that he never got paid neither, so one thing led to another – us drinking hard, and the more we talked, and the more we drank, the more it seemed like we were owed. Like I said, I ain't a good bloke and never been averse to a bit of thievery, so it was decided. That night we were going to take what was ours.

"God's honest truth, though, burglary was all I had in mind. I took my maul and chisel, thinking we'd maybe need to break open a few strong boxes and the like. But things played out different from how we planned. Very different.

"We arrived at Cable Street gone midnight. A light was still burning in front and I figured, maybe another hour and the whole house would be asleep. But Charlie had his blood up and a sudden mind to have things out with Jameson, so he hammers on the door. The man opened up sharp enough and, after a bit of chat, he let us in.

"At first it was real friendly. He'd just become a father, he said. Let bygones be bygones, he said. Have a drink, he said. Wet the baby's head, he said. But then Charlie starts asking about his missus. Wants to see her, pay his respects. Jameson's edgy, like, and Charlie won't take no for an answer, and pretty soon things start to get heated. He seizes the lantern, pushes his way past the counter and into the back room, heading for the stairs. Jameson follows, grabs him, and the two start to tussle. I get between them, and it's then that things go south.

"There's a boy out back, locking up. He's a thin streak of nothing but he's got gumption. He sees what's going down and makes a grab at Charlie. Takes him by the coat sleeves. Jameson slips through my outstretched hands and pretty soon, the two of them are hauling Charlie out the back door. All the time, Charlie's yawling like a cat on heat for me to help him.

"By now my blood's pumping, head's spinnin'. I'm panicking about the noise. About the neighbors hearing. Calling the peelers. Putting me back in the hulks. Seems like I can't think straight. All I know is my mate's in trouble and I just do it. I grab the maul that's lying heavy in my jacket and I swing it at the kid. It catches him under the chin and he drops with an 'orrible crunch. Charlie dashes back into the house, leavin' just Jameson and me.

"He roars at me and I swing again. And again. And again. It's like I'm watching myself. Like the whole 'orrible nightmare is happening to someone else and I can't stop. Then, suddenly Charlie's back at my my side, pulling me out the door. The maul slips from my hand, slick with brains.

"The rest of the night's a blur. I stumbled out the back door. Fell. Smashed the glass in the little transom window. Sliced my hand right open and didn't even feel it.

"Charlie's pale, gabbling. Says we need a stake. Some money to get away. Start fresh. We haul up, over the back wall, and he leads me through the street. All the time I'm shaking my head like some mad elephant. Trying to clear my thoughts. But all I keep seeing is my maul smashing into the wreckage of that face, over and over.

"We arrive at Black's place. Charlie breaks a window, climbs in, and I follow. The strong box is in Black's bedroom. I lead Charlie up. I figure the apprentice sleeps opposite and I go in to check on him. Make sure he don't raise the alarm. I'd swear on The Bible, that all I gave was him a little tap, just enough to put him down, but then Charlie reappears and I hear him say 'Saints Alive Davy, you're a murderous beast and no mistake'. And I look down and I see that young boy, lying broken beyond all repair, and I knew then that there'd be three ghosts following me to my grave and calling for my damnation.

"So we ran. Ran for hours it seemed. By sun-up we were on a train bound for Portsmouth. From there we bought passage to Calais. Worked our way as far away as we could from the unholy mess we'd left behind. Ended up in Australia. It was only a few years ago that I learnt what Charlie had done. Those women. That baby. I swear, if I'd known at the time, I'd 'ave done fer him myself. But by then he was dead and it was left to me to put things right."

Mathers finally stopped his pacing and looked at Holmes with a sort of hungry desperation.

"And you can do that now, Davy. I have all the proof you need," Holmes whispered as though reluctant to break the spell that Mathers' tale had woven. "I have your testimony, confirmation of the all details it has been possible to corroborate, and Abless' thumb imprint to compare with yours. The one taken when we met, and the one on the boy's nightshirt. They match."

Mathers sighed and nodded. "Call the police then. I'll be waiting in my hotel. All I ask is two things. Give Mr. Abless a decent burial. I've money set aside for that that. And you write to my daughter in Adelaide once the courts have done with me. You tell her the truth. The papers are bound to make a sensation of it. Her old dad weren't a good man, but he were a better man for her being in his life and I'd like her to know that."

I sat by the fire long after Mathers had left, deep in thought.

"You believe I should have sent him away?" Holmes eventually asked. "Refused to help?"

I honestly didn't know. It felt right, that Abless' name would be cleared, that the real murderer would finally face justice, but part of me wondered about Holmes. He had been working for weeks for a murderer! Invited him into our home, treated him like a guest.

Holmes paused, then nodded thoughtfully.

"To do what I do," he said, "I must separate the crime from the criminal. I can never never let myself be carried away by the heat of the moment. I must be led by facts, or I am no better than the magistrate who allowed Able Abless to be hounded to his death."

"But do you not feel . . ." I began . . . not altogether sure where my question was heading.

"Yes, Watson, I do feel!" Holmes replied, in a measured tone laced with heat, "and I tell you this: Though you may think me an automaton, a calculating machine, had I a sister, a daughter, or a loved one who had been so cruelly slaughtered, I would burn the world to its foundations to uncover the truth. I confess that I might even take the law into my own hands. Yes. I might even do that. Would that, then, be the *human* thing to do?

"What of the man who murders the one who kills his wife? He's not an evil man. Not likely to kill ever again. What does the world gain by his death? Should I let him go free?

"What is moral? What is fair? How do I balance justice with vengeance? Is that even my job?

"I have encountered creatures whose very presence fills me with the same creeping sensation as you'd feel watching a python digest a meal. Although I can prove no wrong-doing that any court of law would accept, I know them for the villains they are. But, here, a murderer comes to me, confesses his crime, and asks for my help. Do I turn him away in disgust, in horror, or do I seek justice? Not just for his victims, but for the man who has spent forty years in a suicide's grave for a crime in which he had no part?"

There were no easy answers to Holmes's questions and I confessed as much. But I recalled how Mathers had looked as his left our rooms. A man who, it seemed to me, was curiously light on his feet for someone who was surely walking towards the gallows. And as I glanced at my friend Sherlock Holmes, I knew that, whatever his failings, I could trust him to do what was right.

NOTES

This story was inspired by a visit to The Thames River Police Museum. Formed in 1789, the River Police were London's first police force. The Curator, Robert Jefferies, was incredibly helpful, and shared a lot of material from the archives, which gave me an insight into early police procedures. Evidence collecting was surprisingly diligent in an era of minimal forensics – if not officially, then unofficially. Souvenir taking was a "thing". The archive even included a blood-stained flag which had been used to wrap a body and kept as a memento. Our ancestors, it seems, had quite different sensibilities about death.

The infamous Ratcliff Highway murders were the seed for the tale, and some of the details I've included reflect real-life events. The only witness did escape the murderers by climbing from his bedroom window using his bedsheets as a rope. A carpenter's maul was believed to be one of the murder implements. The accused – John Williams – who few genuinely believed was guilty, was found dead in his cell under suspicious circumstances. His corpse was paraded through the streets and publicly whipped before being interred, at a crossroads, as described. He was unearthed in the 1880's by a company laying gas pipes and his head was displayed for many years in the nearby Crown and Dolphin Pub. Alternative suspects included two men: One lame, the other a seaman called Ablass.

Experiments on pig corpses have shown that quicklime can indeed act as a preservative. Its use in burials is likely to come from the attempts to stop bad smells – the "miasmas" which were believed to cause disease.

The real Dr. Faulds fought long and hard to be recognized for his work on finger-printing. His article in *Nature*, "On the Skin-Furrows of the Hands" from October 1880, describes the technique used in the story. Faulds even suggests its use on mummies and in identifying the owners of bloody prints left at crime scenes.

Why a mummy? "The Sussex Vampire" plays with vampire legends. "The Creeping Man" has always seemed to me like a werewolf story. Pharaoh Seti I's amazingly preserved mummy was discovered in 1881 – so with Mummy mania at its height, it seemed only fair that Holmes should have a mummy of his own to play with.

The Piccadilly Poisoner
by Roger Riccard

Chapter I

Shortly after I took up residence with the consulting detective, Mr. Sherlock Holmes, at 221b Baker Street, I found occasion to involve him in a case with a patient I came across while working rounds at St. Bartholomew's Hospital.

The person in question was a young woman named Mrs. Bertram Morgan, *née* Dinah Patel. She was a dark-haired beauty in her early twenties, with a trim figure and a heart-shaped face that set off her doe-brown eyes and flashing smile. While she was of Indian descent, her skin tone was of a lighter shade than most of her people, due to her mixed Anglo-Indian parentage.

Her husband was a wealthy East India importer who was well known for his travels to the Orient and the unique items he was able to provide to the London elite, in addition to his standard imports of teas and spices. He was also nearly twenty-five years older than she, being a widower now on his second marriage. His first wife, who was of an equal age to himself, had died of a heart ailment almost four years earlier. After a suitable year-long mourning period, he began courting Miss Patel, the daughter of one of his Indian suppliers. They married some eight months later – much to the consternation, it was rumored, of his now twenty-year-old son, Whitaker.

Now she was in hospital, complaining of abdominal pain, fever, and skin irritation. My questioning of her activities and diet led me to believe she was suffering some type of food poisoning, perhaps brought on by improperly prepared meals of her largely Oriental diet. Therefore, I questioned her about her recent meals and activities.

"These symptoms have been present before over the past several weeks, but the pain was not so great and I thought it may have been my attempt to acclimate myself to English food. Last night, however, we had a traditional Indian meal. My husband and I had the same dishes, and he did not become ill."

"Were there any other persons eating with you? Some guests, perhaps?"

"No, just my stepson, Whitaker. But he does not partake of Indian dishes. He has never developed a taste for our food as his father has. He had a beef stew instead. I think he does these things just to insult me, knowing that I do not eat meat from cows."

I gave her a sympathetic look as she winced in pain, then enquired, "Your stepson is not cordial toward you?"

She frowned in reply, "His prejudice is obvious when we are alone. He never got over the loss of his mother, as if it were my fault that she had a heart attack. In public he puts on a show of respect, but that is all and such occasions are rare. Even Bertram and I do not go out together in public often. Usually we just visit his more tolerant friends, who are accepting of our marriage."

Having served with Her Majesty's Army in India, I was well aware of the racial tensions that mixed marriages incurred, and a nagging thought found its way to my tongue. "Who prepared your meal last night, Mrs. Morgan?"

"My maidservant, Bala. She has been with me for years, long before my marriage."

"Did anyone else have access to the kitchen?"

"It's certainly not guarded, Doctor. Any of the household staff can come and go as they please. But she is very particular

220

about being left alone to concentrate when she prepares our meals. The staff knows not to bother her while she's cooking, so if you are thinking she may have been distracted and did something wrong, I assure you that it's not possible."

Not wishing to overly concern her, I amended the conversation. "Of course, most likely it is just a case of a spoiled ingredient. Or perhaps something entirely different. A bug bite, or some form of bacteria. We'll keep an eye on you for the next day or two and see what transpires."

She looked at me with exasperation in her eyes, "Must I stay here, Doctor? Bala is quite capable of looking after my needs at home."

I sympathized, but preferred to be cautious and replied, "While the symptoms are uncomfortable, it is important that your body expel the poisons from itself I'm recommending that we keep you here until you feel stronger. I'll have your diet restricted to bland foods, and water or ginger ale. You should be up and about tomorrow or the next day."

In spite of my comforting words to the lady, when I left her I immediately went to the hospital library to consult some medical journals. Her symptoms, thus far, could indicate a number of ailments. However, the fact that she was the only one affected concerned me that poison could be involved. Perhaps it was my new daily exposure to the life of Sherlock Holmes and the criminal elements with which he dealt which was jading my thoughts. For the time being, I resolved to keep an eye on Mrs. Morgan until I was certain that she was in no danger.

That evening when I arrived home, I found Holmes in our sitting room in his shirtsleeves. His right hand was soaking in a basin of water filled with Epsom salts and there was a bruising of his left cheek.

"What happened?" I enquired. "Did one of your cases turn violent?"

"Not a case, Doctor," he replied, as he lifted his bruised knuckles from the basin and inspected them before re-submerging them. "I occasionally engage in a bout of fisticuffs to maintain my fighting skills and make a little money on the side to assist with the rent. Unfortunately, today's opponent slipped under one of my jabs to his jaw, causing me to bounce my fist off his rather hard skull. I prevailed in the end by wearing him down, as I avoided his punches over time. By the eighth round he was too tired to keep his guard up, and I ended it with a knockout blow."

I stood above him and bent to examine his cheek. My touch brought about a wince and I noted, "It appears that you didn't avoid *all* his punches. Let me get some ice from Mrs. Hudson for that bruise."

After I ministered to Holmes's wound, I sat by the fire and took up an evening paper. Mrs. Morgan was still on my mind, however, and I decided to broach an idea with the detective.

"I say, Holmes. I've observed you consulting your collection of indexes from time to time when you've been on a case. Do you have any file of information on a fellow named Bertram Morgan? He's an importer of Oriental foods and commodities."

He took his hand from the basin and dried it as he replied, "The name is not completely unfamiliar to me, Watson." He rose and stepped over to the shelves where he pulled out a volume in which he had pasted several articles on various people and subjects which he felt might be relevant to his work at some point. Flipping through pages, he finally settled on one and read as follows:

Morgan, Bertram. Born May 1st, 1836. Only child of Henry and Mary (née Reston). Oxford, degree in finance. Married Susannah Concord May 10th, 1857. One child, Whittaker Henry, born August 25th, 1860. Wife Susannah died of heart attack February 2nd, 1878. Remarried Dinah Patel, age twenty, daughter of Arjun and Harriet Patel (nee Osgood), November 1879 in Chennai, India. Importer of spices, coffee, tea, and unique Oriental arts and goods. Successfully survived the great coffee rust plague and converted to importing tea. Method and terms of doing so are vague, but no criminal activity has yet come to fore.

"Anything more specific about the son?" I asked.

"I've only recorded the fact of his existence. He has exhibited no behavior worth noting as yet."

He snapped the book shut with his uninjured hand, deposited it on the shelf, and returned to his chair, where he took up his pipe and asked, "So what has happened to Mrs. Morgan that merits your inquisition, Doctor?"

"Why did you presume that Mrs. Morgan was the subject of my interest?"

"Your tone when you asked the question," he answered. "Also, when you bent over me to check my cheek, I noticed a distinct scent of a perfume common among Indian women. It was, therefore, likely then that you were in close proximity to such a person. As your character would eliminate such intimacy with a married woman, I deduced that she was a patient of yours."

"As usual, you are correct on all counts," I replied. "She was in hospital today with symptoms that could be linked to poisoning. When I questioned her about her home life, she indicated that there were some issues of racial bias among their societal circles with which she has had to deal. She's also especially concerned about her stepson, Whittaker, who has never taken a liking to her."

"A natural occurrence among stepchildren who are closer in age to their new stepmother than their father is. Add in the racial factor and the situation is ripe for dissent. Tell me what you know."

I explained what the lady had told me and Holmes puffed thoughtfully on his pipe for several minutes in thought. Finally, he spoke. "There are many ways that poison can be administered, both deliberately and accidentally. If you like, Doctor, I am currently without a case and could look into the matter for you."

"If you would be so good, Holmes," I said. "It would ease my mind and could well assist my diagnosis."

"Consider it done. Now here is what I propose . . . ."

Chapter II

By the end of the next day's rounds, Mrs. Morgan was doing much better and I agreed to sending her home. However, I included the *caveat* that I would be coming around the following day with a specialist who would be looking in on her. She hesitated, but I insisted, and she acquiesced.

The following morning, Holmes and I arrived at the Morgan home in Piccadilly. He had affected mutton chop whiskers and a moustache to disguise himself and hide his boxing bruise. We were greeted at the door by Dugan, a proper butler of rotund proportions, who spoke with a trace of an Irish accent. He took our hats and coats and showed us into the sitting room, where Mrs. Morgan sat reading a letter by the fire. She was so absorbed in her activity that she reacted with a start when Dugan cleared his throat to announce our presence. Efficiently slipping the letter back into its envelope and then into a book on the end table next to her, she rose and held out her hand in greeting.

I introduced Holmes to Mrs. Morgan as "Dr. William Scott, an expert in internal medicine". As Holmes bowed over her hand she declared, "Oh dear, I do hope I am not causing you so much trouble, Doctor. I am feeling much better today."

"Nonsense!" Holmes declared. "We cannot have such a lovely woman as yourself succumbing to conditions in London that you would have no worries of in your home country. The Queen's subjects must feel safe wherever they live."

The lady tilted her head in gratitude and invited us to sit down as she asked Dugan to stir up the fire. "I do admit I like a good warm fire," she said. "This English weather takes much getting used to after growing up in the tropics of my homeland. Would you care for some hot tea, gentlemen?"

We declined her offer, then Holmes continued, "I understand your acclimation difficulties completely. Has the chill ever affected your health? Made you more susceptible to catching cold or that sort of thing?"

She looked pensive and then recalled, "I did have a severe cold the winter before last. I took to my bed for several days. But nothing since then until these latest symptoms. Do you suppose the weather could be the cause, Dr. Scott?"

"Highly unlikely, madam," he answered. "Though I would like to rule out any external factors, if I may. Bacteria could be airborne, or transmitted by touch. With your permission, I would examine the kitchen, your bedroom, and rooms such as this, where you spend significant time. Even your water closet could be a source of this malady."

"Is that really necessary, Doctor?" she asked, appearing skeptical.

"Oh, I assure you, Mrs. Morgan, I have found breeding grounds for disease in the most inconspicuous of places."

She pondered that as she sat back in her chair. Finally she replied, "Very well, but I must insist that you conduct your investigation while my husband is at home. He would not care for strangers wandering about the house unattended. Can you come back tonight, after eight o'clock? We should be finished with dinner by then and he can escort you about the place himself."

Holmes bowed to her condition, "That would be quite satisfactory. If Dr. Watson is available, I should welcome his assistance. I assure you that you will not be double-billed for this service."

"Thank you, Dr. Scott. I shall see that all is ready for you."

Her demeanor indicated that our interview was at end, so we rose, bid her good day, and left to return to Baker Street. I had no rounds that day, my position at St. Bartholomew's hospital being intermittent. Therefore, Holmes and I sat down to enjoy tea and biscuits prepared by Mrs. Hudson.

"So, 'Dr. Scott'," I began my enquiry. "What do you think of Mrs. Morgan's situation?"

"I found her very interesting, Watson. Tell me her symptoms again, when you first examined her."

"Abdominal pain, fever, and skin irritation." I recounted. "She also exhibited diarrhea while in hospital, but that was gone by the end of the first day."

"What sort of skin irritation?"

"An irregular patch of redness, roughly seven inches in diameter, on the right side of her abdomen."

"No blisters or warts?"

"Not yet."

Holmes proceeded to stuff and light his old briarwood pipe and settled back in thought. After several minutes of this posture while I read the morning paper, he finally spoke. "I believe I shall take a visit to the London Library and drop across the street to the East India Club as well."

"Is there anything that I can do?"

He stood, went to the coat stand to prepare for his journey, and merely stated, "I shall need your assistance in distracting members of the household during my searches this evening, Doctor. You may contemplate some plausible excuses to keep them engaged."

With that odd request, he was out the door and gone for most of the afternoon. He returned just after five o'clock with a look upon his face which I could not quite comprehend. "Did you discover something significant?" I asked

"Consider," he stated, as he removed his outdoor garments and flopped into his chair to light a cigarette. "We have a household with a wealthy middle-aged husband who deals with Oriental goods and spices. By all accounts he is an honest man, but his success has sparked jealousies among his competitors. He is married to a woman young enough to be his daughter and she is much resented by his son. I verified these facts while I was at the East India Club. She has a servant, whom she claims to be of unwavering loyalty. This fact I must observe for myself, but do you agree to this likely scenario so far?"

"That seems to align with what I have observed and been told," I concurred.

"Therefore, we have much data to still gather," he declared. "With just these few pieces to the puzzle, I can surmise more than a half-dozen theories to explain her situation."

"Oh, come now, Holmes!" I scoffed. "Six possibilities? Surely not!"

"Watson, you are a good and gentle soul," he sighed, with what seemed to be genuine concern. "I can only hope that your exposure to my world does not blemish you. But in my occupation, I am forced to consider the darker sides of every person, and the unlikely, but still possible, circumstances of every event or contingency. Allow me to elucidate.

"First, the benign possibility that she has merely been exposed to spoiled food, bacteria, mold spores, or some other aspect of her environs. Second, her stepson resents her and has poisoned her. Third, her maidservant secretly resents her and wants to go back to India, which would be a likely result if her mistress dies. Fourth, the butler resents this foreign influence in this once proud and noble house."

"The butler, Holmes?" I interrupted. "That seems far-fetched."

"You would be surprised, Watson, at how deeply some long-standing servants will go to protect the family honor. I am aware of at least one case where the major-domo arranged an 'accident' for the heir apparent because of his shameful public reputation, which allowed the more suitable younger son to ascend.

"But allow me to continue. Fifth, Mr. Morgan himself. Perhaps he has found the whims of his lustful decision to no longer outweigh the demands or personality of a younger wife of a different culture. Perhaps he did not realise how much resentment he would incur among his peers in marrying outside his race and now regrets his rashness. Sixth, Anti-Indian radicals, concerned over the spread of Oriental religions by high placed immigrants, have succeeded in infecting her in some fashion.

"I could go on, Watson, but that would be a futile exercise. After we gather more facts tonight, we should be able to narrow the field considerably."

228

Having finished his discourse, he sat back and casually blew smoke rings into the air. I shook my head slowly and rose to pour myself a brandy at the sideboard. Then I resumed my seat and contemplated my role in what would certainly be an interesting evening.

Chapter III

Our cab delivered us to Piccadilly at precisely seven-forty-five. In spite of Mrs. Morgan's request to arrive after eight o'clock. I questioned my friend as to his disobedience.

"When dealing with suspects, Watson, one must use any means to keep them off balance. If the entire household is expecting us at eight o'clock, their demeanor will be building in anticipation of that event. Mentally, they are fifteen minutes from being fully prepared. For the innocent this will merely be inconvenient, but adaptable. For the guilty, depending on their personal discipline, it could fluster them into a mistake."

He rang the bell as I nodded, but I still asked, "Wouldn't they have made their preparations as early as possible? Surely they would not wait until the last minute to hide or destroy evidence."

His answer was curtailed by the opening of the door by Dugan, who seemed to take our early arrival in stride. "Dr. Scott, Dr. Watson. Please come in, gentlemen. The family is still at dinner, but you may wait in the parlour while I announce you."

"Thank you, Dugan," said Holmes. "We apologize for our early arrival, but our previous meeting at the hospital ended early. We certainly don't wish to curtail the family meal. If you would be so kind, would you ask permission for us to begin our examination of the kitchen until it is convenient for Mr. Morgan to join us?"

"Very good, sir," he stated as he took our hats and coats. He left us standing by the parlour fire. The moment he was out the door, Holmes bid me to play lookout while he made a quick surveillance of the room. In the space of less than two minutes, he noted wear patterns in the carpet, dust levels on the bookshelves, and even the location of a safe behind one painting, before I signaled that Dugan was returning. The butler found us standing where he left us, warming our hands by the fire.

Dugan was not alone, however. Young Whitaker was with him and addressed us as soon as he entered. "Doctors, I am Whitaker Morgan. My father has asked that I escort you during your examination of the house. I understand you wish to begin in the kitchen?"

His tone was polite and showed no hint of exasperation or annoyance at our presence. He was a fine figure of a lad – athletic build, clean-shaven with brown wavy hair, roughly five-foot-ten. His handshake as we introduced ourselves was firm and self-assured. Holmes actually took his hand and turned it palm up in examination, much to our host's surprise. "What is it, Dr. Scott?"

"May I see your left hand as well, Mr. Morgan?" said Holmes. The boy held it up and Holmes clicked his tongue and pronounced, "You are a golfer, I perceive. I could recommend something for your callouses, if you wish."

Whitaker smiled as Holmes let go of his hands, "No need, Doctor. With the warmer weather approaching, I'll be playing often enough to toughen them up against blistering. But how did you know it was golf and not cricket, or some other club-wielding sport?"

Holmes smiled and raised his forefinger as if in lecture, "The single-handed sports, such as polo or tennis, were eliminated by the presence of wear on both your hands. Cricket

230

would be less likely to cause such extensive damage, as you would take far fewer swings and of much lesser force. This pattern is much more common among golfers."

"Well done, sir," admitted the Morgan heir. "I hope such powers of observation will allow you to put an end to Miss Patel's misery, for my father's sake and the peace of the household. Come, I'll show you to the kitchen."

As we walked I broached the fact of his using his stepmother's maiden name. "If I am not being too indelicate, Mr. Morgan, may I ask why you referred to your stepmother as *Miss Patel*?" We had arrived at the kitchen and Holmes was beginning his search. I hoped this distraction was something he could use.

Whitaker turned to me with his back toward Holmes and replied, "I was not present at the so-called 'wedding', which I understand was performed under her religion and not my father's. Nor have I seen any British government document legitimizing their union under English law. And she will certainly *never* replace my mother!'"

This last was said with a vehemence that hinted at a hidden temper under those gentlemanly manners he exuded thus far. I nodded in understanding and what I hoped he would assume was silent agreement. All the better to maintain communications.

In reply I merely stated, "The actions of middle-aged men are often . . . questionable."

"Damned foolhardy, if you'll pardon my language, sir. I love the man, but this decision was absolutely intolerable. I moved out of the house upon his return and only come by for dinner two or three times a week, just to make sure he is healthy and that business goes well."

"You fear for his health?" I asked, somewhat surprised.

"Not to put too fine a point on it, Doctor Watson, but I can only see one reason for him to marry her. Whereas there are several hundred thousand reasons for her to marry him."

Somewhere in the house a clock was striking eight and a young Indian woman came in with a cart, piled with dirty dishes from the evening meal. Master Morgan called out at her arrival and said, "Doctors, please meet Bala, Miss Patel's maidservant and cook. Bala, this is Dr. Scott and Dr. Watson. They are here to try and find out what is making your mistress ill."

The lass was dark-skinned, much more so than Mrs. Morgan, and appeared slightly younger. Her black hair was tied up behind her head to keep it out of the way as she worked. From its volume, I imagined it would be quite long when let down. She was a bit stout, though not obese, and stood about five-foot tall. When she spoke it was very proper English, with a deference in her voice that bordered on fear, I thought.

"Good evening, Doctors. I pray you will be successful. May I assist you?"

Having finished examining the cupboards, Holmes was about to enter the pantry, but stopped and smiled at the young woman. "Yes, Miss Bala. Could you show us the steps you took to make dinner the other night? The meal before she went to hospital."

"Certainly. Did you wish me to actually prepare it?" she asked.

Holmes smiled at her cooperativeness and replied, "No, that will not be necessary. I would just like to see from where you took all the ingredients and examine the containers themselves."

She took us through the process and Holmes whispered to me to note the combinations, as my service in Her Majesty's Army had taken me into that realm and made me more familiar with Indian cuisine. I only questioned her on one particular ingredient, but she explained that her mistress preferred her food less spicy than normal and this herb would reduce the harshness of some of the traditional ingredients.

Holmes followed her about like a hound on a scent, examining each box, can, and jar. In the pantry he also noted the placement of all the items and what they were next too. In addition, he took a mental inventory of all the goods therein and examined the air vent and floor as well.

Bala was thorough in her explanations and Holmes asked one more question, "Does your mistress ever assist you, or come in to check on you, while you are preparing the meals?"

Bala nodded, "Yes, quite often, though not every time."

Holmes thanked her for her cooperation, and then suggested an examination of the bedroom vents and windows. Whitaker replied, "I assume you mean where she sleeps. Follow me." He led us upstairs and into a bedroom with a single bed, but several dressers, a large wardrobe, and a rocking chair with a reading lamp.

"Certainly this is not the master bedroom," I commented.

"No, Dr. Watson, that door over there leads to my father's bedroom. He is a prodigious snorer and both my mother and Miss Patel have used this room in order to be able to sleep. It used to be my nursery."

"Where is your room now?" asked Holmes.

"It's the next room over, though I've moved most of my things out since I rarely spend the night here anymore."

"I see," answered Holmes as he looked about the room. "I notice there is a connecting air vent. Just to be safe, we should examine your room as well."

Whitaker shrugged his shoulders, "Anything that will put this silliness behind us. I don't know how father puts up with her constant whining."

Holmes tilted his head non-committally and began an examination of the former nursery, checking the vents, opening the window to check the sills, inspecting the bedding, carpets, and the closets, looking for any sign of mold or infestation. We followed the same procedure in the master bedroom and then took up Whitaker's old room last. In this room, Holmes again opened the window and examined the sill with his magnifying glass, as he had the others. Looking out he noted, "This room is directly above the kitchen, I see."

Whitaker smiled, "Yes, Dr. Scott, a distinct advantage when I was growing up and mother was baking fresh bread or sweetmeats."

Holmes nodded, then proceeded to the open closet where, to our surprise, an orange tabby cat lay curled up on a blanket on the bottom shelf. It snapped its head up at our approach, then stretched languidly and walked out to rub against Whitaker's leg. He knelt and picked the creature up, who responded by nuzzling the young man's jaw.

"This is Marmalade," he said by way of explanation. "She's the one thing I miss about this house. She slept curled at my feet, or up against my stomach during the night, and always jumped in my lap any time I tried to read. Her brother, King George, is a grey tabby and usually roams the kitchen and dining room when he's not curled by the fire in the parlour. But this one likes hiding in closets and under beds."

He nuzzled the feline and set it back down. Holmes asked, "Are they good mousers?"

"King George is quite the hunter. I don't believe we've had any sort of creature stirring downstairs, at least not for long, since he took up his post. Marmalade usually stays up here and I've never seen a mouse, dead or alive, on this floor."

"That bodes well for that aspect of any disease," replied Holmes as he looked back into the closet. Then he said to me, "Dr. Watson, would you hand me your medical bag, please?"

I had been carrying it throughout our excursion and obediently handed it over to him. Thinking he may have found something significant, I again engaged Whitaker in conversation.

"So, have you ever accompanied your father on any of his trips to the Orient?"

"Once, when I was sixteen, mother and I both traveled with him," answered the young man. "I remember that it was a long and arduous trip. Mother and I were seasick for much of the voyage. After getting our land legs back again, we did enjoy many of the sights, and certainly the warm weather compared to the winter we had left behind in London. But once was enough, I wouldn't care to make that trip again."

I agreed with him and went on to tell him of my service in Her Majesty's Army, which he found quite interesting. By the time I had completed my tale of escape from the Battle at Maiwand, Holmes had finished and declared that he had enough information to test some theories regarding the maladies reported by the mistress of the house. Whitaker led us downstairs and to the parlour, where his father and my patient were waiting, along with King George curled up by the fire.

He left us there to find Dugan in order to retrieve our hats and coats. Bertram Morgan introduced himself and shook our hands. "Well, Doctors, did you find anything that may be causing Dinah's symptoms?"

Holmes took the lead and replied, "The ingredients in the kitchen and the pots, pans, and utensils all seem in order. There is a bit of mold on the pantry floor, apparently seeping in from outside. Similarly, I discovered some on an upstairs windowsill and in Master Whitaker's closet along the floor of the exterior wall, but none in either of the other two rooms. I was happy to see that the poisons were stored away from any foodstuffs and the mousetraps were all clean. That's probably thanks to this fine fellow," He nodded toward the cat.

Continuing, he said, "I have samples which I will test in our laboratory. In the meantime, Mrs. Morgan, I suggest that you keep to the diet which Dr. Watson has recommended for the time being and report any new symptoms immediately."

We took our leave when Dugan arrived with our outerwear. As we walked out to the pavement, we were followed by Whitaker, who was also leaving for the evening. We allowed him to take the first cab and I noted that Holmes took special notice of the address given. Then we hailed a cab for Baker Street. As we rode along, I asked my friend, "Well, did you learn anything? Have you narrowed your half-dozen theories down to a manageable number?"

In reply he tapped my medical bag and said, "I have a strong suspect now, Watson. It all depends on the test results of what is in here."

"So, it is deliberate then? Who's doing it? Whitaker?" I asked.

"All in good time, Watson. We must wait for *Dr. Scott's* test results."

Chapter IV

Once again in our rooms, Holmes retrieved the few samples he had secreted in my bag – two of which, I surprised to see – were small phials of white powder. These he carefully took out and placed on his makeshift laboratory table.

"Where did those come from?" I asked. "The pantry?"

"A moment please," he answered. Holmes then placed some of the powder from one phial in a beaker and added some other chemicals to it to observe the reaction. Then he did the same with powder from the other, which reacted less violently than the first. At last he spoke, "One from arsenic in the pantry and one from a box labeled '*Arsenic*' in Whitaker's closet next to a mousetrap."

"I see," I said. Then after a moment corrected myself, "Actually, I don't see. What is the significance of that?"

He had interlocked his fingers and, with his elbows on the table, was holding his hands under his chin in thought as he replied. "It is not uncommon to cover the bait in mousetraps with arsenic or some other poison, as the creatures quite often snare the tidbits without getting caught. I found it unusual, however, that the box should be left in the closet of Whitaker's room. Why was it there if a cat is on guard? Why wasn't it put away? And why is this particular batch so weak?"

"Do you have a theory as to that?" I queried.

He stood, walked over to the mantel, and stuffed his old clay pipe with tobacco from the Persian slipper, along with the previous day's dottles. Lighting his pipe, he settled into his chair and finally replied, "I must smoke a pipe or two on it, Watson. My findings point toward a theory that seems too fantastic, but still may be the truth, and I need to consider all the factors at hand before pursuing further. I beg you not to speak to me for at least one hour."

I poured myself a brandy and settled down with a cigar and an evening paper, turning the pages as quietly as possible so as not to disturb my friend. Finally, he stood and rushed to the door, throwing on his hat and overcoat. "I'm going out for a bit, Watson. I shouldn't be long, but don't wait up."

I've seen him make these abrupt exits before and have come to accept them as a quirk of his personality. At least this time he acknowledged my presence before departing. As it was now well after ten o'clock, I decided to take myself off to bed in preparation for early morning rounds at Barts the next day. As I drifted off to sleep, all the possibilities that Holmes had enumerated circled about my brain and I attempted to use my observations of the evening to pin down the proper explanation, but sleep came long before an answer.

The next morning, I arose and found Holmes at the breakfast table, ignoring Mrs. Hudson's preparations and opting for just coffee. As I sat with him, I picked out some bacon slices and wrapped them in a warm slice of bread. I poured myself some coffee as well, before finally enquiring, "How did your evening excursion go?"

"Satisfactory for now, Doctor. I've enlisted an ally in our quest, but I also need to conduct more research at the hospital library. Would you mind sharing a cab this morning?"

"Certainly not. You're most welcome. Is there anything that I might be able to answer for you?"

He shook his head slowly, "If my suspicions are correct, the question itself would be beyond the comprehension of most medical men, and would likely not be something that they could answer without conducting the same research, which I shall perform this morning. Thank you, but I would rather not expose you to the dark recesses of the diabolical plot that I fear, until I'm sure of all the facts."

Arriving at the hospital, we went our separate ways. After about two hours, I ran into him again as he was on his way out. Without breaking stride, he merely said, "Pieces are falling into place, Watson. I now have a desire for some Indian cuisine, which I believe shall be best served at the East India Club. I shall meet you back at Baker Street when your shift is done."

The rest of my day, however, was anything but routine. Just after lunch, Mrs. Morgan, accompanied by Bala, was again brought in to an examination room. Her symptoms presented the same as before, though not quite as severe. During my questioning, it occurred to me to ask, "The last time you came in, you said your husband ate the same food as you, but Master Whitaker had a more traditional English meal. Did the same thing occur last night?"

Sensing her mistresses' distress, Bala answered instead, "Yes, Dr. Watson, sir. He came to the kitchen while I was preparing dinner and picked out his own food for me to cook. The same thing happened the other night."

"I see," I said, nodding in thought. "Your husband is feeling no ill effects this time either?"

Clenching her stomach, my patient answered through gritted teeth, "No, he's fine!"

I decided to admit her again overnight with some prescriptions to address her discomfort. As I pondered her situation the rest of the day and considered what I had learned the previous night, it seemed too coincidental that her attacks occurred each time that Whitaker joined them for dinner. Bala's statement that he had been in the kitchen also supported the possibility of an opportunity for him to administer the poison. Given that, and the fact that a box of arsenic was found suspiciously in his closet, a circumstantial case was building against him, though I did wonder why the poison in his room was weaker than that found in the kitchen. Was he only trying to make her sick without killing her? Was he building up a case of long-term exposure that would eventually lead to her demise? Even with his obvious dislike of her, I found it incongruous that the young man I met last night could devise so deadly a plot.

239

Yet, by the time I met up with my companion back at Baker Street, I was convinced that this was the most likely scenario. I expressed my concerns to Holmes as we sat by the fire. He looked at me with a bemused expression, which I thought in poor taste, considering the subject of our discussion.

"Watson, dear fellow, I daresay you have put together a circumstantial case and have not allowed your personal judgement of the man's cordial personality to cloud your judgement of what seem to be incontrovertible facts. For that, I congratulate you."

In spite of the meaning of my conclusions, I found myself momentarily pleased at his acknowledgement of my summation. Then he spoke again.

"You are, however, not in possession of all the facts which I gleaned last night and have leapt to an erroneous conclusion. I take full responsibility for this, in that I did not share everything I learned with you – a habit that I developed long ago, I'm afraid."

My countenance fell momentarily, but rebounded when I realized this meant that young Whitaker was innocent. "Well, who *is* the culprit?" I countered.

Instead of answering immediately, he asked a question of his own. "When do you expect to release Mrs. Morgan from hospital this time?"

I pursed my lips in thought and replied, "Her symptoms are not quite so severe on this occasion. I imagine that she'll be out by tomorrow afternoon. Why?"

Holmes consulted a calendar and finally replied, "Then I believe that we shall have our answer this coming *Sunday*. I have arrangements to make, but that can be done in the morning. I do need you to do one thing for me, Doctor."

He made his request and I protested that such an action would be completely unethical, but he calmed me and stated,

"I assure you, Watson, you will not be performing such a procedure. I just need Mrs. Morgan to *believe* that you will, so she will take that news to her household when she goes home."

"Very well, Holmes," I agreed, reluctantly. "I hope you know what you're doing."

"Always a method to my madness, old chum. For tonight, I suggest a quiet evening enjoying the healthy repast of Mrs. Hudson's roast chicken and a good book."

Chapter V

Come Sunday evening, Mrs. Morgan had been discharged from the hospital for three days and was home again. Holmes left me at Baker Street at about five o'clock with instructions that I should engage a cab and have the driver take me to the Morgan home and wait outside at precisely seven o'clock. I would be joined there at that time by Inspector Lestrade of Scotland Yard. At shortly after seven, Holmes would come out and retrieve us.

I arrived as scheduled and was soon joined by the weasel-faced inspector, who peppered me with questions. "Do you know what he's up to, Dr. Watson? He'd better pray he's not wasting my time on a Sunday evening. I get little enough time off work. All he told me was that he needed me to make an arrest."

I advised the Scotland Yarder of the situation and that Holmes expected to unmask a potential murderer before the deed was done. I also had to admit I did not know precisely who the culprit was, only that it was likely a member of the household or staff.

Lestrade sniffed in displeasure, "Your friend always plays his cards close to the vest. Someday that will cause him more trouble than he can handle."

I attempted to placate the man's mood by offering him a cigarette, but he politely declined and we waited in silence. At about ten minutes past the hour, the butler, Dugan, came out of the house and approached our cab. Seeing me, he announced, "Dr. Watson, your colleague has just announced that he is really Sherlock Holmes, some sort of detective. He requested your presence in the dining room. Is this the police inspector?"

"Yes," I replied. "This is Inspector Lestrade of Scotland Yard."

"Very good, sir. His presence is requested as well. If you will follow me?"

We disembarked the cab and were on Dugan's heels as we entered the house and were shown to the dining room. The scene there was one of dismay and agitation. Bertram Morgan was sitting at his place at the head of the dining table. His plate pushed away and food untouched. The look on his face one of disbelief and shock. Whitaker was standing to the side of the fireplace, fists clenched and face red in anger. Holmes was between the fireplace and the dining table, standing with arms folded and maintaining his calm yet firm disposition. Directly in front of the fire was Mrs. Morgan, looking hot with rage and holding a poker like a cricket bat, as if to stave away any attempt to subdue her. Her eyes flashed from Holmes to Whitaker until she saw us.

"Dr. Watson!" she shouted. "Tell this fool he is insane!"

Lestrade took the lead and stepped forward. "All right then, Mr. Holmes, would you care to explain what's going on? Just who am I here to arrest?"

Before Holmes could reply, the lady of the house pointed at Whitaker and screamed, "Him! He's been trying to kill me! He keeps poisoning my food!"

"Calm down, madam," ordered the inspector. "I'll take all your statements, but first I want Mr. Holmes's explanation."

Knowing that Whitaker was on guard against any movement by his father's wife, Holmes strode over to stand between us and the senior Morgan, still sitting in shock, and began his case.

"When Dr. Watson came to me with his suspicions of the lady being poisoned, I agreed to look into the matter. Certainly Master Whitaker had reason to be rid of his stepmother, but after observing the man, examining the house, and conducting discreet investigations at the East India Club, I was fairly convinced of his innocence.

"But there were troubling issues here in the house itself. Most notably, when I found a box of arsenic in Whitaker's old room, where it did not logically belong."

"See!" cried Mrs. Morgan. "That proves it! He's been the one poisoning me!"

Holmes gave her a look and Whitaker took a step toward her, causing her to raise the poker even higher. She fell silent and the detective continued his report.

"I determined that the box had been planted there, next to the mousetrap so it would appear it was just forgotten. I deduced that the son would not do so, as he was aware that Marmalade was a sufficient deterrent against rodents in that part of the house. However, as with many containers of powdery substances, having been opened and used, there was a slight residue on the outside of the box. Perfect for retaining finger marks. My examination revealed that the marks left behind on this box were far too small to be those of Whitaker Morgan. They were more the size of a woman. The only other woman in the house is Bala, the maidservant and cook. She, however, is of a stout nature with much shorter and fatter fingers than the impressions I found. That left only Mrs. Morgan.

"Chemical tests of the arsenic in that box compared to arsenic taken from the box in the pantry revealed a much weaker strain. One which would cause illness, but not necessarily death, especially to one who had been exposed to arsenic poisoning in her childhood in India."

He looked pointedly at the lady and she lowered the poker and brought her fist to her mouth, where she nervously began biting her hand in fear of being exposed.

"That information I gained through associates at the East India Club, where I also heard rumors of her having a young suitor, before she was married off to Mr. Morgan as part of a business deal."

Now the lady sank to the floor and buried her head in her hands, clearly undone.

I spoke up and asked the obvious, "Do you meant to say she was poisoning *herself*, Holmes? To what end?"

"Her mind has a devious bend, Doctor. Just as in the boxing ring, where I feign injuries as being much more serious than actual, then strike at the opportune time, she made it *appear* as if she were the intended victim. In reality, she planned on using the fatal act as a botched attempt on her life that went awry. She would frame the son for the murder of his father as an attack that was meant for her. Bertram would be dead. Whitaker would be sentenced to either death or life imprisonment, and she would be free to use the Morgan fortune as she chose, likely to return to India where her true love was waiting."

Lestrade then asked, "Obviously the man is still sitting here quite alive, Holmes. Where is your proof?"

"If you will confiscate Mr. Morgan's dinner plate, you will have all the proof you need, for it contains a high concentration of arsenic, hidden by the mixture of spices. But

244

in case you desire more, I witnessed her place the poison in the food myself."

"Impossible!" she shouted, in one last attempt at pleading her innocence.

Holmes turned to me, "Doctor, you recall my saying that I had enlisted an ally to our cause?"

"Yes, you told me that the other day, but didn't say who."

He pointed to Whitaker, "Our friend here was more than eager to help, once I explained my suspicions. He drilled a hole in his closet floor so that I merely had to move an old pair of shoes and I could see directly into the kitchen. He let me in through the back door well before dinner, and I was clearly able to watch her add the arsenic from the full-strength box to her husband's meal while Bala's back was turned."

A groan came up from Bertram and I feared that he might faint, so I went to his side and handed him his wine glass, first ascertaining from Holmes that it was not poisoned as well. Then I asked, "How did you know she would administer the fatal dose tonight?"

"The power of suggestion and manipulation of circumstances, Watson. When I asked you to tell her that if another bout of illness occurred you would need to perform exploratory surgery, it pressed her to action. She could not pull off another weakened attack on herself, so she would have to charge forward with her final move. Of course, it had to be on a night when Whitaker was invited to dinner, so she would have her Judas to blame. I suggested to him to make it known that he was leaving for a three month trip to Europe on business. That set the stage for him to come this evening for a final meal and she, fearing this would be her last chance for months, fell into the trap."

Lestrade stepped forward, took the poker from Mrs. Morgan's hand and pulled her up from the floor. "Dinah

Morgan, I hereby arrest you for the attempted murder of Bertram Morgan. Anything you say will be taken down and used against you. Time to come with me."

He handcuffed her hands behind her back and led her out of the house to the police van that had been waiting since he joined me in my cab. Holmes and I followed with the poisoned dinner plate in a box provided by Dugan. With his prisoner and evidence in hand, the inspector bid us a good evening and directed the driver back to Scotland Yard.

We returned to the house to offer our condolences to the Morgan men. We found the father embracing his son and apologizing profusely. Seeing us, he released Whitaker and came over to shake our hands, taking special effort with my companion.

"Mr. Holmes, I am in your debt. You saved my life and my son. Whatever fee you deem appropriate, please send me your bill."

We took our leave and returned to Baker Street, where we sat with our evening brandies in front of a warm fire. Holmes took out his index book and made a few notes. I also jotted down the facts he had revealed that evening which I have recorded here. It struck me amusing that here were a former army surgeon and an up-and-coming detective, both under the age of thirty, sitting like a couple of old college professors making notes for a lecture. I raised my glass in Holmes's direction and declared, "To you, Mr. Sherlock Holmes! Congratulations on solving a most singular case!"

My friend acknowledged my praise with his own raised glass, "Thank you, Watson, but really, once I had all the facts, it was quite elementary."

"My collection of M*'s is a fine one,"* said he. *"Moriarty himself is enough to make any letter illustrious, and here is Morgan the poisoner . . . ."*

– Sherlock Holmes to Dr. Watson
in *The Empty House*

The Adventure of the
Modest Inspectors
by Derrick Belanger

"The situation is impossible," grumbled Holmes, "and now a killer roams free."

We were sitting by the fire, still in our dressing gowns, enjoying some leisure time on a cool fall morning. My friend had been reading a lengthy piece in *The Telegraph* on the apprehension of eighteen members of the McLeod Gang, a criminal syndicate that had infested Lapham and Battersea. The gang had been using extortion to collect protection fees from businesses. If a business refused to pay, the owner would be severely beaten, often in the streets to be shown as an example to others who might argue about the exorbitant fees. Because of fear of retribution, no one would speak against the tyrants, and so they had been able to work openly. The syndicate had spread their reach across the Thames and were beginning to move into Chelsea.

However, the article explained that none other than Inspector Lestrade had infiltrated the gang. He had taken on a false identity and reported on the criminals' movements to the Force. Somehow, McLeod had gotten wind that there was an informant, so the Yard had to act fast. Using Lestrade's information, the police had captured eighteen of the members of the gang who were holed up in a tenement basement near Chelsea Pier. The villains were taken by surprise and overwhelmed by the Yarders. Miraculously, no one was harmed in the operation.

"I believe you are unfair to the Yard," I countered, "particularly Inspector Lestrade. Surely you can see from the news that he did yeoman's work in infiltrating and bringing down the McLeod gang."

Holmes was sitting in his armchair, his legs stretched out slightly, his hands clutching the paper which he held up blocking his face. He had been muttering about the incompetence of the Yard since he started reading the article. Usually, I concur with my flat-mate's opinion. However, I felt that this was one occasion where the officers deserved praise for their work and continued telling him so.

Upon hearing my remarks, Holmes lowered the paper so that his face was visible to me. His pale cheeks flushed, and his eyes became slits as he examined me, much like an entomologist studies the patterns of an insect. My friend tossed the paper to the floor and stood. He tightened the rope of his purple dressing gown and stepped to the hearth. "Incompetence," my friend muttered to himself. "Pure incompetence." Holmes grabbed some coal and tossed it into the fire. The flames crackled as they began to consume the fuel.

The detective turned from the fire and returned to his seat. "After all I said," he muttered again to himself, ignoring the fact that I was sitting across from him. He picked the newspaper off of the floor, folded it neatly, and put it on the side table. It was not until he had leaned back in his chair, stretched his hands out before him, and settled himself that my friend responded to me.

"Minnows," he said sharply.

"I beg your pardon."

"All that effort just for minnows. They could have had Poseidon!" Holmes hit the side table with his fist. Fortunately, we were done with our tea and no china was there to be smashed. That could have been a last straw for Mrs. Hudson.

I had been living with Holmes for not quite a year, and there had been many times that I thought Mrs. Hudson might have thrown us out on the streets. Between the fumes from Holmes's science experiments, the indoor ballistics tests, and the street Arabs whom Holmes would summon at all hours of the day or night, our landlady would have good reason to send us packing.

I, too, found my good friend trying at times. While his mind was brilliant, his manners were often uncouth – particularly in his interactions with officers of the law. The detective was a perfectionist when it came to solving crimes. Any sign of error – whether it be sheer incompetence or overlooking a trifle – was met with harsh disdain. I had quickly learned in our brief time together that Holmes was an exceptional detective, the best in London and quite possibly the world. Yet anyone that performed beneath him was an amateur in his eyes.

"You are far too harsh on the Yarders. Surely, arresting eighteen criminals is praiseworthy. Besides, McLeod is now the most wanted man in Britain. He may as well be arrested already. He can't extort payments out of businesses anymore. Anyone that he harassed would go straight to the police."

Holmes let out a deep sigh and shook his head. "Watson, you are far too kind in your praise of the Yard, for all they have done is wounded a hydra. Eighteen heads were severed, but more shall grow in their place."

It was now my turn to get angry. "Really, Holmes! Can't you give any credit to the Yard? They've destroyed a horrible crime syndicate, and with McLeod's face in all the papers, he won't be free for long. Lestrade deserves a medal for his work, and I shall tell him that when I commend him the next time that I see him." When I finished talking, my fists were clenched, teeth gritted, and I was shaking from anger.

My friend paused a full ten seconds before responding. He spoke slowly in a soft voice which helped to lower my blood pressure. "I agree that London is safer with those criminals behind bars. But I know McLeod. He is a smart man, Watson. He has escaped the law on several occasions. He will seemingly be trapped and then slip out through some window or door, disappearing into the ether. He has done so again and will continue his crimes from the shadows, extorting businesses through his underlings. He now knows the police are onto him, and he will make certain not to repeat the same mistake twice. If Lestrade had only listened to me, then McLeod would have joined the rest of his gang in irons."

"Listened to you?" I questioned. "Do you mean that you knew of Lestrade's undercover work?"

"They both did," Holmes explained. "Lestrade and Gregson. Had they heeded my advice, worked together instead of against each other, I can assure you that London would be a much safer city for its merchants and proprietors."

"The paper mentioned nothing of Gregson. How was he involved in this operation?"

"Very simply, he *wasn't*, and therein lies the problem." A deep frown etched into the detective's face, and his grey eyes looked distant for a moment as his mind retraced his interactions with the inspectors.

I was baffled. I knew nothing of the details of the matter beyond those provided by the news. "You need to explain this to me, Holmes. I'm scratching my head in puzzlement. How was Gregson involved – or I suppose I should ask, how *wasn't* he involved?"

Holmes stretched his bony fingers before him, allowing them to crack. "It started a few weeks ago. Both men came to me, separately. Both were working different angles of the same case. Lestrade was trying to infiltrate McLeod's gang while Gregson was trying to get some of the gang's victims to become informants. Both were making adequate progress. I know you think me derisive towards the Force, but I do at times respect Gregson's methods and Lestrade's hard work. I advised the two inspectors to combine their efforts. Lestrade could infiltrate the gang while Gregson could get several witnesses lined up for the court trial. It would work perfectly."

"It makes sense," I concurred. "So, what happened?"

Holmes shook his head slightly, a touch of red returning to his cheeks as he explained. "What happened is that the two men had their egos in the way. Lestrade, as always, was eager to prove himself. He wanted the sole credit for capturing McLeod, and to get his name prominently displayed in the newspapers as a hero. Gregson didn't want to be shown up by Lestrade. He couldn't have someone of Breton ancestry showing up a Brit, and so he wanted to infiltrate the gang himself."

"I see. And what did their superiors think of this internal conflict?"

"They feigned disdain at the inspectors. I'm sure they groused and grumbled a bit, and told the two to play nice. However, I know that the Chief Inspector over them concurs with Gregson's opinion of the French. Alas, I fear because of such sentiment Lestrade may end his career as a mere inspector and never advance beyond that rank." Holmes paused for a moment, and I noted remorse in his voice, a sadness that Lestrade would be judged not by his merits but by his ancestry. "The chief also made the mistake of believing that two different approaches to taking down McLeod were better than one – that if one failed surely the other would succeed. I fear the incompetence of the Yard spreads to every level."

"So what happened?"

"Gregson and Lestrade undercut each other, as did their men. Word of the operations became well known in the Force. As you know, Watson, not all officers are honest. McLeod clearly became aware of the movements of the inspectors. I'm sure, to Lestrade's good fortune, McLeod never learned his secret identity amongst his cronies. If he had, I daresay that Lestrade would no longer be walking upon the Earth.

"McLeod did know he had to do something soon to save his enterprise and prevent a rope around his neck. So, he staged a win for the Yard and allowed some of his underlings to be arrested. That way, everybody wins. The Force looks good in the eyes of the public, and McLeod can continue his reign of terror. He will stay in hiding for a few months, and then re-emerge into the light. For now, he shall spend his time in the shadows, continuing to work his operation."

"And this is all because of Lestrade's background? Gregson couldn't work with a Breton?"

Holmes let out one of his odd silent chuckles. "Yes, my friend, though you are giving Gregson too much blame and Lestrade too much credit."

"I feel like you are explaining in riddles today, Holmes. What do you mean?"

"Only that Lestrade's personality and that of Gregson would clash, no matter Lestrade's ancestry. Lestrade always feels that he has something to prove, and he comes across as antagonistic to his colleagues and superiors. He is a good man who pushes others away. Instead of collaboration, his equals are met with condemnation. Gregson, though he calls Lestrade a silly Frenchman, does not have this same contempt for other Bretons in the Yard. It is my belief that if both men were a little less centered on themselves and a little more centered on solving crimes, they would be much better law officers."

"That's too bad," I said with remorse in my voice. "You know, I knew many in the war like those two. Be they officers, soldiers, or fellow medics. Always needing to cut others down to rise in the ranks. It's a tragedy, Holmes. Why, we probably would have won the war much sooner if everyone just worked together."

My friend was about to comment when we heard a commotion from the bottom of the stairs. Mrs. Hudson was yelling about it not being polite to enter a domicile without first knocking. Two familiar voices were arguing with each other. Neither one replied to Mrs. Hudson. Climbing the stairs to our sitting room were none other than Inspectors Lestrade and Gregson.

The two men burst in upon us, unannounced. "I tell you if your men hadn't intervened, then we'd have McLeod in custody!" snapped the mousy-faced Lestrade.

"And I say that your men let him escape!" spat the gruff Inspector Gregson. "He must have walked right past them!"

"Gentlemen, please," said Holmes, standing from his seat and stepping in front of them, making them stop in their tracks.

"Mr. Holmes, Dr. Watson," said Lestrade with a slight bow, remembering his manners. Gregson just nodded. He was enraged from his argument with Lestrade.

"I see you have a bit of a quarrel going on here involving the McLeod gang." I thought Holmes was going to chastise the men for letting McLeod go free, but instead he stayed proper and courteously asked, "How may I be of service?"

"I'm afraid there isn't anything you can do Mr. Holmes," grumbled Gregson, "besides explain to this poor excuse for an inspector that he let McLeod escape from our clutches once again."

"Me!" snapped Lestrade his face turning the color of Mars. "You have some nerve accusing me when I had the man cornered. It was you – *you* – who let the murderer escape! Catching McLeod may be impossible now that he's escaped twice."

"This case was impossible only because *you* were involved in it!" barked Gregson. He held his square handed fist up to Lestrade's face, and I thought we might have a match in our sitting room.

"Gentlemen, please stop your bickering," Holmes pulled Gregson's hand down and pushed the two inspectors away from each other. "You came here for a reason. I may be able to offer some assistance," Holmes encouraged. "You have both brought me what you have said were impossible cases in the past, and I have found that with a slightly different take on the evidence, the solution to those problems was attainable after all."

The two men paused and glared at one another uneasily. Still, they both nodded their heads, conceding that my friend was correct.

"All right, Mr. Holmes," said Lestrade.

"Fine," said Gregson.

"Good, good," smiled Holmes. "Now where shall we begin?"

"With me," answered Lestrade. "And I would have arrested the fiend if it wasn't for him!" Lestrade snapped pointing his finger in Gregson's face.

"Me?" Gregson retorted with a snort. "You couldn't have arrested him if he turned himself in!"

The two then began bickering again, calling each other names, and insulting each other's men.

"Gentlemen, gentlemen, please!" Holmes said, stepping between the inspectors and again pushing them slightly apart. "I can't get anywhere if you keep interrupting each other. Now, Lestrade let me hear you first. Gregson, I ask you to be quiet until Lestrade has finished."

They both cursed each other under their breath but conceded to Holmes's request.

255

"As you know, I had infiltrated McLeod's gang. My guise was that of an Italian named Maroni. Due to my successful effort," Lestrade said haughtily, "we arrested some of the gang's worst members. But I wasn't done with my work yet, Mr. Holmes, for I knew that I could still get McLeod.

"When the police rounded up the criminals, I stayed as Maroni, and I, too, was one of those arrested. I had made a friend of one of McLeod's main underlings, James Davies, a rugged Welshman, who was known for his brutality in enforcing extortion payments. If one of the business owners complained or didn't have the money to pay McLeod's safety fee, they'd be dragged out into the street by the ear and pummeled by Davies' massive fists. The spectacle would shut down any possible rebellion by the others who had yet to pay their protection money.

"While Davies' muscles were strong, his mind was weak. He obeyed orders and didn't ask questions, which is why McLeod liked him. When we were thrown in jail, I made certain that Davies and I were put in the same cell, away from the other gang members. You see, Mr. Holmes, I have my own cunning ways." Lestrade smiled, showing his teeth. With his ferret-like features, he reminded me of an illustration out of a children's book where an animal has been crossed with a man to be more appealing to youth.

"Go on," quipped Gregson, "and get to the part where you lose McLeod."

"If my colleague would keep his tongue still 'til I am finished," insisted Lestrade with a sharp edge to his voice, "then I will get to the part where he stopped me from arresting McLeod."

Gregson was going to comment again, but Holmes held his hand up, motioning him to be quiet and let Lestrade tell his tale. The other inspector would get his turn in a moment.

"May I continue?" asked Lestrade. He was almost taunting Gregson. For his part though, Gregson stayed his anger and just gave a silent nod of his head.

"Well, I knew if I was in a cell with Davies and the others together, I couldn't get Davies to talk. One of the other men would tell him to be quiet, and I'm sure that they would suspect me of being the informant. But being alone with Davies, it was easy to get the giant to speak. I told him that one of the men must have informed the police, and he concurred, cursing and raging at this unknown informant. I told Davies that I feared McLeod would be caught. The giant let out a barking laugh and told me I had nothing to fear, that McLeod was in a safe house in Smith Street. I told Davies that I was still worried, that the police would find him. He told me not to worry, that McLeod was staying with a dentist who was beyond suspicion. McLeod was probably having tea   or something stronger, he joked – while we were sitting in the cell. He also assured me that he was the only one arrested who had any knowledge of McLeod's whereabouts, and he wasn't talking to no one.

"Once I'd tricked Davies into giving me this information, I waited a bit then signaled to our guard. In a quarter-hour, he and several men came and took me out of the cell. They made up some murder I had supposedly committed that they wanted to question me about. It was a good lie, for when I left, I looked back at Davies who was returning my gaze with a look of utter respect."

"Well done, Inspector," Holmes told Lestrade, and my friend meant it. I had never seen my friend look so respectful towards the policeman.

"Thank you, Mr. Holmes," Lestrade replied with a slight bow of his head. "There is more to my story. After gaining the general whereabouts of McLeod, my men and I tracked down the dentist and made a move. We surrounded the house and a small group of constables forced their way in the front door. We didn't anticipate that the dentist and his wife were well-armed savages. The couple and McLeod kept my officers at bay for close to an hour. In the end, my men killed the dentist and his wife, and they wounded McLeod, but in the melee, he managed to escape out a first story window. Fortunately, none of the officers were seriously injured in the conflict."

"That is auspicious," Holmes concurred. "How was McLeod wounded?"

"He took a bullet to his left arm."

"Ah, that would slow the man down."

"One would think, Mr. Holmes, but McLeod is a slippery fellow. We pursued him on foot for several blocks, until he disappeared into an alley behind a row of terrace houses. We had him surrounded. Both ends of the alley were covered, and so the villain burst into the rear entrance of one of the residences. We heard shouting from inside, and then we followed into the back of the house. That's when we found Gregson."

"You found Gregson?" asked Holmes with surprise.

"Yes, Mr. Holmes," Gregson said. It was the tow-headed inspector's turn to continue the narrative. "Coincidentally, the next-door neighbor, a Mrs. Lapham, had reported her husband had gone missing. Constable Reynolds and I were interviewing Mrs. Lapham when we heard a shriek and a call for the police.

"We ran next door, came in the front entrance, and found the missus shouting. She pointed up the stairs and said that a man brandishing a gun had broken into her home. That's when I saw Lestrade and his men as well."

"What happened next?"

Gregson continued. "We both pursued McLeod up the stairs. He had knocked over a bookcase, blocking our path, but it didn't take long to right it. Then we continued all the way up to the roof. We never saw him after that."

"From the roof, did you see any signs of him?"

"We saw traces of blood on the stairwell, but it stopped on the roof. We saw no sign of him running across rooftops. No blood splatters elsewhere. We did a thorough search of the premises, and the surrounding houses. We found no sign of McLeod. It was like he disappeared into the ether."

"Which, as you've said earlier, is an impossibility." Holmes paused for a moment, his eyes looking upward, his brain analyzing the situation. Finally, he asked Gregson, "What do you think happened to McLeod?"

"Why, Mr. Holmes, I think it obvious. He somehow slipped out the back. Climbed down to the alley and escaped."

"Ridiculous!" snapped Lestrade. "I kept a man in the back watching the alley the entire time. Clearly, he somehow escaped out the front of the building."

"And I kept Reynolds out front. That constable is my best man. McLeod could never have escaped past him!"

"And, are you certain he did not leave by entering another residence?" asked Holmes.

"Yes!" both Lestrade and Gregson said together.

"We searched the adjoining homes," continued Lestrade.

"Besides, the residents were at home. They would have seen or heard something," finished Gregson.

Holmes looked serious and thought for a moment. "Are your men still there?" he inquired.

"Yes, I have Reynolds out front," said Gregson.

"And I have a man both on the rooftop and in the alley."

Holmes's lips curled into a slight smile. "Gentlemen, you have acted quite responsibly. I am impressed."

"Then you have an idea of McLeod's whereabouts?" gasped Gregson.

259

"I do."

"Why, then, tell us man!" burst out Lestrade excitedly.

"Just a moment," said Holmes. "I shall give you your answer, but I do have a favor to ask.

"Anything," said Gregson.

"Yes, anything," agreed Lestrade.

"Very good," said Holmes. "To start, you are going to pay for a cab to bring Watson and me to the house that you have under surveillance. If what you have told me remains true, then I know the whereabouts of McLeod. If there has been an error on either of your parts, I am still confident that we shall be able to capture the wounded McLeod fairly easily."

"That is all you request for payment?" asked Gregson. He and Lestrade exchanged looks of puzzlement.

"No, that is not all that I require." Holmes paused and held up a bony pointer finger. "There is one more thing that I shall ask of you both, but I will tell you it once we have captured McLeod."

"Now," said Lestrade, "the whereabouts of McLeod."

"I have to question both of your men first before I know anything for certain," replied Holmes.

We had arrived at the house and found Gregson's man, Reynolds, standing guard out front. Holmes asked if he had seen anything unusual. The constable said that it had been quiet. It was a bit chilly, and so most people were staying in their homes by the fire. A few people had walked by, bundled up, but they had clearly come from one side of the street towards the other. No one had appeared out of a side alley, left through a window, or even walked out of one of the surrounding residences.

After questioning Reynolds, Holmes asked Lestrade and me to step off to the side for a moment while Gregson talked with his constable.

"Do you believe Constable Reynolds?" Holmes asked Lestrade.

Lestrade looked taken aback. "Why, of course. I have no reason to doubt his word."

"Excellent. Then we both agree that Reynolds has done a good job keeping watch over the front of the house."

Lestrade was puzzled. "Yes. I don't see why you'd think I'd doubt the man."

"I just wanted you to acknowledge that Gregson's man did his job. Now, let's move to the back of your house to speak with the constable that you stationed there."

He led us to the rear of the house and gave a similar round of questions to Lestrade's man. Like Reynolds, the officer assured Holmes that he had seen no one enter or leave the back alley. "The only thing I've seen is the light from my cigarette," the constable assured him. "The only way I can stay warm in this blasted cold."

"Thank you, Officer," said Holmes then he turned to Gregson. "May I have a word with you, Inspector?"

Holmes pulled Gregson aside and asked him if he doubted the word of Lestrade's man.

"Not at all," the steel jawed inspector said in his deep voice. "I am sure he is telling the truth."

"Very good," concurred Holmes. "You acknowledge that Lestrade's man kept watch and did his job. I concur."

"Now, are you satisfied?" asked Gregson. "We kept our men posted where we told you, so please enlighten us and tell us the location of McLeod."

"Patience, Inspector." Holmes called Lestrade over and told both men. "I still would like to speak with the lady of the

261

house before drawing any conclusions." Lestrade and Gregson grumbled but acquiesced to Holmes's request. We all went inside and Holmes spoke to the lady, Mrs. Eabourne, who gave an account of the events from her perspective. She had been at home, alone, while her husband, a merchant specializing in spices from India, was travelling on business. Mrs. Eabourne then explained that she saw a man enter her home through the rear entrance. She had never had any issues before and didn't think to keep it locked during the daytime. One additional piece of evidence she provided was that the man was unarmed when he entered.

"Aye, that's very good news, Watson," Holmes said to me. "A wounded man with a gun is very dangerous. One without, particularly with significant blood loss, should be quite easy to capture."

Afterwards, Holmes thanked Mrs. Eabourne for her time and scolded her for keeping her rear door unlocked while her husband was away. He led the inspectors to the house's stairs.

"Now Mr. Holmes, you have questioned both our men and the lady of the house. Could you please be so kind as to tell us the location of McLeod?" Lestrade asked sarcastically.

"Ah, yes," said Holmes. "You have wisely kept the building secure. Without keeping your men posted, I'm sure McLeod would have escaped. Because of your forethought, you two have assured the capture of the notorious criminal. Gentlemen, it is time for me to tell you of the rest of my payment for my services."

Lestrade and Gregson warily eyed one another, wondering what my friend would ask of them. "Go on," said Gregson.

"When we have captured the man, the newspapers will most assuredly speak with you about the arrest," Holmes started.

"Of course, Mr. Holmes. They'll want the rest of the story about how I captured the criminal," boasted Lestrade.

"And instead of giving them that piece of information, you will tell them of Gregson's involvement in the arrest."

"I beg your pardon?" Lestrade said, wide eyed and looking rather offended.

"You heard me, Lestrade," Holmes continued. "You will tell the press how Gregson and his man Reynolds helped you catch the crook."

Lestrade's face had the pained expression of a woman giving birth. But he swallowed hard at Holmes's words, and said dismissively, "Bah! Very well!"

"Excellent," said the detective, a smirk upon his face. Then he turned to Gregson, "And you, Inspector."

"Yes?" Gregson's voice was filled with trepidation.

"You will tell the reporters how Lestrade showed true initiative in capturing McLeod – how, because of his cunning, one of London's most dangerous criminals is behind bars."

Gregson looked as if Holmes had asked him to sign away his soul. The inspector murmured a bit under his breath, but acquiesced at the request.

"Good. Very good." Holmes was beaming with pride over sealing this gentlemen's agreement.

"Now, Mr. Holmes," Lestrade practically begged, "would you kindly tell us the location of McLeod?"

"Yes, let us away to the rooftop. All shall be revealed there."

We climbed the stairs to the exit upon the roof. It was a flat, square gravel roof with several drains upon the sides to prevent flooding. Lestrade's other man, a short officer, stood outside, his arms clutched around his sides, trying to keep warm. Holmes beckoned for the officer to join us and once

263

again made certain that the constable had seen nothing suspicious since he was guarding his post.

"All right, Mr. Holmes, where's the criminal?" barked Gregson.

"Gentlemen, I believe it is time to reveal the location of the villain," Holmes began. "McLeod is a wiry man, capable of hiding in many small places."

"But we searched the premises," Gregson interrupted.

"Please, permit me to finish. I believe you searched every corner of the home and the residences nearby."

"That is correct," answered Lestrade.

"Very good," said Holmes. "Then there is but one place left where you will find McLeod."

"Where?" they asked together.

"The droplets of blood on the rooftop indicate that McLeod is still here."

"But you heard my man, Mr. Holmes. He saw no one up here, and he heard nothing suspicious."

"Follow me," Holmes motioned.

Holmes led us all to the small brick chimney flue on the North side of the roof. While smoke was billowing out of the chimney on the South side of the building, this one was not in use. I surmised that it connected to Mrs. Eabourne's bedchamber in the first floor. Since she wasn't using it, there was no reason to waste the wood heating it.

"You believe the scoundrel to be down there?" asked Gregson, a look of shock on his face as he spoke what we were all just coming to realize.

"Of course," said Holmes. He was looking fully into the darkness of the chimney. I did the same, and could see nothing. "MacLeod is a wiry man. Some of his past encounters escaping the law indicate that he is good at slipping through a small window," Holmes paused and used his arms to measure the dimension of the flue. "It is as I thought, about a square foot. Just wide enough for McLeod to slither down. With your man on the roof Lestrade, and Mrs. Eabourne in her home, someone would have heard the man come down the chimney or make an exit. I'm sure he is still down in that hole."

"There's an easy way to test your theory," I told my friend, and I reached down and grabbed a fistful of grit from the rooftop. I tossed it into the hole and waited a second. Then we all heard the echo of a small cough.

The next morning as we breakfasted, Holmes was in a jolly mood. The morning edition had a lead article about the capture of the notorious criminal MacLeod. The villain was in extremely poor health when he was finally pulled from his chimney hideaway. Sallow and pasty faced from excessive blood loss and the bitter cold, he was barely conscious when the police had him in custody. He was being treated for pneumonia, though I wondered if it was worth the doctor's time, since MacLeod would most certainly recover, only to find his neck broken by a rope.

What caused Holmes to have high spirits, however, were the article's quotes from Lestrade and Gregson. Lestrade said how he couldn't have caught McLeod without Gregson's support, and Gregson said that Lestrade had the brains behind the operation. The article concluded by saying, "*The citizens of London can rest easy knowing such modest inspectors as Lestrade and Gregson are on the Force.*"

The Case of the
Melancholic Widow
by Deanna Baran

Although Holmes's name is now a byword throughout our fair Island, the Continent, and beyond the farthest reaches of our Empire, I recall the lean and obscure days of our early association. His great intuition and observation allowed him to earn his bread and cheese, as it was, but Fame had not yet spread his repute far beyond certain circles within London. Between the remuneration from his clients and the limits of my pension, we were in no danger of actual want, but it is human nature to chafe at the restrictions of one's pocketbook. Thus it was that once my health allowed me, I lost little time in easing myself into practice, taking on light hours at St. Bartholomew's surgery at first, and then accepting what *locum* work came my way as my strength returned.

It was within the teaching hospital that I encountered a former colleague of mine, who now had a civil practice along Lupus Street, and had stopped in for a personal errand. He recognized me, and we spent a good number of minutes catching up on the state of his practice, his wife's precarious health, and congratulating him upon their newly-born twins. It happened that we were standing in a public place, and Holmes had chosen this day to visit those great halls. Naturally, I hailed him and introduced him to Finch, not quite sure of the extent to which their paths had previously crossed.

"I have heard your name, though I have not ever had the pleasure of meeting you in person," said Finch, shuffling his burden of a book and a bottle to his left hand and extending his right. "Still haunting the pathology laboratory, I presume? What experiments are you running today?"

"Dr. Finch," acknowledged Holmes. "No, today I planned to visit the library to transcribe a few pages of *specilegia* for my own personal notes. I'm sorry that your wife is unwell."

"Ah, you must have heard us discussing it?" I asked, although I knew better. Holmes merely smiled and allowed the comment to pass without explanation.

Finch nodded somberly. "Indeed. You will understand my wife has been a delicate creature since childhood. It is painful to be away from home so much during this critical time, but you understand the demands upon a professional man."

"Patients do not cease to be ill merely because it is inconvenient for us to attend," I sympathized. "But surely you could find someone to stand in for you for a few days, until you feel more secure regarding your family's well-being."

"In a normal time, I would, and for the most part, I have," said Finch. "However, there is one case in particular of which I can make neither heads nor tails. I hesitate to refer it to anyone without being clear as to what, exactly, is occurring. A burn patient, *chincough*, a case of gangrene – the treatments are straightforward enough to trust anyone and not worry a moment whether my patients are in good hands. And those, I've just now entrusted to Morley. He's a reliable man, as you well know. But Mrs. Mellor – I suppose it's my own distraction that prevents me from seeing the obvious, but frankly, I'm baffled, and hardly know where to begin, despite having dedicated my energies upon her case for the last eighteen months. It is fortunate she is well-off, for this mystery illness would have drained anyone else's purse with all the failed cures we've attempted."

I glanced at my friend Holmes. I knew he was anxious to get on with his research in the hospital library, but was lingering for the sake of courtesy.

"Perhaps you should describe the case to me," I said, a silent glimmer of challenge in my eye. Holmes's deductions regarding hats and eye-glasses and trouser-knees were fine enough as they were, but the inscrutable mysteries of the human anatomy should remind him of humility! "Perhaps an idea may occur to us, when you put your observations into words."

Finch consulted his pocketwatch. "Perhaps you're right," he said. "Mr. Mellor made his fortune in printing pleated-paper boxes for manufacturers. He died almost two years ago, and Mrs. Mellor has suffered from lethargy ever since. It's a normal enough thing – you lose a beloved spouse, and life is never the same afterwards." His voice caught slightly. "But it goes beyond mere common melancholy or low spirits. Headaches. Dizziness. Confusion. Shallow respiration. Not all at once, mind you, nor all the time. It comes and it goes. Some days she is nearly her ordinary self, and other days, she is very poor indeed.

"I've recommended three or four different specialized diets that have previously given good results for female patients. I've given regimens of rest and relaxation and shower-baths. But no degree of country air or country diet has had any permanent, lasting benefit. Perhaps I ought to prescribe Blandford's regimen of alcohol-and-opioids. You know the thing – rum and milk in the morning, sherry at dinner, port at supper, ale and chloral at bed-time."

"Have you considered the curative properties of exercise?" I inquired.

"Neither hunting nor fishing nor hiking nor boating nor travel have provided any permanent cure," he said. "She spent six weeks taking the waters at Bath, and suffered impaired consciousness – the local physician wondered if it was apoplexy. That troubling experience has rather discouraged her from traveling too far afield since."

"I can understand that."

Holmes inquired, "Has she always been like this? Melancholic, languid, vexed by aches?"

"On the contrary," replied Finch, "she has always been a spirited woman. She and her husband both came from solid country stock. They saved enough to purchase a failing printing press operation in London and made a respectable fortune themselves. She was energetic enough to work at her husband's side when they had little to spare for wages, and she was healthy enough to give him six sons, now all grown to adulthood. The eldest has stayed on to work the presses and continue the family business. Another son is a country vicar assigned to a small northern village. Two are in the Navy: One in Ceylon, and the other in one of the colonies somewhere around Jamaica. One son is in the Army, stationed at Bombay. The youngest is an articled clerk in Dover. They're all hale, hearty, and successful, each in his own way. Not one of them has caused her a moment's sorrow, to the best of my knowledge."

"On the contrary!" remarked Holmes. "How distressing that, of all her six sons, not one of them seems to have stayed close at hand to encourage her during her period of grief and bring solace to her mourning! Instead, one tends his flock but neglects his parent, another supervises the business but is inattentive to his mother. Two are in Asia, and another to the Caribbean, and a third practically in France!"

"And she would have it no other way!" said Finch, his spirits momentarily rising as he parried this thrust. "For, out of her benevolence, she has taken on a companion-secretary, a poor niece, the daughter of her own brother. He lacked the good business sense of his sister and brother-in-law, and instead became the dupe of swindlers, lost what little he had, and died without a farthing to leave to his offspring. Mrs. Mellor took her in six years ago and gave her employment filling orders and bookkeeping at the factory. For the last two years, however, since the onset of illness, Miss Glover has hardly left her side, except in the course of her ordinary duties, which take her to and from the factory to deliver her aunt's messages and instructions. Otherwise, she has dedicated herself wholeheartedly to the courageous and selfless nursing of her aunt! Little did that woman know how her kind charity would be repaid when she took in her poor relation!"

"But surely Miss Glover will eventually tire of wasting her youth in nursing an invalid," objected Holmes. "Perhaps you ought to prescribe an attendant from one of the large nursing institutions, and give Miss Glover a reprieve from her own self-sacrifice. Especially if, as you say, her aunt's fortune can withstand the additional expense."

"It gives Miss Glover pleasure to be of service. She possesses a generous spirit. I shouldn't like to upset the household more than it already has been by this insidious illness. Mrs. Mellor would object to the substitution of a mere hireling for her trusted companion, and I genuinely believe Miss Glover derives a greater amount of satisfaction in the opportunity to repay her aunt's initial gracious gesture."

Holmes appeared to have abandoned the point, for he merely inquired, "And does Mrs. Mellor have any grandchildren in which she may take some delight?"

"The three military sons are unmarried, as is the articled clerk. The vicar is married, but they have no offspring. There had been great expectations for several years for the eldest to marry Miss Glover, but instead, he took up with a young widow in millinery and married her a few months before Mr. Muller's final illness. They are also childless as of yet."

"We seem to be drifting from the patient into the realm of gossip," I said. "I would hardly think that her son's love life or a lack of grandchildren would manifest itself today as confusion and shallow respiration. Perhaps it is not a physical ailment, but is more mental in nature. You ought to find a good alienist to examine her."

"On the contrary," said Holmes. "My dear Doctor, you have some time upon your hands, and I can see that you are anxious to do what you can for your colleague, so that he may attend to his own personal circumstances."

I felt ashamed, for I had almost forgotten why we had begun discussing Finch's patient in the first place.

"If, as you say, Morley is already engaged as your *locum* for your other patients, I would be more than pleased to offer you my own services to allow you time with your family," I said. "If you will authorise me to practice in your stead for such time as you determine, I will see what I can do for Mrs. Muller."

"I could hardly impose upon you, Dr. Watson – "

"I insist! No harm will come of it, and perhaps some good," I said, with more confidence than I felt. "If you will set it all down in writing – "

Thus it was that I acquired a new patient. Holmes, however, insisted on accompanying me in the guise of my assistant, under the name of Osborne. We took the train by way of Victoria Sloan Square to that district of London to which the socially optimistic refer as "South Belgravia", but the less-elastic mapmakers label as Pimlico.

As we passed the streets and squares, I said, "By-the-by, Holmes, how did you know of Mrs. Finch's poor health?"

271

"Although both were black patent leather, did you observe that his boots were not of a pair?" Holmes inquired. "There could be any number of explanations for such carelessness in a doctor – for the fact he was a doctor, of course, was self-evident. He may have been hastily roused to attend an emergency. He may have something occupying his mind. He may have dressed in the dark. And when I see a doctor carrying a bottle of ergot alkaloid, it is true that it may have been obtained on behalf of anyone in London, although the patient is most generally a woman in childbed. But did you happen to note the title of his book?"

"I can't say that I did," I said. "I think it was brown. Possibly reddish-brown."

"It's a popular manual right now that was issued by one of the ladies' housekeeping journals," explained Holmes. "It includes several essays on home management for families of a particular range of income. How to manage one's cook. How to manage one's nurse-maid. How to manage one's offspring. A primer for domestic economy. Now, why would a man of his age have a sudden enough interest in the running of his household to justify the purchase of a popular book on the topic?"

"It's no crime for a man to be interested in the mechanics of his own household, seeing that his wages are what allows it to run," I said.

"Indeed, you are correct," said Holmes. "There are various explanations that come to mind. Perhaps he has a young wife who doesn't know how to manage a household of that caliber. Yet his wedding-ring was not new, as his finger had been smaller at the time of its original purchase. Perhaps he has a wife who is unable to keep within her budget, and requires additional education in economising. Perhaps his wife merely requested it as a useful present or a resource, and he was solicitous enough to purchase it personally for her, rather than having her delegate the item to the servant's marketing list. But perhaps his wife is usually the one to interact with servants, with the housekeeper, with the cook, with the wet-nurse, or with whomever their domestic staff consists, but she is unable to do so at this moment in time, and the unfamiliar burden has shifted upon his own shoulders. A doctor, anxious to consult an authority upon domestic mysteries in a discreet manner, would naturally turn to – where? This, in conjunction with other small signs, was the situation I mentally conjured as I approached and observed the scene *in toto*: A medical man in distress over his wife's difficulty in child-bed, with no prospect of her returning to her usual duties in the near future. Yet both his hat-band and cravat were a green paisley silk. Had he actually been left a recent widower, black would have been the more appropriate colour."

"Clear as day, once you explain it, Holmes!" I said.

"As ever. By the way, Doctor, when you attend your patient, I pray you pay close attention to the colour of her fingernail-beds, and possibly her lips. If my hypothesis is correct, they will have a distinct bluish tinge."

The address was in a square surrounded by tasteful edifices equipped with modern amenities, neither ostentatiously vulgar nor unduly economical in appearance, although it was clear from Finch's description that the occupants could have afforded far more fashionable quarters. We were expected, and were shown promptly to the sick-room, where the patient lay weakly in the shadows of close-drawn drapes, a damp cloth upon her forehead, her companion seated nearby and embroidering upon a hoop.

"I pray, do not strain your eyes," said Holmes solicitously, opening the drapes to allow daylight to penetrate the chamber.

"Oh, but Auntie does have such constant head-aches," said Miss Glover. "I wouldn't dream of aggravating them by allowing her to rest in a sunny room."

It was no wonder that Mrs. Mellor suffered from head-aches, I thought. The room was close and stuffy and heavily scented with patchouli.

"We'll close them soon enough," said Holmes kindly. "But the doctor needs light for his examination as well."

"Thank you, Osborne," I said, rather self-consciously, before turning to the patient and settling down to business. It was the first time that he had ever accompanied me on my own endeavours in a professional capacity, and, for natural reasons, it has rarely occurred since. However, I soon forgot my audience as I began the usual routine of questions and answers, examination and consideration.

I undoubtedly would have noted it myself, even had Holmes not drawn my attention to it beforehand, but Mrs. Mellor's nail-beds indeed had a distinctly blue cast to them. I glanced at Holmes. He had observed them as well. With a meaningful glance, he drew my attention to Miss Glover. I dropped my eyes to her own hands, which still busied themselves amongst her embroidery silks. Discernable in the natural light, her fingertips were tinged with the faint lingering stains of purple ink, although the smudges were old enough that they did nothing to mar her careful handiwork. I turned my attention back upon my patient and continued my diligent queries, taking careful note of her symptoms. Miss Glover was anxious to be of assistance, and was very thorough in making sure Mrs. Muller's case history was related in exhaustive detail. A cynic may have interpreted her contributions as, perhaps, being more of an exhaustive case history of Miss Glover's own attentiveness and sacrifice, but I felt sympathy towards the poor creature, and decided it was only human to desire credit where credit was due. I complimented her diligence perhaps more than was necessary, and she was plainly pleased by the attention.

Holmes, on the other hand, had long since wearied of our joint consultation. I allowed him a few opportunities to contribute his own line of questioning, but he merely asked, "How often do your sons visit you, Mrs. Muller?"

"Most of them are abroad, doing sundry and various," said Mrs. Muller, looking petulant at the reference to her isolation. "Theophilus is the only one who has remained within London, and ever since he married, poor Teddy rarely visits beyond Christmas and Easter. If Lottie didn't run messages back and forth from the factory, I wouldn't know a thing about the circumstances of his life these days. Or the status of the business, either, for that matter."

Beyond that, he had remained silent. Perhaps it was the tiresome dwelling upon aches and pains, which is frequently a tedious subject for healthy men to suffer through, or perhaps the patchouli was giving him a head-ache of his own.

"Osborne," I said, as soon as the conversation lulled and a sufficient pause presented itself, "there are a number of salient points which I wish to discuss with you in private in order to obtain your opinion. Mrs. Muller, is there a place to which we may retire and discuss the particulars of the best course of treatment?"

"Most certainly," said Mrs. Muller. Turning to Miss Glover, she said imperiously, "Lottie, take them to the library."

She leapt up, ever obliging, and led us down a short corridor into a cool, shadowy room lined with books. The volumes were clean and dustless, but the room gave the impression of an empty stage-set rather than a place that saw much use. However, there were several comfortable seats, and

Miss Glover waved us to them before she turned to go. However, Holmes beckoned to her to join him.

"Miss Glover," he said, "You are a bright young woman. Do you ever miss your days bookkeeping at the factory? Being amidst the bustle of London, and reigning over your office realm?"

"Oh, no," she said. "It's nice to be of use wherever I'm most useful, if that makes sense. At one time, I could help with the books. Now, I'm more needed at home by her side, and I'm happy to remain there. I'm happy to go where I can do the most good. It brings me joy, even when the circumstances are grim or the hours long."

"That's very self-sacrificial of you," said Holmes, and she preened beneath the compliment. "You've been with Mrs. Muller since the onset of this anguish. Have you a hypothesis as to how it all began?"

"I expect it was a condition she may have always had," said Miss Glover thoughtfully. "Except, perhaps, when she was married, and building her life, and building her business, and building her family, she never noticed it. But when her children grew and left home, and the business was able to run without her, and her husband passed away, then perhaps a lifetime of melancholy caught up to her all at once, and has prostrated her ever since."

"Ah! So you would prescribe matrimony for Mrs. Muller, then? Or a new business venture?"

"Oh, no, I didn't mean that!" exclaimed Miss Glover quickly. "No, I think that would be a very poor idea. Because, you see, now she is a wealthy widow. She would never be able to know the difference between a man who loved her for herself, versus a mere fortune-seeker, with which I expect London is teeming."

"No quarrel with you there," agreed Holmes. "I suppose the easiest test would be whether or not her future husband had more money than she did. If she married a man who was wealthier than she, then she would know he had married down out of love, not for fortune."

"This conversation is becoming rather vulgar rather quickly," said Miss Glover. "I don't believe I care to continue along those lines. Although the obvious counter-argument would be, of course, that a man with a greater fortune than she had would worry that Auntie was the fortune-seeker . . . and I have no doubt London is equally full of adventuresses as it is of their male counterparts."

"Full of adventuresses who are far younger and more attractive than Mrs. Muller," agreed Holmes cheerily.

Miss Glover stared at him coldly, then moved to withdraw.

"I shall leave you to your consultation with your colleague."

"No, I insist, this is to be a three-way consultation," said Holmes. "I implore you to stay. You have been the constant in Mrs. Muller's sad and lonely path since the onset of her illness, and you undoubtedly have made valuable observations. Dr. Finch is a fine doctor, just as Dr. Watson is a fine doctor, but had he paid more attention to your thoughts upon the matter, I'm sure the situation would have made far more progress by this point. I don't intend to allow us to make the same mistake. I pray, please posit your hypothesis regarding the situation."

Miss Glover visibly warmed beneath the kind speech, and relenting, came to join us.

"I've noticed," she began hesitantly, "that Mrs. Muller's symptoms appear to improve and decline upon a fairly regular pattern. Perhaps every month?" Her voice lilted at the end, in an uncertain question. "Within those four or five weeks, she

277

might spend a week or two in moderately good health, and she may spend part of a week in perfect misery, and the remaining time may be either spent in decline or in recovery. Last week, she was in complete anguish, but the past few days, she's recovered enough for broth and is progressing towards heavier fare. I expect within the next three or four days, her headache will relent, her appetite will fully recover, and things will be normal for a while longer. And then it will begin again."

I frowned. "Mrs. Muller is not within the usual age limits you would expect for ordinary female problems. And her symptoms are not the usual symptoms one associates with – " I began, but Holmes waved me to silence.

"What an excellent diagnosis," said Holmes. "Now, I shall make a wager with you, Miss Glover. Oh, don't worry, I'm not making a vulgar proposition again. Now, listen. My hypothesis is this: When your aunt gets better with this next cycle of illness, there will be no reoccurrence of the usual symptoms when the time comes for the next go-round. Do you comprehend?"

"I'm afraid I don't," said Miss Glover, looking startled at this turn of conversation.

"Then allow me to speak more plainly," said Holmes. "Dr. Watson is going to leave you a receipt for a curative soup, if you don't already have one of your own. It will merely be an ordinary broth, and nothing else. You, with your own hands, will daily prepare and serve this curative soup for the next fortnight. At the end, Mrs. Muller will find herself to be cured. Do you know why she will be cured?"

"I'm afraid I don't," repeated Miss Glover.

"Because she is suffering from aniline poisoning," said Holmes seriously. "Symptoms include cyanosis, the blue coloration of the skin and lips. Sufferers deal with dizziness, confusion, lethargy, headaches, and other trials. When the dosage is strengthened, those who suffer from aniline poisoning risk convulsions and coma and death. Did you know something else about aniline poisoning?"

"I don't know anything about aniline poisoning."

"Indeed. After death, an autopsy will discover the blood has the color of chocolate. An autopsy will discover kidney damage. An autopsy will examine the bladder, and discover little ulcers with decayed tissue in them. And then there will be no doubt at all. Does that sound nice?"

"It doesn't sound nice at all," she shuddered.

"Poisoning is never nice," said Holmes. "Especially long-term, chronic exposure to poison. Now, after Mrs. Muller's death, and after her body has been examined by the coroner to ascertain its causes, the Good Doctor and I will step forward. We will testify that, upon this day, we ascertained from her own lips that her own sons, who stand first to inherit and would be naturally most suspect, have generally absented themselves from the maternal domicile for the last few years. Three of them are abroad, in Her Majesty's service, in service to the Empire. Another is in Dover, surrounded by law books. One son is daily tending his flock in a little village. There are dozens of reliable persons who will vouch for their daily movements. The only one who has remained in the immediate vicinity has not visited since Easter, and then before than, was last here at Christmas. Hardly a frequent enough visitor to poison someone on a monthly basis, and possessing neither access nor opportunity to taint food or drink."

Miss Glover merely looked at Holmes.

"At the same time, the Good Doctor and I will testify that upon this day, we ourselves saw the mark of purple aniline ink upon your fingers. Faded, but still present, despite diligent hand-scrubbing. I presume you obtain your samples of aniline upon your regular errands to the factory. It isn't a difficult thing to steal, if one has the mind to. It is a bit oily, granted, but it isn't a difficult thing to administer, either topically or internally, depending on how one goes about it.

"However, that information will only come to light in the case of your aunt's continued ailment, or in the case of her unexpected demise. I would much prefer to return home, check in weekly on your aunt's progress, hear your praise upon your aunt's lips, and discover that the curative broth has worked its wonders. And when Dr. Finch resumes his attendance, he will be amazed to discover that all is well, and his services are no longer needed."

She held his eye. "I expect the soup shall perform as expected."

"Most excellent. Watson, a prescription. Shin of beef soup. I expect you are familiar with its preparation?"

"I am."

"I'm sure it will do. Doctor, let us proceed to inform Mrs. Muller of this *Wunderheilung* which we are leaving in Miss Glover's capable hands. This course of treatment shall begin today."

It was not until we were ensconced within a cab, rattling our way back to Baker Street, that we had our next opportunity in which to communicate privately.

"That was a bold move," I remarked. "It seemed to be very precarious reasoning, indeed! Purple ink!"

"It had to be bold," replied Holmes sedately. "I would far prefer to prevent a death by poisoning than to catch and punish a murderess. I do not think that Mrs. Muller's life was actively in danger, except through an accidental miscalculation on Miss Glover's part. Such a thing may have happened at Bath, or perhaps it was on purpose, to make a point. I do not know, but her intent is of no import."

"How did you come to deduce that it was a poisoning in the first place, rather than an ordinary malady?" I asked.

"My dear Watson, if a patient tells you, 'I have red spots', do you not begin a process of deduction yourself? Are pimples the same as measles? If a man tells you, 'I have a rash', are you not capable of discerning between one who has grown overly warm, versus a man suffering from pox? Any number of things might cause a headache. Any number of things might cause shallow respiration. Any number of things might cause confusion. Any number of things might cause lethargy. But when taken as the sum of its parts, instead of a hodge-podge of miscellaneous aches and pains, one calls to mind aniline, and looks for confirmation of one's hypothesis."

"But what motive on earth would have led Miss Glover to deliberately torment her aunt at such lengths? She must have hated her, despite the goodness shown her."

"I do not think hatred entered into it at all," said Holmes. "It may be that she achieved a psychological benefit from it. Or perhaps her actions had more of a financial motive behind them. Either could be argued. On the one hand, you have the poor relative who was taken in on charity, and now is indispensable. Her aunt constantly relies upon her. The doctors see her and marvel at her self-sacrifice. Did you not observe how she fed upon praise like a cat upon cream? On the other hand, you have a wealthy widow. She will not live forever. But her possessions will be divided six ways. Would she rob her own children by creating a seventh division? Or does she expect her niece be grateful for the bounty she enjoys during her lifetime, with no expectation of additional benefits from beyond? If you were a young woman in such a precarious situation, what would you do? You would look to marry well to secure your future, and cousin-marriage is not unheard of. But of the eligible brothers of the household, the one she

281

thought the likeliest and pinned her hopes upon ended up marrying another. She could not secure her share of the fortune by marrying it directly, but she could increase her chances of reward by creating a situation whereby she would earn years of gratitude from the matriarch. I do not think it a coincidence that the poisoning began not only after the death of her husband, but also after the marriage of the eldest son."

"How cold-blooded of her, if you put it like that," I said.

"Regardless of the specifics of her motive, it was plain enough to see, and she was the only one with opportunity, presuming that Mrs. Muller was not afflicting herself for the sake of attention. That was made clear in the absence of her sons: A lonely woman craving notice is hardly likely to be content with the mere attention of a poor niece, and she would have found a way to insist upon additional attendants. Likewise, in my search for suspects, it was relatively easy to disregard the servants, as the most serious wave of her illness occurred while she was away at Bath."

"There is suffering enough in this world without having people artificially inflicting it upon each other," I remarked. "Speaking of which, I wonder how Mrs. Finch is progressing through her own crisis. It can be daunting for a physician to tend those closest to him."

"Regardless, Dr. Finch will be pleased to remove this other patient from his burden," said Holmes, with a gleam of something akin to humour. "When he marvels at the miraculous results you have obtained, you must take care to remain humble, for fear of treading the path Miss Glover so recently walked."

Angelique
by Mike Hogan

Billy opened the door and gasped. "Thank goodness you're here, Doctor."

I hung my hat, scarf, and coat on the hall stand and handed the boy a package tightly wrapped in oilcloth and string. "To be placed on a high shelf in the scullery and not touched until I request it."

Billy took the package and offered me our correspondence tray with a trembling hand. I considered the telegram on the tray for a moment before pocketing it and climbing the stairs to the sitting room, one hand on the bannister and the other holding my cane. Just over a year or so after suffering my wound, I still found myself a trifle unsteady on chill and windy days.

I stepped carefully around our maid Bessie sitting on a step halfway up and sobbing with her head in her pinafore. Then I paused as I heard contentious voices and a shrill cry.

"You oppress me with your unwanted attentions, Madam. Begone!"

Mrs. Hudson thundered down the stairs carrying a food tray, cheeks aflame and apoplectic beyond speech. I stopped her and relieved the tray of a steaming mug of beef tea. "Deep calming breaths," I advised our landlady. "And if Mr. Holmes does not want that slice of buttered toast, I will claim it, as I missed breakfast." I balanced the side-plate on the mug. "Might I trouble you for a cup of coffee – in your own time, of course."

Mrs. Hudson leaned towards me and murmured. "We were wondering about knock-out drops, Doctor. To give the household a few moments of blessed peace."

I smiled and continued carefully up to our sitting room, where I ate the toast before I opened my medical bag, retrieved my thermometer, and tapped on my fellow-lodger's bedroom door. I heard a low groan that I interpreted as permission to enter.

"How are we this sharp, windy morning?" I asked, peering into the dimly lit room.

Sherlock Holmes blinked at me from where he lay in bed, propped up by pillows, with a night light on the table beside him. He opened his mouth, but before he had a chance to form a reply, I stepped across to his bed and inserted my thermometer under his tongue.

He mumbled a low groan.

"Tut, tut, Holmes," I said. "I was away a scant hour and you have alienated the affections of our landlady, maid, and even our pageboy, whom I had thought impervious to human emotion."

I held up the steaming mug of beef tea and placed it on the bedside table.

Holmes gargled a remark I couldn't catch.

I removed the thermometer and peered at the scale in the candlelight. "A touch higher." I smiled a bright smile, soaked a linen cloth in a basin of water, and dabbed Holmes's brow. "I predict our fever will break tonight, or early in the morning, as is inevitably the case. Another nice bolus from the chemist will help it along."

"'Our' fever?" Holmes grimaced. "You are most welcome to your share."

"And as a treat for luncheon," I continued, "I'm having an eggnog made up. I have permitted a dash of sherry."

Holmes grimaced again. "I loathe eggnog."

"Just sit up now and let me auscultate you once more."

I listened through my stethoscope as I thumped Holmes's back. "Nothing amiss."

I sat in the chair by the bed, beamed at my patient, and handed him the mug of beef tea. "We'll have you skipping around in two shakes of a lamb's tail, or no more than three."

Holmes glared at me, but he accepted the tea. "I heard the doorbell earlier."

I adopted an innocent expression. "Did you?"

"The telegraph boy. I know his ring. Give."

I leaned back in my chair. "You must understand that I act not as your fellow-lodger, but as your doctor." I wagged an admonishing finger. "And you must obey doctor's orders."

"In ancient Rome, doctors were considered lower than barbers on the social scale, utterly without imperium of any kind," Holmes said fiercely. "And you impede Her Majesty's mails. I could have you taken in charge by a constable without the necessity of obtaining a warrant. Give it here." He put his mug down and attempted to heave himself out of bed, but subsided, breathing heavily. "I am weak as a kitten."

"I must insist that you remain calm, Holmes. No excitement is the rule. You must be placid while Nature, with what help I may offer, takes her course."

Holmes glared at me and again attempted to wrench back the bedclothes.

"Very well, if you absolutely insist." I stood. "With your permission, I will open the telegram and if it is not too stimulating, I will read it to you."

Holmes waved a limp hand.

I ripped open the envelope and frowned at the telegram flimsy. "The writer begs leave to call here at eleven in the morning. It's signed 'Lestrade'."

"A case." Holmes smiled. He lay back and sipped his beef tea.

I checked my watch. "It's almost eleven."

The doorbell rang on cue, and I heard Billy usher a visitor up the stairs and into the sitting room. I slipped out of Holmes's bedroom, closing the door behind me.

The pale-faced police agent who had visited the house several times in the nine months or so since Holmes and I had lodged together in Baker Street warmed his coattails before our sitting room fireplace and flicked through a thin, official-looking file. Our page stood by him in his too-big buttons uniform, looking apprehensive.

"Ah, Doctor," Inspector Lestrade said. "The boy tells me Mr. Holmes is unwell. Nothing serious, I hope."

"While I should not put it past Mr. Holmes to have contracted something unknown to medical science, I believe that he is suffering from influenza, or a touch of the bronchials, no more. It's going around."

"Carried on this equinoctial gale, I make no doubt. We've half the Yard on the sick list. Our offices at Whitehall are damp and draughty, worse than the Clink. There's talk of shifting us to new premises, but it never comes to aught." Lestrade frowned at a muffled cry from the bedroom. "My business is with Mr. Holmes, Doctor."

I sorrowfully shook my head. "And yet, the malady is so very contagious."

Lestrade blinked at me.

"I would not attempt to hinder the solemn processes of the Law, Lestrade," I continued, "but if you really must enter the sickroom, I insist you on no account excite my patient, and were I you I would cover my nose and mouth with my handkerchief. As a physician, I am protected by my Hippocratic Oath."

I led the reluctant detective into Holmes's bedroom.

"A missing person, in suspicious circumstances, Mr. Holmes," he said through his handkerchief.

"What? What?" Holmes barked. He lay back, his hand to his forehead and gasped. "Speak up and take off that silly mask."

Lestrade blinked at me, and I shrugged.

"A missing person, Mr. Holmes." Lestrade said, removing his kerchief. He consulted his notebook. "Mr. Berenger, the manager of Jay's, the big haberdasher's on Oxford Street, was interviewed by a local inspector at his house in Fulham a week or so ago regarding the disappearance of his wife, Angelique, and then again by me this morning. Both Mr. and Madame Berenger are from Jersey in the Channel Islands. They were married there four years ago, coming then to London to set up their household by Saint Luke's Church off the King's Road. Mr. Berenger is fifty-four, and his wife is seventeen years younger."

"Fulham, you say?"

"A four-story townhouse opposite the churchyard, Mr. Holmes, very well appointed. I expect he gets wholesale price on furnishings."

Holmes waved for Lestrade to continue.

"The lady's niece, a Miss Ward, daughter of a high-class pharmacist – "

"What has she to say?" Holmes snapped.

"Miss Ward claims to be intimate with Madame Berenger, meeting regularly for shopping expeditions and concert-going. She states they had an appointment to see the Sullivan play at the *Opera Comique* on a day three weeks ago, but Mrs. Berenger missed the appointment and Miss Ward has heard nothing from her aunt since then – an unheard-of occurrence." Lestrade frowned at his notes. "She visited the Berenger house twice and each time was told Madame was not at home. On her third visit, she demanded an audience with Mr. Berenger."

"What said he?"

"He intimated to Miss Ward that his wife had been diagnosed with a bronchial ailment requiring immediate treatment at a Swiss sanatorium. He showed her a picture postcard he had received from Mrs. Berenger as she travelled to the Continent."

The inspector opened his file and passed Holmes a postcard. He glanced at it and flicked it to me.

"The picture shows the South Eastern Railway ferry at Boulogne." I turned it over. "Chatty inscription extolling a turbot luncheon in Folkestone while waiting for the ferry. The frank is blurred."

"Miss Ward was unconvinced?" Holmes asked.

"She reported the matter to the local police station," Lestrade said. "She declared it inconceivable that her aunt would leave the country without informing her, and she hinted that Madame Berenger's affections may have been directed towards a person other than her husband. An inspector visited the house and interviewed Mr. Berenger. Under questioning, the gentleman confided he was ashamed to admit that his wife had run off with an unknown companion, and he hid the matter from friends and servants by inventing the sanatorium story. He said the postcard, which arrived in the post two days after the lady left, gave him the idea."

"Madame sent her deceived and abandoned husband a postcard describing her railway luncheon. That is hardly solicitous of his no doubt bruised feelings." Holmes sipped his beef tea. "Did she leave a farewell note?"

"In the usual style, sir. She mentions 'another', so that confirms infidelity was a factor."

Holmes snapped his fingers and the inspector handed him a sheet of pale-blue paper. He peered closely at it. "The notepaper is two inches shorter than standard. A heading has been removed."

Holmes turned to me. "Doctor, kindly light the oil lamp."

I did so most reluctantly. "You must not exert yourself, my dear fellow."

Holmes ignored me and held the note to the lamplight, narrowing his eyes. "Female script, written in a tense hand, the nib bruising the paper. We have a watermark, I see an '*N*', a '*T*', and an image of a bird."

He turned back to Lestrade. "What else?"

"Well, that's the thing, Mr. Holmes, I don't know. I'm run off my feet with this Irish dynamite business, and we're short-staffed, as I told the doctor here. My superior maintains there's little in the evidence to suggest anything other than a domestic spat and he has ordered me to drop the case." He flapped the thin file. "This is all I have."

Holmes snapped his fingers for the postcard and he examined it in the lamplight.

"It doesn't feel right, Mr. Holmes," Lestrade continued. "My nose tells me there's something rotten in the borough of Fulham." He tapped the prominent appendage between his eyes. "If I may offer a theatrical reference."

The inspector put on his bowler. "But I see you are unwell, sir, so – " He opened the bedroom door, paused and tut-tutted to himself. "Pity, really, with Miss Ward concerned enough in the matter to offer a hundred guineas for the finder of her aunt or a resolution of the case."

"I may be physically incommoded, but my mental faculties are razor-edged." Holmes said in a querulous tone. "And I am bored. Doctor Watson shall act as my agent, my sleuthhound."

I gaped at him. "Me, Holmes? But I know nothing of detective work."

"You kept up well enough during the Lauriston Gardens case a few months ago." He sniffed, "Almost kept up. And your job is to bring me raw data – you need not indulge in analysis." His hands scrabbled at the coverlet. "Of course, if you cannot furnish me with assistance, I shall have to make other arrangements." Holmes again heaved at his bedclothes. "Call Billy."

Lestrade turned to me, eyebrows raised.

I considered. "Well, I am at something of a loose end just now with only one patient to minister to – although he is a handful."

Holmes subsided against his pillows, a faint smile hovering on his lips.

"I can introduce you to the *dramatis personae*, as it were," Lestrade said. "Then I must devote all my energies to the Irish. They threaten more outrages."

"Where do the Berengers bank?" Holmes asked.

Lestrade consulted his file. "Miss Ward mentioned Hoare's in the Strand. She and Madame Berenger would sometimes meet there before a shopping trip."

Holmes turned to me. "Notepaper and pen, if you please. I shall dictate."

I followed the inspector downstairs and met Mrs. Hudson in the hall. "I have prescribed beef tea or vegetable soup at regular intervals," I informed her. "I require that the patient refrain from rich food."

Mrs. Hudson frowned.

"I would make an exception for your delectable liver and bacon, Mrs. Hudson, but I suggest a small portion of deboned whitefish seethed in milk for breakfast, and a slice of chicken stewed in its own broth for dinner for the next few days. We must rebuild Mr. Holmes's battered constitution until it is sufficiently robust to appreciate more flavoursome food. Remember, feed a cold, starve a fever. He must drink plenty of barley water and, like it or not, an eggnog for luncheon and tea. On that diet, I am sure Mr. Holmes will do very well."

Mrs. Hudson folded her arms. "He'll take his eggnog or I'll know the reason why, Doctor."

"That's the spirit."

Lestrade and I crossed the pavement, our hands on our hats in the biting wind, and climbed aboard his police van. "We'll start with Miss Ward, and then Mr. Berenger, if that suits, Doctor?"

The inspector and I perched on a wicker sofa amid ranks of aspidistras and palm trees in lace-frilled pots.

The lobby of the ladies' hotel in a side street behind Trafalgar Square in which Miss Ward resided was alive with the rustle of crinoline and the chatter of a myriad of members of the gentle sex, young and of a certain age.

The inspector had confirmed the details of the statement that Miss Ward, a florid-faced young lady in a voluminous hat, had made to the police, but her excited demeanour suggested she had more information to impart.

Our witness peered around us as if searching for eavesdroppers before she began. "Before Angelique's disappearance, I was at the Canterbury Music Hall across the river with my friends Mr. and Mrs. Rains, a very respectable couple. Mr. Rains travelled in Sheffield plate for forty years, and we were celebrating his retirement with a modest dinner at the theatre." Her voice lowered to a murmur. "I saw Angelique at another table."

"Mrs. Berenger?" Lestrade asked.

"Dining with a gentleman – a military man by his bearing." Miss Ward lowered her voice to a whisper. "Not her husband or anyone I knew." She looked up and continued in a wondering tone. "Angelique left the hall on the gentleman's arm and passed close to our table on the way out."

I elicited a description of the man and noted it in pencil on my shirt cuff.

"On what date was this?" Lestrade asked.

"September eleventh."

"Did you greet your aunt?"

"Oh, no, Inspector. According to the most respected guides to etiquette, the correct procedure in such awkward circumstances (a lady discovered in intimate circumstances with a man who is not her husband or a close relative) is to bow to the lady, taking no notice of her companion. One does not care to create a scene, particularly not on a Sunday."

I glanced at Lestrade and raised my eyebrows.

"I see," he said.

"However, the very next day, when Angelique and I were taking luncheon at the ABC café opposite St. Clement Danes Church, I did touch on the matter." Miss Ward leant forward conspiratorially. "It was naughty of me, but I asked Angelique whether she had enjoyed the entertainment at the Canterbury!"

Lestrade and I frowned.

"She answered that she had, very much!"

We took leave of Miss Ward and strolled to Trafalgar Square, where Lestrade and I stood on the pavement for a moment lighting our cigarettes and observing the traffic weaving in frantic patterns around the fountains. The wind had died, but the grey sky was darkening and I wished that I had brought my umbrella.

"I thought while I have you with me, we might look in at Hoare's," I said. "*Cui bono?*"

"Who benefits?" The inspector checked his watch. "I can only give you half-an-hour, Doctor."

We were surprised to be directed from Hoare's back to Trafalgar Square and to the City and Suburban Bank branch in Shaftsbury Avenue.

On production of Lestrade's identification, Mr. Lucas, the gaunt and *pinze-nez'*ed chief cashier of the bank, offered us chairs before his desk.

"I have a note here from Mr. Holmes, the inquiry agent," I said, passing it to him. "It is addressed to the manager at Hoare's, but he directed us to you."

Mr. Lucas raised a deprecating eyebrow but took the note. He read it and returned it to me. "I do not know Mr. Holmes."

"You have seen my identification, Mr. Lucas," Lestrade said. "I am investigating a missing person case. A Mrs. Berenger. I understand she and her husband bank with you."

"They do. Mr. and Mrs. Berenger opened a joint account at this branch in January." Mr. Lucas leaned back and regarded us with a stern mien. "I can offer you only very general information, Inspector. Nothing of amounts paid in or out. Not without a warrant."

"We'll get one if we need it," Lestrade answered shortly. "Tell us what you can, sir."

"Mr. and Madame Berenger opened the account in the first days of this year with a token amount. The account lay dormant until a month ago, when we were informed by letter that certain of Madame's Berenger's French properties had been sold on her instructions and the proceeds would be forwarded to this bank and deposited into the account she shared with her husband. The transfer was duly made, and the money was immediately translated into bearer bonds, again on instructions in writing signed by both Mr. and Mrs. Berenger."

"How was her French agent instructed in the property sale? Did she visit or were the transactions authorised by mail?"

"I do not know, Inspector. Transactions on the other side of the Channel are conducted according to Continental regulations with which I am unfamiliar." Mr. Lucas sniffed. "As I'm sure you are aware, foreign banks may play fox-and-hounds with any sums under their control almost without oversight. I very much doubt that any British client sees more than eighty percent of his dividends from non-imperial investments. French banks are particularly rapacious in both foreign currency rates and transaction charges."

"Were the amounts in the Berenger transfer large?" I asked.

Mr. Lucas hesitated for a moment before he nodded curtly.

"More than, let us say, a thousand pounds?" I asked.

Mr. Lucas did not deign to answer. He turned to Lestrade. "Letters of authority signed by both signatories to the account were required before the Bank released the funds as bonds. The signatures were checked against the original specimens we obtained when the account was opened in January."

"Did Mr. and Madame Berenger attend the bank in person?" the inspector asked.

"Both parties opened the account here in my office in person and provided all necessary documentation to prove their *bona fides*. Their banking reference was from Hoare's." Mr. Lucas consulted the file. "On the day in question, September twelfth, the bearer bonds were issued to their representative, a Mr. Grant. Again, with written authority. I supervised the transaction myself."

"Is it usual for a husband and wife to open a joint account?" I asked. "Aren't they the preserve of business partners?"

"That is so," Mr. Lucas answered. He stood, saw us to the door of his office and across the marble floor to the revolving doors. "I hope your enquiry is not in connection with anything irregular? We have received no complaint from the holders of the account. Mr. Berenger said nothing of the matter on his last visit."

"No, no. Just a general enquiry," Lestrade answered. "Thank you for your help."

Lestrade smiled as we shook hands on the pavement outside the bank "The Chief Cashier supervised the transaction himself, Doctor. He would not have done so for a paltry amount. We may have a motive for skulduggery."

I accepted custody of the thin Scotland Yard file on the case, took a cab at the Charing Cross rank, and prepared to beard Mr. Berenger in his den in Fulham.

The butler showed me into a pleasant drawing room where a tall, well-built, middle-aged gentleman with a trim moustache and an erect military posture stood before the fireplace smoking a cigar. He frowned at me, and I at him.

"I believe I have seen you before, sir," I said. "At my club, The Junior United Service."

"That may be so," he answered, a little warily. He held out his hand, "Berenger."

"Watson. I was an Army doctor in Afghanistan."

A question hung in the air for a moment until Mr. Berenger replied. "I served as a captain in the militia – retired a couple of years ago." He glanced at my walking stick. "Maiwand?"

I nodded.

Mr. Berenger banged his fist into his hand. "I would have given all I have to be on the field of battle on that day. What bravery! What glory!" He shook his head. "But I had not the financial means for a commission in the regular army. I had to content myself with the militia."

"Bravery at Maiwand?" I considered. "It was a given, I suppose. But I saw very little glory to be had amid the dust and blood. There was none at all in the medical tent. Even when the chief medical officer shot our wounded one by one to keep them from falling into the hands of the Afghans, the bravest act I have ever witnessed, there was no glory."

I felt a sudden hot flush, a shaft of pain ran down my leg, and I found myself swaying. Mr. Berenger helped me to a chair and rang for a servant. "Brandy," he ordered.

"Just a glass of water, if you would be so kind. I do apologise. My wound acts up at any change in temperature, and today has been chilly."

Mr. Berenger handed me a tumbler of water and I took a sip and thanked him. "I should explain that while I have no official position in this matter, I act for Mr. Sherlock Holmes, the private enquiry agent. The police and a concerned relative of your wife have encouraged Mr. Holmes to take an interest in her disappearance."

"I very much appreciate Mr. Holmes's involvement, Doctor," Mr. Berenger answered. "Rumours abound. One's neighbours and even one's servants look at one oddly. And the inspector this morning seemed utterly disinterested in the matter, merely going through the motions. You will understand that I need to clear my name and for that reason alone I welcome an investigation. Above all, I ache to know the whereabouts of Angelique." He looked down at his toes. "So I might reason with her, you understand."

He looked up. "I would be happy to place the matter in Mr. Holmes's hands at any reasonable fee the gentleman would care to name."

"Mr. Holmes is unwell, and he has deputed me to act in his behalf."

Mr. Berenger pursed his lips.

"He will evaluate any information I gather," I said, somewhat tartly.

"I see." Mr. Berenger leaned against the mantel and regarded me with an aloof expression.

"You opened a new bank account at the City and Suburban Bank in January." I said.

"My wife and I did so in order to facilitate the transfer of the proceeds of certain property sales on the Continent. We were advised the City and Suburban has connections in France that would facilitate the transaction."

"The money was transferred to your joint account in that bank."

"It was." Mr. Berenger answered. "And immediately withdrawn as bearer bonds on the day my wife left. I did not sign the withdrawal slip or authorise the bonds. My signature was forged."

Mr. Berenger unlocked a bureau and took a note from a drawer. "I found this in my wife's writing desk." He handed me a sheet of paper covered with signatures.

"These are your signatures?" I asked.

"They are copies of my signature. Practice makes perfect, Doctor."

I frowned. "Why did you not inform the police of this when you were interviewed this morning?"

"I was already on my back foot over my foolish attempt at hiding Angelique's, ah, elopement. The inspector's questions were sharp and focussed on my prevarications. We did not discuss finances."

I shook my head. "I am puzzled, Mr. Berenger. Under English law, the French money would have become yours as soon as it reached our shores. Your wife would no longer have any claim on proceeds of the sale of her property. What was the purpose of the joint account?"

Mr. Berenger indicated a decanter on a side table. "Would you care for some refreshment, Doctor? Sherry perhaps?"

"Thank you." I accepted a glass of sherry and took a sip – a cool, nutty amontillado.

"The French property was my wife's and the money morally hers," Mr. Berenger continued. "I believe marriage is a partnership, Doctor, not a dictatorship. I arranged a joint account in both our banks, with equal access for Angelique and myself. The foreign proceeds were withdrawn from the City and Suburban Bank using subterfuge, but it was Angelique's money. Our joint account at Hoare's was not touched."

"Your salary from Jay's is paid into that joint account?"

"Of course not." Mr. Berenger sniffed. "I have a personal account."

I considered. "Do you know Mr. Grant, who purported to be your financial agent when he drew up the bearer bonds at the L. and C. bank?"

"I do not."

"If I might trespass on the personal, Mr. Berenger. "Have you any idea who 'another' might be?"

"No. I had no idea my wife was unfaithful to me. She had not been entirely comfortable with our move from Jersey to England, but these past months I noticed an uplift of her spirits and I was sure she had become more accustomed to life here."

"Miss Ward saw your wife dining with a gentleman at the Canterbury music hall on the evening before she left you." I

298

read out the description. "She suggests the man had a military bearing."

"I have no idea who he might be."

I received permission from Mr. Berenger to show Holmes the signature paper and I took my leave.

I checked my watch on the pavement outside the Berenger house. It was just on the luncheon hour.

"Junior United Service Club," I called to my cabby, and I settled back on the bench with a certain sense of achievement. If there was, as Lestrade suggested, skulduggery in the case, the proceeds of the French property sale offered a clear motive. I frowned. But for what? Madame Berenger had left for the Continent (established by her postcard from Boulogne) presumably accompanied by "another". Why had she transferred the proceeds from her French property to England? Why had she withdrawn the money in bearer bonds, faking her husband's signature? And who was Mr. Grant? There was much in the case that did not make immediate sense.

Walters, my usual waiter when I dined at the Club, leaned close to me as he served my leek and potato soup as he answered my murmured query.

"Mr. Berenger was a member of the United Service Club while he was in the Militia, Doctor, but after he left the military he was obliged to resign. Only Militia officers who have also served in the regulars may continue as members after they retire. He still dines here occasionally."

"As whose guest?"

"Lord Frederick McFarlane, sir, of the Scots Guards. The gentlemen are on intimate terms."

I requested a description of His Lordship that I checked against the notes on my shirt cuff. "Thank you, Walters."

299

I was served the second of a two-course *table d'hote*, an excellent grilled chop and roast potatoes. Walters then brought me a bowl of rice pudding, knowing it to be a favourite of mine, asking if I would kindly try the dish, as the cook feared he had added too much nutmeg. In fact, as I willingly informed Walters with a wink, the pudding was perfect.

I laid a two-shilling tip next to my plate, then I thought on the McFarlane disclosure, the free pudding, and Miss Ward's hundred guineas and I replaced the shilling coins with a half-crown. I was about to stand when I recalled the paltry eleven-shillings-and-sixpence I received daily from the War Department and I retrieved the half crown and replaced it with the two shillings. I made a discreet gesture to Walters as I heaved myself up.

The club commissionaire fetched my hat and cane and escorted me to a hansom.

"Wellington Barracks, Birdcage Walk," I called as I struggled aboard, favouring my leg and several pounds heavier than I had been before luncheon. As I settled on the bench, I have to say that an ignoble, uncivil worm of thought reminded me of Holmes's luncheon eggnog and I almost chuckled. Lodging with Holmes for the previous nine months had rarely been dull, but his bohemian habits were a little wearing on a sensitive constitution, rubbed raw by recent catastrophe. I admit I rather welcomed an opportunity to display my professional expertise – turning the tables, as it were.

"Lord McFarlane?" Major Fraser frowned.

The adjutant of the Scots Guards had allowed me a few moments of his time when I turned up unannounced at the barracks. In my note requesting an audience, I had made much of my recent military connections.

The major, in his befrogged undress uniform coat, sat back in his seat and offered me snuff from an ornate box. I demurred and he inhaled an ample pinch, gasped like a guppy for a moment or two, then dabbed his walrus moustache with his handkerchief. He flapped stray grains of snuff from his tunic as I explained the reason for my visit.

"His Lordship is visiting his estates in Scotland for a month," the major said in a mild Scots brogue. "Many of our officers have obligations in that regard, and the Regiment is understanding. The French are in their usual political muddle and we don't expect any infernal capers from them this campaigning season or even next."

He fitted his monocle into his left eye, peered down at my note and then glanced at my walking stick. "You were a medical officer with the 66th in Afghanistan." He pursed his lips. "Maiwand?"

I nodded.

"I lost a cousin in the battle. Captain Marsh, Horse Artillery."

"I knew him, sir." I recalled a slight youth with a shock of blond hair. "He was a prime polo player. A musket ball broke his femur and I prepared him for surgery a few minutes before I was wounded myself. I do not know his fate."

"Afghan fiends, Doctor Watson! Savages, as steeped in blood as the most ferocious Apache on the American Plains, or even the damned Boers. We must pay them back in their own kind and raze Kabul to the ground. *Carthago delenda est.*"

I nodded agreement, although I could not find in my heart much enthusiasm for more bloodshed.

Major Fraser sighed. "Well, there we are. Now, this lady – your witness – saw Madam Bergerer – "

"Berenger, sir."

"On the arm of a young man of military bearing. Her description fits McFarlane and probably half the young officers in the Army. I would not trust a civilian to distinguish between a Gurkha and a Grenadier – "

"If I may say, Major, I have other information suggesting Captain McFarlane is a close friend of Mr. Berenger. And Madame Berenger may be a lady of considerable means. I want to be able to eliminate Lord McFarlane from our list of suspects in the matter."

"And how many names are on your list?"

I coloured. "One."

The major stood, paced to the fireplace, and warmed his hands. "Let's be frank, Doctor Watson. Officers of Her Majesty's Guards are warriors, not saints. Liaisons occur, even with the wives of brother officers, but no officer of the Guards would run off with the wife of a comrade in the Regiment, or any other. The sacrament of marriage is sacrosanct."

"Mr. Berenger is a retired militia officer."

"A civilian then." Major Fraser shrugged. "The point remains that Captain McFarlane may not marry a divorcée and stay with the Colours – not in this regiment, at least not while I am adjutant. And whatever peccadillios the young man may have committed, his life is here with us. His parents are deceased and he has no close relations. We are his family. I cannot conceive he would give us up for a floozy, however nimble and however well-padded with Bank of England notes."

The major brightened. "Is the husband in Society? May we expect an encounter? If so, and McFarlane prevails, he may marry the widow. If not . . . ?" He shrugged again.

I stood, leaning on my cane. "Thank you for your time, sir."

Major Fraser shook my hand. "You knew young Marsh, eh? Damn shame."

He saw me to the door. "McFarlane is a good officer, but he holds himself back by neglecting his military duties for his nautical interests. I've had to pull him up on it."

He smiled at my frown of incomprehension. "I don't know if you play at this angling lark, Doctor. His Lordship invited me to fish in a lake on his Scottish estate and from his boat on the Thames, but I don't see the point – a lot of sitting around getting one's posterior damp. If I fancy a kipper for breakfast, I'll order it from the mess steward, not catch it myself, eh, eh?"

I stopped at the door. "I have one more favour, sir. May I speak to His Lordship's man? Is he with Lord McFarlane in Scotland?"

The major narrowed his eyes. "You had a soldier servant during your service in Afghanistan?"

"I did, sir."

"Then you understand the relationship between an officer and his man is a close one, particularly with a company officer, and even more on active service. They learn a great deal about each other – a lot of good to be sure, but perhaps things that might be considered questionable in other walks of life." He chuckled. "If my man had made public half the things I got up to when I was a young officer, well, I should not be where I am today. Do you follow?"

"I perfectly understand, Major. My soldier servant, Murray, saved my life at Maiwand."

"Did he so?" The adjutant stood erect and his eyes glistened. "I rely on your discretion, Doctor. If you'll wait for a moment, I'll speak to the duty sergeant."

The adjutant returned with a sergeant, resplendent in scarlet and gold.

"Private King is on guard duty at the gate, sir," the sergeant said. "I'll have him relieved and sent to the Mess anteroom. It'll be empty after luncheon." He turned to the adjutant. "I'll move King to night guard, sir."

The major again held out his hand to me. "Saved your life, eh."

"Thank you for your help, sir," I said, shaking it.

I met Lord McFarlane's soldier servant in a large wood-panelled room with cases of sporting and military trophies along two walls and crossed polo sticks, pikes, and swords adorning another. A frieze of stag heads, their horns intertwined, was wrapped around the walls, and heads of buffalo, rhino, and other big game looked down on us. According to a sign, closed double doors led to the mess and dining room.

King was a tall, well-built young fellow in full uniform with a ready smile. He stood at attention, holding his bearskin hat under his arm.

"Are you happy in your profession?" I asked, after putting him at ease.

"Better than beggary, sir," he answered in a thick Scots accent.

"True enough." I said. "Are there any photographs here of your master, the captain?"

"Let's see, sir."

We browsed a wall of framed photographs of gentlemen standing by the corpses of big game or on the hunting field, in rugby kit and cricket whites, on polo ponies and performing at equestrian events. A single photograph at the end of a row showed a young man in a marine cap aboard a yacht of twenty feet or more in length.

"A fine-looking fellow," I said. "Major Fraser mentioned fishing, and I imagined a much smaller boat."

304

"His Lordship's yacht, *Caroline*, sir."

I made a note of her name in the last patch of free space of my shirt cuff. "Do you know where she is moored?"

"At the captain's yacht club at Gravesend, sir. The New Thames."

"His Lordship did not request you accompany him to Scotland?"

"No, sir. Lord McFarlane has staff at his castle. I serve him here in barracks, on campaign, and on his yacht."

"Do you know Mr. and Mrs. Berenger?"

"I do, sir, as friends of His Lordship. They would sail together in the season, and dine frequently."

"With the captain's lady friend, I imagine."

King said nothing.

"Did His Lordship ever dine *tête-à-tête* with Madame Berenger to your knowledge?"

King came to attention and stayed silent.

I furrowed my brows. "In my regiment, a man might be severely punished for dumb insolence."

King remained silent.

I smiled. "I'm not going to prise Lord McFarlane's secrets from you, am I, King?"

He returned my smile. "The captain's stood by me, thick or thin, sir – only right I do the same for him."

King showed me to the barracks gate, where I picked up a cab, and in the relative privacy of my hansom I rubbed my hands together. I had cause to be rather pleased with the information that I had accrued so far. It seemed highly likely Mrs. Berenger had left for the Continent with her fortune in bearer bonds. Whether her lover, Lord McFarlane, would join her after he settled his affairs in Scotland had yet to be determined.

"You are wearing carpet slippers, Billy," I said when the boy let me into the hall at 221b. "Where are your boots?"

Billy softly closed the front door and put his fingers to his lips.

I lifted the boy's chin and frowned at him. "And you are looking pale."

"I feel pale, Doctor," he replied in a faint whisper. "Up and down the stairs twenty times or more. Move the lamp closer, fetch his magnifier, bring the railway guide, and a dozen telegrams to be run to the post office and back in the freezing cold. I'm fagged out, sir."

"Did Mr. Holmes take his eggnog?"

Billy looked down at his toes.

"You recall the oil-cloth package that I requested you deposit in the scullery?" I asked. "Fetch."

I climbed up to the sitting room, treading softly on the stairs, and I peeped into Holmes's room. His counterpane was piled with books, papers, magazines, and volumes of his Index, but under it he slept soundly. I replaced the cloth across his brow with a fresh one, closed the door, and tiptoed into the sitting room.

Billy handed me the parcel I had bought earlier, and I peered at the pestle and mortar on Holmes's laboratory table. "Has Mr. Holmes been mixing anything deadly recently?"

The boy shrugged. "No more than usual. He sent me out for a flask of sulphuric acid last Wednesday, and powdered galls and green vitriol the day before yesterday."

"No eye of newt and toe of frog?"

Billy blinked at me.

I sniffed the pestle. "I'm sorely tempted to leave it to Dame Fortune, but you might give both pestle and mortar a thorough scrub in the scullery, just in case. And bring me the honey jar."

306

Billy tiptoed downstairs and I took a half-dozen medicine bottles and flasks from my medical bag and spread them on Holmes's laboratory table.

Billy returned with the honey and pestle and mortar. I poured measured amounts of various medicines into the bowl and ground them together.

"The bolus I had put up by the chemist next to the station was ineffective," I told the boy. "I am mixing my own recipe." I indicated two small bottles labelled with skulls and crossbones. "Many elements in nature have the power to cure, and also to kill. Antimony and arsenic, Billy, are two of the most potent. Do you know St James's Powder?"

"Of course, Doctor. My ma used to take it regular."

"Regularly. The powder is mostly antimony, a potent poison. It undoubtedly kills more than it cures."

The boy gaped at me.

"But in very small doses, antimony is a potent antipyretic. It lowers fever." I spooned a generous dollop of honey into the bowl. "Honey to bind the medicine, trick the taste-buds, and help it slide down easily." I spooned a little of the mixture and offered it to Billy.

He tasted, licked his lips and grinned. I held the boy's wrist, checking his pulse, and peered into his eyes. "Feeling all right?"

Billy stared at me in horror and pulled away. I chuckled and tasted a spoonful of the mixture myself. "Just right."

I undid the parcel that Billy had brought from the scullery and took out a square, green bottle. "Fling the windows wide open," I commanded as I uncorked the bottle and, holding my nose with one hand, dripped a thick liquid into the bowl. The smell was disgusting. I quickly corked the bottle, shaped the contents of the bowl into two boluses, and covered them with a cloth.

Billy gaped, holding his nose.

"I'll let you into a little medical secret, Billy. The more vile the medicine, the more the patient believes it's doing him good." I grinned. "And the more motivated he is to get better. A little tincture of asafoetida works wonders."

I had the boy close the windows and I knocked gently on Holmes's bedroom door.

"I'm awake," Holmes cried.

I opened the door and found my patient glaring at me. Beads of perspiration mottled Holmes brow. His eyes were bloodshot and his breathing shallow.

"How could I rest with you and the rest of the household thundering around like a herd of rhinos and screeching to each other like macaws?" Holmes grimaced. "What is that stink?"

"You must take your nice bolus, Holmes."

"It is not nice – it is utterly disgusting. And if I may correct you, Doctor, '*viler*' is the correct grammatical form, not 'more vile'. Vile is a single-syllable adjective not requiring adverbial support."

"Very well." I leaned over my patient and offered the spoon. "Then you must swallow your nice bolus to prevent you becoming iller."

I held Holmes's nose and slipped the bolus into his mouth.

He gulped, spluttered, swallowed, coughed and gave me a fierce look. "What in heaven's name is in it?"

"A potent decoction of poisons. We'll follow with a second dose in an hour or two."

Holmes lay back with a long sigh and I moved to leave.

"What of Mr. Berenger?" Holmes said.

I suggested Holmes might want to wait, taking things easy. We could examine the case after his fever had broken, and after a period of convalescence.

"What of Mr. Berenger?" he insisted.

I sat at Holmes's bedside and summarised my interview, handing him the signature sheet.

"Ordinary letter paper, no watermark," he said. "Signed a couple-of-score times with a broad-nib pen and inferior black ink. An attempt by Mrs. Berenger to copy her husband's signature. Or a mis-clue from Mr. Berenger to implicate her."

"Lord McFarlane of the Scots Guards is a close friend of Mr. Berenger and he fits Miss Ward's description perfectly," I said. "His adjutant at Wellington Barracks seemed unsurprised that he might be in an affair with a married lady." I smiled. "According to the major, if the lady divorces her husband and Captain McFarlane marries her, he would have to send in his papers and resign, but if he kills the husband in a duel, he may marry the widow and continue his Army career."

"I'm not sure that is official War Office policy, but I imagine it reflects the view of the Guards."

I wiped Holmes's forehead with a towel and took his temperature.

"Anything else on McFarlane?" Holmes asked as I peered at the thermometer.

"His Lordship's soldier servant mentioned a yacht club with premises at Gravesend."

"Did you note the details?"

I frowned. "Both my cuffs were full. I shall have to buy a notebook."

"Billy!" Holmes cried.

The boy peeked around the door jamb. "Fetch the Red Book," Holmes ordered.

Billy took the book from its shelf, handed to me, and scrambled downstairs. I flicked to the appropriate page in Debrett's *Peerage*. "Lord McFarlane has held the title since the death of his father a year ago. Address: A castle in Fifeshire. Hobbies: Yachting, fishing, and hunting. Here we are – Clubs: Junior United Service, New Thames Yacht Club!" I smiled. "New Thames – *NT*. The clubhouse in Gravesend is where, according to his man, Lord McFarlane moors his yacht, *Caroline*."

Holmes demanded a telegraph form and scribbled on it with a pencil.

"Billy!"

Our page stomped up the stairs, took the form and coins, sighed a long sigh, and stomped down again.

"What of the postcard?" I asked.

Holmes smiled. "A forgery. The perpetrator of this postcard did not know, but I do because I keep my Bradshaw up-to-date, that the boat train timetable from Folkestone to Boulogne changed this season. Passengers no longer take their luncheon at Folkestone between the arrival of the boat train and the departure of the ferry. They must wait until the ship docks in France."

"So, the chatter of turbot luncheon at Folkestone is untrue."

"No, no – true, but on an earlier date."

"Yes, of course, I see it now. The postcard is genuine. The frank and date have been smudged to suggest they were posted after Madame's disappearance."

"Exactly. It is astonishing how much one may discover from a few key references without venturing from one's den – or bed as in this case."

I raised my eyebrows.

"If one has a faithful bloodhound, and access to the post office." Holmes grinned. "Did Madame Berenger take her things with her – jewels, dresses, and so on?"

"I didn't ask."

Holmes sighed. "What had the servants to say?"

I sat back in my chair. "I did not discuss the matter with them. Would that not be perilously close to mere gossip?"

"Catnip to the detective mind, Watson."

I restrained myself from a rude reply.

"Did you visit the nearest public house?"

"I did not."

Holmes sighed. "And His Lordship's man would not cooperate?"

"There is a bond of comradeship between an officer and his soldier servant, Holmes. My man, Murray, dragged me from the battlefield when I was wounded. He found or stole a packhorse, slung me on it, and led me to safety. Seven-hundred-and-fifty British officers and men were killed at Maiwand. I was not among their number entirely due to Private Murray's devotion to duty."

Holmes nodded, but he drummed his fingers on the counterpane. "King is hiding something. If he will not cooperate, we must find another way to the truth."

I held up an admonitory hand. "Calm, Holmes. Your fever is rising again. Your brow is wet with perspiration and your complexion is reddening."

I swept the papers off the counterpane and into Lestrade's folder and piled the books on the carpet. "I must insist you remain perfectly calm and forget all this until the morning." I smiled. "Another bolus should see you through until the crisis, which invariably comes in the early hours."

Holmes lay back, breathing heavily. "Was Mr. Berenger calm?"

"Remarkably calm until I told him the police were still reluctant to become involved and you were not directly engaged in the case due to illness. He blanched."

Holmes smiled his jaguar smile. "Then I believe we may soon expect a break not only in my fever, but in the case." He shook his head. "I see only one solution, Doctor. You must speak to the servants and to Mrs. King."

"Behind her husband's back? Is that a gentlemanly thing to do, Holmes?" I started at a thought. "I have no idea where Private King lives."

"Billy!" Holmes cried.

I went to the door, but a flicker of suspicion made me turn. "Did you drink your eggnog, Holmes?"

He avoided my eyes. "I came to a compromise with Mrs. Hudson. She now offers the eggnog in its constituent parts rather than intemperately mixed into an indigestible glue. The whipped egg I disdained in its raw form, but accepted as an omelette. The sherry I enjoyed as an aperitif."

I turned to the door and paused again. "Powdered galls? Green vitriol? I hope you are not dosing yourself."

"What a suspicious mind you have Doctor. Mix two pounds of galls, a pound of green vitriol, and eight ounces of gum. Two ounces of the mixture make a pint of fine, black ink for everyday use."

I pursed my lips. "I believe I shall have to make up something a little stronger for you if we are to root out this fever."

Holmes lay back on his pillows and closed his eyes. "Remember: Raw facts, my dear fellow. Do not expend your energy in analysis – leave that to me."

I walked from South Kensington Station to the Berenger residence.

"The master is not at home, Doctor," Briggs, the butler said, barring the pass.

"I wish to interview the servants, not Mr. Berenger. I act for Mr. Sherlock Holmes, the inquiry agent."

"I'm not sure, sir – "

"And Inspector Lestrade of Scotland Yard."

I followed Briggs downstairs to the kitchen and waited while he gathered the house servants. The maids lined up beside the cook and footmen, and I barked at them in my best impersonation of a Prussian sergeant major, demanding immediate disclosure of anything relevant to their mistress's disappearance. None spoke.

I pointed to the youngest of the maids, who was avoiding my eyes. "Who are you?" An elderly lady, evidently from the keys at her belt the housekeeper, answered. "Ruby, sir. Madame's lady's maid as was."

"You are holding something back, Ruby," I said in a gentler tone.

"Madame's necklace, her favourite one, sir," the housekeeper said. "Ruby found it this afternoon on the carpet in one of the bedrooms."

"Madame Berenger's bedroom?"

The housekeeper gave me a significant look. "No, Doctor, in the master's bedroom. I am at a loss to understand why it was not discovered before. Madame would never go anywhere without it."

"What was Ruby doing in Mr. Berenger's bedroom?" I asked.

"Working off her notice, sir. With madame absent, there was no need for a lady's maid, so I put her on dusting."

I considered for a moment. "Had you cleaned your master's bedroom since your mistress left?"

"The house has been up, down, and sideways since then," the housekeeper replied.

"I see." I frowned and narrowed my eyes. "You have not answered my question, Madam. Has the master's bedroom been cleaned regularly?"

"Yes, sir."

"Very well. And yet nothing was found?"

The housekeeper looked at her toes.

"Where exactly was the necklace discovered?"

"Under the master's dressing table."

"Where it lay undiscovered for the three weeks since Madam Berenger's departure? I find that difficult to believe."

The servants started at the sound of a bell.

"The master's back," the housekeeper said.

"One more question. Did any of you have any inkling Madame Berenger was contemplating such a fateful step?"

"When she first come, sir, she was happy as a lark," Ruby said, "but from last summer to Christmas of last year, or longer really, she wasn't." The other girls murmured agreement.

"She was morose?"

The girls blinked at me.

"Sad," the housekeeper translated.

"In tears some of the time. And there were rows," another maid said. She blushed and put her apron over her face.

"But she perked up since the New Year," Ruby said.

The servants streamed out to their various duties, but I stopped Ruby with a raised hand. My eyes flicked to the butler, who seemed to hang back.

"Thank you, Briggs."

He left, closing the door, and I directed Ruby to a chair and sat opposite her.

"Now, Ruby, you gave your notice when?"

"On the day Madame left, sir. Three weeks or more ago. My last day is Saturday."

I frowned. "You knew Mrs. Berenger was not coming back. That she looking forward to a new life with Captain McFarlane."

Ruby's hands flew to her lips.

"Madame left you a remembrance, did she not?" I gestured towards a fine ruby ring on the girl's finger.

"And a hundred pounds, along with a character, sir." Ruby smiled at the ring. "Mr. Briggs lets me wear the ring downstairs as I'm on notice anyway." She dabbed her eyes with a handkerchief. "Madame means the world to me, sir."

"And the master?" I softened my voice. "Come my dear, you must be truthful and tell me everything, or what will become of you?"

I returned upstairs and waited in the hall of the Berenger residence while Briggs announced my presence. I followed him into the same study I had visited earlier in the day.

"I didn't think it relevant," Mr. Berenger answered my inquiry about the necklace. "Angelique obviously decamped in a hurry and one item of jewellery was accidentally dropped. The matter is of no importance."

"It was found in your bedroom by Ruby, your wife's lady's maid."

"Angelique entered my room to leave a note on my dressing table. Perhaps she had the jewels in her hand. I don't know. I fail to see what relevance this has."

I too was puzzled, but I gave Mr. Berenger my best impression of Holmes's jaguar smile. "May I see the necklace?"

Mr. Berenger unlocked a bureau, removed a white leather jewel case about the size of a book, and handed it to me. I opened the case and revealed a gold necklace studded with small brilliants from which a glittering pendant formed of larger stones hung. "May I show this to Mr. Holmes?"

Mr. Berenger agreed and I wrote a receipt on a page from the notebook that I had purchased at the station book stall. "Tell me how you came by the postcard," I asked.

"It was delivered normally, through our letter box a couple of days after Angelique left. Briggs brought it to me."

I considered. "But you knew from the farewell note that your wife had left you with another. You knew she was not on her way to a sanatorium on the Continent. The postcard makes no sense."

Mr. Berenger shook a cigar from a packet on the mantel and raised his eyebrows.

"No, thank you."

He struck a match, lit his cigar, and slumped into a chair opposite me. "I thought that Angelique was attempting to mitigate the terrible blow she'd had me endure. My wife was a kind soul who would not hurt a fly on purpose. I saw in the postcard a way to allow myself time to reorganise my life after her departure, and I hit on the notion of her trip to the Continent for medical reasons. I did not know what I was doing. I was at my wits end, in shock."

"Did your wife visit France recently?"

"Several times. A dozen or more since our marriage. More often since her father died last year and she had to see to his affairs."

"One final question, Mr. Berenger. Where were you on the evening of September twelfth?"

"I had purchased tickets to the Gilbert and Sullivan frivolity at the *Opera Comique*. The plays are not to my taste, but Angelique adored them. I had thought we might dine at the Criterion Grill." He took a long puff at his cigar. "But Angelique was unwell, with a touch of this fever that's going around. She begged me not to stay at home on her account as she would have an early night. It was Cook's night off, so Ruby made her a cold collation."

Mr. Berenger puffed on his cigar. "I dined at a chop house in the Strand, and went on to a show."

"*Patience*?"

"One of the can-can establishments near Trafalgar Square, if you must know, and then to a certain house by Covent Garden."

"Are you well known there?"

"No. It's dimly lit, and one uses a false name. Lotty's is not a champagne-and-caviar establishment – more claret and anchovy toast. One picks a girl from the line-up and one is allocated a cubicle." He grimaced. "You must understand that my wife had not been well enough for intimacy for some time – since Christmas."

I stood. "Thank you, Mr. Berenger."

He showed me to the door. "Are you a married man, Doctor Watson?"

"Alas, no." I shook his hand. "And you have no notion who 'another' might be?"

Mr. Berenger shook his head. I was tempted to confront him with my suspicions, but I followed Holmes's precept of holding back evidence until the dramatic *denouement*.

Despite a faint twinge from my wound, I descended the steps to the pavement with a light step and set off towards the station.

Billy yawned as he opened the front door. "Telegrams to Scotland, cups of coffee, cigars, more rooting through newspapers, holding the lamp high while he looks through his what-do-you-call-it."

"Steady the Buffs, Billy."

Holmes's counterpane was even more cluttered with papers and reference books and his microscope lay on the floor. His face was redder than earlier and his eyes were bright. "What news?" he asked.

317

I removed a half-smoked cigar from his hand. "Despite my injunction to rest, you have been busy."

Holmes tapped the Red Book interleaved with telegram forms that lay on his coverlet. "Berenger and McFarlane. Their fathers were at Harrow School together, and so were the boys. Berenger's father married his milkmaid with predictable results. His heart gave out after a year, leaving his son with a pitiful allowance and a widowed step-mother of a low caste with whom he had nothing in common. He did not have enough money for the university or the Army."

I shook my head. "He descended into trade."

"McFarlane bought a lieutenancy for four-thousand guineas just before the practice was discontinued," Holmes said. "He has evidently thrived in the Army, transferring to better regiments and rising to captain. His father died last year, leaving him with their castle and estates."

Holmes waved a cable flimsy. "My sources in Paris tell me Madame Berenger inherited considerable property in France on the death of her father last year, including a chateau near Perigord – vineyards and so on."

He smiled. "I have my worms burrowing into the City, and a connection with the *Sûreté* in Paris. The amount transferred to London was in excess of twenty-thousand pounds."

"But if his wife had such riches, why was Berenger still working at Jay's more than two years after their marriage?"

"Rents accrued in foreign banks are outside the jurisdiction of the British legal or banking system. Madame's husband owned all her worldly goods by English law, but he had no access to the French property."

I brightened. "It would be natural for Madame Berenger to return to France if she were unhappy in her marriage. Should I investigate in France? In Paris perhaps?"

Holmes waved my idea away with a limp wave and picked up the farewell note. "I have examined the watermark with my microscope and confirmed the first two initials are '*N*' and '*T*'. The image is a phoenix, which adorns the burgee of the New Thames Yacht Club."

"What gentleman steals club notepaper for use at home?" I frowned. "To what purpose? Parsimony?"

"And how would his wife get it?" Holmes asked. "And why use this paper for a farewell note? Venom?"

"Perhaps so. Writing a final farewell note to one's spouse on a scrap of paper is a gesture of contempt."

"Using a laundry bill or the back of a used envelope would have made the point more obviously." Holmes smiled. "What of the postcard?"

"Anyone could have deposited it in the letterbox, including Mr. Berenger."

I laid the jewel case on Holmes coverlet, explaining how it had been found.

He opened the case and his eyes sparkled. "Pass me my jewellers' loupe from my drawer."

"I will do no such thing. You are flushed and breathless. You will rest, or my name is not Doctor John Watson."

"Billy!" Holmes cried.

"Oh, very well." I fetched Holmes's loupe from his desk and watched as he peered at the diamonds, muttering to himself. He lay back, gasping. "Paste. This is a fake."

I gaped at Holmes. "It's Mrs. Berenger's favourite piece of jewellery. Are you sure?"

"Were Madame's jewels part of her trousseau or later purchases or gifts?" Holmes asked.

I frowned.

"Tut, tut, Watson. What of the servants?"

"Madame's lady's maid admitted she helped her mistress pack her things, including her dresses and jewellery, and that she received a considerable remuneration. A hundred pounds and a ruby ring."

"French?"

"From Ipswich. She has given a month's notice and found a new position with Lady Kennedy."

I held up my hand and stood. "Medicine time. Another bolus, and I will order your eggnog."

Holmes grimaced. "I should relish a dish of grapes."

I blinked at Holmes. "Grapes?"

"Green ones. Why do you look so startled, Doctor? I am not requesting . . .

> . . . *the fruit*
> *Of that forbidden tree whose mortal taste*
> *Brought death into the world, and all our woe,*
> *With loss of Eden.*"

"I'll see what I can do," I answered.

He handed me the necklace case. "The imprint on the inside lid is that of Asprey of New Bond Street."

Holmes requested my notebook and a pencil, and he scribbled a note. "Speak to a Mr. Redmond."

I administered the bolus and took Holmes's temperature again. "Your fever is proving stubborn, old man. (Why am I surprised?)"

I made my way downstairs. "Billy, run to the greengrocers and see if they have a pound of grapes – green grapes."

"Already been, sir, on Mr. Holmes's orders and come up empty-handed. Grapes is not to be had anywhere in the borough. According to the grocer, an unseasonable frost and political goings on in the Mediterranean have withered the neglected vines. Him and the other fruiterers have petitioned Mr. Gladstone to send a gunboat."

Mr. Redmond, the manager at Asprey, recognised the necklace immediately. "The original was of French manufacture. We made this copy."

"For Mrs. Berenger?"

Mr. Redmond hesitated.

"Mr. Sherlock Holmes sends his regards." I handed him the note.

The manager read it and nodded. "Very well. Yes, Mrs. Berenger ordered the copy. Many of our clients require a facsimile of their jewels for everyday wear, keeping the real thing for levces at the Palace, *etcetera*, and so forth. Insurance costs are significantly diminished."

"Do you know Mr. Berenger?"

"Both Mr. and Madame Berenger are regular clients, always served by a senior assistant or by me." Mr. Redmond again hesitated. "Three of our senior men went down with this fever that's been going around, as did I myself for a day or two. One of our juniors attended Mr. Berenger when he called in last month for a snuffbox he'd had us engrave."

Mr. Redmond sighed. "The junior informed Mr. Berenger that the copy necklace and a ring his wife had ordered were ready and asked if he wished to take them with the snuffbox, or have the items delivered to their residence."

The manager mopped his brow. "It was a considerable breach of trust. We take very great care to keep our clients' affairs – I mean transactions – separate, even if – especially perhaps – when we deal with a married couple."

I did my best to appear understanding.

"According to the junior assistant, Mr. Berenger seemed perplexed at the suggestion that he collect the necklace. I don't believe that he knew of the copy."

"The ring featured a ruby?"

The manager nodded. "A small one. A present, Madame Berenger said. She will allow no stones other than diamonds or pearls to touch her skin."

"How did Mrs. Berenger pay for her purchases?"

"A transfer from the Banque de Paris."

"And Mr. Berenger?"

The manager flicked through his account book. "A cheque on Hoare's."

I made a note in my book. "And the snuffbox – do you have details of the engraving?"

Mr. Redmond consulted a huge ledger. "We were instructed to engrave a thistle and the motto '*Nemo me impune lacessit*'."

Inspector Lestrade sat on the chair by Holmes's bed when I returned home. A bowl of green grapes lay on the side table beside Holmes's open hypodermic case.

I glared at both grapes and the hypodermic on its blue velvet cushion.

"From the intrepid inspector," Holmes said, waving a limp hand at the grapes. "Inspector Lestrade does not know the meaning of defeat."

"I've spoken to my superiors," the inspector said, "and in the light of Mr. Holmes's revelations regarding the postcard, the fraudulent withdrawal, and the fake necklace, we are treating the lady's disappearance as a possible crime. I've been moved off of the Irish inquiry (thank the Good Lord) and assigned to the Berenger case."

"Holmes," I said, indicating the hypodermic, "have you, umm . . . ?"

Holmes overrode me. "What had Asprey to say?"

I summarised my conversation with Mr. Redmond.

"*Nemo me impune lacessit*," Holmes said, smiling. "The motto of Scotland, and thus of the Scots Guards. We can thus surmise that up to a month ago, Mr. Berenger considered Lord McFarlane a close enough friend to have a silver snuffbox made up for his birthday, October 3rd, as I recall from the Red Book. But the necklace and ring made him suspicious."

I checked my patient's pulse (normal) and temperature – again up. "I must know, Holmes," I said sternly, "Are you indulging in self-medication against the express wishes of your doctor?"

"You refer to cocaine? South American peasants are brought up on the drug and they remain disease free and sharp-witted. I use it as a pick-me-up, not a medicament."

Holmes turned to Lestrade. "You are looking a little peaky, Inspector."

Lestrade stood and backed towards the bedroom door, looking wide-eyed at the open hypodermic case. "No, no, not at all, sir. I'm in the very best of health – Why this morning I ate a dozen rashers of bacon, three eggs, and a quarter-pound of kidneys fried by my mother, with buttered bread and three cups of tea. If that is not evidence of a sound English constitution, then I'm the Tsar of Russia." He giggled nervously as Holmes filled the hypodermic from a small bottle and plunged the needle into his arm.

"Or Chang the Chinese giant," Lestrade said, opening the bedroom door.

"Close the door after you, Inspector, I am highly susceptible to draughts," Holmes said, pressing the piston of his hypodermic.

"Holmes . . . ." I said as Lestrade left, closing the door.

"Doctor?"

I threw my hands in the air and retreated into the sitting room.

"Billy!" I heard behind me.

I helped myself to the last drops in the brandy decanter, added soda, and took my seat by our empty fireplace. I picked up the day's *Times* and glared at the front page.

"Doctor Watson?" I blinked awake at a faint cry from Holmes's bedroom.

I leapt up and went to the bedroom door.

Holmes smiled at me. The bed was cleared of books and telegrams and the hypodermic case was nowhere to be seen. Holmes lay with his blankets up to his chin, looking cherubic.

"I do hope I am not being a nuisance, Watson. You know how much I abhor putting people to any inconvenience."

"Not at all, my dear fellow-lodger," I answered. "And I hope that you will understand that I am a little out of practice with domestic medicine. The last time I was called upon to minister to a patient, he had been hit by a jezail bullet and required immediate amputation of an arm. Without anaesthetic." I frowned at a recollection. "Or was it a leg?"

Holmes had the good grace to look abashed.

I softly closed the bedroom door. Billy stood before me holding out a telegram. I opened it to find the home address of Private King.

"Mrs. King?" I asked as the door of a small cottage in a side street off Covent Garden opened. "I am Doctor Watson. I met your husband earlier today – "

Mrs. King looked at me wide-eyed.

"No, no, Madam, Private King is hale and hearty, on duty at the barracks. I am here on a matter to do with Lord McFarlane. May I?"

"Is it about the package?"

I narrowed my eyes. "It may well be."

I was shown into a neat kitchen. "Only, we're not supposed to give it to no one. We are to open it on the last day of the month and put the envelopes into the post." She looked at me and smiled. "Might be worth a pound or two."

"I take it Lord McFarlane gave your husband the package when he left for the North."

Mrs. King folded her arms over undoubted signs of a late-term pregnancy. "Charlie and me have done nought wrong, Doctor. Just looked after His Lordship's parcel as he instructed."

"That is perfectly correct, my good woman," I suggested. "But circumstances have changed – "

"How much?"

I turned away and checked the meagre contents of my waistcoat pocket, slipped out three sovereigns, and held out the coins. "Three-pounds-ten."

"Done." She took the money and put on her shawl. "Charlie's on late tonight. I've to catch him before he goes off duty, 'cos if he gets to the counter of the Merry Widow, he'll not leave till he's spent ten bob or more and lent as much to his so-called friends. His Lordship left him fifty pounds when he took off, and how much is there after less than a month? Thirty-three quid – all I could take from his hiding place after he'd spent the rest."

She laid a hand on my arm. "He's not a bad husband, Doctor. Just weak, like all men. I don't have a problem with floozies. Just the drink and his good nature."

"The package, Mrs. King?"

She busied herself at a Welsh dresser and returned with a sealed brown-paper-wrapped packet that she passed to me.

"Is Lord McFarlane a kind master?" I asked at the door, more from curiosity than any detective motive.

"He is. It will surprise you, sir, that His Lordship wasn't above coming here now and again to have a cup of tea or a glass of stout and talk over this and that with Charlie."

She frowned at me. "Are you Army, Doctor?"

"I was, until recently. Overseas."

She nodded as she put on her pelisse.

"One more question, Mrs. King, and it is in your interest to answer me with complete honesty if you and your husband are to come out of this affair unscathed. I want the truth. Did you or your husband put a postcard through the letterbox of Mr. Berenger's villa in Fulham on the orders of your husband's master? Think before you answer, for a man's life may depend on it."

She frowned. "No, sir, we did not." She hesitated.

"Go on."

"The last errand Charlie done for His Lordship on the day he left was to order a food hamper from a posh shop up West."

"Fortnum and Mason? For delivery to a station? A train to Scotland?"

"No, Doctor, to his boat."

I engaged a steam launch at Westminster Pier and ordered the engineer to head for Gravesend.

No New Thames Yacht Club officials were available to speak to me, and the barman and waiters were tight-lipped, so despite the chill evening, I took my glass of wine outside onto the terrace and ambled down to the landing stage. Lines of boats of all sizes were moored on either side of a jetty and a glowing brazier showed where the watchman sat in his hut.

"*Caroline*, as was?" he answered my enquiry as he held his hands out to his brazier. He took a long pull on his pipe and nodded towards the jetty. "She was moored over there – or used to be.

"As was?" I asked. "Used to be?"

"She was christened *Caroline* after His Lordship's mother, Lady Caroline. A fine lady." The watchman shook his head. "She died of the bloody flux in '70. And the captain's father last year, of high blood."

"And the *Caroline*? Is she here?"

"She was sold, and is to be repainted and renamed." He shook his head. "Doesn't do, sir, messing with the name of a boat."

"Would that repainting work be done here?"

"No, no, sir. We do regular maintenance and that, but a big job would go to one of the yards upstream. Atkin's maybe – They built the *Caroline* – or Waller's, or maybe Jacobson's opposite The Tower."

I made a note. "Atkins?"

"In Limehouse. Off Narrow Street."

The boatyard owner at Atkins Yard answered my knock wearing a napkin around his neck. He was clearly not best pleased to be interrupted during his evening meal.

"His Lordship sold his sloop," he said in answer to my inquiry. "The other party wanted her new furnished, painted, and rechristened. I was at it most of August."

A delectable smell wafted from the open kitchen door behind him where a side of roast beef graced the kitchen table, and the family were gathered, frowning at me. My stomach growled. "I do apologise – I'll come back tomorrow."

Mr. Atkins smiled. "I hope I'm not being impertinent, Doctor, but I know you medical gents are often called out at awkward times, missing your dinner like. Might my good wife and I offer you a seat at our humble table?"

"I accept, Mr. Atkins, with the very greatest of good will."

"We've no champagne, Doctor, but I find a glass of porter goes well with the roast."

I enjoyed a fine dinner and pleasant company, chatting with Mr. Atkins on the doings of river folk. "These parsnips are the best I've ever had," I said to a beaming Mrs. Atkins.

"They must be well-buttered. That's the key, sir."

Roly-poly pudding and custard ended our meal, and while Mrs. Atkins put the children to bed, I took a fill of Ship's tobacco from her husband and we lit our pipes and gazed out over the lights of a myriad of craft on the great river.

"Now that we are replete and in a better frame of mind, I'll show you *Caroline*'s draft, sir. She was constructed here by my grandfather and father for His Lordship's father." Mr. Atkins led me to a shed, lit an oil lamp, and unrolled a diagram on a long table.

"Sweet lines, as you see, sir. She's now in light blue, set off with white. A handsome sloop – Bemuda-rigged as you see – and with new sets of sails, Manilla cordage, and extra brightwork. No expense spared." He winked. "And despite the new owner being quite an elderly gentleman, the aft sleeping cabin's been made pink and frilly sir – prepared for a lady, if you catch my drift."

I held out my hand. "Thank you again, Mr. Atkins, both for your and your good lady wife's kind hospitality, and for the information."

Mr. Atkins ushered me to the landing stage and hailed a steam launch.

I turned at a sudden thought. "How do you know the new owner is elderly?"

"The gentleman came to inspect the work, sir. The day we were due to move her to a mooring opposite The Tower as Lord McFarlane had instructed us to do on completion. The gentleman had a long look around and pronounced himself main happy with our work, only suggesting we test and grease the seacocks. He said we should go ahead with His Lordship's instructions, leaving the spare cabin keys under a coil of rope up forrard as arranged."

"What day was that?"

"Three weeks ago. September twelvth."

I elicited a more complete description of the elderly gentleman. "Did he leave a name?"

"Might have been Edwards, or Edgar, or maybe Woodward, I don't recall. He was a most affable, generous gent, and free with his praise for the workmanship "

"I understand the yacht has been renamed."

"Yes, Doctor. She's now the *Angelique*."

"How is our patient?" I asked Billy as I slipped through the front door into the hall.

"Very quiet, Doctor. Inspector Lestrade is waiting for you upstairs."

I peeked in on Holmes. His face and arms were pale in the lamplight, sweat beaded his brow, and his pulse was racing – the fever had not yet broken. I considered mixing another draught, but concluded a roborative sleep was the best medicine in the circumstances and that I should not disturb my patient. I replaced the damp towel across his brow with a fresh one and softly closed the door.

Inspector Lestrade sat at the dining table and Billy tended the flickering fire.

I placed a bottle of cognac on the table. "I picked up a bottle of Napoleon from the merchant by the station. A sip or two can be efficacious if the crisis is prolonged." I smiled. "And very welcome to those on vigil."

"The finding of the fake necklace is dubious, is it not, Doctor?" Lestrade said as he accepted a glass of brandy soda.

"It could be perfectly innocent," I suggested. "Madame Berenger was not as careful with the copy as with the genuine necklace and it was left behind on her rushed departure. But what of the postcard? If it were sent by Madame on a previous visit to France, it would be in the possession of the addressee, her husband. Yet according to the butler, it arrived through the letter box in the days after Madame's departure. Of course, Mr. Berenger may have slipped it onto the hall mat without being seen."

"Or Madame rooted it out from where her husband stored it and had someone slip it into the letter box. Do you hide postcards you have received, Doctor? Do you keep account of them? No, you toss them into a box or your bureau or the kindling bin."

I took a sip of brandy and summarised my visits to King's house, Gravesend, and the Atkins boathouse.

"What of the new owner of the yacht," Lestrade asked, his pencil poised over his notebook.

"Heavily bearded, dark coat, top hat, spectacles, and elderly stoop. Spoke fondly of Lord McFarlane and knew the *Caroline* well. He inspected the work, tipped the crew, and told them to follow His Lordship's instructions and move the yacht to a new berth opposite The Tower, leaving the spare keys in a safe place." I considered. "Might be Berenger in disguise."

"Or McFarlane, pretending to be Berenger to implicate him."

I smiled. "The yacht has been renamed *Angelique*."

Lestrade returned my smile. "That settles any doubt about McFarlane being 'another'."

I laid the package that I had received from Mrs. King on the table.

"The envelope is unstamped." The inspector opened it and shook the contents onto the table.

I picked up two letters. "One for Major Fraser and one for the colonel of the Scots Guards," I said. "We cannot open them, Inspector. They are stamped."

"But not franked."

I frowned.

"If you are ever to thrive in the sleuthing business, Doctor, you must learn to be less punctilious."

"I intend to thrive in my own profession, Inspector." I smiled and tapped my knee. "Once I get back on my feet."

"I do apologise, Doctor Watson. I meant no offense."

"None taken."

The inspector stood and declaimed. "As a duly accredited officer of the crown – "

"Shh." Billy and I hissed. We pointed to Holmes's door.

"Sorry," Lestrade murmured. He sat and continued in a whisper. "I hereby, by order of Her Majesty *etcetera* and *etcetera*, open these mails and record Doctor Watson and young Billy as witnesses to same."

He slit the envelopes and laid a sheaf of papers on the table. "Resignation letter addressed to the colonel, letter of apology and thanks to the adjutant, receipts for His Lordship's mess bill, all paid up, and various subscriptions cancelled. McFarlane cites unforeseen circumstances as the reason for his resignation – no mention of the lady."

The inspector shrugged. "The captain made plans to elope with Madame Berenger, and she made sure of her fortune in France by selling the property and converting the proceeds into bearer bonds that could be cashed anywhere in the civilised world without question of identity or provenance."

331

I frowned. "If Madame was going to the Continent with her lover, why sell her properties and transfer the funds to England? It makes no sense."

Lestrade threw up his hands. "What does?"

I heard a groan from Holmes's room.

I strode to the bedroom, the inspector following me. My patient's forehead was burning, his pulse was racing, his eyes were unfocussed and bloodshot, and he muttered disjointed, senseless phrases. I dribbled a shot of brandy between his lips and he quietened.

Lestrade watched from the doorway, his face pale.

"Holmes's pulse is now weak and thready," I said. "His temperature is up again. I believe we are very, very close to the crisis. I must tend to my patient, Inspector."

He nodded. "Until the morning, then."

I followed him onto the stair landing.

"Madame concocted an elaborate plan to implicate her husband in her disappearance, suggesting murder," Lestrade said. "That is unusual. I do believe this is the first such conspiracy it has been my good fortune to unravel."

"Our," I said stiffly.

"Oh, once again I must apologise, Doctor. The question is why did she do so? Was Berenger a cruel husband?"

"Perhaps Mrs. Berenger's lust for her younger *amour* engendered an equal and opposite feeling of loathing and hatred for her husband. There have been some interesting studies in the medical press. On the Continent, naturally – "

"Or more simply, Doctor, she wanted to marry her paramour and had to get her husband out of the way."

"With a capital charge hanging over him? That is cold."

We shook hands. "I have a question," I said. "Can one use 'elope' in these circumstances, with a married lady involved?"

"Yes," came Holmes's cry from his bedroom.

I found him sitting up, his eyes blinking and rivulets of perspiration coursing down his face. "The word is neutral as to the marital status of the elopers." He flopped down onto his pillows and closed his eyes.

I smiled. "Our resident Doctor Johnson has arisen."

"Doctor Johnson?" Lestrade asked.

I wiped perspiration from Holmes's face and helped him sip some brandy before his head nodded to his chest and he fell asleep.

"Billy!"

I woke, tried to stand, and slumped back onto our wicker sofa with a swingeing headache.

"Watson!"

"Our fellow over-egged his pudding," Holmes said as he sat up in bed, bright-eyed, his pupils wide, devouring a kipper on a breakfast tray. "He thought that he was dealing with the second eleven."

He held up his hand to stop my interruption. "I say what Berenger thought, Watson, not necessarily the true state of affairs." He laughed. "Only yesterday did he disclose the false signature attempts. The miracle of the necklace was a desperate move. Ha ha!"

Holmes took a gulp of coffee. "Naturally Berenger agreed to the change of banks. He expected to take control of his wife's funds. No matter what airy notions he may have suggested on partnership and sharing, under English law once the money reached English jurisdiction, it was his to do what he would." He waved the signature sheet. "His wife had other ideas."

I considered. "A remark of the manager of the London and Colonial Bank stuck in my mind, Holmes. He said there had been no complaint on Mr. Berenger's last visit to the bank."

Holmes smiled. "I telegraphed this afternoon to ascertain the date of that visit. It was on the day Madame disappeared, just after so-called 'Mr. Grant' left with the bearer bonds on the afternoon of Monday, September twelfth. Berenger asked for a balance on the account, but made no remark on the missing French funds."

I indicated the signature sheet. "Is that a fake? I mean a double fake?"

"No, no, this is a genuine attempt by Mrs. Berenger to imitate her husband's signature. That is how she had the money from her French properties translated to bearer bonds – both signatures were required."

"And that's why she insisted Mr. Berenger move their account to a new bank, whose staff would be unfamiliar with them as clients."

Holmes paused, his knife and fork in the air. "You are coming along, my friend. Have a grape. The paste necklace ordered at Tiffany started a worm of suspicion in Berenger. We know his wife and her lover were indiscreet. His adjutant suspected, and I believe Miss Ward, King, and the Berenger servants know much more than they have been prepared to share with us – you."

I sniffed.

"Madame took her dresses and furs," Holmes continued. "She had help from her maid and others. The servants said their mistress's sad demeanor changed with the New Year. I believe that is when this plan was hatched. The French properties took time to liquidate – it was a long-laid plot."

Holmes sipped his coffee. "Berenger bided his time, keeping a close watch on his wife. He knew from the bank that the money had been withdrawn, and from the boat-builder when the yacht was moved to its mooring opposite The Tower, and that all would be in readiness. On the evening of

September twelfth, he suggested a night out with his wife. She demurred, and Berenger expressed an intention to dine at the Criterion, see a play, and overnight at his club."

Holmes cupped his hands over his mouth. "Billy!"

The boy scrambled up the stairs and peeked around the door.

"More bread and butter, fresh coffee with a cup for the doctor, and fetch *The Times.*"

"She pleaded a headache, or some slight indisposition, but begged him not to miss the play on her account," I said.

"Berenger over-egged his pudding with his brothel admissions, and especially with the necklace." Holmes frowned at me. "Did you ask the name of the girl he supposedly went with?"

"I certainly did not!"

Holmes attacked his kipper with gusto. "Never mind. We should leave some morsels for Lestrade to grub up."

I took my scalpel from my medical bag and stropped it on a leather strap.

Holmes paused in his meal and watched me, narrow eyed.

"Often fever patients are over-excited after the crisis," I said with a smile. "Bleeding is required to restore calm. Perhaps you would prefer leeches?"

Holmes leaned back against his pillows. "My pulse against yours for sixpence. Slowest wins."

I checked Holmes heart-rate against my watch. "Seventy."

I checked my own. "Seventy-two."

"Ha! Put your bright blade away or the dew will rust it. Is there any pudding?"

I admitted defeat and closed my medicine case. "Clytemnestra," I said. "She sought to kill her husband, did she not?"

"Mrs. Berenger? More like Marie Antoinette," Holmes answered. "She wanted her cake, and to eat it too. She knew Miss Ward would start a hue-and-cry. The ridiculous postcard forgery would be exposed, offering circumstantial evidence her husband was attempting to cover up a crime. And the necklace would be found hidden among his things. Damning evidence against him."

"So, Mr. Berenger is innocent and the real jewels, and the bearer bonds are on board the *Angelique*, bound for Scotland – or so we may presume."

Holmes smiled. "I don't believe so. We must await Lestrade's report."

The doorbell rang on cue and Inspector Lestrade joined us, accepting a cup of coffee.

"The evidence is circumstantial, Holmes," I said. "What if Berenger is innocent? Can we develop a set of circumstances that would exonerate him? You said Mrs. Berenger planted the fake necklace."

"Good for you, my dear fellow. There speaks an Englishman." Holmes chuckled. "Berenger and his wife both made stupid mistakes." He handed me the jewel case. I opened it and frowned at the glittering necklace.

"Remember exactly what the servants told you. Ruby said she found a necklace in Mr. Berenger's bedroom. Not a jewel case, a necklace."

I gasped. "There was no mention of a case!"

Lestrade smiled. "I interviewed Ruby this morning, Doctor. She confirms she found the necklace with no case."

"So how did Berenger come by it?" I asked.

"I shall ask him in his cell at the Yard," Lestrade answered, "where he is held on two charges of murder."

I blinked at the inspector.

Holmes smiled at my confusion. "His wife planted the incriminating evidence while she thought he was at the *Opera Comique*. In fact, he was lying in wait aboard the yacht at the appropriately named Gravesend." He held up a telegram. "From the Thames Division. A thorough search of the estuary has retrieved gear from *Angelique* washed up on the Sands."

"And Mrs. Berenger and Lord McFarlane?"

"At the bottom of the Thames, I'm afraid. I have no doubt Berenger sank the launch to hide his traces. I had my searchers scour the docks – in her new livery she would stand out. And Lestrade alerted the French and the east coast ports with no result. Berenger killed his wife and her lover and sank the *Angelique*. Remember his was a double betrayal – his wife and a close friend."

"Mr. Atkins at the boatyard said that the elderly gentleman urged him to check and grease the seacocks of the *Angelique*."

"We know Berenger was away from home until late on the day his wife went missing," said Lestrade. "He unlocked the *Angelique* using the builders' keys and lay in wait."

Holmes nodded. "The couple arrived, breathless with excitement at their successful elopement. They entered the cabin and met their doom, whether immediately or after a period of recrimination we cannot say."

"After the dread deed, Berenger took a cab home and went quietly to bed," I said. "What a terrible affair."

"Berenger returned home with the real jewels and bonds the morning after the crime," Holmes continued. "He found the fake necklace hidden among his possessions, but where it would be easily found."

Holmes smiled. "You will ask why, three weeks later, he put the necklace in his bedroom and implicated himself? Lestrade?"

337

"The tension was getting to him, Mr. Holmes. Berenger wanted his wife's conspiracy discovered, and by implication, his innocence proved."

"Exactly," Holmes answered. "He needed the police to expose the necklace and postcard as fakes. The practice signatures would lead them to the French money and bearer bonds. Simple enquiries would point to McFarlane as 'another', to the renaming of his yacht."

"Not exactly simple, Holmes."

Holmes raised his coffee cup to Inspector Lestrade. "The inspector will shatter Berenger's bawdy house alibi into fragments of prevarication."

Billy brought in a bowl of stewed pears. "If I were you, Lestrade," Holmes said, "I'd look again to Madame's maid. Ruby is the obvious candidate for Berenger's spy in her mistress's camp. He was far too sanguine with regard to the withdrawal of the bonds and the elopement in the *Angelique*. He had inside knowledge. Focus on Ruby, and through her you will gather enough evidence to hang Berenger."

That dark thought lay between us for a moment.

"If I may ask, Holmes," I said when the inspector had made his *adieu*, "in this sort of case, brought to you by the police, how would you usually be compensated, if not for Miss Ward's hundred guineas?"

"*Quid pro quo*, old man. There may come a time when I will need the advice and sage wisdom of the inspector or one of his fellows at the Yard. *Manus manum lavat*, as the Old Romans had it. One hand washes the other."

I frowned. Was there was a tinge of irony in my friend's tone?

Holmes peered at me over his glass and smiled. "Are you thinking of putting up your brass plate as an investigator, Doctor?"

"No, no, of course not. I ask out of idle curiosity, no more."

Holmes smiled. "My professional advice, my dear doctor – and I speak as a grateful recipient of your medical care – would be for you to stick to your present profession and leave sleuthing to me."

"I thought I did rather well," I said stiffly. "Particularly so as I was also attempting to bring succour to a fevered soul,"

Holmes smiled. "If you were told by your wife, assuming you had one, that she intended to elope with 'another', what would you do?"

I considered. "As a first step, I would use all my resources to discover his identity, then I would punch him on the nose. If that did not settle the matter, and my wife were still unhappy with her marriage, I would of course release her from her bond to me." I sniffed. "Then I would punch 'another' on the nose again."

Holmes toasted me in coffee, and I him.

About the Contributors

The following appear in
Volume I:

Deanna Baran lives in a remote part of Texas where cowboys may still be seen in their natural habitat. A librarian and former museum curator, she writes in between cups of tea, playing *Go*, and trading postcards with people around the world. This is her first venture into the foggy streets of gaslit London.

Brian Belanger is a publisher and editor, but is best known for his freelance illustration and cover design work. His distinctive style can be seen on several MX Publishing covers, including *Memoirs from Mrs. Hudson's Kitchen* by Wendy Heyman-Marsaw, *Sherlock Holmes and the Menacing Melbournian* by Allan Mitchell, *Sherlock Holmes and A Quantity of Debt* by David Marcum, *Welcome to Undershaw* by Luke Benjamen Kuhns, and many more. Brian is the co-founder of Belanger Books LLC, where he illustrates the popular *MacDougall Twins with Sherlock Holmes* young reader series (#1 bestsellers on Amazon.com UK). A prolific creator, he also designs t-shirts, mugs, stickers, and other merchandise on his personal art site: *www.redbubble.com/people/zhahadun*.

Derrick Belanger is an educator and also the author of the #1 bestselling book in its category, *Sherlock Holmes: The Adventure of the Peculiar Provenance*, which was in the top 200 bestselling books on Amazon. He also is the author of *The MacDougall Twins with Sherlock Holmes* books, and he edited the Sir Arthur Conan Doyle horror anthology *A Study in Terror: Sir Arthur Conan Doyle's Revolutionary Stories of Fear and the Supernatural*. Mr. Belanger co-owns the publishing company Belanger Books, which released the Sherlock Holmes anthologies *Beyond Watson, Holmes Away From Home: Adventures from the Great Hiatus* Volumes 1 and 2, *Sherlock Holmes: Before Baker Street*, and *Sherlock Holmes: Adventures in the Realms of H.G. Wells* Volumes 1 and 2. Derrick resides in Colorado and continues compiling unpublished works by Dr. John H. Watson.

Thomas A. Burns, Jr. is the author of the *Natalie McMasters Mysteries*. He was born and grew up in New Jersey, attended Xavier High School in Manhattan, earned B.S degrees in Zoology and Microbiology at Michigan State University, and a M.S. in Microbiology at North Carolina State University. He currently resides in Wendell, North Carolina. As a kid, Tom started reading mysteries with The Hardy Boys, Ken Holt and Rick Brant, and graduated to the classic stories by authors such as A. Conan Doyle, Dorothy Sayers, John Dickson Carr, Erle Stanley Gardner, and Rex Stout, to name a few. Tom has written fiction as a hobby all of his life, starting with The Man from U.N.C.L.E. stories in marble-backed copybooks in grade school. He built a career as technical, science, and medical writer and editor for nearly thirty years in industry and government. Now that he's truly on his own as a novelist, he's excited to publish his own mystery series, as well as to contribute stories about his second-most-favorite detective, Sherlock Holmes, to *The MX anthology of New Sherlock Holmes Stories*.

Chris Chan is a writer, educator, and historian. He works as a researcher and "International Goodwill Ambassador" for Agatha Christie Ltd. His true crime articles, reviews, and short fiction have appeared (or will soon appear) in *The Strand*, *The Wisconsin Magazine of History*, *Mystery Weekly*, *Gilbert!*, *Nerd HQ*, Akashic Books' *Mondays are Murder* web series, *The Baker Street Journal*, and *Sherlock Holmes Mystery Magazine*.

Harry DeMaio is a *nom de plume* of Harry B. DeMaio, successful author of several books on Information Security and Business Networks, as well as the ten-volume *Casebooks of Octavius Bear – Alternative Universe Mysteries for Adult Animal Lovers*. Octavius Bear is loosely based on Sherlock Holmes and Nero Wolfe in a world in which *homo sapiens* died out long ago in a global disaster, but most animals have advanced to a twenty-first century anthropomorphic state. "It's Time" is Harry's first 100% traditional pastiche featuring Holmes and Watson, after his story "Doctor Bear, I Presume?" (*Sherlock Holmes: In The Realms of Steampunk*) featured the duo encountering Harry's ursine detective. A retired business executive, consultant, information security specialist, former pilot, and graduate school adjunct professor, he whiles away his time traveling and writing preposterous articles and stories. He has appeared on many radio and TV shows and is an accomplished, frequent public speaker. Former New York City natives, he and his extremely patient and helpful wife, Virginia, and their Bichon Frisé, Woof, live in Cincinnati (and several other parallel universes.) They have two sons living in Scottsdale, Arizona and Cortlandt Manor, New York, both of whom are quite successful and quite normal – thus putting the lie to the theory that insanity is hereditary.

Sir Arthur Conan Doyle (1859-1930) *Holmes Chronicler Emeritus*. If not for him, this anthology would not exist. Author, physician, patriot, sportsman, spiritualist, husband and father, and advocate for the oppressed. He is remembered and honored for the purposes of this collection by being the man who introduced Sherlock Holmes to the world. Through fifty-six Holmes short stories, four novels, and additional Apocryphal entries, Doyle revolutionized mystery stories and also greatly influenced and improved police forensic methods and techniques for the betterment of all. *Steel True Blade Straight.*

Richard Gutschmidt (1861-1926) was the first German illustrator of The Canon, providing over eighty drawings for twenty Canonical adventures between 1906 and 1908.

Paula Hammond has written over sixty fiction and non-fiction books, as well as short stories, comics, poetry, and scripts for educational DVD's. When not glued to the keyboard, she can usually be found prowling round second-hand books shops or hunkered down in a hide, soaking up the joys of the natural world.

Mike Hogan writes mostly historical novels and short stories, many set in Victorian London and featuring Sherlock Holmes and Doctor Watson. He read the Conan Doyle stories at school with great enjoyment, but hadn't thought much about Sherlock Holmes until, having missed the Granada/Jeremy Brett TV series when it was originally shown in the eighties, he came across a box set of videos in a street market and was hooked on Holmes again. He started writing Sherlock Holmes

342

pastiches several years ago, having great fun re-imagining situations for the Conan Doyle characters to act in. The relationship between Holmes and Watson fascinates him as one of the great literary friendships. (He's also a huge admirer of Patrick O'Brian's Aubrey-Maturin novels). Like Captain Aubrey and Doctor Maturin, Holmes and Watson are an odd couple, differing in almost every facet of their characters, but sharing a common sense of decency and a common humanity. Living with Sherlock Holmes can't have been easy, and Mike enjoys adding a stronger vein of "pawky humour" into the Conan Doyle mix, even letting Watson have the second-to-last word on occasions. His books include *Sherlock Holmes and the Scottish Question*, the forthcoming *The Gory Season – Sherlock Holmes, Jack the Ripper and the Thames Torso Murders*, and the Sherlock Holmes & Young Winston 1887 Trilogy (*The Deadwood Stage*, *The Jubilee Plot*, and *The Giant Moles*), He has also written the following short story collections: *Sherlock Holmes: Murder at the Savoy and Other Stories*, *Sherlock Holmes: The Skull of Kohada Koheiji and Other Stories*, and *Sherlock Holmes: Murder on the Brighton Line and Other Stories*. *www.mikehoganbooks.com*

David Marcum plays *The Game* with deadly seriousness. He first discovered Sherlock Holmes in 1975 at the age of ten, and since that time, he has collected, read, and chronologicized literally thousands of traditional Holmes pastiches in the form of novels, short stories, radio and television episodes, movies and scripts, comics, fan-fiction, and unpublished manuscripts. He is the author of over fifty Sherlockian pastiches, some published in anthologies and magazines such as *The Strand*, and others collected in his own books, *The Papers of Sherlock Holmes*, *Sherlock Holmes and A Quantity of Debt*, and *Sherlock Holmes – Tangled Skeins*. He has edited nearly fifty books, including several dozen traditional Sherlockian anthologies, such as the ongoing series *The MX Book of New Sherlock Holmes Stories*, which he created in 2015. This collection is now up to 18 volumes, with several more in preparation. He was responsible for bringing back August Derleth's Solar Pons for a new generation, first with his collection of authorized Pons stories, *The Papers of Solar Pons*, and then by editing the reissued authorized versions of the original Pons books. He is now doing the same for the adventures of Dr. Thorndyke. He has contributed numerous essays to various publications, and is a member of a number of Sherlockian groups and Scions. He is a licensed Civil Engineer, living in Tennessee with his wife and son. His irregular Sherlockian blog, *A Seventeen Step Program*, addresses various topics related to his favorite book friends (as his son used to call them when he was small), and can be found at *http://17stepprogram.blogspot.com/* Since the age of nineteen, he has worn a deerstalker as his regular-and-only hat. In 2013, he and his deerstalker were finally able make his first trip-of-a-lifetime Holmes Pilgrimage to England, with return Pilgrimages in 2015 and 2016, where you may have spotted him. If you ever run into him and his deerstalker out and about, feel free to say hello!

Robert Perret is a writer, librarian, and devout Sherlockian living on the Palouse. His Sherlockian publications include "The Canaries of Clee Hills Mine" in *An Improbable Truth: The Paranormal Adventures of Sherlock Holmes*, "For King and Country" in *The Science of Deduction*, and "How Hope Learned the Trick" in *NonBinary Review*. He considers himself to be a pan-Sherlockian and a one-man Scion out on the lonely moors of Idaho. Robert has recently authored a yet-unpublished scholarly article tentatively entitled "A Study in Scholarship: The Case of the *Baker Street Journal'*. More information is available at www.robertperret.com

Roger Riccard of Los Angeles, California, U.S.A., is a descendant of the Roses of Kilravock in Highland Scotland. He is the author of two previous Sherlock Holmes novels, *The Case of the Poisoned Lilly* and *The Case of the Twain Papers*, a series of short stories in two volumes, *Sherlock Holmes: Adventures for the Twelve Days of Christmas* and *Further Adventures for the Twelve Days of Christmas*, and the new series *A Sherlock Holmes Alphabet of Cases,* all of which are published by Baker Street Studios. He has another novel and a non-fiction Holmes reference work in various stages of completion. He became a Sherlock Holmes enthusiast as a teenager (many, many years ago), and, like all fans of The Great Detective, yearned for more stories after reading The Canon over and over. It was the Granada Television performances of Jeremy Brett and Edward Hardwicke, and the encouragement of his wife, Rosilyn, that at last inspired him to write his own Holmes adventures, using the Granada actor portrayals as his guide. He has been called "*The best pastiche writer since Val Andrews*" by the *Sherlockian E-Times*.

Matthew Simmonds hails from Bedford, in the South East of England, and has been a confirmed devotee of Sir Arthur Conan Doyle's most famous creation since first watching Jeremy Brett's incomparable portrayal of the world's first consulting detective, on a Tuesday evening in April, 1984, while curled up on the sofa with his father. He has written numerous short stories, and his first novel, *Sherlock Holmes: The Adventure of The Pigtail Twist*, was published in 2018. A sequel is nearly complete, which he hopes to publish in the near future. Matthew currently co-owns Harrison & Simmonds, the fifth-generation family business, a renowned County tobacconist, pipe, and gift shop on Bedford High Street.

The following appear in
Volumes II and III:

Ian Ableson is an ecologist by training and a writer by choice. When not reading or writing, he can reliably be found scowling at a clipboard while ankle-deep in a marsh somewhere in Michigan. His love for the stories of Arthur Conan Doyle started when his grandfather gave him a copy of *The Original Illustrated Sherlock Holmes* when he was in high school, and he's proud to have been able to contribute to the continuation of the tales of Sherlock Holmes and Dr. Watson.

David B. Beckwith was born in the U.K. region of Cumbria. His family emigrated to Western Australia in 1969. He studied Mathematics, Middle English, Music, and Philosophy at the University of W.A. He is now a retired I.T. Professional. He started writing about Sherlock Holmes in 2010, he has now written twenty short stories and one long story, published three Holmes books, and a fourth book is in preparation. David lives in a rural region bordering to the metropolitan area of Perth where he and his wife grow vegetables and raise chickens for eggs.

S.F. Bennett has, at various times, been an actor, a lecturer, a journalist, a historian, an author and a potter. Whilst some of those things still apply, she has always been an avid collector, concentrating mainly on ephemera and other related items concerning Sherlock Holmes and British science-fiction of the 1970's. To date, she has written articles on aspects of The Canon for *The Baker Street Journal, The Sherlock Holmes Journal*, and *The Torr*, the journal of *The Sherlock Holmes Society of the West Country*. When not collecting, she can be found writing science-fiction and mystery stories, and has contributed to several anthologies of new Sherlock Holmes pastiches. Her first novel was *The Secret Diary of Mycroft Holmes: The Thoughts and Reminiscences of Sherlock Holmes's Elder Brother, 1880-1888* (2017). She is also the author of *A Study In Postcards: Sherlock Holmes in the Golden Age of the Picture Postcard* (*Sherlock Holmes Society of London*, 2019).

Emily J. Cohen lives in Rhode Island with her fiancé and her tiny dog. She received a Master of Fine Arts in Creative Writing from Lesley University and her work has appeared in *JitterPress Magazine* and *Outlook Springs*. A self-described geek, Emily enjoys Doctor Who, anime, and competitive video games.

Sir Arthur Conan Doyle also has stories in Volumes II and III.

Tim Gambrell lives in Exeter, Devon, with his wife, two young sons, two cats, and seven chickens. He contributed "The Yellow Star of Cairo" to *Part XIII* of *The MX Book of New Sherlock Holmes Stories*. Outside of The World of Holmes, Tim has written extensively for Doctor Who spin-off ranges. He has recently had two linked novels published by Candy Jar Books: *Lethbridge-Stewart: The Laughing Gnome – Lucy Wilson & The Bledoe Cadets*, and *The Lucy Wilson Mysteries: The Brigadier and The Bledoe Cadets* (both Summer 2019). He also has a novella, *The Way of The Bry'hunee*, for the Erimem range from Thebes Publishing, which is due out in late 2019. Tim's short fiction includes stories in *Lethbridge-Stewart: The HAVOC Files 3* (Candy Jar, 2017), *Bernice Summerfield: True Stories* (Big Finish, 2017), and *Relics . . . An Anthology* (Red Ted Books, 2018). Further short fiction will feature in the forthcoming collections *Lethbridge-Stewart: The HAVOC Files – The Laughing Gnome*, and *Lethbridge-Stewart: The HAVOC Files – Loose Ends* (both due later in 2019).

Jayantika Ganguly BSI is the General Secretary and Editor of the *Sherlock Holmes Society of India*, a member of the *Sherlock Holmes Society of London*, and the *Czech Sherlock Holmes Society*. She is the author of *The Holmes Sutra* (MX 2014). She is a corporate lawyer working with one of the Big Six law firms.

Arthur Hall was born in Aston, Birmingham, UK, in 1944. His interest in writing began during his schooldays and served as a growing ambition to become an author. Years later, his first novel *Sole Contact* was an espionage story about an ultra-secret government department known as "Sector Three" and has been followed, to date, by four sequels. The sixth in the series, *The Suicide Chase*, is currently in the course of preparation. Other works include five "rediscovered" cases from the files of Sherlock Holmes, two collections of bizarre short stories, and two novels about an adventurer called "Bernard Kramer", as well as several contributions to the ongoing anthology, *The MX Book of New Sherlock Holmes Stories*. His only ambition, apart from being published more widely, is to attend the premier of a film based on one of his novels, ideally at The Odeon, Leicester Square. He lives in the West Midlands, United Kingdom, where he often walks other people's dogs as he attempts to formulate new plots. His work can be seen at *arthurhallsbooksite.blogspot.com*, and the author can be contacted at *arthurhall7777@aol.co.uk*

Stephen Herczeg is an IT Geek, writer, actor, and film-maker based in Canberra Australia. He has been writing for over twenty years and has completed a couple of dodgy novels, sixteen feature length screenplays, and numerous short stories and scripts. Stephen was very successful in 2017's International Horror Hotel screenplay competition, with his scripts *TITAN* winning the Sci-Fi category and *Dark are the Woods* placing second in the horror category. His work has featured in *Sproutlings – A Compendium of Little Fictions* from Hunter Anthologies, the *Hells Bells* Christmas horror anthology published by the Australasian Horror Writers Association, and the *Below the Stairs, Trickster's Treats, Shades of Santa, Behind the Mask*, and *Beyond the Infinite* anthologies from *OzHorror.Con*, *The Body Horror Book, Anemone Enemy*, and *Petrified Punks* from Oscillate Wildly Press, and *Sherlock Holmes In the Realms of H.G. Wells* and *Sherlock Holmes: Adventures Beyond the Canon* from Belanger Books.

David Marcum also has stories in Volumes II and III.

Mark Mower is a member of the *Crime Writers' Association, The Sherlock Holmes Society of London* and *The Solar Pons Society of London*. He writes true crime stories and fictional mysteries. His volumes of Holmes pastiches include *A Farewell to Baker Street, Sherlock Holmes: The Baker Street Case-Files*, and *Sherlock Holmes: The Baker Street Legacy* (all with MX Publishing) and, to date, he has contributed many stories to the ongoing series *The MX Book of New Sherlock Holmes Stories*. He has also had stories in two anthologies by Belanger Books: *Holmes Away From Home: Adventures from the Great Hiatus – Volume II – 1893-1894* (2016) and *Sherlock Holmes: Before Baker Street* (2017). More are bound to follow. Mark's non-fiction works include *Bloody British History: Norwich* (The History Press, 2014), *Suffolk Murders* (The History Press, 2011) and *Zeppelin Over Suffolk* (Pen & Sword Books, 2008).

Will Murray is the author of over seventy novels, including forty *Destroyer* novels and seven posthumous *Doc Savage* collaborations with Lester Dent, under the name Kenneth Robeson, for Bantam Books in the 1990's. Since 2011, he has written fourteen additional Doc Savage adventures for Altus Press, two of which co-starred The Shadow, as well as a solo Pat Savage novel. His 2015 Tarzan novel, *Return to Pal-Ul-Don*, was followed by *King Kong vs. Tarzan* in 2016. Murray has written short stories featuring such classic characters as Batman, Superman, Wonder Woman, Spider-Man, Ant-Man, the Hulk, Honey West, the Spider, the Avenger, the Green Hornet, the Phantom, and Cthulhu. A previous Murray Sherlock Holmes story appeared in Moonstone's *Sherlock Holmes: The Crossovers Casebook*, and another is forthcoming in *Sherlock Holmes and Doctor Was Not*, involving H. P. Lovecraft's Dr. Herbert West. Additionally, a number of his Sherlock Holmes stories have appeared in various volumes of *The MX Book of New Sherlock Holmes Stories*, as well as the anthologies *Sherlock Holmes: Adventures Beyond the Canon* and *The Irregular Adventures of Sherlock Holmes* from Belanger Books. He is best known as the co-creator of the character Squirrel Girl for Marvel Comics with artist Steve Ditko.

Sidney Paget (1860-1908), a few of whose illustrations are used within this anthology, was born in London, and like his two older brothers, became a famed illustrator and painter. He completed over three-hundred-and-fifty drawings for the Sherlock Holmes stories first published in *The Strand* magazine, defining Holmes's image forever after in the public mind.

Tracy J. Revels has been a Sherlockian from the age of eleven. She is a professor of history at Wofford College in Spartanburg, South Carolina. She is a member of *The Survivors of the Gloria Scott* and *The Studious Scarlets Society*, and is a past recipient of the Beacon Society Award. Almost every semester, she teaches a class that covers The Canon, either to college students or to senior citizens. She is also the author of three supernatural Sherlockian pastiches with MX (*Shadowfall*, *Shadowblood*, and *Shadowwraith*), and a regular contributor to her scion's newsletter. She also has some notoriety as an author of very silly skits: For proof, see "The Adventure of the Adversarial Adventuress" and "Occupy Baker Street" on YouTube. When not studying Sherlock, she can be found researching the history of her native state, and has written books on Florida in the Civil War and on the development of Florida's tourism industry.

GC Rosenquist was born in Chicago, Illinois and has been writing since he was ten years old. His interests are very eclectic. His twelve previously published books include literary fiction, horror, poetry, a comedic memoir, and lots of science fiction. His works include *Sherlock Holmes: The Pearl of Death and Other Stories* MX Books, and his Belanger Books children's novel *The Tall Tales of Starman Steve* and his adult novel *33 Tall Tales of Lake County, Illinois*. He has had his work published in *Sherlock Holmes Mystery Magazine* and several volumes of *The MX Books New Book of Sherlock Holmes Stories*. He works professionally as a graphic artist. He has studied writing and poetry at the College of Lake County in Grayslake, Illinois, and currently resides in Round Lake, Illinois. For more information on GC Rosenquist, you can go to his website at *www.gcrosenquist.com*

Annette Siketa is totally blind and lives in Adelaide, Australia. She first came to Holmes by accident – that is to say, someone "dared" her to write a Sherlock Holmes story. Since then, she has written over fifty Holmes stories, including the full-length novel, *Chameleon – The Death of Sherlock Holmes*. The books *The Failures of Sherlock Holmes* and *The Untold Adventures of Sherlock Holmes* will be released in early January 2020, and will be available through most online retailers except Amazon.

Matthew Simmonds also has as story in Volume III.

Robert V. Stapleton was born and brought up in Leeds, Yorkshire, England, and studied at Durham University. After working in various parts of the country as an Anglican parish priest, he is now retired and lives with his wife in North Yorkshire. As a member of his local writing group, he now has time to develop his other life as a writer of adventure stories. He has recently had a number of short stories published, and he is hoping to have a couple of completed novels published at some time in the future.

Kevin P. Thornton has experienced a Taliban rocket attack in Kabul and a terrorist bombing in Johannesburg. He lives in Fort

McMurray, Alberta, the town that burnt down in 2016. He has been shortlisted for the *Crime Writers of Canada* Unhanged writing award six times. He's never won. He was also a finalist for best short story in 2014 – the year Margaret Atwood entered. We're not saying he has luck issues, but don't bet on his stock tips. Born in Kenya, Kevin was a child in New Zealand, a student and soldier in Africa, a military contractor in Afghanistan, a forklift driver in Ontario, and an oilfield worker in North Western Canada. He writes poems that start out just fine, but turn ruder and cruder over time. From limerick to doggerel, they earn less than bugger-all, even though they all manage to rhyme. He also likes writing about Sherlock Holmes and dislikes writing about himself in the third person.

D.J. Tyrer is the person behind Atlantean Publishing, was placed second in the Writing Magazine "Local Reporter" competition, and has been widely published in anthologies and magazines around the world, such as *Disturbance* (Laurel Highlands), *Mysteries of Suspense* (Zimbell House), *History and Mystery, Oh My!* (Mystery & Horror LLC), and *Love 'Em, Shoot 'Em* (Wolfsinger), and issues of *Awesome Tales*, and in addition, has a novella available in paperback and on the Kindle, *The Yellow House* (Dunhams Manor) and a comic horror e-novelette, *A Trip to the Middle of the World*, available from Alban Lake through Infinite Realms Bookstore.
His website is: *https://djtyrer.blogspot.co.uk/*
The Atlantean Publishing website is at *https://atlanteanpublishing.wordpress.com/*

I.A. Watson is a novelist and jobbing writer from Yorkshire who cut his teeth on writing Sherlock Holmes stories and has even won an award for one. His works include *Holmes and Houdini, Labours of Hercules, St. George and the Dragon* Volumes 1 and 2, and *Women of Myth*, and the non-fiction essay book *Where Stories Dwell*. He pens short detective stories as a means of avoiding writing things that pay better. A full list of his sixty-plus published works appears at:
http://www.chillwater.org.uk/writing/iawatsonhome.htm

A Special Thank You
to Our Backers

This book could not have been a success without the support of our Kickstarter Backers. We would personally like to thank the following:

Wanda Aasen

Charles C. Albritton III

Dean S Arashiro

Ron Bachman

Barak Bader

Howard J. Bampton

Chris Basler

Chad Bowden

Michael Brown

Rachel Burch

Alessandro Caffari

Mark Carter

Chris Chastain

Ivan Cobham

Gina R. Collia

Craig Stephen Copland

Terry Cox

Scott J. Dahlgren

Christopher Davis

Harry DeMaio

Michael Demchak

Edward Drummond

Derrick Eaves

Griffin Endicott

Fearlessleader

Rich Friedel

Tim Gambrell
Jacinda Gift
Brad Goupil
Richard L. Haas III
Paul Hiscock
Scott Jackson
Dave Jones
Melanie K
Miles L
Anthony & Suford Lewis
Debra Lovelace
Anthony M.
James J. Marshall
Scott Vander Molen
Mark Mower
Richard Ohnemus
Mike Pasqua
Robert Perret
Gary Phillips
David Rains
Mary Ann Raley
Michael J Raymond, PhD
Ray Riethmeier
Steve Rosenberg
Eric Sands
Steven Sartain
Scarlett Letter
Eric Schaefges
Evan Schwartzberg
Steven M. Smith
Danny Soares
Bertrand Szoghy
David Tai

Tom Turley

Ida Sue Umphers

Carl W. Urmer, MHS

Karly VK

F Scott Valeri

Douglas Vaughan

Sriranga Veeraraghavan

L.E. Vellene

David A. Wade

Joseph S. Walker

Michael Walker

Charles Warren

Deb "IGrokSherlock" Werth

Anton Wijs

Seow Wan Yi

David Zurek

Belanger Books

Printed in Great Britain
by Amazon